ADAMA

LAVIE TIDHAR was born just ten miles from
Armageddon and grew up on a kibbutz in northern
Israel. He has since made his home in London,
where he is currently a Visiting Professor and Writer
in Residence at Richmond University. He won the
Jerwood Fiction Uncovered Prize for Best British
Fiction, was twice longlisted for the International
Dublin Literary Award and was shortlisted for the
CWA Dagger Award and the Rome Prize. He co-wrote
Art and War: Poetry, Pulp and Politics in Israeli Fiction,
and was a columnist for the *Washington Post*.

ALSO BY LAVIE TIDHAR

Maror

ADAMA

LAVIE
TIDHAR

An Apollo Book

First published in the United Kingdom in 2023 by Head of Zeus,
part of Bloomsbury Publishing Plc

9 7 5 3 1 2 4 6 8

A catalogue record for this book is available from the British Library.

ISBN (HB): 9781804543467
ISBN (XTPB): 9781804543474
ISBN (E): 9781804543443

Cover design: Ben Prior
Typeset by Divaddict Publishing Solutions

Printed and bound in Great Britain by
CPI Group (UK) Ltd, Croydon CR0 4YY

Head of Zeus Ltd
5–8 Hardwick Street
London EC1R 4RG

WWW.HEADOFZEUS.COM

CONTENTS

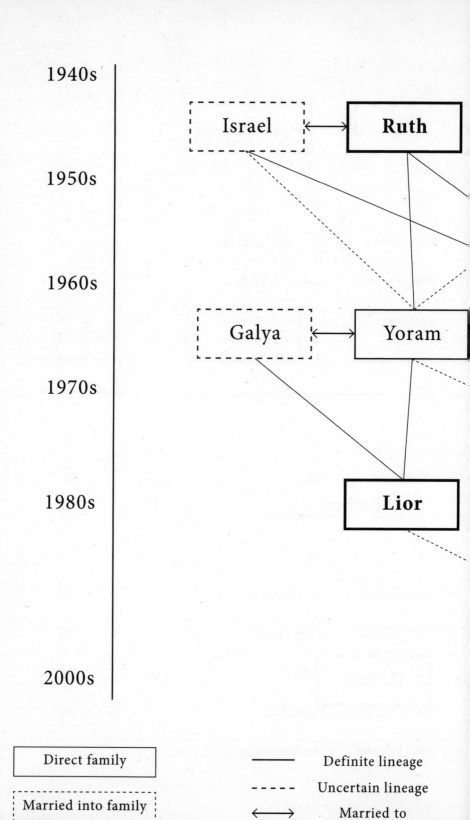

1940s	
1950s	
1960s	
1970s	
1980s	
2000s	

Israel ←→ **Ruth**

Galya ←→ Yoram

Lior

Direct family	
Married into family	

—————— Definite lineage

– – – – – Uncertain lineage

←——→ Married to

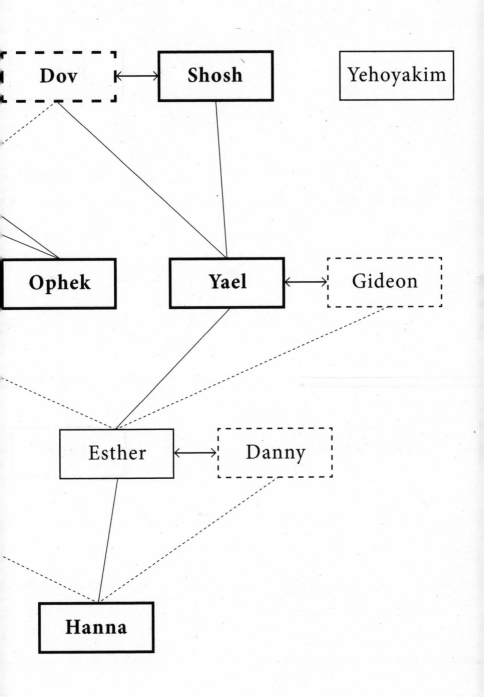

FAMILY TREE

PART ONE

THE END

Hanna

Miami, 2009

1

ON THE AFTERNOON HANNA'S MOTHER DIED THE HOUSE DREW
itself into an early dusk. The sharp Miami sunlight struggled to
break through dirty glass, bounced off dust motes and drew faint
bars across the faded pictures on the wall. The shadows curled in
the corners like sleeping black rat snakes.

They had argued, earlier, a listless fight without much in it.
Esther sat propped up in the bed, wrapped in blankets despite the
heat. Hanna lit a cigarette.

'I told you not to smoke,' Esther said.

'You don't tell me what to do.'

Esther's head was framed in the small bedroom window. The
dim light put a halo over her head.

'Bring me a tea,' Esther said. 'The way I like it, with a slice of
lemon, like back home.'

'This is home,' Hanna said.

'I know,' Esther said. Her face was pale and Hanna saw the fine
hairs on her temples were damp.

She said, 'I'll get the tea.'

She went into the kitchen and smoked, tapping the ash into her
mother's old brass ashtray, the cheap one that had *Palestine* etched
on the bottom, and that always sat on the windowsill.

Hanna smoked and the house drew itself into an early dusk
and a silence settled. Hanna looked out of the window. Mrs
Noyman's gardener was trimming roses in the heat, across the
road. Mr Shulman, the dentist, drove by in his iridium-silver

Mercedes on his way to the clinic. A blue sky stretched over white houses slumbering in the heat. Palm trees with fleshy green leaves barely stirred. Why was her mother drinking tea with lemon all of a sudden? Why was she talking about back home? She never mentioned the place she'd left behind her. It wasn't even a topic.

Hanna pinched the cigarette and stubbed it out in the ashtray. The water boiled. She poured it into a glass and steeped the tea. She sliced a lemon. She took the tea back to the bedroom.

Esther lay in the bed. Her eyes were closed.

'Ima?' Hanna said. 'Ima?'

She put the tea and saucer down carefully on the bedside table. She sat on the side of the bed. She took her mother's hand in hers. There were a thousand things she suddenly wanted to say and yet none at all.

The doctor had come and gone and the circus of verifying and authorising a death had concluded. Hanna made coffee and when they all left she sat and smoked in the kitchen.

The doctor was a small, no-nonsense woman. She wrote *cancer* under Cause of Death and patted Hanna's hand, and Hanna remembered when she was small and went to see her, how the doctor always smelled of menthol cigarettes and always had a sweet in her pocket, ready for Hanna.

'Any relatives, anyone to inform?' the doctor asked.

Hanna shook her head. 'My sister,' she said unwillingly. 'But she's in...' She tried to remember. 'An ashram somewhere and they don't have phones.'

'Anyone else? Family, relatives?' the doctor said.

'Not that I know of.'

'There must be someone, no?' the doctor said.

'She said they were all dead.'

The doctor nodded then. She touched Hanna's hand briefly again, and then she left. Hanna didn't want to sit in the room where her mother lay. So she smoked until the car from the funeral home pulled in outside and she watched them later as they took Esther with them and drove away.

It was so silent in the house. What *did* she know about her family? There must have been someone, no? But they were all dead. How selfish was her mother? How could she just up and *die* on her like this? She wasn't even old. She just got sick. It was so stupid.

Hanna started crying, but silently, just sitting there at the kitchen window. Later she emptied the ashtray into the trash. She turned it over when she did it. That old etching underneath: *Palestine*. She thought of her mother's strange accent, which she never lost. The bits of Hebrew. Bedtime songs in a language neither Hanna nor her sister spoke. Nonsense words, really. Something about the wind in the cypress trees. Or so her mother said.

Hanna went into the living room. She turned on the television. She watched *Desperate Housewives*. She wanted to call out to her mother. 'Ima! Your show's on!' Why was the house so *quiet*? She got up. She went into Esther's room. The bed covers were pulled back. She sat on the edge of the bed. She put her hand on the indentation in the mattress where her mother had lain.

'Oh, Ima,' she said. She felt the tears come on then and this time she broke the silence with it, crying with great big gulps of air, snot running down her face, and she blew her nose noisily on her sleeve. She curled into the spot on the mattress where Esther had lain and she closed her eyes. She could smell her mother's Lancôme as she fell asleep.

The funeral came and went the next day. Esther's friends from Ocean View came. Esther had worked at the hotel for fifteen years. The neighbours came. People from the gun club.

Aunty Maria, from the hotel, gave Hanna a big hug.

'It's always the good ones who're taken early,' she said.

There was no rabbi. The cemetery's ground baked hot in the

sun. There was a grave and Esther was put inside it and then she was covered up with dirt.

Afterward, in the house, Hanna felt she moved like a ghost between the mourners who came. There was coffee and cake. Aunty Maria stopped her, said, 'She was so beautiful.' She moved a strand of hair from Hanna's face gently.

'You have her eyes,' she said.

Hanna's phone rang when she was in the bathroom. Her sister, who'd finally got her message. They cried on the phone.

'You should have come,' Hanna said. 'I would have waited.'

'Death is just a state of change,' her sister said. She must have been quoting someone.

'Whatever,' Hanna said.

They chatted briefly. Hanna flushed the toilet. She went back into the house. She supposed she should sit shiva, but the thought of being stuck there in the house for seven days seemed preposterous, and her mother was never religious. Aunty Maria got a little drunk on the cupboard sherry. She hugged Hanna, tears welling and leaving a damp spot on Hanna's top.

'Call me, anytime,' Aunty Maria said.

'I will,' Hanna promised.

The sun shone brightly outside. The guests left one by one, until soon they had become an exodus, like a flock of black birds fleeing the gloom back into the sunlight. Soon there was nothing left but empty plates with crumbs on them and dirty cups that once held coffee. Hanna washed them in the sink, left them to dry, and wondered what the hell she was going to do now. She had nowhere to go back to.

The lawyer came in the late afternoon, the hybrid car drawing into the driveway with a soft hum. It sounded like a golf cart. The lawyer was a woman in her fifties, her hair dyed a bright red.

'I am sorry for your loss,' she said.

'Thank you,' Hanna said. She felt very alone at that moment, and suddenly angry. She knew the day was coming, had moved back in with Esther less because of the illness and more because she had nowhere else to turn just at that moment, but it still came as a shock to find her mother so unmoving in the bed the day before. Now everything had changed and yet, somehow, everything was just the same as before.

'I won't keep you,' the lawyer said. 'The house is rented, so you'd need to change the agreement if you want to stay.' She looked at Hanna critically. 'You grew up here?'

A series of apartments and houses, of which this was the last – 'It's just a house,' Hanna said.

'She had a little in savings, not much,' the lawyer said. 'It will go towards settling her bills and the funeral costs. So you don't have to worry about that. Other than that there's just this. She left it with me but didn't leave instructions.' She passed over a small wooden box.

'I guess it's yours,' she said.

'Thanks,' Hanna said. She took the box without thinking. It looked like an old tea box. It said *Wissotzky* on the cover.

'Well, that's that,' the lawyer said. 'Again, I'm sorry for your loss.' She shook Hanna's hand briskly.

'Thank you,' Hanna said. She put the box on the kitchen table. She escorted the lawyer to the door. She watched the car drive smoothly down the road. She reached for a cigarette, then let her hand fall. Esther had always smoked, before the cancer.

Hanna sat down on the hard chair and listened to all that immense silence, pressing down on her, crushing her.

She opened the box. An old Israeli passport, long expired. She opened it and made a little abrupt sound, caught in the throat, when she saw her mother's photo, so young that for a moment it was like looking at an old picture of herself. Her mother looked into the camera, lips closed, eyes wide and nervous.

Hanna put it to one side. If she'd hoped for gold coins or some other heirlooms she was disappointed. There was nothing of value inside the box. She took out an old photo of her mother, in khaki uniform, holding an army rifle. She was posed somewhere in a desert, against the dunes. Esther, the soldier.

Another photo, Esther with a small fat baby in her arms. She looked tired. It all looked like it belonged to another era, the colours muted. Her mother's hair was roughly cut, like it was done with blunt scissors by someone who knew nothing about cutting hair. Esther wore shorts and a white blouse. She was pretty.

Did Esther have secrets? She never talked much about what came before America. She always worked. In the hotel she started as a maid and was promoted to receptionist. She never complained about the work. There was always food on the table. She kept a gun but then this *was* Florida. The gun was somewhere in the house. Hanna made a note to do something about it. Esther never talked about any relatives and Hanna had found in herself a resistance to ask. Sometimes Hanna wondered what it was like, to have grandparents, aunts and uncles, cousins – a family. She put the box down and called Alexandra.

'Hanna?' It rang seven times before Alex finally answered. 'What do you want?'

'I miss you,' Hanna said.

'Yes, well.'

Hanna could hear music in the background, people talking, laughing.

'My mother died.'

A silence on the other end. Then, 'I'm sorry,' Alex said.

'Yes, well.'

'Listen, Hanna,' Alex said. She was somewhere on the beach, Hanna could tell. Old anger surfaced. 'I can't talk right now—'

'Are you on a date?'

'Listen, Hanna—'

'I just thought you might—'

'We're not together anymore.'

'God damn it, I *know* that, Alex—'

Some girl somewhere was laughing and Alex spoke low, she must have covered the phone with her hand, before getting back on.

'I'll call you,' Alex said. 'Are you OK?'

'Not really.'

'I'm sorry.'

'Look, it doesn't matter,' Hanna said. She stabbed the phone and cut the call. She sat there breathing heavily. Stupid. Stupid!

She lit a cigarette. Fuck it, she thought. She emptied the rest of the box on the table. A photo that must have stuck to the bottom fell out. Hanna turned it in her hands.

A long table, a woman at the head of the table, the adults sitting along both sides, a couple of young mums with fat little babies, matzos and small plates of gefilte fish on the white cloth. Hanna grew up in Florida, she knew gefilte fish when she saw it. Bottles of cheap red wine and a stain already on the white tablecloth. Everyone looked happy. She turned the photo over and looked on the back.

Passover Seder, 1965.

She looked closely at the picture. If her mother was there maybe she was one of the babies.

'Fuck this,' Hanna said aloud. She shovelled everything back into the old tea box and shut it. A new recklessness took her. There was nothing for her here. The last few months already seemed like a strange, unpleasant dream. Esther, wasting away in the bed. The petty arguments.

Hanna suddenly felt free.

She went through the house, opening and closing cupboards, but it was all just crap. She went into her room and pulled her clothes out of the wardrobe, found her bags and shoved everything in. Armed with her possessions she went out to the car and put them in, then went back and searched again.

She found the gun inside a shoe box in Esther's closet. She

stared at it for a moment, checked it for bullets, then shrugged and put it back. She didn't need a handgun. Finally she went back to the kitchen, washed the coffee cup and emptied the ashtray and put it back on the windowsill. She bit her lip, thinking. Then she took the tea box with the photos. She went outside, locked the door to the house and got in her car.

Moonlight on asphalt and the palm trees silent. Hanna eased the car onto the road and put on speed. She wound the window open. She listened to the quiet.

The city ended. The darkness swallowed her. She drove in silence, with nothing but old ghosts she'd never met to keep her company.

PART TWO

LIOR'S RETURN HOME

Lior

Kibbutz Trashim, 1989

2

THE BLACK TELEPHONE RANG ON THE DRESSER. IT RANG TWICE before Lior picked it up. The blind beggar outside was singing. No one could shut him up.

'Hello?'

He could hear her breathing.

'It's Danny,' she said. 'He died.'

Lior stood very still. Cars passed outside on Allenby. The blind beggar sang his song. Lior wanted to beat the receiver against the wall. He wanted to beat it against the beggar's skull until he shut up for good. He stood very still.

'Hello?' she said. 'Are you there?'

'What happened?' Lior said.

'Does it matter?' she said tiredly. 'He's dead.'

'It matters,' Lior said.

'He was found in the khirbe with a bullet in his head,' she said mercilessly. 'The boys found him. They think he shot himself.'

'And what do you think?' Lior said. He spoke with some effort. It had been a long time since he last saw the boys. He wondered what they were doing in the khirbe in the first place.

He watched the whores outside under the neon light for the Pussycat Club. Not for the first time, he thought he needed a better place to live.

'He was alone, it was his old service revolver,' she said. 'He still had it in his hand. Listen, Lior. I just called to let you know, is all.'

'So now I know.'

'Yes.'

Too late, he said, 'I'm sorry.'

'Yes,' she said.

'How are you, Esther?'

'I'm...' She fell quiet. He could hear a baby crying in the background. 'It's too soon,' she said. 'I don't know how I feel. The funeral's tomorrow.'

'I'll come,' Lior said. He didn't know why he said it.

'You don't have to.'

'He was my friend,' he said.

'Yes, well. You left,' she said. 'You left and we stayed.'

Lior thought of the old place. He swore he'd never go back. There were all kinds of reasons. Her voice brought them back. He could hear her breathing on the receiver. He tried to picture what she looked like now.

Good, he thought. She looked good.

The silence of the kibbutz spread out behind her. Lior could hear it, a silence that was like a negative force. Crickets, soft footsteps somewhere in the darkness, a scooter bike engine starting up suddenly a few rows down on the road that circumnavigated the kibbutz. He tried to picture where she lived now. They must have given them a family room.

'I'm sorry,' he said.

'I have to go,' Esther said. She hesitated for a moment. 'Goodbye.'

She hung up quickly. Lior just stood there. A police car cruised slowly down the street, its lights flashing, and the whores went deeper into the shadows and waited for it to pass. The blind beggar kept singing. He'd been singing since before the war.

Fuck him, Lior thought savagely. His hands shook. He lit a cigarette. The beggar had his war and Lior had his. He was barely more than a kid when they sent him into Lebanon. He stuck his head out of the window.

'Shut up!' he screamed.

'Leave him alone!' one of the whores shouted back. She was

barely more than a shadow. Lior closed the window. He sat down. He stared at the cigarette in his hand.

Who killed Danny?

He should have been there. They wouldn't have dared to mess with him, not if Lior was there. He thought of a night in the children's house, the three of them the only ones awake.

He and Danny and Esther.

'Lior, you awake?'

'Yeah. Esther?'

'I'm awake.'

They got up and snuck out of the room, the lamplight from the road outside the only illumination, and their shadows crept beside them on the wall. No night watchman, not tonight, and the intercom on the wall was silent. Lior's heart beat fast. They weren't supposed to be up at night and out of their beds. They couldn't afford to get caught.

They made it to the door and hesitated.

'Come on!' Danny said.

Lior pushed the door and they went outside. Beyond the children's house the kibbutz lay sleeping in the moonlight. There was no one around. A crooked moon hung in the sky. It watched them as they made their way along the pavement, the asphalt warm under their bare feet. They went past the ugly concrete sculpture of a faceless, lumpy man, one of the many dotted around the kibbutz and made by Shraga, the sculptor who worked in the sheep pens. In the distance the peacocks cried out from the children's zoo, the sound strange and piercing, and Esther gave a little jump in the dark.

'I hate the peacocks,' she said.

They passed the basketball court and now came to the beginning of houses, some with lights still on behind windows, and so they kept to the shadows, following a shortcut up the hill and through the manicured grass before the pergola that separated the social club from the singles club and down the hill and on to a main road with houses sloping down it.

This was the most dangerous part.

Lior heard footsteps and then laughter and he pulled Esther back just in time. They hid behind rose bushes as they saw Mitzi, the kibbutz's hairdresser, and Aharon from the falcha go past, arm in arm, both of them smoking, and as they walked past Mitzi dropped her cigarette on the ground carelessly. She wasn't kibbutz-born, she only joined because she married Uli, the mechanic, after her army service.

Danny darted out onto the road and grabbed the cigarette, which was still smoking. He brought it back and took a drag and coughed, and Esther said, 'Be quiet!' but no one noticed them. Danny passed the cigarette to Lior and he nervously put it to his lips. He held it there a moment and passed it to Esther.

'You didn't even smoke it,' she said.

'Yes I did!'

'Did not.' She lifted the cigarette and took a drag and blew out smoke and smiled at him through the smoke and he thought his heart would burst.

'Come on,' Danny said.

Twice more they had to hide, once when a foreign volunteer drove by on a bike, weaving drunkenly across the road, and a second time when a car came down the road from the gate. The dining room was ahead of them then but still everything was quiet and they slipped through the bushes to the complex of buildings that housed the laundry and clothes depot.

In front of them stood the kolbo, the little store that dispensed sweets and small personal items of all sorts to the members on their allowance. Danny led them to the back of the building and up the concrete steps to the second floor. Here they saw the window to the kolbo was open: just like Danny said it would be.

'You go first,' Lior whispered. Danny smiled. He dangled over the railings and made the leap easily, then slithered through the open window. Esther followed him and then it was Lior's turn.

It was dark inside. He turned on his torch.

In its light they could see cardboard boxes piled up everywhere. A crate of vodka sat in the corner, two boxes of Noblesse cigarettes, boxes of bamba and bisli snacks that made Lior's mouth water just looking at them, boxes of coffee and chocolate bars...

Esther ripped open an Elite box and Lior watched as Twist and Ta'ami bars cascaded onto the floor. The torchlight shuddered and then went out as they fell to their knees, reaching for and ripping wrappings, and Lior shoved chocolate into his mouth until he couldn't fit it in anymore. It tasted so much better for not being allowed.

They were stealing from the collective.

But he didn't think about that, only the taste of the chocolate, and he could have as much as he wanted, they could have everything, and he looked at Esther, and he looked at Danny, and they started to laugh.

'Who's there!' someone shouted. Lior froze. A grownup outside, and a light sweeping against the window. The night watchman. They would be discovered, there would be consequences—

Esther mewed. The sound was eerily accurate. The man outside stopped on the stairs, tried to shine the torchlight into the room. The three of them moved against the wall and the light caught only the open box, the spilled chocolates.

'Yob tvoyu mat,' the man said, cursing in Russian. 'Someone's going to have to clean this up. Here, pussycat, here...'

Esther mewed. Lior tried not to laugh. He shoved his fist in his mouth and bit his knuckles. The man cursed again, but evidently did not want to bother with a lost kitten and an open window. The torch turned elsewhere. They heard his footsteps going down the stairs and then a silence.

They waited in the dark. Lior stirred first. He crawled to the window, stuck his head out. He was afraid of being discovered at any moment but there was no one there and the silence lay over the sleeping building, the concrete steps and the black pavement. He climbed out and Esther and Danny followed him.

Then they ran all the way back to the children's house.

3

LIOR PICKED UP THE RECEIVER. HE DIALLED A NUMBER, listening to the dial winding back slowly after each digit. The beggar kept singing outside. The phone connected at last.

'It's me,' Lior said. 'I can't do the job tonight.'

He waited.

'I have to go to a funeral,' he said. 'It's up north.'

The voice on the other end sounded angry.

'It's family,' Lior said.

He put the phone down.

He took off his shirt, stripped and stepped into the tepid shower. A cockroach watched him from the corner. After the shower Lior put on clean clothes. A white shirt, a black jacket. Black trousers and nice polished shoes. He packed a light bag. He took his gun. He took his keys. He locked the door behind him, not that there was anything to steal. He went down the stairs to the street.

The blind beggar was propped against the wall, dead or asleep. Lior almost felt bad for shouting at him earlier. He dropped a shekel into his bowl. How did the old joke go – how can you tell a kibbutznik? Someone who gives a beggar a shekel and asks for change.

'Hey, Lior!'

It was one of the working girls. Lior looked up. She leaned against the wall with her arms crossed, not wearing very much. She looked at him without expression. 'Buy me a drink?' she said.

'I'm leaving town for a while,' Lior said.

'Too bad,' the girl said. 'I was just starting to get used to you.'

Lior got in his car. Night-time on Allenby, drunks outside the strip club, someone scoring dope in an alleyway. A police car cruised past and turned on Balfour. Lior drove slowly, the city calling out to him. He loved Tel Aviv and the night that was never quiet, that was always alive. The silence on the kibbutz could be overpowering, crickets and moonlight and the little cries of the other kids asleep in their beds. Gadi who always wet his mattress. Once there was a storm outside. They were only small then. A tornado that came inland from the sea and swept up trees and tractors, in the morning the smell of tree sap was everywhere and the workmen in their blue overalls came to cut the wood but the broken tractor they used to play on remained on its side half buried in the ground for weeks after. They had all woken up, crying, alone, all but for Gadi, who slept soundly through the tornado. Around midnight a night watchman stuck his head in through the door, swept torchlight around them and left.

Why was he thinking about the old days? He drove along the coast and the sea was on his left as he headed north.

Tel Aviv receded behind and fragmented into suburbs. Eventually they, too, stopped, and the land became a darkness of fields and train tracks, of orange and avocado groves. Sleeping settlements came and went, ghostly lights in the darkness, and the isolated streetlights whooshed by as he drove past. The air turned cooler by degrees. It was late, and he thought about Danny, Danny with his gun in his hand and his head blown off, slumped by the khirbe. As kids they used to go on hikes there, to the abandoned Arab village, with its ruins of houses where wild cactuses grew red prickly fruit. They'd drunk fresh water from the source, where the old well was, and collected fat blackberries in the summer.

What was Danny even doing there?

Lior knew what they were going to whisper Danny did. He

could tell even Esther believed it. They would call it an accidental discharge, of course. No one was going to say 'suicide'. But that's what they'd believe. And then they'd sweep it under the carpet like they did everything else. The first rule of the kibbutz was that you didn't wash your dirty laundry in public. What happened at home stayed at home. And you never involved outsiders.

His fingers tightened on the steering wheel. The Hadera chimneys came into view on his left then but he could smell them even before he saw them, that awful stench of the coalworks. His employers in Tel Aviv had business dealings in Hadera. He drove on, past Caesarea, past the fish ponds where they found that dead girl back in '75. He stopped at the petrol station between Arab Fureidis and Jewish Zikhron Ya'akov and stretched his legs, unwilling for the moment to go any further. He went in and got a coffee and lit a cigarette and breathed in that humid sea air and the smell of oil and warm asphalt. He remembered this petrol station from all the summer trips to the beach in Tantura, from all the times he hitchhiked a ride to Tel Aviv with one of the members who got car keys for that day, and every time, before the army, that they themselves drove to get wasted in the pubs in Zikhron Ya'akov. And he remembered a night much like that night, his hair was long, before the army shaved it off, and Danny was leaning against the hood of the car, smoking, and looking at him with a goofy smile, and he remembered thinking, this was it, that moment, that was as good as it got, with that same damn smell of salt air and oil and asphalt.

He tossed the cigarette and got back in the car and drove down the dark road with fields on both sides and no more lights on the road and only dark dirt track turnings into the fields. Then he saw a flashing blue light and a siren started up and Lior slowed down. He watched the unmarked car in the rear-view mirror. The siren didn't let up and he reluctantly slowed and then stopped on the side of the road. He didn't get out of the car, but waited. The police car behind him stopped and sat there a while and then a man came out and approached. He shone a torch through Lior's window.

Lior wound down the glass.

'Cohen,' he said. 'What are you doing here?'

'Keeping the peace,' Cohen said.

'My friend is dead,' Lior said.

'Don't get any ideas, Lior.'

'Like what?' Lior said.

'Exactly.' Cohen studied him, then sighed. 'Pay your respects,' he said. 'Then go back to Tel Aviv and there'll be no problem.'

'They say he shot himself,' Lior said. He couldn't help it.

'He did,' Cohen said.

'Why would he do a thing like that?'

'We have it down as an accidental discharge,' Cohen said. 'On account of the arrangements.'

'What if it wasn't a suicide?' Lior said.

Cohen shook his head.

'Don't go causing trouble, Lior,' he said. Warning him.

'Who would want to kill him, Cohen?' Lior said.

'No one,' Cohen said. 'You have a good kibbutz there, Lior. A quiet, peaceful place.'

Lior couldn't read him at all.

Cohen knocked on the roof of the car.

'Drive safely, now,' he said.

Lior nodded.

He rolled up the window.

He hit the gas.

4

COLD MOON, A SILENCE IN THE CYPRESS TREES. WHAT WAS THAT song about the wind in the tops of the trees? Something with campfires and a girl pining for her man to come back from war. He couldn't remember. There was always a song about cypress trees and men going to war. He drove the last mile across empty road where he knew every feature and bump, past the intersection and the corn field and the dirt track turning to the khirbe, the Arab village that was no longer there, until he came to the turning for the kibbutz. The factory rose above him then, tall silos belching out a chemical stench. He drove past the sheds where he fell as a child onto a coil of barbed wire, past the small apple orchard, the wadi down the hill below him on the right, until he reached the gate.

A watchman in the guard booth watched him sleepily. He ambled out with his rifle, shone a torch at the licence plate. Lior knew him: Malachi Uzan, who worked in the sheep pens. He rolled down the window.

'Lior?' Uzan peered at him behind his bottle-top glasses.

'Get that fucking light out of my face, Uzan,' Lior said.

'Sorry, sorry. What are you doing here at this hour?'

'Just open the gate, will you?'

'Sure, sure. Haven't seen you in, what, how long has it been, Lior?'

'Not long enough,' Lior muttered.

'I remember when you were a little boy running around in the sprinklers,' Uzan said, and scratched his eye behind the glasses.

He was better with sheep than with people. 'You going to see your grandma?'

'Yeah.'

'You heard about Danny?'

'Yeah.'

'Terrible, what happened.'

'What happened, Uzan?'

'Well, I mean...' Uzan said. 'You know.'

'I don't know,' Lior said.

'I thought you said you heard,' Uzan said.

'Depends,' Lior said. 'What's to hear?'

'Nothing, nothing,' Uzan said. 'I mean... He wasn't himself recently, you know? But I never thought...'

'Thought what, Uzan?'

'Well, you know. In the khirbe? Well, it must have been an accident, that's all. Terrible thing. And with a young wife and a small child and all. We mourn as a community.' He said that last one with the devout sincerity of someone who learned the words by heart.

'You're going to the funeral tomorrow, Uzan?' Lior said.

'I would, but I got rotated nights for guard duty, didn't I,' Uzan said.

'So you're not going.'

'I will try to make it. At such times as these we must—'

'Come together as a community,' Lior said.

'Exactly.'

Lior thought of the sign that hung in the communal dining room.

'The road to ourselves begins with others,' he said.

'Exactly!'

'What was Danny doing, Uzan? What was his job?'

'His job? He worked in the factory, Lior.'

'What was he doing there?'

'He was the supply manager or something.'

'How's Esther?'

'I haven't seen her, Lior.'

'Alright. Let me in?'

'Sure. Say hi to your grandmother for me.'

Uzan went into the guard booth. He pressed a button and the gate lifted. Lior eased the car through. Uzan waved goodbye. Lior didn't wave back. He found a parking spot outside the administration building and got out, smelling cut grass, late blooming jasmine and eucalyptus. The eucalyptuses were brought from Australia back in the nineteenth century and planted in their millions in an attempt to dry the malarial swamps. Now they were everywhere. A cat watched Lior from the doorway of the administration building. Lior stared back until the cat blinked and looked away.

He hadn't been back in years but he knew every inch of the damn place. He found himself walking by habit. Here he waited for the bus to the regional school where they lived and worked from the age of thirteen. Here was where he pushed Merav into the rose bushes once. He came to the kolbo and the laundry building and remembered again the taste of that stolen chocolate, and how good it was. No one around, and for a moment he was tempted to pick the lock and go in, as if it would somehow bring Danny back from the dead. He walked on and hesitated outside his grandmother's room. The light was on inside. He went in past the untended garden and let himself in quietly.

The light was on and Ruth sat in her armchair despite the hour. She was reading a book by Kaniuk.

'Lior? Why did you come back?'

She put the book down and watched him in that way she had, eyes bright and intense, and he marvelled at how lined her face was now, and how light she seemed.

'I came back for Danny.'

'You came back for Esther, you mean,' his grandmother said. She shook her head. 'Are you staying here tonight?'

'I was hoping to.'

'You can take the sofa. What are these clothes you're wearing?'

'It's just a jacket, Savta,' he said.

'A jacket! You look like an undertaker.' She dismissed it with a wave of her hand. 'Could you make me a cup of tea?' she said.

'Sure, Savta.'

'Do you have a cigarette?' Ruth said.

'I thought you quit,' Lior said.

'I'll quit when I'm dead,' Ruth said, and laughed at her own joke. Lior took out his pack and shook out a cigarette for her. She took it from him in both hands, put it in her mouth and reached for a box of matches on the table.

'The tea,' she said.

'Right.'

He went into the kitchenette and put the kettle on.

'And don't use a new teabag.'

She lit a match and took a drag. Lior found the small dish with the squeezed used teabags. He took two and dumped them in a mug, added a slice of lemon and one sugar.

'And don't throw the bag away. It's good for one more.'

'Yes, Savta…'

He carried the tea back to her.

'Sit down,' she said.

He sat on the sofa, feeling like a little boy again. Saw the framed photo on the table, the one that was always there. Passover Seder in the kibbutz dining room. 1965.

Ruth sat at the head of the table. Then Yoram and Ophek, her children, on either side. Lior had loved Ophek, the magician. He vanished in 1976. He'd taught Lior how to fire a gun.

Next to Yoram was Galya, looking tired, holding a baby Lior in her arms. Aunty Paula and Aunty Malka, who never spoke, sat together as they always did. A baby Esther and her mother sat near the end of the table, though she wasn't blood.

It always hurt, that photo, seeing his parents so young and alive.

He looked away. There was nothing good in old pictures.

'Are you still working for those gangsters in Tel Aviv?' his grandmother said.

'Savta...'

'So you are.' She nodded, sucked the lemon, stabbed out her cigarette. 'I understand, Lior. When we were kids we left our homes in Europe, our lives, all to come here. We left everything behind. We tried to make a better world, as much as it might be hard for you to grasp just now. A new society. Our children were meant to be better than us. But I think they just tried to please us.' She brooded. 'At least you left. Even if it's to work for those parasites. They were always there, you know. What gun do you use?'

'Savta!'

'Show me.'

He brought out his gun. She took it from him. Old hands held it, old fingers dismantled it expertly. She reassembled the weapon and handed it back.

'Nice,' she said. She patted his hand. 'When you carry a gun,' she said, 'you've got to intend to use it.'

'I just came for the funeral,' Lior said.

'You don't know why you came,' she told him ruthlessly. 'But dead men don't need guns.'

'Danny didn't shoot himself,' he told her.

'You don't know shit about shit, Lior,' Ruth said. 'You've been gone a long time. The kibbutz isn't the same anymore. It's dying. Oh, we've not been hit as badly as the others. The stock market and the bad loans and all of that. We're fine. We're balancing the books. But the soul of the kibbutz is not there. They want to abolish communal sleeping for the children! They're even talking about differential salaries, an end to our entire way of life. Don't you think this is slightly more important than your friend shooting his brains out?'

'No,' Lior said, 'I don't.'

Ruth smiled without amusement. 'I know,' she said. 'You never fit in with the collective, not really. But Danny did. You left. He stayed. Leave it alone. And leave the girl. She doesn't need you pining for her.'

'I'm not... I wasn't...'

'Get some sleep, Lior.' She patted his hand again. She pushed up from the chair and went to the bathroom. When she came back she was in her robe and without her teeth.

'Savta loves you,' she said.

'I love you too,' Lior said.

Ruth nodded. She went to her bedroom. Lior lay on the sofa. He stared at the ceiling. He listened to the quiet. He hated the quiet. Soon he fell asleep.

5

SUNLIGHT BROKE THROUGH THE BLINDS AND BEAT HIM OVER the head without mercy and with it came the crackling music on the radio, and Ruth said, 'Get up, it's time to go.'

'Go where?' Lior said, closing his eyes against the glare, thinking it was much too early, but he couldn't shut out the radio, or the birds outside, chittering on the branches of his grandmother's ficus tree. It drew wasps to it, too. Tree and wasps existed in symbiosis, the insects pollinating the trees, the tree a nursery for the wasps' eggs. Neither could exist without the other.

It was like the kibbutzim and the state, he thought, groggy: the state needed the kibbutzim to settle where it could be of most use, the kibbutzim needed the state to exist in. Socialist wasps in a capitalist body: but now there was an illness in both.

'Stop dreaming and get up,' Ruth said. 'We're going to the dining room.'

'Not the dining room,' Lior said, groaning. The very thought filled him with horror.

'It's not every day I have my grandson come visit me,' Ruth said. 'So get up, wash, and get moving.'

'Yes, Savta…'

He had a quick shower and put on clothes he already knew were too much city. Ruth climbed into her electric buggy and Lior half walked, half ran beside her to the dining room. Members were already heading to breakfast and the road was busy, people calling out hello, the workmen in blue overalls and the falcha and the sheep pen workers in boots and the factory men in chequered shirts. The women wore dresses or shorts or jeans and came from the laundry or the children's houses or the office. The kibbutz might have liberated women from the task of child-rearing, but it still seemed to expect them to look after the kids and do the laundry. Not Ruth, though. She had been a driver and now she drove her electric buggy with ferocious joy, zigging and zagging as fast as the small electric engine would let her. Lior felt horribly conspicuous jogging beside her.

'Sit next to me!' Ruth shouted.

'No, thank you!' Lior said.

'Hey, Lior!' Lior slowed down and the man, his one-time youth leader in the movement, beamed at him and shook his hand. 'Uzan said you were home again but I didn't believe it.'

'I'm here for the funeral.'

The man lost the smile. 'Of course,' he said. 'Terrible, what happened. We mourn—'

'As a community,' Lior said. 'Listen, I have to go. My grandmother—'

'Of course. Ah, Ruth. The very bedrock of our little community,' the man said, and Lior remembered him suddenly and with aching clarity on a night, long ago, when they'd found him spying through the window into the girls' showers.

They never said anything, of course. What difference would it make if they did? He jogged after his grandmother but she was already parking the buggy by the steps to the dining room.

More people stopping him, a girl from his class pushing a pram with a fat little baby, one of his teachers, Mitzi the hairdresser, Mordechai who taught Lior how to drive a tractor, and all this before going in through the doors. Then inside the cavernous space of Brutalist Soviet-style concrete, with the sign overhead that said 'The Road To Ourselves Begins With Others'.

He felt ten years old again. One summer he had had to work

in the dining room, cleaning up after everyone left. He still remembered spraying the metal food carts with the hose and watching all the cockroaches scuttling away.

Ruth was already sitting. The kibbutz elders sat at a couple of long tables, chopping salad. It was a point of pride for them to chop cucumber and tomato as small as possible, to make an Arab salad, *baladi*, and they sat focused on the task at hand, patiently cutting the vegetables into smaller and smaller chunks. Ruth had her coffee in front of her and a hardboiled egg and a slice of bread. She sat apart from the others. Lior came and sat beside her. He drank instant coffee. He tried to see if Esther was there somewhere in the hall but she wasn't.

'You don't eat?'

'I'm not hungry.'

'You should eat,' Ruth said.

He went to get food. Aunty Paula and Aunty Malka served behind the counter. They didn't speak, but when they saw him they gave him something almost like a smile. They weren't family, but Ruth had raised them like her own.

They gave him an extra helping of hardboiled eggs: their way of showing affection.

He put the tray next to his grandmother's and went for another coffee.

He stood by the giant samovar and when he finished he turned; turned, and saw the boys.

They loomed, bigger than he remembered them, the casual meanness of youth transformed by elite army units and the war in Lebanon into a hardness in the eyes that wasn't there before.

Big Dick Yuval. Gadi the Ginge. Pushyou Peleg. Everyone on a kibbutz was given a nickname. Sometimes no one could remember afterwards what their real name had been. They weren't particularly imaginative, most of the time. Yuval had a big dick. Gadi was ginger. Peleg liked to push people. He pushed Lior now.

'Lior. Heard you were back.'

'I guess word gets around,' Lior said. He looked to see if they were carrying. They looked too, to see if he was.

'What are you, an undertaker now?' Yuval said, looking at his clothes.

'In a way.'

'Big city guy, huh? So why'd you come back?'

'You know why I came back.'

'Danny, right. It's sad what happened.'

'You found him?'

'We did. It was a mess, too.'

'Real mess,' Gadi said, and made a face.

'What were you doing in the khirbe in the first place?' Lior said.

'What business is it of yours?' Gadi the Ginge said.

'Calm down, Ginge,' Yuval said. 'We were on patrol, Lior.'

'What patrol?'

'We're in the security committee,' Yuval said. 'Been a bunch of sheep thefts recently and we're not far from the Green Line, you know. What with the recent kidnappings and all, we have to be careful.'

'Protect the kibbutz,' Pushyou said.

'Didn't protect Danny, did you,' Lior said.

'Listen, asshole—' Ginge started, but Yuval cut him off.

'He killed himself, Lior,' he said. 'End of story. And you don't live here anymore. You left. So pay your respects and say your goodbyes and fuck off back to Tel Aviv. Alright?'

Lior nodded.

'Right,' he said.

'See you at the funeral.'

Peleg pushed him again, for good measure. Then they turned and went back to their table. He hadn't seen any of them since, what was it? The Siege of Beirut in '82.

Shit. They were only kids then.

*

They were moving street to street and house to house, clearing out hostile elements. One house a frightened grandmother; another children hiding behind their mother's dress; in yet another a group of hostiles returning fire. The soldier behind Lior got it straight in the chest and dropped. Lior threw a grenade inside. The men shouted. An explosion started small then rocked the house and blew up the roof: it was packed with explosives.

Lebanon, man. Shit. They had no idea what they were doing there. Arik Sharon with his mad dream of taking Beirut and fucking Yasser Arafat right up the ass. Seventy-two hours and we'd be out of Lebanon, he said. In and clean.

Instead, this.

Another house, kick down the door, go room to room, 'Clear!' and move on, past burned cars, stepping over corpses. The worst were the snipers, shooting at you from the rooftops, shooting at you from fuck knew where, and the soldier beside Lior dropped and Lior took cover – he couldn't even remember the dead guy's name.

House to house and street to street, clearing the perimeter. The navy blockaded the city out to sea, the tanks and artillery rolled to position: choking the city in an iron grip.

And there he was fresh out of basic training and into this. He sweated and smelled smoke and fumes and hot metal and blood. Fucking Beirut. Fucking Arik. At last he stopped and didn't know where he was anymore. Soldiers streamed past him, an officer barked orders. Lior fell back. He found a café, still standing. Three guys sitting there cool as you like, smoking a sheesha pipe.

'Hey, dickhead, are you going to sit down or what?'

Ginge grinned at him; Pushyou sulked. Yuval was indifferent.

He came and sat down with them. What else was he going to do?

'What the fuck are you doing here?' he said.

'Enjoying the show.'

They'd gone to the army a few months before him. He hadn't been back to the kibbutz since the thing that happened. Once he joined up he was gone for good.

'What show?' Lior said.

'This.' Yuval pointed. Overhead mortar flew. The explosions rocked the city. Plumes of smoke rose like a field of wild mushrooms. 'We're going to fuck them up so good,' he said.

'Who are you with?' Lior said.

'None of your fucking business,' Pushyou said.

Ginge laughed.

'Classified,' he said.

They'd joined some commando unit, Lior knew that. While he was just a regular grunt. They were still more boys than men. But men without morals made good in a war without merit or sense.

'Alright,' Lior said.

'You want some?' Ginge said, passing him the pipe. He wiped the mouthpiece with his sleeve. 'It's clean.'

'No, thanks.'

'Come on, boys,' Yuval said. They stood up. 'See you, Lior.'

'Yeah. I'll see you.'

He watched them go, then got curious enough to follow. They didn't go far. A man in civilian clothes met them down an alley. He pointed to a garage. When they opened it there was a nice car inside it. A Mercedes. Yuval smiled when he saw it. Pushyou and Ginge went over the car. Lior watched them from the shadows. They wired it up, strapped explosives under the chassis and under the hood and ran wires. They looked like they knew what they were doing. The civilian was gone. Mossad, or Shin Bet. Something like that. Yuval went into another room and came back with a skinny fucker who looked like he was high on hash. Lior knew what hash smelled like, it smelled like Lebanon, there was so fucking much of it. Yuval talked to the guy and the guy shook his head and Yuval slapped him. The man nodded and got behind the wheel of the car. Yuval took a briefcase and opened it for him. Cash. The man nodded. Yuval shut the briefcase.

'Yalla, yalla,' Pushyou shouted. The driver hit the gas.

Ginge mimed 'Boom'. The boys laughed.

They took the briefcase with them.

6

SUNLIGHT OUTSIDE. COOL AND LOUD IN THE DINING ROOM.
Everything on the kibbutz was a room. A house was a room. The
communal classrooms and dormitories for the children were a
room. The vast dining hall – a room. Volunteers from Scandinavia
occupied two long tables near the back. The fug of cigarette smoke
hung above the smokers' section. Workers in blue overalls argued
over the latest news in the *On Guard* newspaper. 'For Zionism,
Socialism and Solidarity Among Nations', its masthead declared.
A kid at a nearby table mashed a hardboiled egg with a fork and
mixed in olive oil and salt. Lior looked away. Arab workers from
the factory sat separately at two tables of their own. Ruth finished
her coffee.

'Well?' she said. 'We have a funeral to go to.'

He wasn't really sure *how* old his grandmother was. She still
worked – of course she did. She'd never stop. The elders of the
kibbutz could not contribute in the way they did before but they
could still do something. Now she met with all her old friends
every day in a nice, comfortable room where they packaged
products from the factory: simple, easy work, but work all the
same. Work was the ultimate value on the kibbutz. To be a worker.
If you did that then you were somebody, you were not a parasite,
a word Ruth spat out like the worst insult, worse than anything.
And if you worked hard then whatever else you did didn't matter.

He went out with her and accompanied her to work, still feeling
conscious in his white shirt and black trousers and black jacket

36

and his shiny shoes – a parasite in his fashion, here among all the
blue overalls and khaki shorts, and with his hands too smooth.

He watched Ruth work. She worked with the same quiet,
ferocious determination she always had, frowning in concentration
putting labels onto boxes, labels onto boxes, labels onto bo—

The nurse tapped him on the shoulder gently, jolting him
awake.

'Coffee?' she said. She was not a kibbutznik, he could tell
straight away.

'Please.'

'No problem. You are visiting your grandmother? She is a dear,
isn't she?'

No one had ever called Ruth a dear.

'She's something,' he said.

The nurse brought him coffee and sat down with him on the
sofa.

'It's good they work,' she said. 'Packing those little gift bags. It
gives them purpose. The ones who can still work, at least…'

'You've been here long?' Lior said.

'A couple of years, now.' She smiled. 'I like it here. I'm Ronena,
by the way.'

'Lior.'

'She never mentioned you.' Ronena frowned. 'I don't think she
ever mentioned her family.'

'The kibbutz is her family,' Lior said.

'They all say it,' the nurse said, 'but not many of them mean it.
Many of them don't *have* family anymore. Kids grown up and left,
they don't even come to visit. These are the lucky ones, they still
have each other. You visit often?'

Lior said, 'No.'

She nodded, accepting it for what it was. 'The ones who are
further gone, I just sit with them. They cry at night, sometimes.'

'Like in the children's house,' Lior said, without mercy.

'What?'

'Like they did to us, when they left us in the children's house, alone. Crying into an intercom for the night watchman... That's you, now, I guess. You're the person on the end of the intercom.'

'You sound bitter.'

He rubbed his face.

'I guess so,' he said. 'I've been away a long time. I don't think about it, usually. It's just this damn place brings it back.'

'I like it here,' Ronena said. Just then Motti who used to work in the avocados called out to her. His bladder gave out and he sat there looking upset.

'I liked it here, too,' Lior said. But he said it quietly, and anyway the nurse was gone by then.

'What if you become a ghost and never leave this place?' Esther said. They were in the room and it was dark. No more adventures outside. A dog barked in the distance. The moon cast shadows from the trees outside. Esther sat on the bed hugging her knees. 'What if you die here and you never get to leave?'

'There are no ghosts,' Danny said. 'When you die, you die. My grandfather says that's non-reductive materialism.'

Danny's grandfather fought with the partisans in Europe during the war. He said things like 'non-reductive materialism' and 'the dictatorship of the proletariat' and he had a moustache like Stalin.

'When you die you die,' Lior said, agreeing with him. He saw Ulrik's corpse before his funeral. Ulrik rode a tractor and the tractor overturned and Ulrik went under it. When Lior saw the body he thought if Ulrik had a soul it got crushed right there under the tractor with him. So that was that.

'But what if you don't?' Esther said. 'What if when you die your soul can't go to heaven and it stays where you are, and you can't—'

'My grandfather says the notion of heaven is bourgeois and the

38

only heaven is the one we can make right here on the kibbutz,'
Danny said.

'Fuck your grandfather, Danny,' Esther said.

That shut Danny up. Lior grinned. But he could see Esther
was serious. Something had spooked her, and she shivered there
on the thin blanket, and the shadows lengthened outside. Then
they heard the footsteps of the night watchman coming along the
corridor, and they froze for just a second before they climbed back
under the covers and pretended to be asleep. Lior tried to control
his breathing. This night watchman was the angry one. Lior could
feel his heart beating, the blood in his ears. He tried to breathe like
he was sleeping.

But the night watchman wasn't angry that night. He was very
quiet. He came to check up on them. He went bed to bed. He went
to Esther's bed last. And there he stopped.

'Wake up, Lior,' Ruth said. 'This is a funeral.'

She was back on her buggy. Lior sweated in the hot sun. The
funeral procession began at the pergola by the social club. The
elders all came on their motorised scooters. Young mothers,
many he grew up with, pushing prams – friends of Esther's. The
kibbutz secretariat, friends of Danny's from the factory, the boys,
a handful of the Scandinavian volunteers, Danny's parents, his
sister Miri, some family from outside the kibbutz who Lior didn't
know. They all added up.

The Chevra Kadisha funeral car drove slowly along the road,
carrying the coffin. Lior walked alongside his grandmother, who
was driving slowly for once. Everything was slow, the procession,
the steps everyone took, the babies who looked half-drugged in the
heat, fat and happy. He saw Esther ahead, walking by the coffin.
He felt that same helpless coil of frustration with the slowness of
it all, the sedateness. He hurried his steps, going to catch up with
Esther, to tell her he was sorry—

'Stop right there, Lior,' Ruth said. He slowed down again, giving in to it, that sense that there was nothing to hurry up for because there was nowhere to go.

What if you become a ghost and never leave this place? he thought.

They passed the library, the playground and the grass where once a year the Independence Day celebrations were held. The fun ride was locked. They only turned it on once a year. As a kid he couldn't understand it, what was the point of a fun ride you could never ride? An Arab gardener weeded the flower beds. They went through the houses, the hill sloping down, past the sports hall where they screened movies on Wednesdays, which as kids they always used to try and sneak in to. The road went up again, past the children's zoo where he'd had to feed the chickens, then more houses until the houses stopped and the pine trees began.

The cemetery gates were iron. The coffin was carried in. Lior walked slowly, so slowly now. His feet trod pine needles. The smell of fresh sap. Weeping boletes grew under the pines. In the autumn they'd always pick them to cook, and everyone knew the cemetery had the best mushrooms. The boys carried the coffin. They made him sick. What was Danny doing in the khirbe on his own? Unless he wasn't on his own when he died. He saw Esther by the grave. She was crying.

Lior stopped when he saw his parents' headstones. Ruth held on to his arm. Yoram and Galya. Rest In Peace.

'Do you ever miss them?' Ruth said.

Lior said, 'No.'

His grandmother sighed. 'You carry all your dead with you, you know,' she said. 'The ones you hurt. The ones you loved. The ones you lost.'

'They're just ghosts,' Lior said. 'Do you miss him, Savta?'

'I miss him.'

Lior put a pebble on the graves, one for each. They went back to the funeral. There were speeches, but short. Esther tried to speak but she was too broken up. There was no ceremony. The coffin was lowered into the ground. Then it was over. They started shovelling earth over the coffin.

Lior picked a handful of earth. There was a little bit of moisture in it. A worm wriggled from where he had disturbed it. He smelled the good, fresh earth. He tossed the handful over the coffin. The boys worked efficiently with spades. He wondered how many they had had occasion to bury. Then it was done, just a mound of earth unmarked amidst the tombstones.

'A good funeral,' someone said.

The kibbutz secretary said, 'Thank you, chaverim, for coming. There is coffee and tea in the social club.'

They started to file out. A man in a suit stood by the gate. It was a good suit. He had good shoes. He was clean cut and clean shaven. Yuval came up to him and they shook hands, then spoke briefly.

Lior said, 'Who is that?'

'Bill Anderson,' Ruth said. 'He's an American.'

'What's he doing here?'

'He's from a big American company. They've been in talks to buy a share in the factory.'

'It's doing that well?' Lior said.

'We're doing alright,' Ruth said. 'Not like some of the other kibbutzim.'

'I read the news,' Lior said.

'Are you coming to the social club?' Ruth said.

'There will be coffee and tea,' Lior said. 'Some cookies too, I bet.'

'They'll be the good cookies,' Ruth said. 'When are you leaving, Lior?'

'I just got here.'

'You're a stubborn ass.'

'Must have got it from someone,' Lior said, and Ruth reluctantly smiled.

'You've got a smart mouth,' she said. 'Alright. But don't come crying to me when it all ends badly.'

'Yes, Savta…'

She got on her buggy and drove off at full speed. Lior stood alone by the gate. Esther went past.

'Esther.' He stopped her.

'Lior.' She looked at his face. 'You didn't have to come,' she said.

'You know that's not true.'

'I'm glad you came,' she said. She touched his hand lightly. 'It's been…'

'How do you feel?' he said.

'Numb,' she said. 'I don't think it's sunk in yet.'

'What happened, Esther? Do you know?'

'He must have… I don't know, Lior. He was distracted recently. Quiet. He was out a lot. I thought it might be the baby, or work, something…' She leaned into him and he held her in his arms as she cried without sound.

'I'm glad you came,' she said. She wiped her face. 'You really didn't have to. When are you going back to Tel Aviv?'

'I don't know.'

'You're staying with Ruth?'

He nodded.

'Maybe I'll see you around then.'

She turned to leave when he put his hand on her arm, stopping her.

'Esther, I don't understand—'

'There is nothing to understand, Lior!' Her voice was raised. People were looking their way. 'There's nothing to understand,' she said, more quietly. 'Shit like this just happens sometimes. Go home, Lior. Go wherever it is you go to at night. And leave me alone.'

This time when she walked away he didn't stop her. The American still stood by the gate. He shook Esther's hand, offering condolences. She nodded, then left. Lior watched them all depart:

the boys, the elders on their buggies, the mothers with their prams, the kibbutz secretary in the second best car from the kibbutz car pool. The American got into a black Buick. The guys from the Chevra Kadisha were the last ones left. They huddled by the gate sharing a smoke. Lior went over and lit up himself. He offered the pack around. They took it gratefully.

'Kibbutzniks,' the one on the left said. 'They don't even bury properly.'

'No kaddish, no nothing,' the one on the right said. 'But they pay like everyone else. You in the business?'

'No, I'm in Tel Aviv,' Lior said.

'The big city,' the one on the right said. 'Pshhh.'

'How come,' Lior said, belatedly realising something, 'the funeral wasn't pushed back?'

'What do you mean?' the guy on the left said. 'You've got to bury the next day, no question.'

'But it was a gunshot,' Lior said. 'Needed an autopsy, a crime scene, something, no?'

'Accidental discharge,' the guy on the left said. 'Medical examiner signed off on it straight away.'

'Best thing for it, considering,' the guy on the right said, lowering his voice. 'You know. Because of the circumstances.'

So the police thought Danny shot himself.

But he knew that already.

'Right,' Lior said.

'Hey, thanks for the cigarette,' the one on the left said as Lior turned to go.

'Don't mention it,' Lior said.

7

THE SOCIAL CLUB WAS THE SAME AS HE REMEMBERED IT. THE sort of space that could be reused for a disco or a kid's bar mitzvah or a memorial service for your grandfather. Tables and chairs, cold refreshments, coffee and tea. The inevitable samovar. Plates of Elite chocolate wafers, and cookies – the good ones.

'Lior.'

It was Roni, the kibbutz secretary. She'd been the geography teacher when Lior was a kid. Then she was the car pool supervisor and then the under-secretary and then head of the decoration committee and then she managed the volunteers for a while and had a baby from a volunteer from Venezuela that everyone knew was his other than her husband. Then she was head of the culture committee and was then elected to the top position of secretary. Now she looked on Lior with something less than good will.

'Roni,' he said.

'I heard you were back. Are you staying with Ruth?'

'Aha.'

'You can't stay long,' Roni said, with the air of a police officer handing a parking ticket to someone who thoroughly deserved it. 'Outside visitors regulations.'

'But I'm family,' Lior said.

'Doesn't matter,' Roni said. 'It's in the bylaws.'

'Well, I'm here now,' Lior said.

'So you are,' Roni said. 'Why, exactly?'

'I came for the funeral.'

'A great sorrow to us all,' Roni said solemnly. Lior wasn't sure she meant Danny's death or his own presence.

'He was my friend,' Lior said.

'Yes,' Roni said. 'I remember you two broke into the kolbo – no, don't try to deny it, Lior. I knew it was you.'

'We were only kids.'

'And the time you stole the car and left it in the field—'

'Well, I mean, we were just—'

'And the time you got drunk and threw up over my dog!'

'It was an accident,' Lior said.

'And then threw him in the kiddie pool to clean him up!'

'Well, it was a long time ago,' Lior said.

'Some children are just born bad,' Roni said, with an air of great sorrow. 'We're not supposed to say it, but there it is. Not everyone can fit the collective. But Danny did, Lior. Eventually. He got over the badness inside him. Danny was a full member. He made a life here.'

'He died here!' Lior said.

'And we mourn his death. But I don't see what it has to do with you.'

'What was he doing, Roni?' Lior said.

'Doing? He worked, he had a family.'

'So why…?' He left the rest of it unsaid.

Roni shrugged. 'I'm sure I couldn't say.' She put a hand on his shoulder gently.

'Make sure to be out by the end of the week,' she said.

Lior smoked. He drank weak coffee. He stared out of the window at the manicured grass. Little fat kids trudged past in swimming trunks on their way to the pool. Around him people chatted in quiet voices, spoons clinked in glasses. It was so much like home and yet he was a stranger. He couldn't stand being there anymore.

He pushed his way out of the room, stood outside breathing in air that was too fresh and too still. Danny didn't kill himself. He knew that. Which meant someone else pulled the trigger, someone else left him in the khirbe with a bullet in his brain. Which meant that somebody knew who, and why.

'Phone call for you, Lior.' It was Uzan, looming out of the gloomy inside.

'Me?'

Uzan nodded. Lior followed him to the black telephone. He picked it up.

'When are you coming back?'

Benny, back in Tel Aviv.

'I'll be a few days,' Lior said.

'Took me forever to track you down. Couldn't remember the name of that kibbutz of yours. Trashim. What kind of a name is that?'

Lior smiled, remembering the story Ruth liked to tell. 'When they first came to settle the land it was nothing but rocks, unsuitable for farming. So they called it Trashim, a land of hard stones, and spent the first two years clearing it.'

'Aha,' Benny said. 'That's what they tell you? Well, I need you back here, Lior. You don't earn if you don't work. And that bank job is almost ready to go.'

'I've got to do this, Benny.'

Benny sighed over the phone. 'I'm sorry for your loss,' he said.

'Yeah,' Lior said. 'Me too.'

'Stay out of trouble, Lior. I can't protect you up north.'

'Protect me from what?'

'From yourself,' Benny said, and hung up.

Lior stared at the receiver. First Cohen popping up on the road to the kibbutz like he knew Lior was coming. Now Benny delivering some sort of fucked-up warning. *Everyone* was telling him to go back to Tel Aviv.

Someone had to know something.

He just had to find someone willing to talk.

★

She sat on her porch with a cool jug of lemonade sweating on the other side of the glass. She was as cool as the ice in the lemonade. She wore a summer dress and stretched long tanned legs and stared at Lior without any obvious expression. Maybe she was bored. Maybe she was curious. Cool ice in the jug and cool mint leaves in the lemonade and her eyes were green like the mint. She watched as he walked past her along the narrow path.

'What brings you back?' she said. She folded one leg over the other. Stretched one arm towards the lemonade jug as though in invitation. Lior stopped.

'Merav,' he said.

'Been a while, Lior.' She wrapped tanned fingers round the glass and took a sip. Her lips were red, redder than he remembered, and she was fuller now, she filled the dress up and didn't leave much for the imagination. He wet his lips. She saw and smiled.

'You thirsty?' she said.

'I guess.'

'You can come over,' she said. 'I won't bite hard.'

She laughed. She looked like she had all the time in the world. Maybe she did. Lior approached cautiously.

'Sit,' she said. She indicated an empty chair. Lior sat. She poured him a glass. He took a sip. It was cold.

'Don't you have work to do?' he said.

'Finished early,' she said.

'What do you do now, Merav?' he said.

'This and that,' she said. 'I help with the accounts.'

'Married?'

'God, no. You?'

Lior said, 'No.'

'Still pining for Esther?' she laughed, but it had a bitter ring to it. 'Never figured out what you saw in her.'

'She was just a friend,' he said.

'How's Tel Aviv?' Merav said. She looked him up and down then. 'What are you, Chevra Kadisha?'

'I do this and that,' Lior said. 'I help with the accounts.'

She didn't smile at that.

'Which accounts, I wonder...' she said. 'You got a cigarette?'

'Sure.' He passed her one, then lit them both up. The cigarette tasted sweeter, somehow, there on the porch with Merav.

'I used to have a crush on you, you know,' she said suddenly. 'You were always so serious. Or angry maybe. You always *brooded*, anyway.'

'I was just a kid,' Lior said.

'Not at the end there, you weren't.' She traced moisture on the side of her glass. 'I wasn't, either.'

Lior contemplated that in silence. Merav sat there, as though she'd sat there all afternoon, as though she was happy to sit there just like this for as long as it took. Lior took another sip. The lemonade made his head spin pleasantly.

'What's in it?' he said.

'Vodka.'

He took another sip.

'You didn't go to the funeral?' he said.

She shrugged. He was very aware of the way her body moved under that thin dress when she shrugged. He didn't think she was wearing anything under it.

'I don't like funerals,' she said.

'What do you like, Merav?'

'Silent men and quiet days,' she said. 'You staying with your grandma?'

'I am.'

'Ruth is alright.' She bit her lip, considering. 'She's cool,' she said, deciding.

'Cool?' he had to smile, both at the English word and hearing it applied to his grandmother.

'Can't say it about many people here,' Merav said.

'If you don't like it here, why do you stay?' Lior said.

'I like it fine, Lior,' she said. 'I like it just fine. People you don't like…' she leaned forward as if to impart a great secret – 'they live everywhere.'

She laughed, close to him. He felt her breath on his face. Minty cool. Felt the heat of her body.

'You want to go inside?' she said.

'Inside?'

'I have some records.'

'Who listens to records anymore?' Lior said.

'I do. They're more romantic.'

'I like it out here.'

'Suit yourself.' She pulled back, took another sip of lemonade. Stretched in her chair, stretched out her legs. He was painfully aware of every motion. She could see it. She smiled.

'There's a disco tonight,' she said.

'Disco?'

'There's a disco every night.'

He remembered the kibbutz disco. Drinks on the account and guys trying cheesy pickup lines on the latest crop of volunteers. Thumping music in a concrete air-raid shelter, some teenagers always throwing up outside. That used to be Danny and him. The thought made him smile.

'It's not like it used to be,' Merav said.

'Why not?'

She shrugged. 'It grew. The boys took it on and now it's paid entrance, every night and into the morning, people come from all over. It's a good money earner for the kibbutz.'

'The boys have been busy,' Lior said.

'Well. You know. They're good sons.'

A good son was someone born to the kibbutz. Someone who stuck around. Could have been Lior, should have been him, maybe. But he left.

'I might swing by, then,' he said.

'I might see you there, then,' Merav said.

'Where is it these days?'

'By the stables.'

'Alright. Is the music good?'

She finished her drink and put the glass down on the table harder than she intended. The sound jarred.

'Who cares?' she said.

Arab workers were busy painting his grandmother's neighbour's house. They spoke softly among themselves. Lior had noticed the Arab workers earlier. Factory workers in the dining room, a gardener. Now this. Kibbutz Trashim sat lonely in the apex of the Manasseh Hills, a short ride from the West Bank and the large Arab towns and villages, still within Israeli jurisdiction, that sat just before the Green Line that demarcated Israel and the Occupied Territories. Lior assumed the labourers came from there.

He needed a way into the factory. He needed to talk to someone who knew Danny. Ruth was sat in front of the television. An old movie was on, and it took Lior only a moment to recognise it as *The Vultures* from '53, starring Bill Goodrich. Some of it was shot on location on the kibbutz, and family lore said that Ruth's sister, Shosh, had been in the crew. It was the first Hollywood production filmed in the then-new State of Israel.

He sat down, letting the film wash over him, his head spinning with a mixture of coffee, vodka and funeral blues. His friend was dead and he'd done nothing about it. On the screen, Goodrich hid in a barn on the kibbutz as mounted policemen surrounded the barn with weapons drawn.

'I wonder if he'll get out this time...' Lior said.

Ruth snored softly. Lior helped himself to some pastrami in the fridge and made a sandwich. He ate standing up. He bit a pickle. Fuck this, he thought. He wiped his mouth and went out. The Arab workers were still outside. Bees hummed in the flowers.

A lone child rode past lethargically on a bicycle. Other than that the kibbutz was still. *Schlafstunde*, the kibbutz elders called it. Everyone else called it the afternoon rest. Between two and four nothing was allowed to stir. The adults downed tools and slept the heat away. In the children's houses the children lay down to sleep. He remembered too many days like that, lying in bed wide awake, the metapelet shouting, 'Lior, face to the wall!'

Schlafstunde. A good time to go poking about, with everyone asleep. He almost went to see Esther. But not now, with everyone there. There'll be time later. He walked along paths he knew too well, his feet leading him. The factory towered ahead on the boundary of the kibbutz, silos jutting into the air. He went to the gates and let himself in like he used to do a thousand times. The factory was its own place. A truck waited patiently as it was loaded with pallets. Arab workers drove front loaders to and from an open warehouse. Lior walked past, like he belonged there. He was a good son once, too. No one would think to stop him.

He went past the old granary where they used to jump in the harvested wheat when they were kids. There were always grain beetles in the funnel and he hated them when they crawled up but he had loved playing in the funnel. Now it was empty and there were no kids around, and the old silo was locked. He went past the lab where the chemicals were tested and wandered past the admin offices. An army jeep was parked outside and a driver in khakis leaned against it smoking. Lior went over and gave him a nod and lit up himself. He couldn't remember when he had his first cigarette. It was just a thing everyone did. Everyone smoked.

'You work here?' the guy said.

'I'm from the kibbutz.'

'Ah.'

'You?'

'I'm just a driver.'

They smoked. Presently an officer came out of the building,

gave Lior a stare, gave the driver a nod. The driver tossed the cigarette and got back in the jeep and they took off.

Lior stared after them. Just then Yuval came out of the admin building. He wore blue overalls stained white.

'What the fuck are you doing here?' he said.

'Just looking around.'

'You don't fucking *live* here anymore, Lior,' Yuval said. He wiped his hands on his overalls. 'And it's dangerous to be here unsupervised. You're not even wearing a hard hat.'

'You're not wearing one, either.'

'You could have an accident.'

Lior nodded. 'Always possible,' he said.

Remembered one night, on guard duty at the gate, before he left. The older guy had to go to one of the warehouses in the factory, it had pigeons living in it. Took Lior with him. He had an air rifle, was a sniper in the army, back in the Yom Kippur War. *Pop!* and a pigeon dropped down. *Pop!* and another one went. Reloaded the air rifle after each time, until the floor of the warehouse filled up with small corpses. Then he went through them methodically, one by one, and shot them again – 'Confirmation kill,' he said, by way of explanation.

'So get going,' Yuval said. 'Man, you were always a pain in the ass.'

'I'm gone,' Lior said. He walked away, purposely slow. Knew Yuval was watching him all the way back, until he turned the corner and was gone from his sight.

He wondered why the old grain silo had brand new locks put in, still shining with oil.

8

HE WOKE UP SWEATING BUT THE NIGHT WAS COOL. RUTH WAS in the kitchen. He could smell frying eggs.

'Eat up,' she said. She slid eggs onto a plate and buttered up toast. Lior ate. Blood pounded in his ears. Ruth helped herself to one of his cigarettes. She lit up and studied him.

'You're going to get yourself killed,' she said.

'Doing what?' he said.

'Whatever it is you're doing.'

He mopped up yolk on the plate and chewed. 'Come on, Savta,' he said. 'I'm only doing what you'd do in my place.'

She watched him through the smoke. Inched her head at last, maybe in agreement. Reached under the table, brought out Lior's gun wrapped in a napkin.

'I oiled it for you,' she said.

He got up, kissed the top of her head. Reached for the gun.

'They don't allow guns there,' Ruth said.

'Guns where?' Lior said.

'The disco.'

'Who said I'm going to the disco?'

Ruth shrugged. 'It's night on a kibbutz,' she said, 'and you're not even married. What else are you going to do?'

He nodded. 'Alright,' he said. 'I'm going to the disco. Like old times.'

'I'll keep the gun for you, then.'

He nodded again. Went out, closed the door softly behind him.

Listened to that goddamned silence. A cat startled him. It rubbed against his ankles.

'Here, kitty...'

For some reason he thought of the khirbe. They'd taken a tractor, they'd both just passed their tractor driving test. They attached a carriage and took turns driving Esther in the back. They drove to the khirbe and picked fruit from the cactuses that grew there. Sabras. Prickly on the outside, sweet on the inside. Danny was learning the guitar back then. He had a cheap acoustic. He brought it out and played as Lior built a fire.

'The wind blew through the tops of the cypress trees,' Danny sang. He had a good voice. 'In the distance the jackals howled. And you were beautiful, so beautiful my darling, sat by the campfire beside me.'

Did it bother Lior, how Esther looked at Danny? Did he put together kindling, make a pyramid of sticks, the old song that was sung a thousand times blowing in the wind and ruffling the tops of the cypress trees, did he bite down on a feeling he would not, could not, acknowledge?

The fire burned. They sang more songs. They made black coffee. They passed around a pack of Noblesse and coughed when they tried to smoke – but they were getting better at it. Was it then Esther spoke? The elders wrote a hundred songs about campfires and cypress trees and going to battle, but never about secrets whispered in the dark; and he knew now that it was because secrets could not be sung.

Secrets could not be celebrated, only endured.

Was it then that they first made their plan?

He shook his head. The cat vanished. He couldn't remember and anyway, what did it matter now? He went along the path and smelled roses, jasmine, mint. Moonlight on black asphalt and that quiet again.

He headed downhill, towards the stables. He began to hear the thumping of a bass. The lights flashed in the distance. A car passed Lior, and then another. He could hear laughter from the open windows. Townies, rolling in.

The disco sat in its own grounds where an empty field used to be. A large parking space was full of cars. The ground was muddy and there was a line at the entrance. Two guys he vaguely knew, they were a couple of years below him in school, took money for tickets. Pushyou Peleg played bouncer. He scowled when he saw Lior.

'My money no good?' Lior said. He flashed him a Ben-Zvi, a full one hundred. Pushyou took the money and pocketed it.

'No, your money's good,' he said.

'Thought so.'

'Enjoy your time, Mr Lior, sir,' Peleg said.

'Fuck off, Pushyou.'

He walked inside, half expecting a shove in the back.

But this was a professional operation. Lior knew professional. His bosses in Tel Aviv had nightclubs and discos all over town. Here there was the intake on the door. There was the intake on the bar. He saw the bar. It was a good bar. A long counter and plenty of top-shelf drinks behind it and kegs of Goldstar and three girls on staff serving drinks. Ginge supervised the money. The bar was packed with a mostly young crowd ordering arak and grapefruit juice, vodka lemonade, beer and a few white wine spritzers. The sophisticates of the lower Carmel and the Jezreel Valley. Lior pushed his way to the bar and bought a beer. He drank it slowly.

The music pumped loud. The dancers danced and swayed. Everything that was fast and loud and in English. Belinda Carlisle and Madonna and Kylie. *They* didn't sing about the fucking cypress trees. They didn't sing about going to war and no girl was waiting for them by the campfire. Lior sipped. He watched couples hook up in the corners. He watched young guys still with long hair inexpertly smoking cigarettes and talking shit. Saw Scandinavian volunteers getting wasted on vodka.

'It's not much of a scene,' a girl beside him said, 'but it's a scene.'

She stood beside him and leaned against the bar. She'd changed her summer dress into a pair of jeans and a black leather jacket. She smelled of Opium perfume. She smelled *good*.

'Merav,' he said.

'You want to dance?'

'Sure.'

She took his hand and led him to the dance floor. He followed. They danced to Donna Summer. The DJ wore sheep pen boots. He put on a slow song. Merav pressed her body against Lior. He felt her breath on his ear. His hands on her waist. He let one lower, pressed her against him, felt her heat.

He watched the disco in action. The dim lights and the smoke in the air, the couples making out. Merav grabbed his ass. She rubbed against him. Lior watched Yuval standing in the shadows. Saw business being done, some townie handing over hundred-shekel bills for a small bag from some kid who waited for a nod from Yuval. Saw the townie pocket the bag and stroll back to his friends.

So that was the action, he thought. It was professional enough. Money on the door, money on the bar, money on the perishables. Maybe it wasn't much of a scene but, like Merav said, it was a scene.

The song ended. Merav pulled away slowly. 'I'm just going for a piss,' she said.

Lior went to Yuval.

'I thought I told you to leave,' Yuval said.

'I know what you're doing here.'

'Is that right? And what am I doing, Lior?'

'Drugs,' Lior said. 'Did Danny find out? Is that what happened?' He grabbed Yuval by the shirt, pushed him against the wall. 'You do him in, Yuval?'

'Fuck off, Lior,' Yuval said. He pushed him off. 'Drugs. Come on. Maybe we grow a little weed out in the far fields. Who doesn't? It's a kibbutz, for fuck's sake. And I told you already, Danny shot himself.' He looked more irritated than angry. 'Enjoy the party or go home,' he said. 'Otherwise I'll throw you out. Alright?'

'Right,' Lior said. Merav came back, zipping her pants. She looked at the two of them.

'Anything wrong?' she said.

'Just catching up on old times,' Yuval said.

'Right,' Lior said.

'Come on, then, Lior,' Merav said. She put her arm through his. 'We have our own catching up to do.' She gave Yuval a smile. 'For old time's sake,' she said.

Lior let her lead him out. Cool air outside the disco, the smell of horseshit, people smoking weed. Merav pushed him against the wall. She leaned in for a kiss.

Her lips were hot.

Lior said, 'I have to go.'

9

SHE STOOD IN THE DOORWAY BEHIND THE MOSQUITO SCREEN. SHE looked at him without expression, like she always knew he'd come.

'I had to see you,' he said.

'It's late.'

'We should talk.'

Esther opened the screen door. He came in. She shut the door behind them. The room was dark. She wore a faded T-shirt and shorts. She looked good. She had always looked good to Lior.

'We have to mourn and move on,' she said flatly.

'Do you miss him?' he said.

'Of course I miss him.' She considered. 'We were married.' She shrugged, like that summed it up. 'You want something to drink?' she said. She didn't wait for an answer. There was a bottle of wishniak next to an old Wissotzky tea box on the counter in her kitchenette. She grabbed the bottle and two cups and carried them over. She poured for them both and downed hers and refilled it. Lior sipped. The cherry brandy made his head spin. It was the sort of remedy every kibbutz elder kept in the cupboard.

'You smell of somebody else's perfume,' she said.

'Esther—'

'I'm not judging.' She looked at him, like she was finally really seeing him. 'Why *did* you come back, Lior?'

'Danny—'

'Danny's dead!' she said. 'Like you give a shit. You never came back when he was alive. You never saw either of us.'

'I couldn't,' Lior said.

'Why,' she said. But it wasn't a question, and he knew she knew.

'Because it hurt too much,' he said.

She took another gulp of wishniak and put the cup down a little hard on the table. 'You're so upset I went with him?' she said. 'That, what, I didn't give you another hand job after high school?'

'Esther!' he said. Thinking of the one time she did. When they had come so close to...

'You're a big boy, Lior,' she said mercilessly. 'I hear in Tel Aviv you do big boy things. Don't sell me your bullshit. Not me. Not now. Why did you come back?'

He whispered, 'Because I still hate them...'

She smiled then. She refilled her glass, emptied it, got up unsteadily and came to him. She sat in his lap. She smelled of sweat and burekas and funeral flowers. She smelled wonderful. She reached for his belt. He lifted her T-shirt, buried his face between her breasts. They didn't speak, not then, not for a while.

When it was done she stood by the window in the dark and smoked one of his cigarettes. He only saw her in silhouette as she stood there. He sat in the armchair with his pants round his knees.

'He was stealing from the factory,' she said. 'From the accounts.'

'What?'

'If they caught him,' she said dispassionately, 'he would have gone to jail for a long time.'

'How much?' Lior said.

She shrugged. 'Millions.'

'And no one saw?'

'Maybe they saw.'

'You knew?'

'I didn't know shit, Lior!'

'Who told you?' he said.

'The boys.'

'They lied!' Lior said.

'Why should they?' Esther said. 'They were trying to help him.'

Lior fumbled for his trousers.

'Danny could have come to me,' he said.

'He might have,' she said. 'He was dumb like that. But even he knew you were just more trouble.'

He didn't know what to say to that. What to think. She wasn't telling him everything. But it was something to go on.

'Where is the money?' he said.

'How should I know?'

She put out the cigarette into an empty coffee cup.

'I think you should go now,' she said.

He stood, reached for her. She pulled away.

'Esther...'

'You should go,' she said again tiredly.

He nodded.

She walked him to the door.

What did Yoram Taharlev write in that poem? How the kibbutz room door only stops mosquitoes, not people's stares?

There was always someone watching.

He wondered if anyone saw. He walked in the shadows, avoiding the lamps.

How was it when he was a boy? When his father was still alive? He'd come to his parents' room at four and at seven he would go back, and his father would walk him to the lamp post, and Lior would beg, 'Just until the next lamp, just until the next one,' and so they'd go from light to light, and at the next one stop, and he would ask again, pleadingly, and in this way from light to light they made their way back to the children's house.

Then with the other boys and girls he brushed his teeth and chewed his fluoride, put his little toothbrush back in its little cup holder next to all the others, then off to bed, to read a while before the metapelet put the lights out in all the rooms. He read *Chasamba* and *The Young Detectives* and other books about gangs of kids who solved mysteries or found treasure, that sort of thing. He was the commander and Danny was his second in command and Esther was the girl, there was always a girl in those books, someone for the heroes to fall in love with. They swore an oath to always be faithful to each other and to fight evil no matter what. They never spoke about the nights the quiet night watchman came. He didn't come often. And when they grew up he supposed they forgot about it. You had to learn to forget.

Eyes watching him. He could go back to Ruth. He stumbled like a drunk. Cut through the old kindergarten where he once lived, a rusting tractor in the yard where they took shelter one summer day when the kids from the adjacent kindergarten attacked with mud balls. Some kids put stones into the mud balls so they hurt bad when they hit you. He remembered crying once when the metapelet made him finish his food, it was some sort of synthetic mash from a bag, he hated the taste of it, but she made him finish every drop. A good boy leaves an empty plate. Who sang that?

The boys were selling drugs. The boys ran the disco. So what? Danny was stealing money from the factory. Maybe. So what? You didn't go to the police with this sort of shit. You never went to the police. You sorted it inside.

So what happened, Danny? What happened for you to end up the way you did?

He got to the parking lot. His car sat there, waiting. He could leave, he thought, he could fucking leave and be done with it. All he had to do was get in and drive.

He saw a big American car come in through the gate. A Buick. Not many of those around. The kibbutz cars around were all Japanese Subarus. The car parked. The American he saw at the funeral came out. Bill something. Bill Anderson.

He passed Lior, nodded politely, said 'Good evening' in English. Lior stared after him. Where was he going at this hour? Suddenly everyone and everything seemed suspicious. He went to the gate. Uzan was in the guard booth. He beamed when he saw Lior.

'I heard you were at the disco earlier,' he said. 'That Meravi of ours needs a man in her life, Lior. It's not good for a gal to be alone.'

'Shut the fuck up, Uzan,' Lior said. He jerked his head the way Bill Anderson had gone. 'What's the American doing here?'

'He has a room on the kibbutz,' Uzan said. 'While the negotiations are ongoing.'

'He seeing anyone?'

Uzan shrugged. 'What a man does is his own business,' he said.

Lior stared out of the glass. Lights were moving along the road to the kibbutz. Headlights. He counted three, one after the other. But they didn't drive up. They turned, heading on the off road that led to the factory gates.

'What's that?' he said.

'How should I know?' Uzan said. 'Deliveries.'

'At this hour?'

Uzan shrugged.

'They come and go,' he said.

'*Who* comes and goes?' Lior said.

'I don't know, Lior. Does it matter?'

Lior left him there. He went out and along the road. He saw the trucks ahead. They waited as the factory's side-gate swung open. They drove through and the gate closed.

Lior went closer. He found a spot and waited. The night was quiet, crickets made their cricket sounds. A frog croaked. He hated frogs. They bred and crawled outside the kindergarten, hiding in shadows. Their bulging eyes stared. He shuddered in revulsion. In time the gate swung open. One truck, two trucks, three trucks came out. They drove away. The gate swung shut.

Something coming in? Or something going out?

He stared after them. It was dark, but he could see their khaki-green.

Army trucks, with army licence plates.

He went back. Uzan was asleep in the booth with his mouth open.

Lior went to his grandmother's. He fell on the sofa and went to sleep.

10

Yafa Yarkoni sang on the radio. Ruth was already gone to the dining room when Lior woke up. He cooked Turkish coffee, mud-thick and black. He fried himself two eggs. Arab workers outside the window painted the neighbours' wall white.

He used Ruth's phone. He made a call. He showered and shaved and went outside. He didn't lock the door. You didn't lock your door on the kibbutz.

He walked past houses and down the hill until the houses ended. He crossed the wadi. The water was dirty with the factory's waste. He climbed the next hill and saw a deer in the distance, framed against the pines. The deer startled and vanished.

No one around. A blue sky above. Golden wheat fields in the distance. Bulbuls sat on the branch of a tree and stared at him dubiously. He remembered as a kid the hunters coming back in the night, jeeps roaring past the stables with a dead boar in the back. He went on, past the ruined old flour mill the army blew up back in '48, when the Arabs all left. He followed the next wadi until he reached the ruins of the Arab village.

It looked much the same as it always did. He picked a pomegranate from a tree and smashed it against a rock. It split open and red covered his hands. He patiently picked at the seeds.

Where was it that Danny died?

A bullet to the head. He started to look. Saw traces of police tape. Came to a place. A dark spot on the ground. Maybe this was it. It told him nothing.

He saw signs of fires around. Rings of stones, dead coal. Remembered again coming here with Danny and Esther. Was it then that they decided to do what they did?

Who killed Danny?

He had a pretty good idea who.

He lit a cigarette and waited. In time he heard the sound of a car engine. He stood and watched the plume of dust as it came nearer. The car stopped and a man got out. He was an old man. He was skinny with a pencil moustache, a bad haircut and bad shoes. His name was Moritz. He stood there and looked at Lior and shook his head.

'You look like shit,' he said. He had an old-world accent he'd never lost.

'Did you get it?'

'Here.'

Yosef tossed him a bag. Lior caught it. It was heavy.

'Who runs things in the north?' Lior said.

'Who is asking?' Moritz said. 'You or Tel Aviv?'

'Me,' Lior said. 'I'm asking.'

Moritz shrugged. 'It's not like down south, where you guys are so organised,' he said. 'Here it's just local families, depends where you are. Haifa's still mine... at least the shit parts. In Afula you have two or three families. You go further, into the Galilee, it's more Arabs there. Down here...' He spat on the ground. 'I don't come here anymore.'

'Why not?'

'Me and your grandma don't see eye to eye.' Moritz smiled suddenly and without warmth. 'Never have.' He shrugged. 'I tell the kids to stay away but they don't always listen. Had some guys, what, three four years back, came down here to rob. I mean, everyone says kibbutzniks don't have anything, but that's bullshit. You have televisions, don't you? Cash. Who knows. They figured it was an easy job. No one locks their doors. Only, my guys never came back.'

'What do you mean?' Lior said.

'Just vanished,' Moritz said.

'Maybe they went somewhere,' Lior said.

'Yeah, they went somewhere,' Moritz said. He tapped his foot on the hard land. 'Who knows what else is buried in all these fucking fields. Anyway, people wised up and they let it alone now.'

'The boys?' Lior said.

'Is that what you call them?' Yosef looked at him sourly. 'What was it like growing up here, Lior?'

'It's like everywhere else,' Lior said. 'You have to grow up somewhere.'

Moritz considered, then spat on the ground.

'You should go back to Tel Aviv,' he said.

'That's what people keep telling me.'

'Just a word of advice. Don't be an asshole like your uncle was.' Lior didn't know what he meant. He let it go. Moritz nodded.

'Well, I guess I'll see you,' he said. 'Unless I won't. If you're ever in Haifa again give me a shout.'

He drove off and Lior watched the plume of dust vanish into the distance. He could see the kibbutz on the horizon, the houses on the hill where the rocks used to be. He ate another pomegranate. Then he went back.

On the way he saw three green trucks come out of the factory. They were agricultural sort of trucks, with agricultural sort of crates in the back. The trucks had writing in Hebrew and Arabic on the side. The writing said *Sunflower Fruit and Veg*.

Ruth sat in the armchair watching the kibbutz's teletext channel. Minutes for the next kibbutz members' assembly were replaced with the weather forecast, then announcements from the decorations committee. Ruth sat still and her lips moved without sound.

'Savta?' Lior said. He knelt by her side.

'Who?' she said. She looked at him with a vacant expression. 'Who?' She raised a trembling hand and touched his face. 'Ophek?'

'I'm Lior, Savta. Lior!'

'Lior?'

Then the sharpness came back into her eyes abruptly and her hand dropped.

'I was asleep,' she said. 'You woke me.'

'You weren't asleep, Savta,' he said.

'Don't Savta me! Don't talk back, it's rude. Where have you been? Your hands are all red. Don't touch the sofa, you'll get it dirty.'

'Where did you put my gun, Savta?'

'Why, you're finally going to use it?'

'Maybe.'

She snorted. 'In the bedroom closet,' she said.

He looked at her.

'What?' she said. 'Leave me alone.'

The bag he'd got from Moritz was lighter now. But he felt better with his old gun. He sat with Ruth and they watched *The Vultures*. It was showing on the kibbutz's television channel every day that week. Bill Goodrich had just come off the rickety old ship he had been travelling on with the other illegal refugees from Europe. They had made it all the way to Palestine, but now the jig was up: British soldiers on the shore had them surrounded.

'You'll never take me alive!' Goodrich snarled. He rammed the nearest soldier, sending him to the ground with the impact, and snatched his gun.

'Come with me!' he cried. He took the hand of the mute nine-year-old girl, Karolina. The soldiers closed on them, the refugees stood with their arms raised, all but for Goodrich. He burst through the soldiers and ran, ran into the dunes, holding the little girl's hand as he sought to save them both.

Lior woke up abruptly, images fading from his dream. Goodrich, hiding on the kibbutz. The mute girl speaking again for the first time. For a short while Goodrich almost had a family again: he fell for the gorgeous kibbutz girl (played by Italian actress Isabella Rossi). Then trouble started…

It was early evening. Ruth sat in her chair, staring into nothing again. He worried about her. He didn't know how to say it. You never really talked about how you felt, growing up on a kibbutz. You had to keep things inside. Keep them contained. You grew up constantly on view. Your clothes came from the communal allocation. You showered with the other kids. You slept in the communal rooms. You ate together, crapped together, picked flowers in the fields for Passover together, went down the rows in the kibbutz dining room during the Seder waving your sad little bunch of flowers for the benefit of everyone to see but at least you did it *together*, and if you had a single thing you wanted to keep, just for yourself, you shoved it deep inside and never let it out.

You didn't say, 'I love you'. You could say you loved your country, you could say you loved this land, this fucking adama that people bled on, died for, killed for, just so you could have a home, a land to call your own. You could love this land. A girl could say she loved you, if you were going to war and you'd already knocked her up. Most of the songs were about that. But you couldn't say 'I love you' to the old woman sitting with a vacant stare in the armchair beside you, slowly forgetting your name.

'See you later, Savta,' he said. Then he got up and took his gun and walked out.

11

He stuck to the side roads but the kibbutz was busy at this hour. Kids stood outside the kolbo eating ice-creams. Mums with prams chatted in groups near the laundry building. Men strolled with that ineffable pace of people who had nowhere to go to and no hurry to get there. Teenagers waited for the bus back to the regional school. It was after dinner. People would be going to the social club or to the library or to take the kids back to the children's houses, late swimmers were still coming back from the pool, the ping pong room would be open now and there'd be some sort of class or lecture for anyone who wanted, on stamp collecting or photography for amateurs or on Ancient Egypt in the Early Dynastic Period. It didn't really matter. There'd usually be something on in the dining room too, later. One week they'd have a stand-up comedian from Tel Aviv, the next a member showing slides of a trip to Africa or a woman from Haifa talking about aliens. It didn't really matter. It was just stuff to do.

The Young Watcher is strong of will. He strives towards physical, mental and spiritual perfection. Lior saw teens in the blue work shirts with the white shoelace hanging around, having just been inducted into the youth movement. He had been in the Young Watchers himself once. It seemed like a lifetime ago.

He remembered his own induction. They were woken abruptly at night and told to come quietly, that no one could know. They were led to a place that was prepared in advance. Everything was ready for a fire ceremony. As the display was lit and the smell of kerosene mixed with the pines they swore an oath, and then they were given their instruction. For the next three months they played at being in the underground, keeping it secret, before they earned their shirts.

The Young Watcher is pure in thought and deed: does not smoke, does not drink and maintains sexual propriety.

How many of the Ten Commandments could he still remember? He looked at the kids. They looked happy. He supposed he'd been happy here, too. All in all it was not a bad place to live.

He passed through among them. He acknowledged the few hellos he got. Remembered nights like this, going with his mother to the kolbo. Getting a chocolate bar. Just hanging out outside. Special moments. Yes, he decided. He must have been happy.

He slid through the gates into the factory. It had shut for the day, all but for the skeleton crew keeping the engines running. What did they even make? Chemicals and shit. The pollutants killed the brook in the wadi. He supposed it was the price of progress. He went unhurried, not worried about being spotted. He was just out for a stroll and he was still a son of the kibbutz. Born here. Not adopted, not joined later, but grown and raised right here. A good son.

He came to the old grain silo. When he ran his fingers on the new locks they came away coated in oil. So there was this. He wasn't in a hurry. He took out the tools Moritz brought him.

They were hard locks, more than just for show. But they were still just locks.

When they snapped open he stood there for a moment breathing before he packed everything back neatly. Then he went inside.

Dark, still with the smell of old wheat lingering. He turned on his torch.

Nothing there. He thought of the trucks the night before, and the trucks he'd seen today.

Something coming in.

Something going out.

He shone his torch around. Three military crates in the back of the silo caught his eye. *IDF* on the side. Army crates. He went over. Knelt down. There was a shipping manifesto on the floor. No mention of what was inside, but a neat accounting of cargo. He took a crowbar out of the bag.

'I wouldn't do that,' Pushyou said.

Lior looked up. Pushyou Peleg stood there holding a gun. The gun was pointing at Lior.

'Why not?' Lior said.

'Because what's inside doesn't belong to you.'

'Who does it belong to, then?'

'It's ours. It's our cut.'

'Now I'm curious,' Lior said.

'You can still walk away,' Peleg said.

'Or else what? You'll shoot me?'

'Aha.'

Lior believed him.

'Would you enjoy it?' he said.

Peleg shrugged.

'I wouldn't lose any sleep over it,' he said.

Lior stuck the crowbar in the crate. He broke the wood open.

'Well, shit,' he said.

'You fucking idiot,' Peleg said.

Lior took out one of the bags. Neat bags of white powder. He weighed it in his hand. Half a kilo right there, he figured. How many in a crate? How many crates in three trucks?

'Heroin?' he said.

'Some of it,' Peleg said.

'What's the rest, hash?'

'It's what they do best, over there,' Peleg said.

'Lebanon?' Lior said.

'Lebanon,' Peleg said.

'Where's the rest of it?' Lior said.

'Gone.'

'Gone where?'

'Gone what do you care where? Stand up. Slowly. I'm going to take you to Yuval.'

'But army trucks?' Lior said.

'That's right. So don't get any dumb ideas.'

'You're smuggling drugs using army trucks?' Lior said. He pushed a nail into the bag of heroin gently. The plastic resisted, then gave way.

'We're not smuggling shit,' Peleg said. 'We're just storing it. It's sanctioned. Is that why you're here? Tel Aviv send you?'

'No one sent me,' Lior said. 'I came for Danny.'

'Stand up slowly. Turn around, you fucker!' Peleg said.

Lior stood up, slowly. He raised his hands. He held the bag of heroin.

Peleg said, 'Drop it.'

'Why don't you fucking take it,' Lior said. And he threw it in Peleg's face.

Two things happened.

One, Peleg's gun went off. Lior fell, but the bullet missed him and hit the wall. The air filled with white powder. Lior covered his nose and mouth with his T-shirt. He saw Peleg above him, choking. The split bag had hit Peleg straight in the face and burst open.

Which was two: the man was covered in heroin.

He grasped around him blindly. Lior got up to a crouch and jumped on Peleg. He brought him down hard. He held the bag over his face.

'Let me breathe, let me breathe!'

'What happened to Danny?' Lior said. 'What happened to Danny!'

'Fuck Danny!' Peleg said. 'And fuck you!'

Lior felt a savage joy as he held the bag over Pushyou's face. He'd hated those three for years. Hated the whole fucking place. Remembered the endless bullying, the pushing, the jeers. The way they'd picked on Esther when they were younger. The way they'd sometimes grab her tits when they thought no one was looking. But they were good sons just like him, they worked in the fields, they were the first to get their tractor licences. Everyone knew they'd go to the elite units later, in the army. Now he held the bag over Peleg's nose and mouth. Let him breathe that shit. What did it do to you, anyway? Could you breathe this stuff?

It didn't really matter. He held the plastic over Pushyou's face. The man tried to fight but it wasn't in him.

The man, Lior thought. But he only saw the boy.

Eventually Peleg settled. His legs kicked once and then his shoulders relaxed and he lay very still. Lior sat beside him in the dark silo breathing hard. He must have pressed harder than he'd thought.

White dust settled over the floor, over the body, over the crates. It looked like a European winter. Lior tried to figure things out.

He still couldn't make much sense of it, but:

The boys were using the old grain silo to store and ship drugs. The drugs came from Lebanon – well, that border was so porous it may as well not exist. Everyone was bringing in drugs – his bosses in Tel Aviv had their own lines of supply going.

But army trucks, and paperwork? He thought of the guy he saw the day before, coming out of the administration building in uniform.

That was the weird thing about all of this: no one was *hiding* anything.

It's sanctioned, Peleg said.

Sanctioned by *who*?

This was not the sort of operation three kibbutzniks could pull off. Lior realised that he believed Peleg.

So they were just the warehouse, a stopping point en route. It made sense. An isolated kibbutz with its own security team. Who would even think to look?

Is this why they killed Danny? He found out and was going to—

What, exactly? Go outside with it?

He wasn't going to find out the answers standing around. He knew that. And he knew they'd be waiting for Peleg to come back with the job done.

They'd known Lior would come: they'd been ready for him.

Well, let's see if they'll be ready now.

He reached in the bag and took out the C-4 and detonator that Moritz got him.

It was only a little bit of C-4.

He fixed it to the wall, activated the timer on the detonator, and ran for it.

The silo went up in a ball of flame behind him. He didn't look back. He only had a limited time and he'd just let them know he was coming for them.

12

FIRE TRUCK SIRENS IN THE DISTANCE. THE SMOKE ROSE OVER the kibbutz. Lior crouch-ran, away from the factory, to the muddy no man's land where the disco stood.

It was not yet open at this hour but he knew they'd be in there. A jeep was parked outside. He supposed it was the one they used for patrols. He hid and watched. The lights were off. It was dark outside. Stars overhead, in the youth movement they were taught the constellations and how to navigate, how to always look for the north star. He felt a little woozy. The gun drooped in his hand. He estimated the distance to the building through the empty parking lot. Maybe they weren't there after all. He made a run for it.

The building was dark and empty. The bar stood unguarded. He poured himself a drink and downed it and felt the vodka burn. He went room to room. A utilitarian office with bills of purchase, an ashtray with a still-warm cigarette stub inside.

They went recently, and they went in a hurry.

He thought of Pushyou burning in that silo and felt savage joy.

One down, he thought.

Only two to go.

Why was he feeling so light-headed? He held on to the desk for support. He shook his head, trying to dispel the feeling. The raw heroin, he thought. He checked the toilets next but they were empty.

All that was left was the cellar.

He went down. The place was old. It might have been what

they used to call a slick, once. A place built to store guns back in the days his grandmother's generation fought against the British. Exposed old brick and old stains on the dirt floor. Now it had casks of beer inside, and crates filled with empty bottles.

He moved cautiously, gun drawn. It smelled of hops in there. It was a pleasant smell. His head swam. He heard footsteps behind him.

Turned, too late.

Yuval, smiling out of the shadows.

The butt of a gun smashed into his face and sent him down a well of black water.

Somewhere a phone rang and rang. Lior woke up in a chair, his hands and feet bound in thick rope from the sheep pens. His vision swam. Ginge stood smoking a cigarette. He watched Lior.

'Couldn't leave it alone, could you,' he said. He shook his head, pinched the cigarette, stabbed it out on Lior's arm. Lior bit on a cry.

'This was a long time coming,' Ginge said.

'You smuggle drugs from Lebanon?' Lior said. 'Wait till the secretariat find out about this.'

'We don't smuggle shit, Lior,' Ginge said. 'We provide warehousing for a classified military operation. That's all. Who do you think keeps the kibbutz afloat? We do! You ever open a fucking newspaper? You see how the kibbutzim are struggling? The bank loans, the debt? Here we still have communalism. Children still grow up the way you and I did. Everyone is cared for. From each according to their ability, to each according to their needs. You *asshole*. I thought you were dumb but I didn't think you were *that* dumb. Blowing up the silo… We'll have to tell them it was a chemical fire. But it doesn't look good on us.'

He scratched his nose. 'Oh, and Pushyou,' he said.

'Bye bye, Pushyou,' Lior said.

Ginge punched him. It was the sort of well-executed, careful punch Lior could almost appreciate. It was the sort that said the man who delivered it had considerable experience with men tied up in chairs. It didn't throw Lior off-balance. It just hurt him. It hurt him a lot.

Somewhere the phone kept ringing. It was never going to stop.

'I can do this all day,' Ginge said.

'What do you want?' Lior said.

Ginge punched him again. Lior's head rocked back. He tasted blood. Then Ginge really went to work.

Lior felt a rib crack. The air was gone from his lungs. Ginge aimed short, brutal punches. Pain became a companion. Ginge took Lior's small finger in his grasp. Left hand. He twisted.

Lior screamed.

Ginge was breathing hard.

'I can do this all day,' he said.

'What do you want!' Lior shouted.

'Who sent you?' Ginge said.

'No one sent me! I came for Danny!'

'Danny was weak,' Ginge said. 'Danny was always weak.'

'You killed him,' Lior said.

Ginge grabbed Lior's ring finger. He pulled. The sound of the bone breaking was drowned by Lior's scream.

'He was weak,' Ginge said. 'That's why he took the coward's way out.'

'He killed himself?' Lior whispered. 'Why?'

'Who sent you? We know who you work for. Everyone knows. You think you're a gangster now? You're just a kibbutznik in a cheap suit, Lior.'

'I swear, Ginge, I didn't know you were running drugs. I wasn't here to muscle in on it.'

'You compromised the entire operation!' Ginge said. He took a wooden stick. The sort, Lior thought woozily, they used back in the Palmach days, the Haganah's Strike Force, when his grandmother's generation trained to take on the British using stick fighting.

The idea, Lior thought. Taking on the British Army with sticks. It always struck him as faintly ludicrous. They used to train in the forests nearby. Ginge took the stick. He hit Lior over the chest with it. He smashed it into Lior's shin. Lior screamed, and Ginge grinned like the jackals that howled every dusk on the hills beyond the kibbutz.

'We can talk about this, Ginge,' Lior said, sobbing. He could barely see now. The room was dark and Ginge was a vague shape standing above him.

'There's nothing left to say, Lior,' Ginge said. And the stick came down on Lior's face.

He woke up surprised to find he was still alive. The phone had finally stopped ringing. There was no one in the cellar room.

He was lying on the ground. The chair had toppled over and no one had bothered to pull him upright again. There was a pool of vomit by his face and the vomit was mixed with blood. Maybe they thought he'd choked on it. Maybe they just didn't care. They were going to kill him anyway.

He supposed at least he'd be buried in the place he used to call home. There were more bodies buried in the hills than in the kibbutz cemetery. But all he'd wanted was to get away from there.

He realised suddenly that he wanted to be buried anywhere else. Anywhere else at all.

He felt the knot in the rope with his good hand. When he tried to move the other the pain shot up his arm and he had to stop himself from screaming. Some of his teeth were broken. A couple of ribs.

He was a mess.

He stared at the door. It must have been a cell once, he thought. Soon they'd come in. Then it would be over.

It was pretty simple. He'd been the guy on the other side of the door before. Now he was on the wrong side of it. It wasn't like he could break the chair or cut the ropes or pull off some magic trick. Maybe Uncle Ophek could have. He was a magician. But Uncle Ophek vanished a long time ago. So maybe he wasn't that good a magician. Some things you just couldn't get out of, unless it was by pure dumb luck.

Danny must have found out about the boys. About the drugs coming through the factory. What did he do? Did he threaten them? Then they must have killed him. They wouldn't have, not unless he was going to go outside with it. He stared at the door. Heard someone coming down the stone steps. Ginge, coming back to finish the job. Someone rattled the doorknob. The door opened.

Lior stared.

Roni, the kibbutz secretary, stood there with a dumb look on her face. Lior thought it was a very dumb look.

He said, 'Help me up!'

'Lior? What is this?' Roni said. 'What are you playing at?'

'I'm not playing, Roni! They tied me up!'

'I don't understand,' she said. She peered at him. 'You look terrible,' she said.

'Untie me!'

'This is really not protocol,' Roni said. She came over to him. 'You look terrible,' she said again. She touched his jaw. Lior closed his eyes from the pain.

'Please,' he said. 'Help me.'

Something in his voice must have gotten through to her at last. When she moved she was efficient. She found a knife and cut the ropes. Blood rushed into Lior's hands. He tried to stand and stumbled. Roni helped him upright.

'What happened here?' she said.

'It will take too long to explain,' Lior said. 'What are you *doing* here, Roni?'

'I came to look for Yuval,' she said. 'About the fire in the silo…'
Realisation of some sort slowed her down.

'They were hiding drugs in there,' Lior said. 'They killed
Danny!'

'What has gotten into you?' Roni said. 'Danny killed himself.
Whatever it is you've got yourself mixed up in, Lior, it's not too
late, we'll just go to the police and—'

'No police, Roni,' Lior said. He picked up the knife. 'Sit down,
Roni.'

'Have you lost your mind?'

'I said, sit down!'

He pushed her in the chair. Tied the ropes around her arms
and ankles, moving as fast as he could, struggling with the broken
fingers.

'You need to go to hospital, Lior. You need a doctor.'

'I'll manage.'

He knew he didn't have long. He'd just got lucky. Stupid, dumb
luck. He found a piece of cloth. He shoved it into Roni's mouth. All
he had was the knife. It would have to do.

He slipped out of the room and closed the door. Listened to the
quiet. Where had they gone? He went to the bar. Took a bottle of
vodka and drank from the bottle. It burned going down and he
almost heaved. He heard a car outside. He waited.

The door to the disco opened. A man stood framed in the
doorway. He walked inside. Lior moved behind him. He put the
knife to Ginge's neck.

Ginge froze.

'Where's Yuval?' Lior said.

'He's at the windmill.'

'The windmill?'

'By the khirbe,' Ginge said. 'It's where we stash our stuff.'

Lior had walked right past it the other day.

'How come you're telling me?' he said.

Ginge licked his lips. 'Yuval can take care of himself,' he said.

'Tell me what happened and I'll let you go.'

'You're full of shit, Lior. You were always full of shit.'

Lior pressed the knife to Ginge's neck. He pressed hard enough to draw blood. It was a nice sharp knife, the one from the bar they used for cutting limes. He liked the feel of the knife in his hand.

'You go back to Tel Aviv,' Ginge said. 'Go back and tell them!'

'Tell them what, Ginge?'

'You can't muscle in on this. It's sanctioned.'

'Sanctioned by who?'

'Don't you *get* it?' Ginge said. 'It's the army. It's been running since *way* before we ever entered Lebanon. There were always drugs coming in. Hash from Lebanon, going through us to Egypt. Well, someone figured out, if we can't stop the smuggling, why should we even try? It was in the national interest to keep the Egyptians doped up. It might as well be… regulated.'

'Bullshit,' Lior said.

'It's true. So once a month army trucks would go to the border, pick up the drugs, drive the cargo straight back to army HQ in Tel Aviv and store it on the base. Then, once a month, the same trucks would go south, deliver to the Bedouins who smuggled it into Egypt. And everyone was happy. The dealers, the buyers – and now us, helping national security while clearing fifteen per cent.'

'*Bullshit,*' Lior said.

'Look it up,' Ginge said. 'Anyway, then came the annexation of the West Bank, and we went into Lebanon, and so the objective… changed. Now it's more heroin than hash, and it doesn't go south to Egypt anymore. All it has to do is go over the Line to the West Bank. And we're right by the Green Line. So now you know, dipshit. You just compromised national security. Not to mention murdered an active intelligence agent—'

'Pushyou?' Lior said. He felt hollow. 'Fuck you.'

'Fuck you, Lior!' Ginge said. 'They're already on the way here, to clean this mess up. So let me go, and *maybe* I'll speak up for you when they put you up for trial—'

He gurgled as Lior shoved the knife in. It went in easy. Lior moved it in a nice quick slash. Ginge dropped to his knees.

'You killed my friend,' Lior said.

He waited, watching Ginge struggle, trying to breathe. But there was no more breathing for Ginge.

Lior wiped the knife on his trousers. He went to the office. He used the black phone on the desk. He made a call. The call was short. Then he went outside.

He found the jeep just sitting there, the keys in the ignition.

He kicked the engine to life and drove out to the khirbe.

13

He parked beside the cactuses. Beyond this point he'd have to walk. His head spun and he dragged one leg behind him. He wasn't in the best of shapes. He figured he had a fifty-fifty chance at most. But he figured he would take it.

He followed the brook to the old mill. It was just a leaning pile of bricks over the brook, all that was left. Once there was a prosperous little village, once there was a mill to mill the flour from the fields. But whoever owned it was gone and no one was ever going to let them come back.

He saw a light ahead. Almost stumbled into Yuval's jeep. How did Yuval drive it up here? He saw a light moving, then vanish. Was there a cellar? He had never seen one before. He always thought...

He went closer, cautiously. Where had Yuval gone? He heard a gun cock and froze.

'You look like shit,' Yuval said.

He came out of the shadows. He held a gun on Lior. Lior held his own gun on Yuval. His hand shook. But he could squeeze a shot, he figured.

'Ginge,' Lior said.

'Ginge,' Yuval said. He shrugged. 'He was the best at interrogations.'

'Is that what you call it,' Lior said.

'You do what has to be done,' Yuval said. 'You know that just as well. There are no innocents here.'

Lior considered it. They aimed their guns at each other. It seemed so stupid suddenly. He wanted to laugh. Then he remembered what they did to Danny and he didn't want to laugh anymore, he wanted to kill someone.

'You're a pain in the ass, Lior,' Yuval said. 'How did you get away from Ginge, anyway?'

'Roni came looking for you and she found me.'

Yuval laughed. 'Nosy cow,' he said. It was only a short laugh. Lior could make his face out in the dark now. Yuval looked furious.

'Why did you do it, Yuval?' Lior said. 'Why did you kill Danny?'

'I told you, he shot himself,' Yuval said. He gestured with a quick nod. 'Over there by the khirbe.'

'You're lying.'

'He found out about the operation,' Yuval said. 'He was going to take it outside. He didn't leave us a *choice*, Lior, do you understand? He went against the kibbutz, doing that. And I still tried to reason with him. He had a young wife, a new child. He would be hurting *them*, didn't he see that?'

'What did you do?' Sudden fear took hold of Lior. The fear of being a small child, of being awake in the dark in the children's house, knowing there was no comfort to come. There was no one to stroke your hair when you cried in the night, no one to sing you to sleep when you woke and were afraid.

'I told him I knew,' Yuval said, and the words stabbed, and Lior's hand shook, holding the gun. He saw Yuval smile.

'I know what you did,' Yuval said. 'I saw you that night when you went down to the wadi.'

'Bullshit,' Lior said. His hand shook. He held the gun with both hands to steady it. 'Don't move!' he said. 'Don't move!'

'I remember thinking, what are they doing now?' Yuval said. 'I never thought you had it in you. I didn't think *she* did.'

Lior froze. Yuval stood there, patient. Yuval knew he was going to shoot Lior, knew Lior was weak, that he had always been weak.

On the kibbutz, only the strong survived. Lior had learned that lesson, had taken it with him. Swore never to be like the weak kids, never again.

You didn't have to be weak, with a gun.

That night in the khirbe, sitting by the fire, Danny playing guitar. It was then Esther told them. It came out haltingly, about the night watchman, what they all knew, what they never said.

And one of them – he couldn't remember who – said, 'Well, why don't we kill him?'

It was just one of those stupid, helpless things to say.

How do you just get up and kill a man?

But as it turned out, it was so *easy*.

Esther went to speak to him. She bumped into him in the entrance to the dining room. She feigned interest. Suggested meeting later that night. The man responded. Like he had never seen her before, but he liked what he saw. Then they just had to wait.

They took him in the dark. They stuffed his mouth with a towel from the kitchen and they dragged him to the wadi, where no one could see and no one could hear. Under dark cypress trees, with no campfire and no singing. Danny stole the gun his father kept in the cupboard in his bedroom.

They held the man down, excited, scared. He looked at them like they were crazy.

'You do it, you do it!' Danny kept saying. Lior held the gun. He aimed it at the man's face. The man's eyes widened. He believed them then, and maybe he thought about why, and maybe he didn't.

Then Esther snatched the gun from Lior and she sat on the man's chest and she looked at his face like she was trying to find something, but she was disappointed, and then without saying a word she lifted the gun and held it in both her hands and the gun fired and the roar of the gun sent the birds in the trees flying into the night, and the man's face burst open and bits of skull and skin and brain flew off what was once a living thing and was now nothing. Then Esther tossed the gun on the ground and without a word she went behind a tree and threw up.

'You couldn't do it,' Yuval said, gloating. 'You were always weak, Lior. *She* had to do it. I bet she didn't even think twice.' His face was ghostly. 'I know where you buried him. Danny couldn't take it. He was weak, like you. So he did the only thing he could think of. He took the same fucking gun to the khirbe, and he blew his own brains out. And that's the truth of it, Lior. I never laid a fucking finger on him. And if you'd just *listened* to what everyone told you, we wouldn't be here right now—'

He looked down, surprised. So did Lior. The shot threw him back and he staggered and fell. Yuval sat down heavily.

'You fucking shot me,' he said.

Lior touched the wet hole in his shoulder.

'You shot me,' he said in surprise.

They raised their guns up simultaneously and fired again.

Yuval fell and he didn't get up.

Lior let the gun drop. He staggered to his feet. He was still alive somehow. His shoulder burned and blood was gushing out. He went to Yuval. He tore his shirt and made a bandage with the fingers that weren't broken and he tied it on himself. He could do it, he thought. He could just make it.

He went into the ruins of the old mill. There was an open trapdoor into an old cellar. You'd never know it was there if it wasn't open. They must have covered it with dirt and rocks otherwise. He didn't go in. Yuval had brought out two bags from the hiding place. Lior opened one. He wasn't surprised to see it was full of cash.

So Yuval looked after himself, too, not just the kibbutz. Lior picked up the bags. Every step he took was a fight now, but he knew he could make it. He just took them one at a time, following the brook, leaving a trail of dark blood as he went.

One step, and another, and another, until he came to the khirbe and there he sat down with his back to a rock, and waited.

The headlights of the approaching car woke him from a nightmare in which he was dying. He wasn't dying. He wasn't even bleeding much anymore. The car came to a stop. He couldn't make it out clearly. It was a big car. Not a kibbutz car. He heard the passenger side door open and close softly as she stepped out.

He saw her only in silhouette. She walked over and when she saw him she gave a small cry and said, 'What happened to you, Lior?'

'It doesn't matter,' he said, and tried to smile. 'What matters is that you came.'

'I had to,' she said. 'I didn't know what—'

He thought being a widow didn't suit her. He tried to get up to his feet, staggered, held himself upright against the rock.

'You're bleeding,' she said.

'You should see the other guy.'

'Don't make jokes!'

'Here,' he said. He pushed one of the bags towards her. 'Just like I told you.'

She opened the bag. She saw the money.

'Where did you get that?' she said.

'They killed him, Esther. They killed Danny in everything but name.'

She shrugged. 'He shot himself, Lior. He was never as strong as—'

She fell silent.

'As you?' he said.

'I had to be,' she said. 'He didn't.'

'We can go away, right now,' Lior said. 'Take the money and go. We could be in America next thing tomorrow.'

'What would we do in America?' Esther said.

He didn't think there was something weird about the way she said *we*. Not until the door of the driver side of the car opened and he saw the tall lanky silhouette emerge.

He finally realised where he'd seen a car like this, only recently. The big American Buick that was parked in the kibbutz parking lot. The car that belonged to the clean-cut American, Bill Anderson.

Then he saw the nasty little Glock Esther had in her hand.

'Esther, no,' he said. The muzzle flashed. The pain ripped his belly apart. She looked at him without much of an expression of anything.

'I'm sorry, Lior,' she said. 'But you shouldn't have come back. All you did was bring back bad memories.'

She shot him again. It went through his shoulder this time. Somehow he was still alive. His vision blurred. He saw her walk away, just this darkened outline of her, and the American held the door for her as she went in the car. He heard a baby cry in the back seat, heard her say, 'Hush, we'll be there soon.'

The American came and got the bags. He loaded them in the back of the car. Then they drove off.

Lior watched the taillights vanish into that great big darkness. His hold on consciousness was weakening.

'We did it, Danny,' he said. Somewhere nearby the campfire burned, and Danny played the guitar. He turned and gave Lior a bright smile.

'I suppose she'll be safe now,' Danny said.

'I suppose she will,' Lior said.

'I liked the way you did for Ginge and Pushyou,' Danny said. 'I never liked them, Lior.'

'I know you didn't, Danny.'

'I hope the kibbutz will be all right,' Danny said, 'now that there won't be all that extra income.'

'They'll sell a share in the factory,' Lior said. 'They'll be fine, all things told. They'll close down the children's houses and have them sleeping at home with their parents and they'll tell themselves it's better that way. They'll have differential salaries and everyone will own their house now, not like before. It won't be a kibbutz anymore, but it will still look the same.'

'It sounds nice,' Danny said.

'They'll say...' Lior coughed. Blood gurgled. 'They'll say it's a good place to raise children.'

'I wish I got to see it,' Danny said.

'Me, too,' Lior said.

He closed his eyes. The wind ruffled the tops of the cypress trees. He listened to Danny sing. He had a nice voice. Lior fell asleep still listening to it.

The night grew long
And soon we'd go to battle
And you would stay behind to wait for me
I took your hand, and led you to the barn house
Remember me, my love, remember me.

PART THREE

TWO LITTLE GIRLS

Ruth

Haifa, 1946

14

THERE WERE TWO PAIRS OF EYES CAUGHT IN THE GLARE OF THE headlights. Ruth slammed on the brakes. The truck, overladen with crates, skidded across the dirt track road.

The eyes stared at her mutely in the glare of the lights. She reached for the Luger. She had just left the kibbutz, the Arab village was on her right now, with only a few coal fires burning outside the houses.

She opened and closed the door, softly. She stepped out, gun extended.

'Who's there?' she called.

No answer, just two pairs of eyes, disembodied. She could not make them out in the dark. A moonless night. Good for a moonless ride on a late-night delivery. She had not meant to put on the headlights at all. She crept closer. Could be an ambush. The night was quiet. But there they were.

'Come out,' she said. 'Slowly.'

Two shadows crept into the beams of light. Ruth held back a Hungarian curse.

Two apparitions, like small and white-faced ghosts. Their faces were devoid of all expression. Two little girls. They stared at Ruth.

'What are you doing here?' she said.

They didn't speak. She tried Yiddish. No reply. She went to them. Took their hands in hers. Their skin felt cold. The girls were barefoot. They wore thin shifts, as though they had just walked right out of bed. She looked at their feet. Held back a breath: the skin broken and bleeding, their toes caked in mud.

In the distance a jackal howled. The girls did not react. They looked lethargic. But they had walked miles, Ruth thought. They must have walked miles to get here.

'Where do you come from?' she said. 'Where is your mother?'

The girls said nothing. The smaller one moved suddenly. She put her arms around Ruth. Ruth held her tight. She felt the little girl's heart beat fast against her chest.

'You poor thing,' she said. 'You poor thing. You're safe.'

The older girl said nothing. She looked at Ruth with eyes devoid of trust or hope.

Ruth turned the girl's thin wrist.

'No number,' she said.

She rose, lifting the small one with her. She clung on to Ruth. Ruth took the older girl's hand in hers. The girl didn't resist. She took them to the truck. She had to make the delivery, she thought. But she couldn't, not now, not with these two girls out of nowhere. She bundled them into the truck. Hit the gas and turned the vehicle round and drove right back to the kibbutz.

It wasn't much of a place to look at. A far cry from the comfortable home she knew back in Hungary, its thick carpets and warm fireplace, the smell of chicken in the oven. Trashim was just a gaggle of tents, a thin wooden fence all around it, a watchtower in its centre. A chicken coop, three skinny sheep, the shower block with some buckets inside. It wasn't much of a place but it was theirs and it was home. The truck bumped over rocks on the way. The guard stood outside the gate, gun at the ready.

'Ruth?' he said.

'It's me, Mishka.'

'Why are you back so soon?'

'Open the damn gate, Mishka.'

He hurried to obey. She drove through and he shut it behind

them. The members were asleep in their tents, all but for the guards by the fire.

'Go wake Fanya up,' Ruth said.

'But she's asleep, Ruth—'

'Now, Mishka!'

Fanya had recently completed a six-week nursing course. She emerged bleary-eyed out of the tent she shared with Shimshon. She glared at Ruth.

'What is this?' she said.

'I found them.'

Fanya opened her mouth to argue, then shut it quickly. She knelt by the girls instead. She wasn't gentle but she was efficient. She cleaned and bandaged their feet.

'Who do they belong to?' she said.

'I don't know.'

'We'll have to report this to the British police,' Mishka said.

'No police,' Ruth said.

'Then to our own people,' Mishka said, capitulating quickly. 'To the Yishuv. Someone must know who they are.'

'We'll get word,' Ruth said. 'I have to go make the delivery. I won't be back tonight.'

'What should we do with them?' Fanya said.

'Put them with the other children,' Ruth said. 'For now.'

'We can barely feed ourselves,' Mishka said. 'Let alone two more mouths.'

'They're children, Mishka,' Ruth said. Fanya glared at him until he nodded.

'But we must put it to a vote,' he said. 'To the members.'

'We will discuss it in the next meeting,' Ruth said.

She went to the girls. 'You're safe now,' she said. The girls looked at her. She wished they would speak. She wished they would tell her where they came from. She said, 'You can sleep here tonight.'

She went to the children's tent. Baby Yoram lay asleep in his cot. She put her lips to his little head, inhaled his smell. He was hers. All hers. But he wasn't. He belonged to the kibbutz. She gave him a quick kiss, no one would see. The metapelet stirred in her sleep next to the children. Ruth closed the flaps of the tent and went outside. She got back in the truck. She drove out again into the night.

This time she kept the headlights off. She knew the road. The stars overhead covered the sky. No moon, the Arab village sleeping. There were five large Arab villages in these hills and Trashim stood alone a Jewish settlement. The road she drove on she had helped build herself. Stone by stone they laid it out. She finally reached the crossing where the dirt track turned onto paved road. She kept watch all the while, for passing cars, for Arab gang ambush, for British police. But the road was quiet and the night dark. She followed the signs to Haifa.

She came on the roadblock without warning. A sudden flare of lights, voices shouting through a megaphone. She slowed down, stopped the car. She waited.

A British policeman shone a torch in her face.

'Your papers,' he demanded.

She handed him her ID document. Kept her face impassive. He studied it.

'Where are you going at this hour?' he said.

'I have a delivery of vegetables,' she said. 'They must be ready for market tomorrow.'

'You drive?' He looked amused. 'They couldn't find a man?'

'On the kibbutz we share all tasks equally.'

'Kibbutz,' he shook his head at this Jews' folly. 'Well, we have to search your truck.'

'I'm in a hurry,' Ruth said.

'And I,' he said, 'am not.'

'Don't spoil my tomatoes,' she said.

He gave her a long, up and down stare.

'Your tomatoes look fine to me,' he said.

She waited with her hands on the wheel. Heard them moving in the back of the truck. Opening crates. But she could tell they weren't going to find anything. She stepped out.

'I tell you you can step out?' the policeman said.

'You got a cigarette?' Ruth said. 'I'm dying for a smoke.'

The policeman relented.

'Here,' he said. He offered her a tin. His cigarettes were already rolled. She always made sure to bum a cigarette from the British. Their tobacco was better than what was sold in the shops.

'Egyptian?' she said. She dragged in smoke gratefully. The policeman nodded.

'It's just tomatoes and cucumbers and shit,' she heard someone say from the back of the truck.

'Vegetables, huh?' the policeman said.

'Why, what are you looking for?' Ruth said.

'Guns,' the policeman said. 'Hashish. The usual.'

'I'm just a woman,' Ruth said. 'I wouldn't know anything about that.'

He nodded. His own cigarette dangled lazily from his lips. He could have been handsome, in a different light. But in the light of the stars over Palestine he was just an occupying Brit, unwelcome and unwanted by either Arab or Jew.

'I don't get this place,' the policeman said. 'I don't get you Jews.'

'What's to get?' Ruth said. 'This is our land.'

'This is a no man's land,' the policeman said, and he spat on the ground. 'I saw less desolate places during the war.'

'You were in the war?' she said.

He smiled, and it made him look boyish. 'Served under Montgomery in El Alamein.'

'I wanted to fight in the war,' Ruth said. She didn't know why she was confiding in him. Finding the girls had shaken her more than she realised. 'My sister, my family, they were in Budapest when the Nazis came.'

'The war is over,' the policeman said, indifferent perhaps. He must have seen his share of horrors, she thought. It was hard to be sympathetic anymore to a stranger's plight. 'You should go out, live a little. Put some lipstick on, a decent dress. You'll be right as rain.'

Ruth nodded. She dropped the cigarette and ground it with her foot. She said, 'Am I free to go?'

'Go,' he said. 'But drive carefully. The road can be dangerous.'

'It's a dangerous land,' she said. 'Thanks for the smoke.'

She got back in the truck. They opened the roadblock for her and she drove through.

This land could be dangerous. There were few lights. She passed Arab villages and Jewish settlements. She passed a British police fortress and one of their prisons. The road was quiet. When she came to the shore road she drove with her lights off. She went on to a dirt track, then sand. Nothing around for miles, and no lights but the stars in the sky.

The beach she was going to had no name. It lay somewhere between Haifa and Acre, and she had had to learn the road by heart or she would have missed the turning. She heard a whistle cut through the dark and knew she'd been spotted. She came to the ruins of an old crusader fort.

The men materialised noiselessly out of the dark. She marvelled at that, their ability to hide. The British still hadn't found this site, it was still a safe harbour for the Jews of Europe to illicitly make landfall.

'Ruth.'

'Avraham.'

He'd lost an eye in '44 to shrapnel from a Stern Gang booby trap. The black eye patch made him look dashing, that and his long hair and that salt-crusted skin, burned too long in the sun.

'How was it?' she said.

'It was hairy tonight,' Avraham said. 'Fifteen boats off the *St Helena* out of Saloniki. We got nine through. The others were all caught by the Brits.'

'We can't go on like this,' another man said. Srulik, who wore a raincoat and sailor boots. He'd served in the Jewish Brigade during the Italian campaign. 'The more we bring them in the more the British send them back. We need them here and we need the British gone. Did you bring it?'

But the men were already offloading her cargo. Hidden in a secret compartment under a false bottom in the back of the vegetable truck were the guns. Clean, oiled and ready to use, guns that had been used and used again before, in other wars, in other places.

It didn't matter who used them before, she thought. It only mattered that they could still be used now.

The men distributed the guns. They vanished into the crusader fort. Old wars had been fought on these shores before. This latest war was merely an extension.

'The refugees tonight,' Ruth said. 'Were there two small girls there? Sisters?'

'How old?' Srulik said.

Ruth thought. They'd looked so small, so thin. It was hard to tell with the refugees from Europe. 'They looked six or seven,' she said. 'Could be older.'

'I don't recall,' Avraham said. 'But we had all of them accounted for.'

'Bullshit,' Ruth said. She knew how the operations worked. You had to get as many people onto shore as you could in one mad rush. It wasn't uncommon for people to vanish in the dunes. And what records were kept weren't exactly reliable.

'Well, I don't remember them,' Avraham said. 'Srulik?'

Srulik frowned, thinking, then shook his head. 'Why do you ask?' he said.

'Doesn't matter,' Ruth said. They couldn't have come off that night's ship, anyway, she thought. They wouldn't have walked all that distance. 'Did anyone report any missing girls from the other ships?'

'I really don't know,' Avraham said. 'You'd have to speak to the contact in Haifa.'

'Alright.'

Srulik took out a tobacco pouch and rolled a cigarette. He handed it wordlessly to Ruth and lit it up for her with a Zippo. She took a deep drag of smoke and sea air. The waves lapped at the shore. Ruth said, 'Anyone from Hungary tonight?'

'Maybe,' Avraham said.

'Where did they go?'

'Where do they always go?' Avraham said. He made a magician's flourish. 'They vanish. They have to.'

Ruth wondered if she'd know her sister again if she saw her. Was she alive still? Would she make it to one of the refugee camps, would she meet the right agents of the Mossad for Aliyah Bet, the network of Jewish smugglers who put people on the rickety old ships that made the journey to Palestine? Was Shoshana still alive, would she try to come, would she make it or drown in the crossing?

And then there was the matter of the man who sold her sister out to the Germans.

She smoked in silence. The sea lapped at the shore. Suddenly she was sick of the sea. She tossed the cigarette and the sea breeze caught it.

'See you, boys,' she said.

She drove more slowly on the way back. The coastal road, past the Check Post crossing and another British barricade, then up the mountain to Haifa.

She left the truck parked by the market.

She climbed the stairs up to the flat that was in no one's name.

She opened the door and saw the bottle of whisky and two glasses on the kitchen table. She smelled Egyptian tobacco and Ascot aftershave.

She smiled and went in and shut the door on the world, for just a few hours.

15

THE HONKING OF TAXI CABS WOKE THEM. SUNLIGHT STREAMED in through the gaps in the blinds. Gulls cried in the distance, over the harbour. Burton said, 'They're not supposed to do that.'

Ruth rolled over, pressed against his warmth. 'Do what?' she said sleepily.

'Honk like that,' Burton said. 'The commissioner doesn't like it. Almost the first job I had in Haifa District was to warn the taxi drivers to keep the noise down.'

'Truly you are a credit to the Crown,' Ruth said.

He put his arm around her. Stretched, and reached across the bed for his tobacco.

'Do you have to go?' Ruth said.

'Do you?' he said.

She laughed, then sat up with him. He rolled them both a cigarette.

'I will miss you when we gain our country back,' Ruth said, and it was Burton's turn to laugh.

'You think we've lost already?'

'I think you will.'

'We're just trying to keep the peace here, Ruth.' He rubbed the bridge of his nose. He was balding on the top of his head. But he was still handsome, she thought.

'Do you think it's easy, trying to keep order in a place like this?' Burton said. 'And every year it seems to get worse. Only last month one of our soldiers was stabbed in Tel Aviv, and the month before there were bombs on the railway tracks when the train to Egypt was leaving. It's a miracle nobody died.' He turned to her, his eyes hard, a policeman's eyes. 'If you know anything about that, Ruth...'

'I don't,' she said. 'I'm not with that lot.' She leaned closer into him.

'Who's Agatha?' she said.

She felt him stiffen. He was suddenly very still.

'I saw her name somewhere. Should I be jealous?' she said.

'There is no Agatha,' he said.

But she saw it, just for a moment. *Operation Agatha*, but nothing else. Burton was careful with his papers. Usually.

'You're planning something,' she said. 'Something big. Aren't you?'

'You know I can't tell you.'

It was her turn to be still. So it was true, she thought. Something big. Something bad. How much did the British know? How soon before it came?

'Can you tell me when?' she said.

'So you could warn your friends?' he laughed softly. 'This isn't how we play this game.'

She knew that. They used each other – that was mutually understood. But it didn't mean they couldn't be cordial about it.

'What about that information I gave you?' Burton said. 'Was it any use to you?'

'What information?'

'About that man you were looking for, Deutsch.'

She shrugged. 'Couldn't find him,' she said.

He looked at her curiously.

'What is he to you?' he said.

'Nothing,' she said. 'He's nothing to me.'

Thinking of a boy with a pale face and a winning smile, who lived over the road. Thinking her sister, Shoshana, who had a special look saved only for Nathan Deutsch, when she saw him. Of her parents, who welcomed him into their home.

Of the last letter from her sister, arriving who knew how, smuggled out of the camp they sent her to, the letter stained and the ink barely legible.

Nathan told them where we were.

'I checked it out,' she said. 'But it didn't go anywhere.'

Burton let it go. He didn't know what Deutsch meant to her. He didn't care. It was useless information to him. And she'd traded him information useless to her in return. The location of a slick, a cache of weapons, belonging to the Jewish resistance. But by the time Burton and the CID found it there was just a handful of old Ottoman-era guns there, more likely to blow up the shooter than the target. It looked good for Burton on the paperwork, though. Which was what counted with CID.

'Did anyone report two missing girls?' she said, changing tack.

'Two missing girls?' Burton looked at her sharply.

'Young,' Ruth said. 'Two sisters.'

She wondered if the mother had been captured while the girls escaped. It made sense to her it would be this way.

But Burton shook his head. He looked at her suspiciously.

'No report,' he said. 'Is there something you want to tell me?'

'If I did, would you do something about it?' she said.

He shrugged, uncomfortable. 'Children go missing all the time,' he said. 'Most of the time they turn up again.'

She thought of that nine-year-old boy who went missing in April. He walked out of the Institute for Defective Children in Giv'at Ha'shlosha and no one saw him since.

They didn't always come back, she thought. And she felt a cold rage.

'We do our best,' Burton said, sensing her mood. 'It isn't easy when no one will work with us.'

'Then leave,' she said. 'Excuse me—'

She went to the bathroom and was sick into the sink.

When she came out he was looking at her differently.

'You're not—' he said.

She smiled.

'No,' she said. 'Don't be silly. It's just something I ate.'

She got back into the bed with him. He was not a bad man. She reached under the sheets, between his legs. His breath came ragged.

'We don't have time,' he whispered.

'No?'

Outside, the taxis honked as loudly as ever. Gulls cried over the harbour. Inside it was warm, and for a while they forgot they were on opposite sides of a war.

The greengrocer spoke Yiddish and had the manners of an Old World farmer. He supervised offloading of the crates. Tomatoes and cucumbers, grown by the sweat of her comrades. Her own hands were calloused now from the hard work on the land. The greengrocer grabbed a tomato, bit into it. Juice ran down his chin.

'Es iz gut,' he said.

He counted money. Ruth took it, counted it herself. He watched approvingly. He wrote the date and the amounts in his counting book and nodded, satisfied.

Ruth waited as the truck was loaded. Sacks of flour for the new baker's oven, with guns inside. She said, 'Herschel, do you have some of the arrivals from last night?'

He frowned, for this was not protocol. But he gave her an address.

She left them to load the truck. The boarding house was nearby, in the lower city. A dilapidated house with geraniums in the windows. She knocked and a heavyset woman answered.

'Herschel sent me,' Ruth said, 'I'm from the movement.'

The woman looked her up and down, then shrugged. Ruth went inside and the woman shut the door. Women and babies sat at the kitchen table, thin, unkempt things, still with the stink of the ship on them. Men sat in a semi-circle, looking overwhelmed.

'We could use good workers on my kibbutz,' Ruth said. The men looked up at her with hopeless eyes. What was 'kibbutz'? they seemed to ask her. What was this hot and dusty land that, like a stone, they'd rolled into?

Ruth sat at the table with the women. They looked at her without curiosity. She had met the refugees from Europe before, had noticed their reticence, this wariness that felt so foreign, as though they had experienced such horrors where they came from that they no longer trusted that the world itself was real.

'Two little girls,' she said. Repeating a mantra she kept speaking now. 'Sisters.'

She watched their eyes to gauge a reaction. But they were not even curious.

'Might have come on a ship a few nights ago.'

If a mother lost two of her children there'd have been an outcry, Ruth thought. But so far nothing. The women shook their heads one by one. They'd lost children before, they seemed to mutely say. They lost mothers, husbands, lives. Now here they were, in a stranger's kitchen, in an ugly old city on the edge of a foreign sea. What life could they possibly make here?

The landlady came back with black tea.

'There were two little girls passed through here,' she said. 'A month or two back. Sisters. But I don't remember where they went.'

'Were they with a mother, guardian, someone?' Ruth said.

'They must have been,' the woman said. She shook her head. 'I'm sorry. In this line of work it is best to forget everything.'

Ruth thanked her. She drank her tea.

Dead ends so far, but she would keep looking. Where *had* the girls come from? Why did they walk, and where were they trying to go? Perhaps they'd speak to her, in time.

The women spoke among themselves in Yiddish. You must speak Hebrew now, Ruth wanted to tell them. You speak the old language of exile, when you must learn the new tongue of rebirth. But her heart wasn't in it, not then, and she did not know where these women would end up and how their lives would be, only that they would not be easy.

She got back to Herschel in the market. Her truck was loaded. She got in behind the wheel and hit the horn, making the greengrocer jump. Ruth laughed and waved. She hit the gas and sped along the narrow roads, beeping at any cars coming her way. Give the British Commissioner something to complain about, she thought. Jews making noise.

The wind brushed her hair. The city receded behind her. The sun shone and she was free. She had dreamed of freedom, back in Hungary. There, she felt constrained by her bourgeois upbringing. She would have been somebody's wife, somebody's mother. But she just wanted to be herself.

On the open road she was free. The green truck swayed, laden with supplies. The sun shone down. Her arms and legs were brown from the sun. She thought of the baby growing inside her. She thought of that name she saw, for just a moment. *Agatha*. So the British planned a big operation. She needed to know when, how secure things were in the movement. The three resistance groups had joined forces only recently. She wasn't sure how long it would last. She checked her wing mirror. A buffed-up Ford was behind her. She thought nothing of it at first. She turned off the coast road onto the road that led back to the Jezreel. The Ottomans had built it back in the first war. The Ford took the same turn and followed.

There were few Jewish settlements on this road. It was why the kibbutzim were built where they were. The Yishuv had to put a foothold in Arab populated areas.

So far, the members of Trashim had a cordial relation with their Arab neighbours. But Ruth knew something, sooner or later, had to give.

The Ford kept behind her. When Ruth slowed the other car slowed. She tried to get a glimpse of the driver but the sun glinted off the windscreen and she could see nothing. She came up to Yokneam. Farms and cows grazing, a single tractor sitting in the sun, some chickens clucking around a water tap. She passed the tin settlement, turned a bend in the road and stopped the car and waited.

The Ford came behind her. It slowed and then it stopped there, keeping the distance between them, and just waited too.

Ruth reached for the Luger in the glove compartment. She stepped out of the car. The Ford just sat there, motionless.

'Well?' Ruth shouted across.

The Ford engine started up. The car edged slowly forward, then turned and went back towards Haifa.

Ruth didn't let the gun drop to her side until the sound of the Ford's engine died in the distance. She leaned against the truck and wished she had a cigarette.

Someone snooping after her because of the guns? CID, or some independent outfit, some splitter assholes from the Stern Gang? But they didn't try to arrest her, or rob her.

A cold certainty washed over her then.

The girls.

She'd been asking questions.

Maybe someone heard. Someone who had an interest in the girls.

She didn't like this. Didn't like the Ford sticking to her like that. Didn't like how it had sat there, watching her.

She got back in the truck. She drove more slowly now, checking her rear-view mirror. But she didn't see the Ford again.

16

THE COMRADES WERE ALREADY IN THE FIELDS, TILLING, AND some were sawing wood and hammering nails into the new cabins that were going up. Ruth parked the truck. Dov and Israel came, nails dark with soil. Dov grinned when he saw her and Israel swept her in his arms for a kiss.

'How was the run?' Dov said.

'Alright.' She decided not to mention the Ford.

'And the Brit, Burton?' Dov said.

'You're not jealous, are you?' Ruth said. Teasing him.

'We're not!' Israel said.

'I think they're planning something,' Ruth said. 'The British.'

'They're always planning something.'

'Something big,' Ruth insisted.

'If it was big we'd know about it,' Israel said. 'We have guys in the police, in all kinds of places.'

'Maybe they're keeping it tight this time,' Ruth said.

They carried the crates of weapons to the bakery. Tuvya, the baker, had already finished his work. Loaves of bread waited inside and the warm interior smelled of yeast and burned crust. Dov reached for the trapdoor and opened it, revealing a ladder set into stone. He vanished inside the slick and Israel lowered the crates down to him.

There was half a loaf of sliced bread on a plate. Ruth took a slice. She felt both nauseous and starving. She put her hand over her stomach protectively. Israel didn't notice. Ruth took the bread and went down the ladder to the slick. Cool stone walls and a dirt floor opened on to a small room lined with shelves. The smell of gun oil and gunpowder and of Dov's sweat. Ruth saw grenades and Bren machine guns. Enfield rifles, Mausers and Lugers. Crates of ammo were crammed into every available space. This was one of the central clearinghouse slicks for the entire north. She put a hand on the wall to steady herself. Dov was by her side in a moment.

'Is anything wrong?'

'I'm fine,' she said. She pushed herself away. 'I just need air.'

She climbed back out. They shut the trapdoor behind them. She stepped outside into hot sun. But there was no time to rest. She went to join the others in the field. They would plant wheat here, cotton, orange trees and pomegranates. But there was no water. The ground was parched and they had to bring in the precious liquid on the back of a donkey. She worked under the hot sun, breaking the hard land before it had a chance to break her in turn. They would do all this, she thought, so that one day this will be a paradise, and her children, born and as yet unborn, would waddle on green grass, on a land that was their own and no one else's. They broke for lunch of bread and olives and went back to work again, until the land, subjugated at last to their will, was tilled in rows, order imposed on the chaos of rocks and dirt. The stones piled up high in mounds.

When work was done her back ached and her hands shook from the hard labour. They went into the showers, two cabins erected and sharing a wall. The women in one and the men in the other, and Ruth let the cool water in the bucket wash over her and borrowed soap, passed it to Fanya who passed it to Greta, who tossed it over the divider to the men at their shouted request. The shower was filled with conversation and laughter. She thought of Dov and Israel on the other side of the wall, their naked bodies, Dov wiry and small, Israel muscled and tall. She loved them both so much.

After the shower she felt refreshed. The children were waking from their afternoon sleep. She scooped up little Yoram in her arms.

'Mummy,' he said sleepily.

'Ruth,' she corrected him. 'It's Ruth.'

His eyes brightened. 'I want to play,' he said.

'Then go play.'

She put him down and he ran off without a backward glance. She went to find the two little girls. They looked better in the daylight. Their hair had been washed and they were given clean clothes, short khakis and shirts. They looked up at her with eyes as bright as her child's, but still said nothing.

'Do you have names?' she said. 'Can you tell me that, at least?'

Fanya touched her on the arm.

'This one's Paula,' she said brusquely. 'This one's Malka.'

'What? How do you know?'

'They told me.'

Ruth looked at the girls. They looked back at her in mute concern.

'What else did they tell you?'

Fanya kept a hold on Ruth's arm.

'Outside,' she said.

Outside was a spot in the shade under a gnarled old pine. Ruth picked up a pinecone and weighed it in her hand.

'Well?' she said.

'How are you feeling?' Fanya said.

'Fine.' She saw Fanya's expression. 'I'm fine!' she said.

'Do they know?' Fanya said.

'Dov and Israel?' Ruth laughed. Even Fanya had to smile at that one. 'They wouldn't have a clue.'

'Do you know whose it is?' Fanya said.

'It's mine,' Ruth said. 'That's all that matters. Now tell me about the girls.'

'They don't talk much,' Fanya said, relenting. 'They don't need to. I gave them a physical.' She shook her head. Ruth felt a sickness inside her that had nothing to do with the baby.

'How bad?' she said.

'Bad.'

'Who?' Ruth had to force the question out.

'I don't know, Ruthie. But it's not safe for them out there.'

'Then they will stay here, with us. They will be safe with the collective.'

'Will they?' When Fanya worried her mouth turned into a thin line. 'What if there's a mother somewhere?'

'Then I will find her.'

'The men who took them...' Fanya didn't finish. Ruth thought of the Ford, the way it followed her. The way it turned back.

'You think they will come for them,' Ruth said.

'They were property, Ruth.'

It was the sort of thing you knew about, you heard about in whispers, but you didn't talk about openly, you didn't write about in the papers. She thought of the boy who vanished from the Institute for Defective Children, and of all the ones you never even heard of, because there was no one to miss them.

They were property, Ruth.

And property had *value.*

'I will kill them,' Ruth said.

'I know.'

'Keep them safe,' Ruth said.

'Where are you going?'

'If there's a mother, I'll find her.'

Fanya let her go. Dov and Israel sat by the fire, brewing coffee for the comrades. The children played in the far field in shade of the pine trees where the first grave of the kibbutz was only recently dug. The two little girls had joined them. Ruth went to the truck. She took apart and oiled and reassembled the Luger.

'Another delivery, Ruth?' Mishka said. He appeared in the window, a greasy notebook open in his hand. 'It's not on the schedule.' He frowned. 'I need the truck to drive to the general meeting of regional coordinators in Megiddo.'

'You can fuck Batya from the central committee another time, Mishka,' Ruth said, 'just make sure she doesn't take minutes. I need the car.'

'But Ruth!'

She almost softened, the way his face fell. But she started the ignition all the same.

The Atlit Detention Camp sat, wrapped in barbed wire, a mere stone's throw away from the sea. For the people imprisoned inside it may well have been miles inland. They could smell the sea, they could hear the cry of gulls; could remember with an aching clarity the terrible voyage that took them across from Europe, crammed into the hull of a rickety old ship purchased on the cheap and crewed by sailors with sometimes more passion than skill. The boats that didn't make it drowned. The boats that did, more often than not, were caught by the British. And the passengers ended up here.

Atlit, with another ancient crusader fort on the shore, and a beach that served the smugglers until the British wised up to it and put their camp there instead. Ruth came often; as often as she could. She drove the truck to the gates and waited as the soldiers checked her documents.

'Bit late for a delivery,' the officer on duty said. His thick moustache was tinged with grey.

'If you got a problem you can raise Burton on the phone,' Ruth said.

The officer shrugged amiably. 'I got no problem,' he said. 'Park it by the hospital tent.'

She drove slowly. They were not unduly concerned. They knew her here. She waited by the hospital tent as one of the nurses came out. The gates closed and locked behind her.

'What did you get?' the nurse said.

'Some toys for the children, some sweets.'

The nurse nodded.

'You want a cup of coffee, Ruth?'

'Please.'

She looked around her. Saw the corrugated metal shacks, laundry hanging on makeshift lines, children playing hopscotch in the sand. But where the camp had been full before it was more than half empty now. And she knew the ships kept coming, and the navy boats kept intercepting them.

And as more and more illegals came, all the same the camp was emptying.

'They're shipping them to Cyprus,' the nurse said. She handed her a mug. Ruth took a grateful sip.

'I know.'

'I'll go with them,' the nurse said.

'We won't let them be sent back to Europe,' Ruth said.

Only the year before the Strike Force broke into Atlit and freed the prisoners. It was a coup for the resistance. But it pissed the British off. A lot. And now the prisoners were being shipped across the Mediterranean to the new Cyprus camps, and no one was going to get them out of there.

Ruth stared at the empty huts and she had a bad feeling nagging her somehow.

'What are they going to use it for?' she said.

'What?'

'What are they going to do with an empty prison camp?'

The nurse shrugged.

'I don't know,' she said.

Unless it wasn't going to *stay* empty, Ruth thought.

Whatever Operation Agatha was, she needed to find out more about it, quickly.

'Any news about your sister?' the nurse said.

Ruth shook her head.

'Did she write to you?'

'No.'

'Maybe she's in one of the camps in Europe,' the nurse said sympathetically. 'It's not always easy to get word.'

'I had a brother, too,' Ruth said. 'Have.'

'What happened to him?'

Ruth shrugged helplessly.

'I don't know.'

She thought of Yehoyakim, the revolutionary. Palestine interested him less than the revolution in Russia. It was just like him, to vanish into the Great Soviet. Not Shosh. She stayed. And she was betrayed, and taken to the death camps. She felt the rage course through her again.

'Well, you can ask around some more,' the nurse said. 'Maybe someone will remember her this time.'

'I will. But I'm looking for someone else, too.'

She explained about the girls. The nurse lit a cigarette, took a puff, offered it to her. Ruth took a drag and passed it back.

'That bad, huh?' Ruth said.

'We get cases from time to time,' the nurse said. 'But I don't know. Your two just don't ring a bell. Let me come with you. See if anyone knows them.'

They finished the shared cigarette and went to the women's side of the camp. They asked everywhere. Two little girls, did anyone remember them, were they on a ship, was there a mother, is anyone missing two girls?

Young women with old eyes stared at Ruth and shook their heads one after the other. The children ran barefoot through this side of the camp. What was it like for them, to grow up behind a barbed wire fence? She wanted to take them in her arms and tell them everything will be all right. But she knew she would be lying.

At last they came to a tent on the edge of the camp where three young women sat separate from the others. They listened without comment, and Ruth thought this was another dead end. But one of the women – a girl, really – nodded. She had listless eyes and her hands were folded in her lap as though she had given up on anything but sitting there, staring at a darkening sky.

'We were on the *Hesperus* out of Burgas,' she said. 'The sea was rough and there were too many of us on the ship. It was an old ship. Too old to sail, I think. But it was all we had.' She closed her eyes, remembering.

'The stench of it,' she said. 'That's what lingers. We were crammed so tight, the babies crying, soiled, if we could we went on deck to breathe the air, but at the end of it, it was all the same. You slept when and where you could, if you could. The ship creaked and swayed. I do not like the sea.'

'What happened?' Ruth said softly.

'There was a woman there, with two small girls like you describe. She didn't speak to anyone. Neither did I. It was hard to speak, and what was there to say? You—' she opened her eyes and looked at Ruth, '—you here don't want to know how it was for us there. You say *over there* like you don't even want to know. And we, we try to forget. I don't know where these little girls were, how they survived. I don't know who their father or fathers were. You do what you have to do, to survive. And the mother, she loved them.'

'Do you know her name?'

'Eva something, I think.'

'What happened to her?'

The girl looked at Ruth. 'She loved those girls. She was going to get to Palestine, she was going to raise them up right. We made it all the way here. All the way across that awful sea in a ship that shouldn't have been sailing. We could see the lights of Palestine across the water in the end. Just a few lights in a great darkness. For the first time we dared to hope. The boats came, running dark. Some of us managed to get on them. Then…' She fell quiet. Her fingers twisted in her lap, helplessly. 'Then we heard the voice on the megaphone. Bright lights blinded us. The boats tried to flee to the shore and maybe some of them made it, I don't know. Eva was in one. I don't know where the girls were. The boat Eva was on… It capsized in the waves from the navy ships. I saw… there was a flare from one of the ships. It lit up the sea like a false sun. I saw Eva fall. I didn't see her come up.' The girl shook her head. 'And that was that,' she said, in the same listless voice. 'The British took us and brought us here. It's not so bad. There's food and clean clothes and we get to shower. Now they say they'll send us to another camp in Cyprus. It doesn't matter. One camp is like another and I have spent my life in camps. We get food and clean clothes.'

'And the girls?' Ruth said. 'What happened to the girls!'

'I don't know,' the woman said. 'I don't know what happened to them, but they weren't on the ship when we were brought here. I guess they got out. So that's good. It's good…'

She didn't speak again. Ruth said, 'Thank you.' The woman didn't reply.

'I'm sorry,' the nurse said, after they went back to the medical tent. 'What will you do now?'

'What do you think happened to them after the *Hesperus*?' Ruth said.

'They would have been sent to a kibbutz, I think,' the nurse said. 'If they made it on shore safely. Unless they weren't. Who is to say? You think they had someone else, someone waiting for them?'

'I don't know.'

'Will you look?'

Ruth nodded. So many were missing, six million Jews in Europe who will never come back again, her mother and father and uncles and aunts, and who knew if Shosh and Yehoyakim survived? Did anyone still live of her family? So many gone, vanished into smoke, and who was there to care about two little girls in all that devastation, if they had no one left in the world? Who, if not her?

'You could try the orphanages,' the nurse said.

★

'We don't allow visitors after six,' the matron said. She had the bearing of a British staff sergeant and the mean bloodshot eyes of a belligerent drunk. The orphanage sat in an abandoned plot of land in the lower city in Haifa. Wild flowers poked out from the dirt and a barbed wire fence enclosed the field. The house itself towered two stories high. Inside, it smelled unpleasantly of soiled nappies and boiled cabbage.

'Two girls, illegals, came off a ship a while back,' Ruth said. 'Mother died in the rescue. Paula and Malka, their names.'

'No visitors after six!'

'I need to know if they were here,' Ruth said.

'Why?' The woman *was* drunk, Ruth realised. She saw the shake of the hands the matron didn't even bother to hide.

'I need to know if they have anyone left.'

'Listen, *suka*,' the matron said. 'If anyone comes here they don't *have* anyone left. And they should be grateful we take them. Do you know how much it costs to feed and clothe these kids? We never have money. No one cares for these children. We're all they've got.'

Ruth looked around her but saw no toys, no books, nothing to indicate children lived here.

'Where *are* the children?' she said.

'In bed.'

'It's only dinner time!' Ruth said.

'They eat early. Now bed.'

'Paula and Malka,' Ruth said.

The matron glared at her. Ruth held her gaze.

'...Maybe,' the matron said at last. She kept stealing glances at a closet door. Ruth bet she had her bottle there. 'Troublemakers. It's no good to have troublemakers here.'

'Why?' Ruth said. The matron looked at her as though she were dim.

'They cause trouble,' she said.

'They're children!' Ruth said.

'Bad children,' the matron said, 'get punished.' She stole another glance at the closet.

'Don't mind me,' Ruth said, and the matron grinned suddenly and reached inside for a bottle of vodka. She took a swig and colour flooded her face.

'You want some?' she said, suddenly generous.

'Thank you, no.'

'Children come and children go,' the matron said. 'It's best not to remember too clearly.'

'What do you mean children go? They're adopted?'

The matron barked a laugh. 'Who would adopt these strays?' she said.

'Then what?'

The matron shrugged.

'I don't know,' she said.

'You don't *know*?'

'They apprentice out, some of them. The older ones. Cobblers and so on. Carpenters. They have to work. The small ones, well... They do well as long as they behave.'

'And if they don't?'

The matron shrugged again. 'Bad children go on the street,' she said. 'And if they go on the street, well, that's no longer my responsibility, is it?'

'So if a child disappeared, you won't even report it?'

The matron openly laughed at her. 'Report to who? The police? Bad children don't go to the police.'

'Then where do they go?' Ruth said.

The matron took another swig and hiccupped.

'They can go to hell for all I care,' she said.

17

'THE ORPHANAGE,' DAVID ALMOG SAID. 'YES...' HE SHRUGGED and took a sip from his cognac. 'It is what it is,' he said.

They were sat in the Casino in Haifa, watching the waves lap against the shore. Big band music came from the dance hall inside, and a big colourful sign advertised an upcoming song-and-dance show by Josephine Baker. The Casino was the place to be if you had money to spend. The only thing it was missing was the gambling.

'You're not drinking?' Almog said. He was a thin, intense man, no taller than her.

'Still thinking,' she said. She was shook up from the orphanage. As she walked out of that building with the smell of despair she swore she saw a pair of eyes staring at her helplessly from behind a grille of rusted metal poking out of the ground.

'Alright.' He lit a cigarette, passed her the box. She took one.

'Are you still looking for that man?' He looked at her curiously. 'Deutsch? Nathan Deutsch? Did you ever follow the lead I gave you on his whereabouts?'

Ruth drew smoke. She shook her head.

'I lost him,' she said.

'Too bad,' Almog said. 'What is he to you, anyway?'

Nathan told them where we were.

'Nothing,' she said. 'He is nothing to me.'

Almog looked like he wanted to follow it up, then saw her face and thought better of it.

'How's Dov?' he said instead.

'He's fine.'

'And Israel?'

'He's fine too.'

'Good men.' Almog broke into a grin. 'And lucky boys,' he said. Almog was former CID. His exploits with the police led a pulp writer called Shlomo Gelfer to start publishing a series of stories starring Almog under the title *The Hebrew Detective*, which proved popular with teenage boys. Unbeknown to the British (who eventually sacked him), Almog also worked intelligence for the Stern Gang on the side. A cop called Morton shot Stern in the back in '42, but the rest of them kept on killing Brits and bombing Arabs until even the Yishuv had enough and started hunting them down. But right now everyone was friends. Right now the resistance movements all worked together. Yet Ruth wondered how long the fragile peace between them would last. The Revisionists didn't like the Social Zionists and the Social Zionists didn't like the Communists but right now everyone hated the British more so there was a détente.

'It's a shame you and I never...' Almog said, and let the thought trail.

'It's a shame,' Ruth said.

'Any chance of...?'

'How about I buy you a drink instead,' Ruth said, and Almog smiled.

'With what, pebbles?' he said. 'When are you going to quit that kibbutz of yours and come to your senses? There's more to life than tilling fields and making babies.'

'Then buy me a drink,' Ruth said.

'I thought you'd never ask.'

She sipped the cognac when it came. A smoke and a drink: that was something they had in common. And the baby wouldn't mind, she thought. It would be a tough baby when it came. It would be a true sabra.

'That orphanage...' Ruth said.

Almog tapped ash into the ashtray. It was a cheap brass thing, with *Palestine* etched on the back. The sort of memento sold in the market that British soldiers bought to send home as gifts.

'It's better than some,' he said.

'It was awful.'

'These are hard times, Ruth. There are a lot of orphans and more coming in from Europe by the day. Most can be absorbed into society, can find a fit into a structure, have... *ideals*. We are nothing if we don't have that, even if we occasionally disagree on them, like you and me. But there are always those who don't fit, who degenerate through blood or circumstance. And then what? The Institute for Juvenile Delinquents? The streets? We must do more to help them, of course we must. But we are a poor nation, and a nation at war. Someone is always going to fall through the cracks.'

'They are *children*, Almog!' Ruth said. Almost shouting. Thinking of that silent orphanage that was more like a prison than a prison could ever be. 'Just little children.'

He pushed the burning stub of the cigarette into the ashtray and ground it.

'I wish I could tell you it isn't like that,' he said. 'But to you I can only ever tell the truth.'

She steeled herself.

'Then tell me,' she said.

'There are men who scout for such children,' he said. 'I had a case like this back in '32. They look for those who have no one and nothing. Who need only a friendly face and a kind word. And when they find them, they sell them.'

Her stomach, why did she feel so sick?

'Where?' she whispered.

'Here, at first. Then, a few months later, they would ship the merchandise,' Almog said. 'Beirut, maybe, or Cairo, where the fleshpots are always in need of fresh supplies. Your girls were smart enough or desperate enough to run before it happened.

Once they'd gone to Beirut not even God could bring them back. Drink up, you look like you need it.'

The cognac burned as it went down. She swallowed, but couldn't wipe off the taste of bile.

Thought of the two little girls and their eyes in the night. No wonder they were mute, she thought.

And they had no one in the world.

No one but her.

'Ruth? What are you doing here?'

Burton, with a face she almost didn't recognise. He marched in with a group of senior officers all in uniform. He grabbed her arm, pulled her aside into a quiet corner.

'I was just leaving,' she told him.

His face relaxed. 'Stay in town tonight,' he said. 'It's late.'

'Is that the only reason?'

'I just… I could see you later,' he said.

'I have to go.'

'Please,' Burton said. 'Stay the night. It's safer.'

'Safer how?' When she looked into his face he looked away.

'What are you planning?' she said.

'Nothing.'

'I see.' She turned to leave.

'I could arrest you right here!' he said.

'Then do it.'

'It's for your own good, Ruth!'

'Let go, James,' Ruth said. She said it quietly. He let go of her arm. She touched his cheek, gently. Leaned in and kissed him right on the lips.

'Thanks,' she said.

'For what?'

'For the warning.'

She walked away without looking back. Expecting any moment he *would* come after her and arrest her—

Because, she realised, the British were running their operation *now*.

She could go back and warn Almog. He would get word out. But word about what? No one seemed to know anything about this Agatha. What *did* they plan? Where would they hit? What did they *know*?

She got back in the truck. The old girl looked out of place parked outside the Casino, next to the Hillmans and Bentleys and Wolseleys. There was nothing Ruth could do but get home. She hit the gas and the truck lumbered along the coast and up the hill. A black car slid into the night a few spaces behind her. It stuck on her tail.

'Son of a bitch,' Ruth said.

She climbed the slopes of the Carmel.

The black car followed.

She tried to lose it in the alleyways around the market in the lower city. She saw armed patrols of khaki-clad Jews, and an Arab sniper post set up on the roof across the street from them. She gunned the engine but the black car followed. She left the city at last, speeding downhill again, and turned off her lights. She drove dark, but the black car behind her did the same and now they coasted at a dangerous speed like two shadows fleeing. A jeep came round the bend with glaring lights, momentarily blinding her, and she swerved and heard a shouted curse as she passed the other vehicle. She tried to outrun the black car back on the stretch of flat ground going out of the Check Post but it stuck fast, until Ruth had had enough and she turned the wheel in one furious motion, rocking the axle and playing havoc with the suspension until she almost toppled over. But the old truck held. Ruth stared through the windshield at the approaching car and gunned the engine until she shot towards the other vehicle.

They came at each other at speed. The other car slowed, and Ruth turned on her lights, hoping to blind the driver. She could see now it was the same Ford that followed her once before. The driver tried to reverse but it was too late. The kibbutz truck hit him sideways. Ruth held on for dear life so she would not fly into the glass. The impact jarred her but she was ready. She kicked the door open and stepped out, Luger in hand.

'Don't,' a voice said.

He slithered out of the driver side of the Ford and stood there in the dark pointing something small and sleek in her direction. It was smaller than the Luger but no less effective.

Ruth pointed her gun at him.

'Anyone with you?' she said.

'My associate, in the back.'

'Tell him to step out, carefully.'

'He's passed out, miss.' He took a careful step forward and she could see him in the glare of her car lights. He was small and thin and urbane, in a suit that came from a good tailor who didn't have the right materials to work with. He reminded her a little of that Hungarian actor, Peter Lorre.

'I just want to talk,' the man said.

'Talk about what?'

'My nieces, miss. My dear nieces. They have gone missing and, well, I am distraught with worry.'

He spoke a native Hebrew, the sort she would never have. He spoke the sort of language they wrote in the newspaper.

'I don't know your nieces,' Ruth said.

'Two little girls,' he said. 'I am all they have left in this world. It is a sad situation, miss. Tragic.'

'What's it got to do with me?'

'You were asking for my Paula and my Malka,' he said. His eyes assessed her. The gun in his hand didn't waver. It was a nasty little gun. 'I wondered why.'

'How did you hear?'

'I hear things, miss. Hearing things is what I do. The hearing ear and the seeing eye, the lord has made them both. *Proverbs.*'

His face shone in the light. She raised the Luger higher. 'Get back in your car and drive away. Now.'

'I want my girls!'

She took a step back. Held the gun on him.

'I'm not kidding,' she said. Her finger tightened on the trigger.

'Alright!'

He held his arms up in a placating gesture. The gun dangled from his index finger. He gave her a smile that was just teeth. Ruth took another step back. She kept the gun on him. She was by the door to the truck.

'I am leaving now,' she said.

'This isn't over,' the man said. Ruth jumped in the truck. She watched him, wondering if he would shoot. But the man just stood there and watched her as she drove away.

18

'RUTH! WHAT'S WRONG?'

Dov and Israel, on her return. Night on the kibbutz, a world away from Haifa with its big band dance halls, cognac and pre-rolled Egyptian tobacco. Just the silence and the stars overhead, the Milky Way like a knife cutting through a dark sky. They both held her, until Miskha came, a hurricane lamp in his hand, and saw the truck.

'What did you *do* to her!' he screamed.

'We have bigger problems,' Ruth said. She told them about the man who'd followed her.

'He wants the girls,' she said.

'Then let him take them,' Mishka said. 'What is he, their uncle or something?'

'He's not their *uncle*, Mishka,' Ruth said, a cold and quiet fury in her voice making even Mishka take notice. 'He's their pimp.'

Mishka turned pale behind the hurricane lamp.

'That can't be—' he said, then stopped. 'These things don't happen here,' he said.

'Don't they?'

'We can keep them safe,' Dov said. 'Do you expect trouble, Ruth?'

'I would say so.'

'Israel, get the boys. Get the guns from the armoury. Keep a double shift tonight. Where are the girls?'

'In the children's house,' Ruth said.

'I'll stand guard there myself,' Dov said.

'What about me?' Mishka said.

'You fix the car.'

'Fix the car? It needs a new fender!'

'We don't have money for a fender. Just hammer it into shape.'

Mishka patted the truck's chassis. 'I'll see what I can do...' he said.

The comrades moved quickly. The trapdoor to the slick was open and guns and ammo were passed up. Ruth went with Dov to the children's house. She went inside quietly. They were all asleep. She found Yoram curled up in his little cot. She kissed him on the forehead, smelled his scent. For just one moment he was hers and only hers.

Then she left him there with all the other kibbutz children. Malka and Paula were asleep, Ruth saw with relief. They were so small and so fragile. But they were safe here. They were all safe. She went outside again, where Dov stood guard, the Enfield rifle strapped to his shoulder.

'Well?' Ruth said.

'Get some sleep, love. If they come it will be before morning.'

'Maybe they won't come,' Ruth said.

Dov smiled.

'Maybe they won't,' he said. 'For now the children sleep, the stars are out and all is well.'

She kissed him.

'I love you, Dov,' she said.

'I love you too. More than you'll ever know.'

She touched his shoulder.

'I'm pregnant,' she said.

His face changed with unspoken emotions. Hope? Excitement? Fear?

'Is he mine?' he said.

She smiled.

She stroked his face.

She said, 'He could be.'

*

She slept. In her dream she was back home, in the old house with the thick carpets that swallowed sound. Shoshana was there, and Yehoyakim, and her mother and father. It was Passover. They sat around the table together for the Seder.

A memory, she thought, still dreaming. The last time they were all together. The Deutsches were there too, as honoured guests. And one seat was left empty for the Prophet Elijah. By the third of the four glasses of wine Ruth's hunger had been replaced with a warm fuzzy feeling. Shosh and the Deutsch boy, Nathan, sat across from each other, laughing at jokes only they understood. The reading of the Haggadah took forever. Later, they walked the Deutsches back and it began to snow.

When the war broke no one thought the Nazis would make it as far as Hungary. Ruth left for Palestine as soon as she turned eighteen. Yehoyakim got into trouble for being a communist and he fled to the Soviet Union. The only one left to look after their parents was Shosh. When the Nazis invaded, they went into hiding. But even as the Nazis rounded up the Jews Ruth thought her family was safe.

Nathan told them where we were.

Ruth tossed, turned. Somewhere outside, the waking world tried to get her attention. But she couldn't wake up. The last letter from Shosh, falling from her hands when she finally got it. That certain knowledge that her family was dead. And that everything she knew had gone up in flames and vanished forever.

'Ruth… Ruth!'

She woke with her heart pounding. Israel above her, his hand on her shoulder.

'What?' she said, for a moment not sure where she was, knowing only the terrible sense of loneliness and loss inside her.

'They're here,' Israel said.

The present washed back in, like a river flooding a cavern. It took away the ghosts and replaced them with the pop-pop-pop sound of sporadic gunfire.

'How many?' Ruth said.

'Three cars, about a dozen men.'

She swore softly. Reached for the Luger.

'Ruth, we're handling it.'

She nodded absently. She walked out into the night. Comrades ran like shadows, holding weapons. All the lights were out. She ran, half crouching, to the children's house.

'We're handling it, Ruth.'

It was Dov, materialising out of the dark. His face was blackened with mud. Only his eyes shone feverish bright.

'Then handle it,' she said.

She heard gunshots, close by. Dov swore. Someone raised a shout in the dark. The attackers had breached the fence.

Dov vanished. Ruth steadied herself against the wall. She peered over the corner. Saw a figure darting in the dark, in clothes no kibbutznik would wear. She raised the gun and fired.

The man dropped. She ran to him, crouched over.

'You bitch,' he said. He spat blood. She peered into his face. She didn't know him.

He reached for his gun so she had to shoot him.

She thought he'd reached for his gun.

It didn't really matter.

He didn't get up again.

More gunfire, the sound of a car engine starting up, then a scream and the engine cut short. Ruth stayed by the children's house. The door opened and one of the girls, Paula, stood there.

'Go back inside,' Ruth said. 'Close the door. Stay low.'

Paula nodded. She shut the door.

Shots coming from the pines. Ruth turned at the sound of footsteps but it was too late.

The man shoved her against the wall. He put his gun to her back.

'Remember me?' he said.

She didn't feel fear. His free hand ran down her body, turning her round roughly. She spun with it. Their bodies were so close they were touching. His face closed on hers. 'I'll fuck you before I kill you—'

He looked surprised. The Luger, pressing against his stomach like an erection. She wasn't even conscious of squeezing the trigger. The gun *kicked*. The man fell to his knees. That look of dumb surprise. The door opened and Paula and Malka stood there, silent as ghosts. They saw the man. They saw Ruth.

The man's lips moved. He tried to pull his intestines back in. Ruth went to the older girl. She put the gun in her hands.

'You have to do it,' she said. The girl looked at her without expression. Ruth led her to the man. Ruth held the girl's small hands around the gun.

The man stared up.

The girl spoke.

'What?' Ruth said.

The girl repeated the words. It was the first time Ruth heard her speak.

'I don't want to,' Paula said.

The man tried to speak. He failed. His eyes begged mercy.

'You have to,' Ruth said. She felt the little girl tremble. Then the hands steadied.

The gun *kicked*.

The smaller girl started to cry.

'Good girl,' Ruth said. She took the gun from Paula's hands. The man's face was spread out against the ground. Ruth pulled Malka to her. She held the two girls close. She hugged them tight.

'It's over,' she told them. 'It's over.'

19

HERE AND THERE SHE COULD STILL HEAR SINGLE SHOTS BEING fired as another of the attackers was tracked down and dispatched. Then there was only silence.

The children were fast asleep in the children's house. The bodies of the men who dared attack Trashim were collected in a pile outside the shack that was the communal dining room.

'Filth,' Dov said. He smelled of gunfire and blood. She hugged him and felt his heart beat against her chest.

'We need to get rid of them before sunrise,' Ruth said. 'Make it so that they were never here.'

'What about the cars?' Mishka said. He had a glazed look of avarice. 'Beautiful vehicles.'

'Get rid of them,' Ruth said.

'I could take them to a chop shop in Haifa,' Mishka said. 'At least the kibbutz will earn money from it.'

'We don't have the time and we can't draw attention. Lose them in the woods near Juara and torch them.'

'It's a crying shame,' Mishka said. 'A crying shame.'

They got to work. It wouldn't do to stuff the bodies in the cars, Ruth thought. Sooner or later someone would find them. But the hills beyond Trashim were bare. They hitched a trailer to the tractor and loaded it up with the dead. They marched in grim silence behind the vehicle, spades in hand. Starlight lit the way. Down by the wadi on the edge of wood they dug and dug. They left the bodies in a shallow grave.

She felt lighter when it was done. If a job was to be done then it should be done well. It was lighter as they began the steep climb up the hill. The first tendrils of the sun put the lie to darkness.

Not the sun. Ruth froze. Lights, moving fast. Lights, bobbing in the distance, getting closer. Heading to Trashim.

'What's that!' somebody called. A whistle of warning came from the watchtower on the hill. Dov swore. Israel took Ruth's hand.

'The British,' Ruth said. The knowledge slid into her heart. 'The British are coming.'

Dov swore.

'Why here?' Israel said.

And Ruth realised then, though it couldn't be, had she only known, had she only realised—

'Not here,' she said.

'Then where?' Israel said.

Ruth said, in awe or horror, she couldn't say, 'They must be coming *everywhere*.'

'The slick,' Dov said. 'The slick!'

'You boys should run,' Ruth said. 'Hide in the hills, they wouldn't find you.'

But she heard the engines now, heard dogs barking, heard boots stomping, guns pumping, the blare of a megaphone, 'Put down your weapons! You are surrounded! By authority of his majesty King George!'

They made it up the last incline and ran straight into armed troops. Dov and Israel were pushed to the ground. A soldier saw Ruth, raised the stock to smash her in the face, she cowered, screamed, 'I'm pregnant!'

'Sorry, miss. Go stand over there with the others.'

The soldiers moved between the makeshift buildings. Men were placed on the ground and handcuffed. The women pushed to one corner under the watchtower. The children came out of the children's house. The soldiers ripped floorboards and smashed walls. They broke furniture and pulled up tents.

Ruth didn't pray, hadn't for years. But she prayed now. That they wouldn't find the slick with all the weapons.

And that they wouldn't find the *other* slick.

The soldiers found the truck and tore it apart in their search. They found the hidden compartment but it was empty.

Inch by inch they searched. They got to the bakery. They went inside. They were there a long time.

'Anything?' an officer said.

'Nothing, sir.'

'Keep searching.'

They went through the whole kibbutz. They took ID papers from everyone.

'Well?' the officer said.

'Sir? Sir, we got something!'

Ruth could only watch. Watch as the officer went into the bakery. The door was open, the daylight that had grown by degrees now illuminated starkly the open trapdoor to the slick. The British officer smiled. It was not a nice smile. Soldiers vanished inside. They brought up Stern machine guns.

The officer's smile grew bigger.

'Arrest everyone on the list,' he said. 'And put them on the trucks.'

Ruth could only watch. The soldiers came. They took Dov. They took Israel. They put them on the trucks. They carted precious guns and ammo. Paid for in blood. Paid for in cash. They took every scrap.

'Well, have a nice day,' the officer said. 'I apologise for the inconvenience.'

And then they were gone, just like that.

★

The news kept filtering in throughout the day. Trashim was not the only, nor the worst hit place. Operation Agatha deployed thousands of British soldiers all across Palestine. They decimated the resistance's arms supplies and arrested half of the Strike Force soldiers and nearly all of the movement's top leadership. Low-flying airplanes circled Jerusalem. A nationwide curfew was declared. Roadblocks shut off all the main roads, and the camp in Atlit filled up with prisoners.

None of that made much difference to Ruth.

Israel and Dov were gone. Even Mishka had been arrested.

She helped with the children and preparing food for the day and then she snatched a few hours of sleep in her tent. She woke up exhausted and threw up outside, but after that she felt better. She could feel the baby inside her, suffusing her with its light. Everything will be fine, she wanted to tell her. Everything will be fine.

The comrades remained by the radio, listening to the news as they came in. No one was going in or out of the kibbutz.

One by one they dropped, went to their tents. The children were asleep. Only a single hurricane lamp still burned. Ruth took it with her.

She made her way along dirt roads marked with stones. To the edge of the kibbutz, where they kept the donkey. She patted the donkey's neck. There was a little stable there, where one day they hoped they'd have horses. There was hay for the donkey, a trough for his water. The mud smelled of the donkey's excrement. There was a small wooden hut where they stored bales of hay. The British had tossed the hut earlier. But they didn't find anything other than shit.

She went into the donkey's enclosure. Went behind the trough. Set down the hurricane lamp and felt in the mud until she found the ring. She grasped the metal and pulled.

A small entrance. She climbed down, pulled the trapdoor shut behind her. It stank underground in that little cell. Ahead of her was a metal door. She reached for her key. She turned it in the lock. She pushed the door open.

A man sat shackled to a chair. His beard had grown wild. There were welts on his face. A bucket of excrement sat by the door. The man opened bleary eyes. His eyes teared up in the glare of the lamp.

'Please,' he whispered. 'Please, don't.'

Ruth picked up a truncheon. She hefted it in her hand.

'Hello, Nathan,' she said.

PART FOUR

DISPLACED PERSONS

Shosh

Germany, 1947

20

'I WISH TO GO TO AMERICA,' SHOSH WROTE. 'BUT THE BORDER to America is closed.' She was writing to Ruth again. She wondered if Ruth was alive. She held the pen, something so simple and yet so precious. It was hard to get, even on the black market. And paper was worse. Even the Amis had paper shortages. The stuff they read was badly printed on cheap paper. No Goethe or Schiller, not even Tolstoy. Their magazines had lurid covers, buxom dames threatened by brooding men with guns. She was lucky she had a fellow who was sweet on her. Even now, even after everything, the camp, she looked good. Frank gave her the pen, and he gave her reading, to help her with her English. *Black Mask* and *Spicy Detective* and *Dime Detective Magazine*. She held the May issue. A girl with *Miss America* across her chest, not wearing very much at all, was threatened by a skeleton in a fedora.

How she wanted to go to America with Frank! Not Palestine, that awful, dusty place where there were nothing but camels, but Hollywood, like in the pictures the WIZO women put on once a week for everyone. She loved George Montgomery, with that easy smile of his, she loved the way the camera framed the characters and the way the shadows fell, the stark lines of sunlight and the darkness that was always there, and the influence of German expressionism on those strange tales captured in celluloid a world away, where palm trees moved in the breeze and the sun was the sort that could erase the shadows.

All around her people were sleeping, crying, farting, fucking, in the freezing cold barracks which were not too long ago the Wehrmacht's, in the shadow of the prison where Adolf Hitler wrote *Mein Kampf.* Now it was her home: the Landsberg DP Camp, and here she was, a DP, Displaced Person, with no home to go back to and nowhere to go. She was nothing but a problem nobody wanted: not the Germans – God, not the Germans! – not the Americans, or the British, or the French or the Soviets. Not that anyone wanted to go to Russia. Anyone with any sense tried to get a visa to America. The rest were mad with Zionism and Palestine, just like her sister was.

The flame from the candle stub shuddered in the cold draught. Makeshift barriers were put up between bunks in the barracks, all for trying to reclaim a tiny bit of privacy, but there was none, only the pretence of it. A baby cried nearby. The smell was awful but she had grown used to stench, she barely felt it, and besides, a baby was a joy. The mother sang softly in Yiddish behind the curtain as she changed the baby. Shosh, too, wanted a baby. It didn't even matter who it was from. Just to give new life, for all the life that was lost. Just to say to the Nazis, you could not kill us all, and now we're here, and we are still alive, and we can still make life. There was something miraculous in having a baby. How a life can come from nothing, like a match being struck and making a flame. When all she could think about were the millions of candles snuffed, just like that.

Remembered arriving in Auschwitz, with Mama and Papa and the rest of the Jews from their town. Then Mama and Papa were taken one way, and she another. She lived and they died. She picked up the pen.

'It is not so bad,' she wrote. She didn't know why she was writing. She didn't know where Ruth was. Every week she frequented the UNRA office, looking for any mention of Ruth, of Yehoyakim, but never a name, never an answer of whether they lived or died. 'It is not so bad, being alive,' she wrote. 'Last week Frank took me in his jeep and we went to the Ammersee. It is a pretty lake and we had a picnic. Frank tried to catch fish but he is no fisherman. It is cold but when the sun shines it is also beautiful. Frank is fond of me and I of him. He gives me extra food...' She trailed off. She was near a skeleton as a human could be and still somehow live when the camp was liberated. Now their rations were macaroni and cheap bread, foods to fatten them without nutrition. There was a riot only the week before over the lack of eggs, of meat, even milk. There were no vegetables. Frank had given her a small pot of jam, as casually as you would pass someone a postage stamp. Shosh took it to the black market and traded it for duck eggs and fresh cheese. She hadn't dared taste the jam, she hadn't tasted jam since before the war. Sometimes Frank gave her cigarette packets. For those she got meat on the black market. For a packet of cigarettes any woman would sleep with a man. This was just a fact of life, but Shosh was lucky to have a good man there. Without Frank she would be much worse off. She would marry Frank if she could, but Frank had a wife back home in Oklahoma. She would marry him if only she could and get a visa to America, but the border to America was closed.

'I hope to find you and to see you soon,' she wrote. The candle shuddered, almost finished. Somebody groaned beyond the divider, a keening sound of loss so awful that Shosh closed her eyes. A sound like that was heard every night in Landsberg.

'I love you. Your sister, Shoshana.'

The candle went out. Shosh folded the cheap pulp paper as neatly as she could. She wrote in the margins of adverts for Eveready Batteries and the LaSalle Extension University of Correspondence Learning, and mail-order items like the Vacu-Matic or body-building manuals, or how to learn to be an electrician at home. The magazines were so full of adverts, and the adverts were so fantastical, that America came alive in Shosh's mind each time she leafed through them. A land of impossible plenty, where everything could be had for the price of a stamp, where no invention was too outlandish, where everyone could improve themselves – their bodies, their minds – from the comfort of their own home. It was incredible. She put the sheets into the envelope and sealed it.

She never sent the letters. She didn't know where to send them to. But writing them gave her comfort.

She took the pen and the envelope and rose from the small table. She shared this makeshift room with six others. Mr and Mrs Gold were asleep. Yankl, the Pole, muttered prayers in Hebrew on his bunk. He did that all night long. Renata was out, she was probably with a guy. Renata always had cigarettes. Shosh stretched out on her bunk. She wrapped the blanket tight around herself but it was cold, so cold in the barracks. She reached in her pocket, took out the small rectangle of paper she had torn out of a magazine called *Adam*. She didn't need to look at it to see what it said:

If Loneliness is Your Only Companion

Why not contact a girl abroad?

Thousands of beautiful girls and ladies in **EUROPE, SOUTH EAST ASIA & LATIN AMERICA** are looking for pen pals, friendship or marriage.

Details and sample photos Free by air mail.

HERMES Berlin 11, Box 17/20 Germany

If only she could get to Berlin. If only she could get out of Landsberg. In the town, the defeated Germans hated the DPs, and of the Amis some were good and some were bad but all wanted something. Frank kept promising to take her to Berlin. If only she could sign on with Hermes, have her pictures taken, maybe a lonely man over there in America would request her details, free by airmail with sample photos. She could get a visa then. She could get a degree with the LaSalle Extension University and buy Eveready batteries and find out what a Vacu-Matic was.

And then she'd be free.

21

'HEY, DOLL.'

Mid-morning and another day of listless existence beckoned. Moritz chewed a blade of grass and leered at her from the top of the cart he was sitting on. 'You want to make some money today?'

'I'm not working, Moritz,' Shosh said. Truth was no one wanted to work, not after Auschwitz, not for Germans, never for Germans. There were classes, yes, the WIZO women held a sewing class and whoever had more than a high school education had a go at teaching classes – in geography, in math, whatever little they could still remember. But mostly they all just… waited. Waited for something to change. Waited to leave, if only there was a place that would take them.

'I ain't talking that kinda work, Shosh,' Moritz said, 'I ain't taking in *washing*.'

The kid was only fifteen or sixteen. Had done a whole year in Auschwitz, hooked up with the Greek crew, the sort of people who always had shoes. You had to have shoes to survive, this was the sort of truism you learned in the camp. You stole or you traded or you did what you could, because if you went without them you died. Moritz was only fifteen or sixteen and looked younger, but he was an old man all the same.

'Then what?' Shosh said.

'You got an in in the kitchens?' he said.

'You know I do.'

'Then you know what's what.'

'Not today, Moritz,' Shosh said. She was tired and antsy, she hadn't slept well, dreams of the camp woke her up again. In the dream the kapo, Anna Klug, hit her again with the soup ladle. It was an awful metal weapon of vengeance, and Anna Klug wielded it with a savage joy in the wounds she inflicted. Two of Shosh's fellow inmates from the same block died at Anna Klug's hands.

'What else you got to do today, Shoshi?' Moritz said. She'd let him feel her up once and he'd had a crush on her ever since. 'You want to be like them?' He gestured at the DPs milling around, women breastfeeding, men reading the Torah or pulp magazines, a mixed group of youths sitting in a semi-circle around one of the instructors from Palestine, who came to tell them about reclaiming the land. They listened avidly. 'You want to be like the rest of the cattle?'

'Shut your trap, Moritz,' Shosh said, angry, and the boy lost his smile.

'You were there,' she told him. 'You should know better.'

'I know. I know. But come on, Shosh! We can make some dough from the dough!'

He's been reading too many of those *David Almog: Hebrew Detective* booklets that passed hand to hand through the camp. Cheap fiction in Yiddish, but the tales came from Palestine, where this Almog was a private detective of some sort, there was a picture of him in a fedora in the booklets. Ruth preferred American fiction.

Still.

She wanted butter, milk, fresh eggs, a steak – no. *Chocolate.* Her mouth watered at the thought. Moritz was right. If there was one thing she had learned back in the camp it's that you had to survive by any means. Rules? Law? Those were polite fictions, fairytales she might have believed in once. Not anymore.

'All right,' she said, 'All *right*.'

'Sixty-forty?'

'Fifty-fifty, like last time. And I'm taking all the risk!'

'Not all the risk,' he said complacently. He jumped down from the cart. A knock-kneed child. His eyes were huge in a face too thin. 'All right, let's go.'

'Give me a cigarette first.'

'Can I feel you up again?'

'*Cigarette*, Moritz.'

'For you, doll, anything,' he said. He took out a packet. It was cheap German shit. But it was better than nothing. He lit her up with Wrigley's gum matches. She took in a drag, coughed. Took pity on the kid.

'Oh, come on then,' she said. She drew him behind the cart with her.

'Just hurry up,' she said.

The kitchens were army built. The huge pots cooked starchy blandness. Heavy-armed cooks stirred the pots. Bags of flour stacked against one wall. Renata in an apron, why *she* worked in the kitchens was anyone's guess.

'We gotta make it quick,' she said, 'before they find out.'

'We've done it before,' Shosh said. 'We'll do it again.'

They picked up a heavy sack of flour and strained to heave it, along the wall and in the shadows, to the back door where Moritz and the cart awaited.

One bag, and then another and another. On the fourth trip one of the cooks went past, said, 'Hey, what are you—!'

Shosh slipped her a packet of Moritz's Ami cigarettes. Moritz always had Ami cigarettes, but never for smoking. Only for this. The cook pursed her lips and moved on. They made another trip, another. Nothing but flour in the whole goddamned place.

'Meet me later in the market,' Moritz said. He took off with the cart and his fucking donkey, Moishel. Even that donkey ate better than Jews.

'I've got to get back,' Renata said. 'Listen, Shosh…'

'Yeah?'

'I think I saw her.'

'You saw who, Renata?'

Renata took Shosh's hand.

'I think I saw Anna Klug,' she said. 'The kapo.'

Shosh started to shake.

'It can't be,' she said.

'I'm not sure. And her name is Klugerman now. But I think it's her. It *is* her.'

'Here?'

'Well, where else?' Renata said. 'She's a Jew. As far as the Amis are concerned she's just another survivor.'

'She's *here*?' Shosh said. 'In Landsberg?'

'I saw her queuing for the showers,' Renata said.

'I can't think about this right now,' Shosh said. 'I can't.'

She kept shaking. Renata held her. They hugged against the cold wall, clinging to each other.

'I'll kill her,' Renata said. 'I'll kill her for what she did.'

'We'll report her,' Shosh said. 'There'll be a people's court. There will be justice—'

'Justice!' Renata spat out the syllables. 'What is that word?'

'I don't know,' Shosh said, 'I don't know, Renata, I can't *think* about this right now—'

'Then go.' Renata released her. 'We'll talk later. Yes?'

'I promise.'

'And my cut!' Renata said.

'Everything,' Shosh said.

Renata squeezed her hand and hurried away. Shosh ran out into the cold sun. She threw up on the ground. Her puke was as thin as the gruel they fed them daily.

She wiped her mouth. She lit up another of Moritz's awful German cigarettes. It was more wood shavings than tobacco. She coughed and took another drag.

Thought about Anna Klug.

★

Anna Klug wasn't a big woman. Maybe she was fat once. Maybe she was thin. In Auschwitz she was just another walking skeleton, but the Nazis made her kapo.

The Nazis ran the camp but the kapos kept internal order. In exchange they got a bit of authority and an extra ladle of soup, and for that they could decide if you lived or died. All day the smoke rose from the crematorium and all day the inmates slaved for the Nazis, and every day they died, and every day more trains came laden with Jews. So many Jews for the ovens, this many Jews to be slaves. Heads shaved, gold teeth extracted, robbed of all they had, even their names. To the Nazis they were numbers, tattooed on their arms, entries in a column in a record book. The Nazis loved their records.

Shosh dreamed of working in the kitchens then. An extra stolen slice of bread. A ladle of soup with a chunk of potato in it. Instead she worked sorting dead Jews' fur coats to be re-sold by the S.S. It was indoor work so it was preferable to the chemical plant or the mines or the Sonderkommando transporting the corpses from the gas chambers to the crematorium. It was a *good* job. Whenever they could, the inmates tried to sabotage the coats. The men ripped the linings and tore the seams. But the women put tiny rolled notes into the pockets of the coats: *German women, know that you are wearing a coat that belonged to a woman who has been gassed to death in Auschwitz.*

Doing this was punishable by death. And Anna Klug was kapo. Shosh witnessed her when she caught one of the women in this act of sabotage. Anna Klug's fury was a terror to behold. She grabbed the woman by the neck and threw her on the ground and kicked and beat her, and then she tossed her out in the snow and the Germans came and shot her. And Anna Klug screamed at the women, and she told them this will be the fate of anyone who was caught.

Shosh didn't hate Anna Klug.

Shosh was *terrified* of her.

22

She met up with Moritz in the market. The market was a black market. *All* markets were black markets. Germans sat on blankets on the floor selling watches and cameras, the family silver, paintings if they had them, daughters if they had those – whatever they had left and could be traded for hard cash. Not the worthless occupation money but *real* cash – cigarettes, mostly. Farmers sold eggs and chickens and butter and milk, all of which they were not allowed to sell, but nobody cared, not here. Amis and Brits and black market speculators of all shapes and sizes – Germans, DPs, whoever had means, motive and opportunity. Ami soldiers walked around and bought German-made watches wholesale. They traded canteen foods and Camels. More money left Germany now than was coming in. Organised gangs shipped German-made goods to the States by the kilo. People were getting *rich*. And at least the Amis paid for stuff. The Soviets just stole whatever they could get their hands on.

Moritz had already offloaded the flour. He counted US dollars in one palm. He handed her the precious, precious currency. You didn't see a dollar every day. With a dollar, you could *be* somebody.

'I'll see you, doll,' he said. He was the hardest-faced kid she ever knew but she liked Moritz. It was just that he never got the chance to be a kid.

An Ami jeep drove slowly into the market. A familiar face smiled at her from the driver's seat.

'Hey, beautiful,' Frank said. 'What are you doing here?'

'Hey, Frank.' He made her happy, just seeing him. He wasn't the most handsome of men and he wasn't the smartest, and she knew that, like everyone else, he was dealing black market stuff. But he thought she was beautiful and, after the camp, no one had called her that, not for a long time. She didn't love him, not the way she had Nathan Deutsch, who she had loved wholeheartedly and even now, and even knowing what he did she couldn't hate him. A love was a love. But Frank made her happy. She only wished he could take her with him to America when he left.

'You busy later?' Frank said. 'Meet me in the usual place?'

'Of course,' Shosh said. Just the absurdity of his asking if she was busy was endearing. No one was busy at Landsberg, unless they were busy counting time. 'I will see you.'

'Super,' Frank said, with that same boyish enthusiasm all the Amis seemed to possess. Shosh sometimes wondered how they ever won the war. She figured maybe it was simply because it never occurred to them they could lose. 'I've got some business to take care of with the boys, but I'll see you after, yeah?'

'Yeah,' Shosh said.

'Super,' he said again, and gave her a glad wave and drove off, deeper into the market. Landsberg was not a large town, just another Bavarian shithole with a river and a prison where the Amis, from time to time, executed senior Nazis. Shosh knew Frank was doing business on the side, but what did she care? He gave her gifts and treated her nice, and what more could a girl ask?

'I remember Mama and Papa and all the happiness we had when we were all together,' Shosh wrote. It was afternoon and she sat in the courtyard outside with all the others. 'Then you left for Palestine and Yehoyakim disappeared with his revolutionary friends and it was just me to be with them. I was with them until the end, Ruth. Until the camp. Do you think of them sometimes, too? Do you think of me? I cannot picture your life in Palestine.

Do you have a family of your own now? I have so many questions. Would we still know each other if we meet again? But then, surely, we must. We are sisters.'

She chewed the pen. The Zionist instructor had the boys in youth movement uniform do physical exercises. How keen they all were. Everyone knew somebody who knew how to get on the aliyah ships to Palestine. Only a fool would try, Shosh thought. And yet the ships kept going, and drowning or getting captured, and all you did was swap one camp for another. And still they went on. She guessed they didn't see another way but to go.

'There was a woman in the camp,' she started. Then she stopped. Her heart fluttered. She wrote, 'I still think of Nathan, despite everything. I hope he is well, for all that he did. He was never a brave boy, and he must have done what he did because he was frightened.'

She knew Ruth wouldn't understand. Ruth had a cold, cruel streak in her. She once beat up one of the boys in their class for picking on Shosh. Hit him with a rock until he almost died. Eye for eye, tooth for tooth, Ruth always said. It was in *Exodus*.

She crossed out what she wrote, scribbled on it with the pen until the squiggly black lines hid the words. Ruth wouldn't understand. Shosh wrote, 'Perhaps you could come and visit me in America one day.'

She signed the letter as she always did. 'I love you. Your sister, Shoshana.'

She folded the letter and put it away. She saw Renata crossing the courtyard. Renata had that pinched, angry face, like when she was sorting the dead women's coats in the camp. The way she marched towards Shosh, people got out of her way.

'What is it?' Shosh said.

'I saw her again. She's in the line for the showers.'

Shosh started to shake. Renata grabbed her by the shoulders, shook her. People looked, then looked away.

'Stop it, Shosh.'

'I don't want to see her,' Shosh said.

Renata took her by the hand. Dragged her across the courtyard. The long line snaking for the showers. Women waiting. This is all you did in Landsberg, waited. Renata said, 'See?'

She pointed.

Shosh looked.

The woman who stood in the line looked no different to the others. Then she turned, and her face caught the sun, the cruel profile softened into just another victim's outline. Shosh's heart beat fast but she stood tall and took it in.

Anna Klug, alive and wearing shower clogs.

'What do we do?' Shosh said. She spoke softly. Renata held her hand.

'You know what we have to do,' she said.

Mr and Mrs Gold were playing cards with Yankl, the Pole. Shosh paced. Nothing to do but wait, and try to wash her dress, her second-best one, and try on the lipstick Frank got her. She checked her hair in the small mirror. She looked good, she thought. Her face had filled out now. The rest of her too. She fit into the dress. Renata came in.

'Are you ready?' she said.

'Gin rummy,' Mr Gold said, and he laid down his card.

Shosh checked her lipstick one last time. She looked good.

'Yes,' she said.

They went away, arm in arm.

The wedding party had already started. There was always a wedding party. People hooked up everywhere, in the kitchens, in the showers, in the halls and in the courtyard, in the tents outside, in the beds inside. People got married and people got pregnant. *Fast.*

The groom broke the glass.

'Mazel tov!' Shosh shouted. There was even wine, cheap wine the WIZO women provided. She and Renata took a cup each.

'L'chaim!'

Someone started playing the hora on an accordion. Everyone danced. The bride and groom kissed, the girl visibly pregnant. A couple making out bumped into Shosh. The serious drunks sat at a table with vodka. The party was turning wild. There was no separation of the sexes. The rabbi sat smoking with the serious drunks. The hora segued into a Spade Cooley number. A violinist joined the accordion player. The beat picked up, couples formed, swirled, Renata took Shosh's hand, pulled her across the dance floor, a man pulled Shosh away, twirled her around, Renata took her back, pulled until they reached the end of the impromptu dance hall, stepped over a couple rolling in the bedding on the floor, walked down a cold corridor with dim light. The music receded behind them. They held hands without speaking.

'Now?' Shosh said.

Renata said, 'Now.'

23

They sent Moritz to do it. They waited in the cellar with the rats. It was cold and it was dark, and Shosh shivered. She held a shiv Renata gave her.

'What for?' Moritz had said.

'Don't you mind what for,' Renata told him. 'Just get her to come down to the cellar.'

'Offer her money,' Shosh said. She pushed a dollar into Moritz's hand. 'She would do it for that.'

'And what do I get?' Moritz said.

'Come on, kid,' Renata said. Moritz looked at them both. Shosh knew what he wanted. She held herself straight. She said, 'Do it for me.'

Moritz nodded. Moritz went. They waited below. At last, footsteps came.

When Anna Klug stepped in through the door it was shut behind her. She peered in the dark, a lone, frightened woman.

'Who's there?' she called. 'What do you want?'

Renata came out to her. She said, 'Hello, Anna.'

'Who are you?' Anna Klug said.

'You know who I am.'

'No. No, I don't.'

'Say it,' Renata said. 'Say it!'

'I don't know who you are!' Anna Klug turned to the door. She started to bang on it to open. 'Help! Help!' she cried.

'There is no help, Anna,' Renata said. Anna turned back to

her. Her face changed then. Shosh took a step forward, and then another. She emerged out of the shadow. Anna Klug's mouth widened in a mocking grin.

'Renata and her little bitch,' she said. 'You think you can take me?'

'You are a murderer,' Shosh said. Where the courage came from she didn't know. She held the shiv. 'A sadist and a collaborator. You deserve to die.'

Anna lost her smile. She reached under her clothes, pulled out a knife.

'You stupid bitch,' she said. 'I *saved* your lives. You stupid cunt. I had to make an example of the others or we would have *all* died there. I did what I had to do, not for me but for all of us! And you dare to judge me? You *live*!'

Shosh gripped the wooden handle of the shiv. She never hated. She *loved*. But suddenly it all came back to her, and she remembered the nights in the camp, in the bunk, in the dark, she and Renata and the other women, telling each other stories. About meals they'd made. Meals they were going to make. Lovingly detailing kugel and lokshen, chola and tshulent. Listing ingredients and family recipes. Learned from mothers and grandmothers turned into smoke. Telling each other, to keep them alive. Her stomach hurt from hunger and desire but they never stopped, and in the night she dreamed of kreplach and rugelach and chicken soup and schmaltz.

She wasn't conscious of advancing on Anna Klug. Was barely conscious of Anna lunging at her, the sharp knife tearing through her dress, and she was taken by surprise as she hit Anna Klug with her closed fist and broke Anna's nose. The other woman stood there, gaping, blood dripping down her face, and Shosh's shiv flashed and sliced through Anna's wrist. Anna's knife fell to the ground. Then Shosh and Renata were both on her, holding her down on the ground, and Renata said, 'Anna Klug, you are found guilty of murder and collaboration in this people's court, and sentenced to death.'

'I... fucking *saved* you,' Anna Klug said, and Shosh stabbed her, the shiv sliding too easily between the kapo's ribs, and Anna Klug cried out, but the cellars were deep and the door heavy and there was no one to hear her cry.

It was over quickly. Shosh's mind flittered like a butterfly into a dark night. She was barely conscious of the blade, rising and falling. She was barely conscious of the blood. Then Anna Klug lay still and her blood no longer pumped, and her eyes went dim, and she just looked stupid lying there. Shosh started to laugh.

'What are you...?' Renata said. Then she started to giggle. Then they were both laughing, laughing and crying both, holding each other's blood-covered hands.

'So, so, *stupid!*' Shosh said. 'Look at her, look at her... *eyes!*'

'We have to... stop it, Shosh, we have to... don't make me laugh! We have to... go.'

Shosh hiccupped. Anna Klug just lay there. She stared at Shosh. Renata said, 'Shosh, are you all r—'

Shosh vomited. The bile rose out of her, burned her throat, fell on the corpse. It was suddenly so cold in the cellar. She started to shiver. Renata said, 'Shosh! Snap out of it!'

'I, I, I, I can't,' Shosh said.

Renata held her. Shosh shivered.

'Why did we do it?' Shosh said. 'Why, Renata?'

'She deserved it,' Renata said.

'She was just trying to survive,' Shosh said. 'Same as us.'

'Not the same as us!' Renata said. 'Never the same.'

'She didn't deserve to die,' Shosh said. 'We're no better than her, we're not—'

'She deserved it for what she did.' Renata dipped her finger in the blood. She drew on the concrete floor. Shosh watched in horrified fascination. A line up, a line down, up, down. Forming a single letter:

M.

'Like in that movie,' Renata said. 'The one with—'

'Peter Lorre,' Shosh said. 'Yeah, no, I get it.'

'We have to get out of here,' Renata said. 'We need to lose the shivs and we need to clean up.'

They knocked on the door, twice in a row. Moritz opened. He took one look at them and didn't say a thing.

'She was a kapo, Moritz,' Shosh said.

Moritz nodded. He put out his hands. Renata gave him her shiv. Shosh gave him her shiv. He wrapped them in a cloth.

'I'll drop them in the Lech,' he said.

They slunk, the two of them, Shosh and Renata, Renata and Shosh, along the cold corridors, against the walls. But no one saw or, if they did, nobody cared. Landsberg's DPs had their own problems, and they had learned long ago not to see too much. Shosh scrubbed the blood off her hands and face in the showers. She stood in her shift and shivered in the cold and scrubbed and scrubbed her dress. The water turned dirty. Renata kept watch. They took turns. In the hall the wedding party was coming to an end. There would be new babies conceived that night, new children to replace all the ones that were lost. Shosh was glad of that. She wanted a new life for herself. She wanted a baby, too. Maybe doing what they did to Anna Klug – maybe that was what she had to do to exorcise the past. Maybe now she could look forward. A new life, a new Shosh. She scrubbed and scrubbed the blood.

'Frank?'

He never ceased to make her smile. She was smiling now, dressed in her second-best dress. She came to their usual meeting place like she'd promised. She looked for his jeep, which was usually parked nearby. The river Lech stretched out into the distance, men fishing on the shore, the sun setting and the light shimmering off the water. Shosh was scrubbed pink. She would tell Frank she *had* to go with him, she thought. He'd understand. He would do what had to be done, she was sure of it.

'Frank?'

She waited, but he never came. The sun went down and the moon rose and it was cold. Shosh went back to the camp.

'Did you hear?' Mr Gold said. 'They found a woman down in the cellars, murdered.'

'Executed,' his wife said and pursed her lips. 'They say she was a kapo.'

'Gin rummy,' Mr Gold said. He put down his cards.

'We are going to Palestine,' Mrs Gold said. 'It has been arranged. You should come with us, Shosh. We are leaving for Italy next week.'

'You got a *sertifikat*?' Shosh said.

Mrs Gold shook her head. 'It's not like that,' she said.

'Then you'll be arrested. Sent back, or put in prison.'

'One camp is much like another,' Mr Gold said. 'We have to try. We must make a new life.'

Mrs Gold put her hand on her stomach. Shosh realised with some surprise that she was pregnant. Mrs Gold saw her look and smiled.

'A new life,' she said.

'But America,' Shosh said.

Mr Gold shook his head.

'There is only one land left for us,' he said.

'What will you do there?' Shosh said.

'Whatever it takes,' Mr Gold said. 'I used to be a diamond cutter. But if there are no diamonds I will sweep the streets, or work the fields, or in a factory. I will do what I have to.'

'There is so much fighting there,' Shosh said. 'War.'

'Then I will go to war,' Mr Gold said.

'I don't want more war,' Shosh said. 'I saw enough of it.'

'You must fight for what you want,' Mrs Gold said. 'And for the children. We will travel on the *Judenstaat* in two weeks' time.

I wish to eat a Jaffa orange. I wish to see the lights of Haifa in the distance, and breathe the warm air... I wish never to set foot in Germany again.'

'I can't,' Shosh said. 'I have...'

She couldn't finish the thought. Hopes? Dreams?

Where *was* Frank?

'I have to go,' she said.

'Just think about it,' Mrs Gold said.

24

SHE WENT LOOKING FOR FRANK. THIS WASN'T LIKE HIM. SHE
went to the barracks but was turned away by the sentries.

'Try the market, or the Dicker Hund,' one said, taking pity on
her.

She went back to the market. Flames burned in torches stuck
into the ground and in hurricane lamps, and the faces of the buyers
and the sellers were shrouded in smoke. Laughter was louder,
arguments coarser, shadows moved through stalls. Watches on
blankets, gold rings and cameras, silver bracelets and paintings,
all manner of things. She pushed through, a man's rough hand
reached to grab her and she turned and slapped the hand away,
ducked and moved on, not looking back. A group of Ami soldiers
stood in one corner smoking cigarettes and counting swag, but
Frank wasn't with them and she went on.

The entrance to the Dicker Hund was set into a stone alcove in
the old part of town. Loud music came from inside. Amis stood
outside leaning against walls with girls who laughed at their jokes.
In the alleyway a private was getting a blowjob. Shosh looked
away. She made to go inside.

'You have money?'

Some stooge of the proprietor stopped her. His ugly fat face was
too much for Shosh.

'Get out of my way,' she said.

'Or what?' he said. 'You filthy DP—'

She kneed him in the balls. The fat man dropped, his face red, and she stepped over him and went in. Stone arches and a long polished bar, Amis in uniforms and girls not wearing very much at all. Shosh didn't often come to places like this. She didn't think it was Frank's sort of scene.

'Suzie,' someone said. She saw a soldier lean against the bar. His name was Jerry, he was a friend of Frank's. He gave her a wary smile. 'What are you doing here?'

'I'm looking for Frank,' she said.

'Didn't you hear?'

'Hear what?' Shosh said. She felt weak all of a sudden. Jerry held her arm, gave her a stool to sit on. He motioned for the bartender and two mugs of beer appeared.

'What happened to Frank?' Shosh said.

'He was in a car accident,' Jerry said. 'He's fine, Suzie. Just broke his legs and has a concussion.'

'Where is he, Jerry?' She grabbed him by the shirt. He let her, then pushed a mug of beer into her hands.

'They took him to Berlin,' he said.

She took a sip of beer. The beer was cold. The beer was fine. She took another sip. She put down the mug.

'What really happened?' she said.

Jerry shrugged, uncomfortable. 'An argument over, you know.'

'Black market goods,' Shosh said.

'We had a decent operation going here, Suzie. A good, clean run. But these new boys, they play rough.'

'They got rough with Frank?' Shosh said.

'They did.'

'And you, Jerry? Where were you!' She was almost shouting.

'I was with him, girl. But I couldn't do nothing to stop it.'

'Who are they?' Ruth said.

'It doesn't matter,' Jerry said. 'What matters is, Frank's gone. I'm sorry, Suzie. I know you liked him.'

'He's not coming back?' Shosh said. The shock of it was slow to hit her.

'He's going home,' Jerry said. 'But listen. Hey. I'm here.' He raised his glass to her. 'We could still have a good time together,' he said.

'You married, Jerry?' Shosh said.

'What's that got to do with anything?' Jerry said.

'Fuck!' Shosh screamed. Heads turned. Bavarian girls glowing with good health glowered at her. The men looked elsewhere. Jerry raised his glass of beer. Shosh downed hers. She chugged the beer. The beer was cold. The beer was good.

'Fucking Amis,' Shosh said. She walked away without a backwards glance.

There was a protest outside the camp when she came back. She felt unsteady on her feet. America, no longer promised, receded from her sight. All that work she spent on Frank – wasted. All that time, gone.

Men and women marched outside the camp holding placards as military police watched. Torches burned. Shosh saw folks from the wedding. Nursing a hangover, nursing a grudge.

'We need food, not pap!'

'We will not live like rats!'

'Open the gates of Palestine!'

'Improve conditions now!'

The mood was dark with anticipation. Shosh could tell how it would go. Night, and the bottled anger they all felt was coming out. The MPs watched at the ready. All it took was a spark for the fire to start.

Shosh saw figures moving in the dark. Moritz passed her, a rock in his hand.

'Fuck the pigs,' he said. Then he threw the rock at the military cops.

Shosh knew to get out of the way. If only she could. The mass of protesters surged forward, people holding whatever makeshift weapons they could find, like the staves they had used for the banners. The MPs had batons out. They looked eager to break bones. Moritz was somewhere in the milieu. Shosh was pushed and shoved in the mass of bodies. She tried to get out. She heard screams. She fell to the ground. Feet threatened to stomp her. She pushed at them, she screamed to get up, but her voice was lost in the noise.

She held on to the nearest man's shirt and pulled herself up and kneed him in the face as he went down, just because. Some do-goodnik in glasses. The glasses broke. She didn't care. She pushed through and found herself on the edge of the mob. The MPs fired bullets in the air.

Shosh ran.

There was no sleep that night. The police swept through the camp. They kicked up beds and beat up anyone who looked at them directly. They were *pissed*.

The agitators had been arrested. There was also the matter of the corpse down in the cellar, but that one got dumped on the Jewish camp cops and they just went through the motions. Everyone knew what that letter *M* was for. No one was going to cry over Anna Klug.

Only someone did.

'Her husband,' Moritz said. He had a nasty cut on his forehead from the riot.

'She was *married?*' Shosh said.

'Every pot has a lid,' Moritz said, and looked hurt when Shosh started to laugh.

'What!' he said.

'Nothing. You sounded like an old grandmother just then.'

'He wants the murderers found. They were newly married. They met right here in Landsberg. Wanted to emigrate to Palestine, start a family. He's a guter mensch, Shosh. Good family, still has some contacts. The policemen might have to move on this.'

'But that's not good,' Shosh said.

'Not for you, no.'

'Meyn gat,' Shosh said. Everything was falling apart. She looked at Moritz pleadingly.

'What about you?' she said.

'Me?' He shrugged his little shoulders. 'I didn't get arrested.'

'I noticed.'

'I'll get by. Only I'm sick of this place. We should go, Shosh. We should go together.'

'Go where, Moritz?'

He lowered his voice. 'Palestine.'

'And eat rocks and shit dust for the rest of our days?'

He looked shocked at her language.

'I can get us on a ship,' he said.

Shosh screamed, 'Fuck!'

25

'Dear Ruth,' Shosh wrote. She stared at the page. What else could she write? The page was blank, its story still waiting to be told.

'I will see you soon,' Shosh wrote. What else was there to say? She signed the paper and put it away.

It was a cloudy day. Seagulls cried overhead as the *Judenstaat* left the port of Naples. They had made their way there with forged identity papers, avoiding borders as much as they could, the Zionist underground leaders even younger than they were but different, somehow. Harder, more self-possessed.

They didn't meet the other groups until they all boarded the ship, at night, displaced no more, for now they had a place to go to. They came from all over Europe, survivors all, the remnants. *She'erit ha'plita*: all that were left. Led by their young shepherds, until they boarded this rickety old ship, crammed inside her worse than in Landsberg.

Shosh had asked Renata to come with her. Begged her, then shouted. But Renata was firm. She'd met a new Ami, and this one was going to come through for her, this one was going all the way. A ring on the finger and a visa to America. She was trying to get pregnant. She drew it all for Shosh. The two-garage house, the white picket fence. Kids playing baseball in the front yard.

Shosh's dream. *Shosh's* plan.

Now she was stuck on a rust bucket on a choppy sea, sailing out of Italy into God knew where. She stared out into the wide open sea. Dark birds circled high overhead. Shosh tried to imagine what Palestine was like, and what sort of world they were sailing into.

And found that she couldn't.

'Gin rummy,' Mr Gold said, and put down his cards.

PART FIVE

FOUR ARAB WOMEN

Dov

The Galilee, 1948

26

DARK BIRDS CIRCLED HIGH OVERHEAD. DOV STARED UP AT THE cloudless skies. He tried to make them out. Large shapes moving in the sky above the battlefield.

Vultures.

He almost laughed. He wished he could tell Israel about it. But Israel was fighting somewhere in Jerusalem last time he heard. He wished he could tell Shosh, but she wasn't there. No one was there.

Now it was just Dov, the corpses, and the circling vultures.

He tried to move. Everything hurt. From time to time a sniper shot rang out and hit one of the corpses. Best not to move, then. Best wait until sundown. He just wasn't sure he had much time left.

How did he get here? It was his own goddamned fault.

The cleansing of the Manasseh Hills, in contrast to *this* fucked-up operation, had gone very well two months earlier. It even got written up in the newspapers after. It was a semi-independent attack by the Revisionists' militia, and since Dov knew some of the guys from their time in Cyprus together he came along. Someone had to, from the kibbutz. The Arab villages dotted the hills and operational policy was to clear as much land as possible. It was hot and dry. Dust coated Dov's shoes. It felt good to be out of prison at last and doing something useful.

He held the rifle and marched with the others. Foot soldiers, with the artillery coming behind.

The villages lay sleeping in the early morning light. The priority was clear. Eliminate fighting men and any resistance, send the rest fleeing, and raze what was left so they wouldn't come back. It was the sort of necessary evil that was, well, necessary. Dov didn't feel bad about that. You did what you had to do or the others would do the same to you. So on he marched, in this land he knew so well, and he could smell the fresh growing za'atar and he saw a porcupine hide in a nook in the rocks when it saw the soldiers go past. They approached the first of the villages and halted as the artillery was put into place.

Then the first mortar whispered.

The explosion raised a cloud of dust far ahead. The order was given then, and Dov and the rest of the mobile force went on foot towards the village. Artillery shells flew overhead, and the explosions woke the sleeping residents and tore new holes in the ground. One hit a house and the artillery men cheered. Dov and the others reached the village. Gunfire welcomed their approach.

'Take cover!'

Dov ducked behind a rock. The enemy were few and ill prepared, but they were still a threat. Dov saw a figure moving, took aim, fired. The man dropped down. Dov ran to the next rock. A shell hit the village's water well. A small kid ran out into the open. A frantic woman ran after him. Dov took aim, fired over her at a man he spotted in a window. The man vanished from sight, the woman scooped up the kid and ran for safety.

'Just run,' Dov said.

They encountered little resistance when they entered the village. Houses lay in ruins. Corpses lay on the ground. The survivors raised their arms when they saw the soldiers.

'Women and children to one side!' the commander barked. Dov saw the kid from earlier, the mother with her three other children. The men they went through one by one. The young defiant, angry. They got tied up. Old folks got sent to the other side. One old man stood alone.

'You're the mukhtar?' the commander said.

'Yes.'

'Go with the women and children,' the commander said. 'You know where to go?'

'Yes,' the mukhtar said.

'Good. Then get going.'

'What about the boys?' the mukhtar said.

'Prisoners,' the commander said. 'Nothing bad will happen to them.'

'Something bad has already happened to them,' the mukhtar said. But he went to his people, and started to lead them away. They streamed out of the village, out of their homes and their lives: women, children, the old and the infirm. They knew where to go – somewhere, anywhere, as long as it was far from here.

The fighters were put on the trucks. The commander gave the order and the destruction of the village began. The bombers placed explosives in the still-standing homes. Dov hummed Chaim Chefer's 'The Bombers' Song'.

It was good stuff. Good for morale. They marched on. The next village lay five kilometres away. They knew they were coming now. It would be a harder battle without the element of surprise. The hills crawled with Arab militiamen. Complete savages, out for Jewish blood. The next village came into view after a long hard march. The mortars spoke louder than words ever could. Dov and the rest of the regular troops stormed the village. They were met with bullets. Took cover. Dov threw a grenade. Dust everywhere, it was hard to see. The commander ordered 'Attack!'

Dov ran into the dust, shooting.

It hurt so much. He blinked sweat from his eyes. The sun overhead and the damned vultures circling. If it weren't for the snipers still filling up the corpses with holes the birds would have been down by now. But vultures were patient. They liked their meat to settle before they settled down to eat. By night the field would be crawling with them. Dov didn't want to become a vulture's supper. He had so much to live for. He didn't want some bird shitting out his liver. Not that he had much of a choice. He had two bullets in him and he was losing blood fast.

Forget the cleansing of the hills, then. That was just a run-of-the-mill operation – and they blew up the Arabs' old flour mills while they were at it, just for good measure. It was a terrific success, as far as an operation ever goes – no casualties on their end, around twenty dead Arabs, a cache of captured weapons and ammunition, and five villages cleared. The rest got the message.

He blinked sweat. The birds circled. Somewhere above him a bored sniper fired shots at the corpses. Making sure no one only *pretended* to be dead. Dov didn't even know if it was an Arab or a Jew who was doing the shooting. He didn't know who won and who lost. It was just his bad luck wandering into the middle of this particular battle.

This war to come was much on Dov's mind when the British sent him to prison in Cyprus at the tail end of '46. Everyone knew it had to come. Everyone knew the British position in Palestine was untenable. Sooner or later they'd have to fuck off. And when they did, Palestine would be left up for grabs.

He was in good spirits at first on the ship out of Haifa. A calm day, and seagulls circled. He liked the smell of the sea, but the sight of the shore receding from view reminded him he was an exile now. The British soldiers guarding the prisoners let them on deck to watch. They weren't going to run off anywhere.

He watched Palestine recede from sight. Then there was just the open sea, or rather the hold where they kept the prisoners. Big Moysh beat off in the dark when he thought no one was looking. Yoskeh had got hold of a bottle of grog from one of the more sympathetic sailors and was drinking like his life depended on it. Without it he got the shakes. He was himself a sailor, one of the guys bringing in refugees on the ships, only he got caught. Shorty Shmulik, who had one leg shorter than the other, played cards with Dan – they were both part of Yoskeh's crew. Got busted together on the *Susannah* sailing out of Metaponto in Italy. They seemed happy enough.

'Relax, Dov,' Yoskeh said. 'Sit down, have a drink.'

'How can you be so calm?' Dov said. 'We're prisoners. We're useless here. We'll be even more useless in Cyprus.'

'A sailor is never useless, so long as he's at sea,' Yoskeh said. He had the jollity of the habitual drunk.

'Susannah Susannah Sus*annah*!' Big Moysh screamed. He zipped up his pants and came back to join them. 'Someone should write a song like that,' he said. 'You should have seen us, Dov. The sea was stormy and the flagpole groaned, the masthead of the ship was all but gone. But Yoskeh had it all well in hand. We were just about to raise another glass to the sea—'

Yoskeh took a swig from the bottle.

'I'll drink to that!' he said.

'When the enemy's ships suddenly appeared,' Big Moysh said. 'And, well, here we are.'

'Here we are,' Yoskeh said and hiccupped.

'Raise you twenty,' Dan said.

'I fold,' Shorty said.

Dan swept matchsticks onto his pile. Shorty started shuffling the cards.

Dov stared at them.

He thought they were all mad, mad down to a man.

He saw her for the first time when he tried to get a pair of thick socks from the supplies officer. She must have been a new arrival. She stood at the barbed wire fence and looked out to sea. He only saw her from behind, but there was something so familiar about her, and for a moment he couldn't, for the life of him, say what it was.

Then she screamed, 'Fuuuuck!' and a flock of seagulls, startled, took to the air and the guards in the watchtower turned to look, then looked away uninterested.

Dov came closer. She turned then, hearing his feet on the gravel.

'What do you want!' she said.

He saw her face. Saw Ruth, somehow, looking back at him. A little younger. A little different. Her eyes were softer and her mouth curved as though she wanted to smile even when she was angry. When Ruth was angry there was no smile and you knew to stay well away.

'Nothing,' Dov said. Mumbled, really. He was kind of shocked. 'I heard you shout.'

'Yes, well, that's why I didn't whisper, did I,' the woman said.

'I'm Dov,' Dov said. 'Do you... You don't like it here?'

She looked at him like he was mad, and he realised how idiotic he sounded. He felt his face go red.

'Like it?' the woman said. 'It's just like where I left, only worse somehow. One camp, another camp, what difference does it make?'

'I'm Dov,' Dov said again.

'I'm Shosh.'

'You look an awful lot like someone I know,' he told her.

Suddenly she was there right in front of him. She grabbed him by the shirt. Her fingers were long and she was strong.

'Who?' she said.

'Her name is Ruth,' he said, and he saw the stillness that overtook Shosh then, and she looked into his face like she was studying some foreign map and trying to make sense of it.

'Ruth?' she said. 'You know my sister? Where is she? How is she!'

He took her hands. Removed them gently from his chest, held

them as he told her Ruth was well. 'She is in Palestine, she is a valued member of our kibbutz community, a real pioneer—'

'What?' Shosh said. 'What the fuck are you talking about!'

Then she was crying, and he was holding her, and the sun slowly set over the sea behind the barbed wire fence; gulls cried overhead and the guards in the watchtower watched as they smoked their lit cigarettes.

It was, Dov thought, kind of romantic.

He put a ring on her finger two weeks later. It was that quick. Love forged behind a barbed wire fence was all the more urgent, and neither of them knew how long they had left. Babies were born all over the Dhekelia camp.

'I want a baby,' Shosh said.

'With this ring you are sanctified to me as my wife under the faith of Moses and Israel,' Dov said, and with that it was done. Their friends cheered as Dov broke the glass. He smashed it with the heel of his shoe. Then he kissed his new wife, lifting her veil, and she returned the kiss passionately, but nobody cared.

That night they made love in the tin hut that was left empty for them on this wedding night. The tin huts were boiling in summer and freezing in winter, and why Dov went looking for thick socks in the first place on the day he met Shosh. Usually he shared the hut with three others. But for tonight, at least, there was only Shosh.

They made love and Shosh's voice was soft against his fevered skin. When they were done he lit them both cigarettes and she reclined on the bedroll and watched him and said, 'In Germany I killed someone.'

She was so like her sister that he almost laughed, and she batted at him fiercely and said, 'What!'

'I'm sure he deserved it,' Dov said, and Shosh nodded, very seriously, and said, 'She did. I think.' She looked into his eyes.

'You have to have a moral code,' she said.

Dov didn't know much about Shosh. She seemed private to him. But he believed she would be happy in Palestine, happy on the kibbutz. He could picture her working in the new sheep pens or helping with the children, and they would have their own children to contribute to the pool of the kibbutz, new sons and daughters, sabras all. He couldn't wait to take her there.

'Do you love me?' he said.

She watched him through the smoke.

'I love you,' she said, 'you funny little man.'

He jumped on her and she laughed, and then their arms closed around each other's bodies and the night was theirs and theirs alone.

He was drifting in and out of consciousness now. Dark shapes moving in the sky above, and the field he lay in was so still, so still with only him and the dead.

'Sir? I want to be of help.'

He was only a kid then. Barely fifteen. At school, before the kibbutz, before he met Ruth. And the commander was tall and strong, his moustache reddish-black, the colour of the juice bleeding from a pomegranate.

'You know what we do, kid?' the commander said.

'Fight for the homeland,' Dov said.

'You know what fighting means?'

Dov didn't. Of course he didn't. But he nodded all the same.

'I want to shoot an Arab,' he said.

'Oh?' the commander said. 'And why is that?'

'I'm underage,' Dov said. 'The British will hang you but they can't hang me.'

He was pretty proud of his logic. And the commander laughed.

'Six o'clock Wednesday night after school, in the gymnasium,' he told him. 'We'll see how you do then.'

So that was his time. Every week after school, a group of them kids gathered in secret. He learned how to disassemble and put together a gun, how to load it, how to fire. He learned how to observe and how to report. He learned codes. Mostly, he learned to do what he was told without asking questions.

Dov got his wish. 'Tomorrow at oh six hundred hours,' the commander said. 'On the corner of the market in Hadar. You see an Arab you jump on your bicycle and let the shooters know.'

Oh six hundred hours he was standing there as the market opened up and traders came from the adjoining villages and from the upper and lower Carmel. Dov was the spotter. The shooters were two, men in their late twenties, standing by the cinema. A gun mole behind them – a girl in a flower-print dress. After the shooting her job was to pick up the guns and put them in her purse. Then everyone was to head off in different directions.

An easy job. He stood there, watching. Israel was spotter number two, on the corner across. Dov waited, tense. He tried to look casual. His palms sweated. His heart beat fast.

A Ford taxi went past. A British patrolman strolled past, eating an apple. A cart carrying tomatoes to market went past. Then he saw one. Had to be an Arab, Dov thought. Dressed in that Turkish fez and a long robe, had to be – but what if he wasn't? Could be a Jew, plenty of them, like Dov's father even, still dressed like the Turks. Dov couldn't decide. The man gave him a friendly look, looked away.

Dov let him pass.

A few minutes later he heard *bang! Bang! Bang!*

He ran to see. He was just a kid. Was it *his* Arab? The shooters were gone, the girl too. Dov saw a man and a donkey, the man on the ground, blood sprouting out of his throat. The donkey was wounded, it cried out in pain. Someone needed to put a bullet in that donkey's head. Someone needed to help that donkey. A woman screamed. Dov stared at the corpse on the ground. It was the first body he ever saw.

The police were going to come. Dov ran.

He met up with Israel later. 'It was my one!' Israel said. 'I gave them the signal, I saw them shoot him!'

Israel's eyes were very bright.

'It's us or them,' he said.

They went down to the harbour together. They found a hut that sold arak to sailors. They got drunk. It was the first time Dov ever got drunk. He was a good boy until then. There were whores. Dov and Israel went with the whores. It was very quick when it happened. Dov threw up in the place where people fucked and people pissed. It made no difference to the smell there, with the ships docked in the harbour, with the moonlight on the waves.

A lot of new things: first body first drink first sex.

They found a doorway and slept there the night. In the morning the shopkeeper kicked them out. Dov staggered into the bright sunlight of a new day. He didn't make it back to school that morning.

'Fuck you! Fuck you, Dov, you awful little man!'

The whole kibbutz could hear her. Pregnant and miserable with it. Her hands callused from the work in the fields. She blamed him for that. She blamed him for everything. He stepped out into the night, wanting to end this, how everyone would talk.

'Shosh, please,' he said.

'Fuck you!' She smashed a plate. He couldn't let her do that, it was communal, it belonged to the kibbutz.

'Shosh, please, calm down!' he said. 'The baby—'

'Is that what I am to you? Someone to carry your precious *baby*?'

'That's not what I—'

'Get out.'

He left. He went to Israel and Ruth's room. Israel met him outside, a bottle of brandy *medicinal* and two cups in his hands.

'It will pass,' he said. He poured them both a drink. Dov downed his and Israel refilled it.

'I don't know, Israel.'

'She loves you. It's a hard pregnancy, is all.'

He poured again. Dov sipped this time. Ruth was inside somewhere. But she wasn't coming out. She had lost her last baby. So many babies were lost. Dov worried.

Ruth chose Israel, in the end, and that was all right. Now Dov had Shosh. Maybe it would all work out, he thought. Maybe it will work out fine in the end.

Dov lay in the sun and stared at the vultures. A daughter or a son? They had got out of Cyprus eventually, went back to Palestine. Shosh was already pregnant by then.

Then the war, just like he knew it would come. And he and Israel picked up their guns and went to fight. So that was that.

And here he was.

All because Shosh was right.

You had to have a moral code.

27

THE VILLAGE WAS SOMEWHERE IN THE UPPER GALILEE AND AT first everything went according to plan. The village was heavily fortified by Arab Liberation Army forces. They were a ragtag bunch of volunteers and deserters from across the Middle East, nothing like the British-trained and run Arab Legion who operated out of Transjordan and were fighting for Jerusalem. But the ALA were heavily armed and they fought to the death all the same.

There were several large villages close together and the Israeli forces had to go slowly. They fired mortar shells and tried to destroy the ALA's base but the ALA shelled them back and Dov's company had to keep moving.

They took over an outlying village and made their base in what was left of the mukhtar's house, it being the largest in the village. The sound of shells whistling overhead and the sound of explosions shook the ground. Dov kept his helmet on. He crouched by the window and looked out at the night lit up with bombs.

Avi and Danny Becker sat with their backs to the wall and shared a cigarette. Their friend Shulman stood with the commander at the kitchen table, studying a hand-drawn map of the area. Dov didn't know any of them well. It was a new unit, hastily put together, part of Operation Broomstick, to sweep away the Arab presence in the Galilee. It wasn't long before they were given their orders. They marched out into the night. The shelling continued and they went on foot, in the dark, sneaking their way to the largest village where the ALA had their base.

They must have been marching over fields, Dov realised. After school was finished, at some point he moved away from the tenets of the Revisionist movement and the allure of the Stern Gang lost its pull. He went to agricultural school and joined with others who wanted to work the land, not plant bombs on crowded buses. When they built the first fence-and-tower post of their new kibbutz he felt as though his life was finally beginning. He had loved Ruth just as Israel did, but they were never jealous of each other. They believed in sharing – land, crops, property and love. The kibbutz was going to be a new way of life, Dov believed in that. No more jealousy and no more *ownership* of things, but somewhere things could be finally different.

And he discovered that he loved the land, the earth he ploughed and the rocks he gathered from it, the good rich smell of it when it rained and the roots took hold. He wanted to put down roots. Their second day on the land he had planted a tree. He wanted to see it grow.

They were trampling fields and he felt bad for the crops they destroyed. Cucumbers, tomatoes, *baladi*, the good sort that was native to Palestine. Watermelons, maybe. He had loved the watermelon sellers in the summer on the beach, in their carts, offering slices. Loved the black seeds that you spat and tossed on the ground, where they might grow new plants. He had been studying the problems to do with water, irrigation, how to carry water to their rocky hill, how to lay down pipes, how to yield a crop even when you didn't have enough water. Kibbutz Trashim was built on a hard land, and it needed hard people to work it. But their folks were good people, idealists, mostly from Europe who came with the movement, left their homes and their lives behind to begin a new one in Palestine. Not like Dov and Israel, who were born here.

This was partly why he found Ruth so attractive. That accent she had, the way she spoke Hebrew. Her children will not sound like her, he thought.

Movement ahead. Dov froze. The older Becker brother, Avi, went ahead. He attacked with the bayonet. Stabbed the patrolman in the heart and signalled for them to move. Then they moved *fast*, flowing over the corpse and this breach in the Arabs' perimeter, only to run into a fucking *machine gun* stationed overhead. Dov dove for cover as bullets strafed the ground.

'Grenade!'

Shulman tossed it high. It arced overhead, landed behind the gunner. The explosion threw the machine's aim, hit a soldier whose name Dov didn't even know. The boy fell and didn't get up. The machine gun puttered to a stop. They stormed the outpost and took control of it and moved on, now with friendly covering fire.

Grimly they went on. Hand to hand and door to door, grenades and bullets. Elkin said, 'Cover me as I—'

And looked surprised with a bullet in the chest. Dov ran on, fired blindly, heard a scream. He tossed a grenade into a house through a window and ran on not waiting for the explosion. Then they came on the main force and took cover as gunfire erupted everywhere.

If he could just make it through this night, he thought, if he could just get back to Shosh, if he could only tell her everything will be different now, if he could only live to see his baby, if only he could—

He heard the whistle too late. A shell exploded and he was thrown violently backwards, tossed and turned like when he caught waves as a kid with Israel. When vision returned a soldier stood over him with a gun and Dov saw death, but Gideon came out of nowhere and gutted the soldier with his bayonet and he fell on Dov. Dov pushed him off and Gideon helped him up.

He said something.

Dov said, 'What!'

'I said, are you all right!'

'I'll live!' Dov said. He laughed hysterically. They ran on, all discipline forgotten, reached the old British police station where the ALA were based.

The battle slowed.

The ALA, surrounded, prepared to hold out in their fortified position.

Then the mortars whispered; and when the dust cleared, the old police station was gone.

'You ever fucked an Arab girl?' Avi Becker said. He stood by what was left of the window and smoked, staring out.

'I wouldn't,' Shulman said. 'I wouldn't stick my dick in one of them.'

'Right,' Avi said. His little brother Danny hopped from one foot to the other, over and over. He listened to music no one else could hear.

'You?' Shulman said.

'Nah.'

Dov was too tired to tell them to shut the fuck up. They had secured the village and when the dust cleared and the fighting finally stopped they had too many prisoners to know what to do with.

This was the thing about war. It had fuck all to do with *rules*.

So they lined them up against the wall and shot them one by one. They managed to dump about ten down the village well before it filled up. Then the commander gave the order and Dov had to get a spade and dig a hole big enough, him and the others, to put all the bodies in. Only the men, so that was all right. The others, women and children and old folks, them they sent north on foot. Let them find a new village somewhere in Lebanon. With any luck, all the new refugees would slow down the ALA fuckers still coming over.

So that was that, and he caught a few hours' sleep while waiting for new orders to come in. The whole of the Galilee was one messy war zone right then.

'You four, seeing as you're up and doing nothing, go on patrol.'

'Sir, yes, sir,' Dov said. The Becker brothers both groaned. And Shulman just shrugged in resignation and reached for his gun.

'An order's an order, boys,' he said.

So the four of them trooped out of the police station into the blood and the mud outside.

'It's a bullshit detail,' Avi Becker said.

'A job's a job,' Shulman said. He looked unconcerned, like he was out for a stroll, not a patrol. He probably had the right attitude. They had the area cleared. It was just killing time until the orders came in.

So there they were, and after a while it *did* get nice. Dov could never get used to how beautiful the Galilee was. It was open, green, with a startling blue sky in which white clouds drifted like delicate scrolls illuminated by the rays of sunlight of the sort that heralded angels.

In the distance the Hermon rose high, shrouded in snow. Pine needles crunched underfoot, and the irises and daffodils that grew in profusion gave the place an enchanted feel, so that Dov momentarily forgot everything, forgot even the war and his parting from Shosh and all his worries, and he was carried along in a reverie in this ancient place—

'Halt!' Shulman said. Dov was startled awake from his dream, to see three soldiers heading their way from further up the incline with prisoners in tow.

'It's just us,' one of them said. Dov couldn't remember his name. Gadi something. 'We caught these four on the perimeter. They might be infiltrators or something.'

There were four women with them. The prisoners. Dov didn't pay much attention. They were different ages, the youngest around fifteen, he made the oldest in her forties. They looked tired and scared. Just then they heard gunshots uphill. Dov made a quick calculation. He said, 'Shulman, you and the Beckers take them back to base. I'll go with this lot, see what's going on over there.'

He knew they weren't going to argue with him. Why run towards gunfire when it wasn't your job for once? He looked back once as he followed Gadi's guys up the incline.

The Beckers, Shulman, and the four Arab women disappeared into the trees.

The shooting uphill turned out to be on account of a deer. By the time Dov got there the deer was filled up with bullets. It lay on the ground in a puddle of blood, one of its horns broken.

Luckily, one of Gadi's boys had trained as a butcher. He had the deer skinned and cut and before Dov knew it they had a fire going and the meat turning on a spit. It was the best meal Dov had had in a long while, even if he had to watch out for bullets while he chewed.

By the time he got back to base he was pleasingly full and warm from the fire. They'd sat around the coals and sang all the good songs.

'The wind blew through the tops of the cypress trees,' Dov sang to himself now. He liked singing. 'In the distance the jackals howled. And you were beautiful, so beautiful my darling, sat by the campfire beside me.'

He was really warming up now. 'The night grew loooong!' he sang, 'and soon we'd go to baaaattle, and you would staaaay behind to wait for me! I took your hand, and led you to the barn house... Remember me, my love, remeeeeember me.'

He didn't know what made him go into the copse of pine trees.

Something in the moonlight, or the very hush of the night, or some nagging feeling, all the same, sparked by the sight of the dead deer on the ground. He didn't know. The copse was dark but moonlight shone through pine needles and bathed his face with a serene calm.

Then Dov stumbled on the first of the corpses.

28

WHEN HE CAME BACK TO THE BASE THE BECKERS AND SHULMAN were there and Dov said, 'What did you *do*?'

His hands were shaking. He saw the way they looked away from him then. The dopey looks, the bloodstains that still looked wet, not dried. Shulman had a couple of scratches on his face. Shulman lit a cigarette.

'There wasn't anything we could do,' he said.

Dov could still see it. Some attempt was made to hide the bodies, but it was desultory. The women had been stripped naked at some point in the night. The fifteen-year-old was lying against a rock. The other two were spaced further apart and the fourth, who he thought was the oldest, was missing most of her skull. All four had been shot in the back of the head. They lay on the forest floor under the pines, four Arab women whose names were lost.

Right then he didn't know what to do, what to think. It was pretty clear what happened. A slow rage built inside Dov. The moon looked down on him and the pines whispered and the women's blood soaked the black earth where they lay. No one would likely find them. And if they did, they would think nothing of it anyway.

'What happened, Shulman?' Dov said. He spoke very quietly. Shulman just shrugged. The Becker brothers both turned and looked at Dov then.

'Oh, fuck off, Dov,' Avi Becker said.

The gun was in Dov's hands before he even realised it. 'Face the wall,' he said. 'Put your hands up.'

Shulman blew smoke.

'Are you out of your goddamned mind, Dov?' he said.

'Do it!'

'Listen here, Dov!' Shulman said. He tossed the cigarette and took a step towards Dov and stopped when the bayonet rose to meet him.

'Against the wall. Now. All three of you. I'm placing you under arrest.'

'You have no authority!'

'Do it!'

They lined up against the wall. He searched them, removed their pistols.

'Stay there,' he said.

'Listen, Dov...'

'What *happened*?' Dov said.

'It wasn't like that, Dov, they tried to escape and we just...'

'You raped them.'

'It wasn't like that,' Danny Becker said.

'What was it like, Danny?' Dov said.

'I just pretended, I couldn't get it up—'

'Shut *up*, Danny!' Avi Becker said. 'Don't say another goddamned word.'

Dov took the other guns out of the room. He went out and locked the door.

'Hey!'

'You can't do this, Dov!'

He left them there. Went to see the commander. Found him by the village water well, which was starting to stink from the corpses. The commander was on the radio. Dov waited until he was done.

'What is it, Dov? I'm busy. We need to mobilise soon.'

'Shulman and the Beckers raped and killed four Arab women, sir.'

The commander was still.

'You have proof?'

'The bodies are in a copse of pines nearby, sir. They were our men's captives.'

'We cannot have our soldiers committing atrocities, Dov,' the commander said.

'Yes, sir.'

'But I need all men for the battle ahead.'

'Sir?'

'I would order a court-martial, but I can't spare them. They can go free if they fight. I will tell them that.'

'Sir?'

'Come with me.'

Dov said nothing. They went back to the room where he'd locked them. He unlocked the door. They went in.

'I see,' the commander said.

The room was empty. The window was open. Dov cursed himself. But he didn't think they'd be *that* stupid to run.

'Deserters,' the commander said mournfully. 'Well, now I'm down four men.'

'Four, sir?'

'Just bring them back, will you? They couldn't have gone far.'

'Sir, yes, sir.'

'And Dov?'

'Sir?'

'Don't do anything stupid.'

'Sir.'

'They're good boys, but bad things happen in war.'

'Yes, sir.'

'Take care of it.'

The commander left.

Dov stared out of the window.

They couldn't have gone far. Sure.

But they could have gone anywhere.

★

When Dov set out, the company was getting ready to move. On to the next village and the next battle, and who could tell who would come back and who would be left behind on the battlefield? It was night time and in the distance the sky was illuminated with mortar attacks as other battles raged, and Dov tasted gunpowder on his tongue.

The deserters would have the advantage of darkness but it would slow them down, too. They went on foot. He tried to think where he would go. South or south-west, he thought. Out of the Galilee, towards the sea or down to the Jezreel Valley. Now that they were no longer soldiers they wouldn't want to be caught in the midst of fighting. Though that might be hard for them to avoid.

He went slowly. He went on foot. The conquered villages vanished behind him. He followed the easy route, downhill, figuring the deserters would have gone down the most straightforward path. He found himself between two hills, with a gentle stream running alongside him. Poppies and bluebonnets grew between the rocks. It felt like untouched land, pristine, where nature was allowed to flourish untouched by human hands. A blanket of stars covered the canopy of the skies, and Dov felt like a boy in synagogue again, contemplating that which was infinite.

It was then that a shape rose out of the darkness, and for a moment he was so wrapped up in his own unexpected rapture that it was only when he saw how it towered over him, and how wide it was, and heard its roar in his ears and felt its hot breath that he realised it was not some demon conjured out of the stories in the Talmud but a wild bear.

Dov cried out and the bear lunged at him, irate, and its claws missed Dov's face. It was a Syrian bear, of the sort he heard lived on the slopes of the Hermon, but what one was doing here Dov couldn't imagine. The bear stopped and regarded the cowering Dov.

What do you want here in this land? it seemed to ask. Why have you disturbed me in my solitude? The bear smelled of animal musk and wet fur, and Dov realised it might simply have been taking a nightly wash in the brook that ran beside them when it was interrupted by Dov. Dov got up and he faced the bear, trying to make himself big, and he spoke to the bear, and he told him about his mission, and how he hunted the men who spilled blood on this land; and maybe the bear understood him; and maybe it grew bored. It grunted and fell on its haunches and ambled away into the dark.

Dov stood there breathing heavily for a long moment, and then he knelt by the brook and cupped water in his hand and drank in this manner, like one of David's warriors who would not put their face in the water but watched out for attack. And refreshed he went on.

He could hear distant battle, then silence. The silence grew and it was all around him. Moonlight illuminated the heights of the Golan and the snow on the Hermon and the slopes of hills covered in pines. He was tired now, and dawn was near, and he could see no sign of the men he tracked. For the moment he had lost their trail.

A hill rose before him, and on the hill were ancient rocks, not of this place, piled up in mounds whose age Dov couldn't fathom. Some ancient men carried them here, before the first verses of *Genesis* were ever written down or spoken, and who they were, these vanished ancients, there was no man alive be he Arab or Jew who would know.

Dov climbed over basalt boulders and scrambled until he stood in the illumination of an early dawn. He could see across this land, from the heights down to the lake, or so it seemed to him. He could see the tiny figures fighting, fleeing, the tiny pinpricks of gunfire and the flames of bombardment and the red of the blood and the black of the earth. He found an enormous stone tablet, fifty tonnes or more, and beneath it an opening into an underground passage. Dov slid down into a Neolithic grave. It was warm and dry in the cavern. Dov lay down and slept.

29

WHEN HE WOKE HE WASN'T SURE WHERE HE WAS AT FIRST. HE stared up at the slab of stone above him. A pattern had been carved into the stone, some message from the ancients, perhaps a spell. Daylight fell down from the grave's opening. Inside it was cool and dark. Dov got his pack and climbed out into sunlight. He took a piss and watched the view. He could hear sporadic battle far away. He wondered how these rocks were carried here. The whole hill was covered in Neolithic structures.

They would try to stay off the roads, he thought. The deserters. Make their way down from the heights, still on a south-west course. They would go at night and avoid the daylight. He had a map but how useful was a map when it was actively being redrawn? Of the villages marked there, how many still survived? He hefted his pack and started to march down the hill.

Bees hummed in the flowers. The land widened, and he could hear the sounds of battle closer by. Then he crested a hill and saw far below him a lake, and knew it was the Hula. The sunlight shimmered off the surface of the water, and he saw a herd of buffaloes grazing far away. Smoke rose at several points around the lake. Dov kept walking.

The ground became marshy and his feet sank in the mud. Reeds and cattails grew in abundance and slowed his way. Mosquitoes began to buzz around him. Their bites covered his face and arms and he was afraid of the malaria he knew they carried. He saw another herd of buffaloes, close by, heard their grunts and went the other way. He came to the lake.

A burned wooden boat lay on the muddy ground near the water. A fisherman's corpse lay beside it. Dov washed his face and arms in the lake. He began to circumnavigate it, away from the columns of smoke he saw in the east. His progress was slow. He chewed on his emergency rations. The lake was full of fish but Dov didn't know how to fish. An otter startled him as it ran in front and slid into the water. Cormorants flew overhead. Dov filled his flask and then he went on. The lake wasn't large but as he left it still heading where he thought the deserters went the marshes began again and his progress was slow. The heat of the day began to wane. The sun dropped lower in the sky. Clouds of mosquitoes rose before Dov, then parted like a dark curtain and he found himself in open land again.

It was then that he first came upon living people. They rose at him unexpectedly, through the shrubbery, and for a moment he thought they were spirits conjured out of the earth itself, they were so quiet. When they came closer he hid at first, then realised they were no danger to him. Women, some in bare heads and some covered, marched grimly across the valley floor, some holding babies in their arms, some pulling small children behind them. Carts, some pulled by donkeys and others by hand, rumbled behind them, and the elderly sat inside with heaps of hastily retrieved possessions piled up in an ungainly way. Dov stepped out and watched them go, but they paid him no mind, as though it was him who was the ghost and they, the living, could not see him. On and on they came in silence, eyes fixed ahead, the smell of smoke and blood on their clothes. On and on they fled.

By the time night had fully fallen the refugees were gone, and Dov found himself on the outskirts of a small village in which nothing moved. A dead dog, a bullet in its head, lay on its back next to the shell of a house and corpses lay here and there, scattered haphazardly like backgammon tiles. He went through the houses methodically, gun held at the ready, but could not find a living being. At last he came to a house that was mostly still standing. He stepped inside, still tense, and went from room to room to secure the property.

When he entered the bedroom he found something at last moved, and his finger tensed on the trigger. A man with his back to the wall, his hands held protectively over his stomach. The moonlight caught his face, and Dov saw the rictus of a smile as the man recognised him.

'Hello, Dov,' he said.

Dov sat on the edge of the bed and lit a cigarette.

'Shulman,' he said.

Shulman didn't move. Dov saw he was trying to hold in his insides, which were attempting to spill out of his gutted belly. He didn't have long to live, and for sure he knew it. Dov took the cigarette and put it to Shulman's lips and Shulman inhaled and shuddered.

'What happened to you, Menachem?' Dov said.

'We had a... disagreement,' Shulman said.

'You and the Beckers?'

'Aha.'

'You were going to go back and sell them out, weren't you,' Dov said.

'I figured... it was best,' Shulman said.

'And they thought otherwise.'

He let Shulman smoke again. The man's hands were covered in his own blood. His breath was weak.

'Where did they go?' Dov said.

'Fuck... you, Dov,' Shulman said.

'Fuck you, Shulman,' Dov said.

He smoked and waited. It wasn't long before Menachem Shulman drew his last breath. Then he was still, and Dov finished his cigarette.

He went outside. He didn't want to sleep in that house. He made his bed under the stars. In the night he was woken unexpectedly. He lay still. Something long and cool slithered nearby. Dov willed himself to lie perfectly still. The snake slithered close. Its tongue flicked out and tasted the air. It was over a metre long. Dov saw the dark diamond shapes on its skin. It was a viper.

The viper studied Dov but did not seem to consider him a threat. It curled up for a moment as though wishing to keep Dov company. Dov stayed frozen. At last the viper lost interest and vanished into the shrubbery. Dov sat up and let out a breath. He was scared of snakes.

He decided not to stay in the village any longer. He had caught a few hours of sleep. That was enough. The night was cooler and he could go quicker. He didn't want to lose the Becker brothers once they hit a city or the coast. He marched on and was relieved when the ruined village vanished from sight.

By dawn he'd made good progress. Twice he saw and heard battle but both times it was distant. It would be near Safed, he thought. He went up and down hills and through a forest and when he came out of it at last, exhausted, he saw a stone structure on a hill above him with stout walls and a domed roof with a cross above it.

Dov went to the gates and knocked and a man came out in a monk's robe and looked at him without expression.

'What do you want?' he said.

'I'm looking for a couple of men. I wondered if they came down this way.'

The monk considered. 'Not many people come this way,' he said. 'Even with the war. We're pretty remote.'

'You're what, Carmelites?' Dov said.

'Greek Orthodox.'

'Do you have some water?' Dov said. 'I've been walking a long time.'

The monk considered again. Then moved aside so Dov could come in.

Inside, chickens ran below a large coop, and monks tended to a vegetable garden. An orange tree grew in the middle of the courtyard. The monk gestured for Dov to sit at a wooden table under the tree. When he came back he brought a pail of water and an earthenware cup. Dov drank greedily. The water was fresh and cold.

'Thank you,' he said.

'Jesus teaches us to care for the man found by the side of the road,' the monk said.

'And did you find two such men before I came?' Dov said. 'I noticed you didn't answer my question earlier.'

The monk considered.

'What is it that you want with them?' he said.

'They have committed a crime,' Dov said. 'It falls to me to find them.'

'You are, what? Their judge? Their executioner?'

'There is no one else.'

'I cannot countenance your purpose,' the monk said. 'You carry a gun. There is blood on you.'

'There is a war going on,' Dov said.

The monk nodded. 'We take no part,' he said. 'This land belongs to God, not people.'

'This land,' Dov said, 'belongs to Jews.'

'By what right?' the monk said.

'By right of covenant,' Dov said. 'And this.' He hefted his gun.

The monk nodded.

'I cannot help you,' he said.

'I understand,' Dov said.

Dov stood. The monk walked him to the gate.

'Be careful who you let in,' Dov said. 'This land isn't safe. Not even for monks.'

The monk considered.

'No land is safe,' he said. 'Not even for monks.'
Dov nodded.
'Go well,' the monk said.
The gate shut behind Dov.
He marched on.

30

THE SOUND OF MORTAR FIRE INTENSIFIED AS THE SUN ROSE higher. Dov knew he was close on the heels of the men he sought now and so he pressed on, even as the sound of gunfire became continuous. Twice he had to hide as armoured trucks drove past. He didn't know which forces they belonged to, Arab or Jew. They were simple vehicles reinforced with metal. This no longer concerned him, not until his mission was complete. This land was rocky and hills rose above and he could hear the sounds of battle everywhere but didn't see the combatants.

Explosions rose to his left and his right, as though the battle raged on two fronts, and he was wading into the no man's land between them. He heard screams cut short and smelled sulphur and gunpowder and jasmine and za'atar. The hills rose ahead and he saw smoke and the outline of houses. Then someone took a shot at him.

Dov dropped to the ground. He heard another shot, saw dirt shoot up into the air about a foot to his left. The vegetation hid him. He crawled on his stomach. A burned armoured personnel carrier lay on its side beside the village and Dov hid behind its dark carcass. The village was just ahead. He stuck his head out and looked.

Ping!

The hidden sniper nearly got him. Dov cursed. He looked at the village, saw two shapes crouched low against the wall of a house that was no longer there. Only the wall remained standing.

Dov calculated distance. Waited.

Snipers were patient. Dov knew he couldn't outwait the hidden gunman. The air was still and he heard bees buzzing in the flowers. The bees did not care about the war. Dov tensed, then ran across the open field. A bullet whistled past his head and he dove the rest of the way but made it safely to a still-standing wall. From here he could see the scattered bodies of the village's one-time defenders and, beyond the corpses, the outline of the two still-living men.

'Come out with your hands up!' Dov shouted.

'Fuck you, Dov!'

The Becker brothers, Avi and Danny, looked in bad shape. They were sat against the defending wall with their guns between their legs, looking thoroughly miserable.

'I came to bring you back!' Dov shouted.

Avi Becker laughed and the laugh was the only sound echoing in that desolate valley.

'We know why you're here,' he said.

When Dov risked a look again the two figures had vanished from the wall. He scanned the village. Where did they go? He gripped the gun, trying to think. He had to factor in the hidden sniper. His shadow lengthened on the ground.

There!

Something moving in the ruins of a house. Dov grabbed a grenade from his belt and pulled the pin and tossed it high. It arced across and fell.

Boom!

The explosion threw up stones and Dov heard a scream of rage and pain.

'Son of a bitch!'

'Did I get you?'

'You're going to die here, Dov.'

He risked a look and saw Danny Becker with his arm at an unnatural angle and his face covered in blood vanishing into the inside of a ruin. Dov calculated, ran. The sniper, this time, didn't fire. Perhaps he was just curious to see where this was going.

A closer gunshot rang and stone fragments flew from the wall just above Dov's head and hit his face. He hid.

'How does that feel!' Avi Becker screamed.

Dov didn't reply. He risked a look and was rewarded with another gunshot. A bomb whistled through the air, high above. Dov looked up. The sunlight caught the metal. The small object began to descend. Dov started to run.

When the bomb hit, the explosion shook the ground and he heard walls crumble. Dust hid everything and for a moment he knew the hidden sniper would be unable to aim. Dov held his gun. He ran into the dust, towards the place where the bomb fell.

Smoke and dust cleared in a gust of wind and he saw the Becker brothers, both ahead, one to his right and one to his left.

He fired just as they did.

Now he stared up at the darkening skies. It was hours later. The vultures circled overhead. Around Dov were the corpses of villagers and soldiers, and of Avi and Danny Becker.

They'd hit him twice but he was faster or luckier and he got them both before he fell.

He wasn't going to make it, he knew that now. Even the hidden sniper stopped taking potshots a while back. There was no one here anymore. Just Dov and the dead and the vultures.

His vision swam in and out of focus. His mind drifted. He thought about Shosh and their unborn child.

It didn't hurt anymore. There was no more pain.

It was so quiet there, under all that sky.

The first of the vultures landed.

PART SIX

THE VULTURES

Shosh

Kibbutz Trashim, 1952

31

THE CORPSES LAY IN THE FIELD AS NIGHT FELL. THE SMOKING ruins of the Arab village stood around them like headstones. The air didn't cool as night fell. A hot, sticky night with no wind, and the flies and mosquitoes buzzed over the dead. Nothing moved on the ground itself. Even the unseen sniper had stopped shooting some time back. Now the first of the circling vultures came in to land.

The bird stood over the corpses.

One of the corpses twitched irritably, then sat up. Bill Goodrich, face smeared in blood and mud, smacked himself on the forehead. He screamed, 'Fuck!'

'Cut!' the director yelled. 'Goddamn it, Bill! We're losing the light!'

'Fuck this, Eddie!' the corpse shouted back. 'I'm getting eaten by mosquitoes here!'

The last of the sun sank behind the horizon. The rest of the corpses sat up, the generator sputtered in its niche of piled stones, the boom operator lowered the mic and the lights cut off overhead.

'Well, what are you standing around for?' Eddie Dmytryk said. 'Go get the star.'

Shosh hurried to obey. Bill Goodrich, a bite already swelling into an uncomely lump on his handsome forehead, looked at her beseechingly.

'Suzie, you life saver,' he said. 'Do you have my tea?'

'Here,' Shosh said. She unscrewed the top of the small thermos she carried just for him and poured. The smell of whisky mixed with the strong black tea. Bill drank greedily.

'Much better,' he said.

'Let me take a look at that,' Shosh said. She felt his face gently, examining the bump. 'It will go down in no time,' she said.

'I had it with this shoot, Suzie,' Bill said. Shosh helped him up. He put his arm through hers and she led him back to the craft services table, where the girls from the kibbutz had set up a buffet of food the likes of which none of them had seen in years. The film crew had been shooting for a week already, and the government gave them a special exception from the austerity laws. Shosh was lucky most days to have bread and olives, an egg three times a week. But on the craft services table were whole roast chickens, buttered potatoes, freshly baked bread, real coffee with as much milk and sugar as you wanted, and an assortment of cookies and sweets. Just the *chance* to be this close to this much food made the job worthwhile.

She could still remember coming out of the camp in '45. Seeing real food again, and gorging until she was sick. Her starved body could not handle the food, and some died after liberation just from eating again. Shosh couldn't bear to be without food. She always kept bread in her pocket. She was always afraid it would run out and she would be hungry again.

The bird man was out in the field gathering the vultures. How he kept the birds, Shosh had no idea. He was a taciturn man from a new kibbutz up in the Galilee, which sat on the lands of an Arab village Dov had fought to liberate during the war. Now Dov was dead and Shosh was a war widow, and she was sick to death of men dying on her. She started heaping food up on a plate for Bill. A chicken leg with crispy skin, a pile of potatoes, a slice of buttered bread. Bill was a good man, but words like 'good' didn't really matter. He was a movie star.

She still remembered watching him on screen for the first time, enchanted, in Landsberg's barracks during one of the

WIZO women's weekly screenings of American pictures. Bill smouldered with unbridled passion opposite Barbara Stanwyck in *Kiss Me Hard*, and the next week opposite Lana Turner in *Bad Girls Don't Cry*. He played bad boys and cowboys. Now he was playing a Holocaust survivor with a dark past trying to make it in Palestine, in a cinematic experience set against the new state's War of Independence, as 1948 was now officially called. The Arabs just called it the Nakba – the disaster. Whatever you wanted to call it, it was an odd choice for an American picture.

But then again, it was an odd sort of crew.

'Well?' Bill demanded. Shosh realised she was daydreaming again. He snatched the plate from her and tore meat and skin off the chicken. Shosh's stomach growled.

'Listen, Eddie,' Bill said, waving the chicken leg, 'you've got to do something about those mosquitoes. And the birds are giving me the creeps.'

The vultures were back in their cages. The bird man stood next to them, a strange, stooped figure. Shosh figured he was a survivor, too. Nobody ever asked. Nobody ever wanted to know. For the new Israelis, these self-styled sabras, those who survived the Holocaust were both victims and suspects. Why did you not fight? And why did you alone survive, when so many didn't? Sometimes she hated them, their casual brutality, the cheery way that they pretended what happened to her wasn't even their concern. They were not weak like the old Jews of Europe. They were new, and hard, and masters of this land, this 'adama', a word she had to learn in Hebrew lessons, which she hated.

'There is no *a-d-a-m-a* without *d-a-m*,' her first teacher told her, proudly. 'Dam' was the Hebrew word for blood.

No land without blood.

And Shosh was sick of blood.

'We'll pick up tomorrow,' Eddie Dmytryk said. He seemed resigned. 'I can't do anything about mosquitoes, Billy. Let's just get through the rest of the shoot and you'll be back sipping margaritas in L.A. before you know it.'

'Screwing Margaritas,' John Hunt, the first AD, said. He came over to join them at the craft services table. 'And Maggies and Mollys and Fays.'

'Come on, guys,' Bill said, 'it ain't like that. You know I'm a good soldier.' He rubbed the swelling on his forehead. 'But this country, I mean… Jesus.'

'We'll use a stand-in for the corpses scene,' Eddie said. 'Then cut for when you crawl out still alive from under the bodies.'

'Well, why didn't we do that in the first place!' Bill said. 'Never mind, never mind. Are we done here, Eddie?'

The director sighed.

'We're done,' he said.

'Good.' Bill finished chewing and pushed the plate at Shosh. 'Bin that, will you?'

'Sure,' she said. She turned from him and handed the plate to Tsilla from the kitchen, who, for the duration of the shoot, was head of craft services. Tsilla nodded. Shosh knew the food would go into a separate container clearly marked 'Rubbish' and, later, they would distribute it discreetly to the kibbutz members. It was hard since the war, with austerity. Only a few months ago the kibbutz near Juara was fined for moving cattle – everyone knew they sold it to black market profiteers. She couldn't blame them, though. They had children to feed too.

She followed Bill. A location scout from Los Angeles had found Trashim a few months earlier on a tour of Israel. He was a mild-mannered American Jew with a Hebrew accent even worse than Shosh's. This was a good place to make a picture, he said. Remote. Rugged. So the kibbutz had a members' assembly and they voted, and the vote was in favour. Now everyone mucked in. And Shosh, who had better English than most on account of the Amis back in Landsberg, got assigned liaison. Which turned out to be mostly looking after Billy Goodrich.

'I thought it would be different,' Bill said. He stopped and she almost bumped into him. With the lights off and the crew packing up the sky was a deep black and a river of stars filled the night from horizon to horizon.

'When I look at it like this,' he said, 'it's almost like this is some other planet, and I crash-landed here.'

'That's a good line, Bill,' Shosh said. She wondered how long he'd been practising it. 'You're a good actor. Hell, you're a movie star.'

'I just thought... Listen,' he said. 'I've got to get out of here. Just for a little while, blow off some steam. Can you do something?'

'I can try,' Shosh said. She had to be careful. Kramer, the producer, was very clear on that one.

'Your job is to manage the talent,' Kramer had said. 'You get him everything he wants. But you keep him out of trouble.'

'What sort of trouble?' Shosh said.

'Trouble,' Kramer said.

'I want to go to a party,' Bill said. 'Somewhere with good coke and big cocks. Do you have somewhere like that here?'

'What's coke?' Shosh said. Bill cracked a smile.

'Come on,' he said. 'We'll take everyone out. What about that set designer who likes you? What's his name, Arty?'

'Art,' Shosh said. 'Arthur Fenwick.'

'That guy, yeah. Why don't we invite him along too? He's been dying to spend some time with you, I can tell. I can always tell.'

'You think?' She found herself blushing. Arty Fenwick didn't say much, and almost nothing to her. She did feel him looking at her, sometimes. He was a few years older than her but there was something boyish and lost in his eyes...

'Sure,' Bill said. 'But he's a pinko, you know.'

'A pinko?'

'A communist.'

'Oh.'

'Half of them are, you know. Eddy, and the writer, what's his name?'

'The writer?'

'Yeah, you know. The guy who wrote the picture.'

'I don't remember,' Shosh said.

Bill waved a hand. 'Well, writers don't matter, anyway. They're all commies. Not me. I don't truck with that sort of thing.'

'You don't believe each should give according to their ability, and each should receive according to their needs?' Shosh said, and Bill Goodrich laughed.

'On what *I'm* making?' he said. 'Are you kidding?'

'I live on a kibbutz,' Shosh said. 'They believe in socialism. My sister adores Stalin. They all do, you know.'

'But do you?' Bill said.

Shosh didn't answer.

'I don't know how you live like this,' Bill said. 'Tea?'

'Sure.'

She poured him a drink from the thermos. Then when he drank it she poured some for herself. They stood in companionable silence and watched the stars overhead.

32

SHE LAY AWAKE ON THE BED IN THE ROOM. THE KIBBUTZ WASN'T much different in a way to Landsberg or the camp in Cyprus. Tin shacks and insects and you could hear people screwing. She'd shared the room with Dov but Dov wasn't there. Ate in the dining room and showered in cold water in the communal showers and ate bread and olives, and eggs three times a week. A teaspoon of jam as a special treat on the Shabbat.

Shosh hated it here.

She hated Palestine. Or Israel, as it was now. They got to name it any way they wanted now. They'd won their war. Hell, Dov won it practically singlehanded. The wind blew through the tops of the cypress trees, and she had stayed behind to wait for him. He took her hand, and led her to the barn house, and knocked her up, and went off to his death.

This was the part the songs never told you about. The songs were for the men. The women just had to be pretty in the light of the campfire.

All she had of the bastard was a faded photo of their wedding day in Cyprus that she kept in an empty Wissotzky tea box he once gave her.

She thought about Yael. How beautiful she was when she came out, and how much it had hurt. Dov never even got to see the baby. He was already dead by then. How much Shosh had longed to be a mother! That moment when she held the baby against her skin, that first time, she never wanted to let her go. Then they took Yael from her, kindly, and put her in the baby room where a nurse fed and changed the babies and the mothers could come just to hold them.

Yael wasn't even hers, *nothing* was *hers*, not as long as she lived on the kibbutz. Now Yael was just another snot-nosed face in the crowd of children, no different to Yoram and Ophek, her sister's little ones. She belonged to the kibbutz. And far more than Shosh ever would.

She tried to sleep but it was hard, Bill wasn't wrong about mosquitoes. Out in their camp the crew had beers and sausages and music, a generator with fuel, a gramophone with records from America. She wished she could be with them, but the kibbutz didn't like the ideological corruption inherent in fraternising with capitalist stooges—

They didn't *all* talk like that. But still. It was a small place to live and you had to pick your battles.

And they gossiped *all* the time! Everyone knew everything. If Shosh were to go with *anyone* from the cast or crew then everyone would know. And it would be out there. And they would look at her. And they would judge.

So she just did the job. And at least everyone was happy about the extra rations.

She tried to sleep. Why was sleep so hard? As a child she always slept so easily. Then when they got to the camp and they took her parents and she went the other way... She never slept well again after that. If she slept she saw them. If she slept she heard them crying in the showers with the gas. Night after night after night.

She tried to tell some of that to Ruth. She loved Ruth. But Ruth was different, or maybe she had always been this way, and the heat of Palestine just stripped away the softer layers that hid her true inside, until now she was like an unadorned blade.

'I know you want to go to them,' Ruth told her, the second or third day of the shoot on *The Vultures*. They stood together on a rise and watched the crew below, moving cameras and equipment, setting up the scene where Goodrich's character meets the beautiful kibbutznik girl he falls in love with. The actress who played her was indeed beautiful, an Italian, and she spoke terrible English that nobody seemed to mind. Kramer said she was going to be the next Gina Lollobrigida.

'You want to go, and I understand *why* you want to go,' Ruth said. Her hand was on Shosh's shoulder. 'What they offer. Life here for us is hard. It requires sacrifice.' She stroked Shosh's braided hair. 'But it's worth it, Shosh. It's a world where everyone's equal, and where we have a land of our own, that no oppressor will ever take from us again. You of all people must see that.'

They never spoke about the war. About the camps. And they never talked about Mama and Papa. It was too hard. Some things were too hard.

'I know,' Shosh said.

'You're strong,' Ruth said. 'I know you. I know how hard you can be. You just have to believe in this place, in the future. If not for yourself then for Yael.'

And Shosh just nodded. You couldn't really argue with Ruth, anyway. Not argue and win.

She tossed and turned. Then someone knocked on the door and she jumped up to open it.

'Someone at the gate,' Mishka said. 'Says he's for you. It's nighttime, Shosh.' He looked at her disapprovingly. 'He tried to give me eggs.'

'Eggs?'

'Dirty speculators,' Mishka said. 'You know him?'

'I think I do,' Shosh said.

She followed Mishka to the gate.

The kibbutz had grown since she arrived in '48. Tents became shacks, shacks became brick buildings. The babies had their own house, and a new dining room large enough to fit all the new members was being planned, inspired by Soviet architecture. There was a chicken coop and several sheep, a new vegetable garden and even a patch of grass almost large enough to play football on. It still had the old tower, and a gate on the only dirt road that led in, and it was still being guarded.

A beat-up British Ford stood behind the gate. A small man stood nonchalantly perched against the hood smoking a cigarette. Shosh ran to him and threw her arms around him.

'Moritz!' she said.

'Hello, darling,' he said, smiling. He'd grown since Landsberg. His face filled in and he had a little moustache waxed with pomade. 'How's life in the countryside treating you?'

'Oh, you know,' Shosh said. 'It's just like everywhere.'

'Aha. They won't let me in. This guy has a real attitude, Shosh. *And* I offered him eggs!'

Shosh looked at him in affection. Moritz took surprisingly well to Palestine. But then, she thought, he was the sort of guy to find his place anywhere. He got his start with a greengrocer called Herschel in the lower city in Haifa. In short time he had his own operation going. He wasn't dressed like a kibbutznik, in khakis and sandals. He wore a nice suit with a pocket kerchief, and the cloth of his pressed trousers didn't come from government stamps. He looked more like the Americans on the film set, who wore new, foreign clothes so casually. Where they came from, everyone dressed like they were rich.

'So you got my message,' she said.

'When you call, I come,' Moritz said. 'What do you need, doll?'

'A party,' Shosh said. 'A party for a movie star.'

'Is it true?' Moritz said. 'You really met Bill Goodrich?'

'He's just a normal guy,' Shosh said.

'Well, what's he like!' Moritz said. 'A guy like that, wow. I mean.'

'I know what you mean.'

'Do I get to meet him, then?' Moritz said.

'If you can help me with the party.'

'Listen, doll, there isn't a party in this country worth a damn unless I'm organising it. What does he like, this Goodrich? What's his poison?'

'Anything and everything, I think,' Shosh said. She lowered her voice. 'He likes guys, though,' she said.

'Guys, huh?' Moritz said. 'That's more tricky. They've got a shtrick in Binyamin Garden in Haifa, I could ask around.'

'What's a shtrick?' Ruth said.

'Where they meet for sex.'

'Well, it has to be discreet,' Shosh said.

'Oh, believe me,' Moritz said. 'Those guys keep it *quiet*.'

'You have a place we can use?'

'I got everything, doll. For a price.'

'They have dollars,' Shosh said.

'Say no more,' Moritz said.

'Give me a cigarette,' Shosh said. Moritz offered her his case and lit up for her. Shosh took a deep drag. *Real* tobacco, not the stuff they sold in the shops nowadays. Her head spun pleasantly.

'I'll make arrangements,' Moritz said. 'When?'

'Friday,' Shosh said. 'And I want you to cut me in for ten per cent.'

Moritz pursed his lips.

'For your kibbutz?' he said.

Shosh said softly, 'For me.'

33

FRIDAY CAME AND ALL OVER THE NEW STATE OF ISRAEL A silence settled as night fell. On the kibbutz a frugal dinner was shared by all. In synagogues men prayed, in the new tenement camps for immigrants women lit Shabbat candles, on the borders the soldiers stood guard, and all was well. All was well.

The truck bounced along the road, Ruth driving. Bill and the boys sat in the back, and Bill raised a bottle of whisky and screamed, 'They'll never take me alive!' – a line from the movie, it must have been – and everyone laughed and cheered. They passed some abandoned Arab village, the houses fallen down. It didn't matter. On Ruth drove and Shosh sat beside her sister. They spoke little.

'I understand what you need to do,' Ruth said. 'But it's distasteful.'

'Keep them happy,' Shosh said. 'That's my job. And the kibbutz earns.'

'I know,' Ruth said.

Ruth drove with her hand dangling out of the open window, a cigarette in her mouth, cheap woodchips and just enough tobacco to make it count. Shosh marvelled at her sister. How strong she was and how little she cared about the things that were so important to other people. She had looked at Bill Goodrich like he was just some guy. *He* looked at her like he wished she *was* a guy.

In the back of the kibbutz's old pickup truck were Bill, John Hunt the AD, and Art Fenwick, the set designer. Kramer, the producer, was in Europe somewhere, and Eddie Dmytryk had stayed behind to set up the next day's first scene.

'I want them back early,' he told Shosh. 'And ready for a shoot by eight a.m.'

'Yes, Mr Dmytryk,' Shosh said.

But now the road stretched ahead, the stars in the sky, the air blowing through the open window, and the night was open with wild possibilities. She kept it in. But her heart beat fast all the same, and maybe Ruth could feel it. But she said nothing more.

They came to the foothills of the Carmel and began the climb up the mountain. Through ancient pine forests and sleeping Druze villages, the beat-up truck struggling with the rises, the Americans in the back getting louder as the bottle was passed hand to hand – even Fenwick, who was usually a quiet guy.

Then they crested the mountain. Below them in two directions stretched the sea, a dark mirror reflecting back stars. The lights of ships bobbed in the harbour. Zim ships, mostly. Israel's new maritime fleet. The same shitty old ships like the one that carried her to Palestine. Now they were used for cargo and passenger services and they were talking about expansion. Shosh imagined purchasing a ticket, going on one of the new routes to Italy or Greece.

Why did she stay here? Because this was where her family was?

Her daughter who barely knew her didn't know another place.

And then there was Yehoyakim.

He showed up one day, after the war was over. In a worn suit jacket and a shirt that was once white, in shoes that had seen better days. But he looked *good*.

How she and Ruth cried when they saw him! They hugged and hugged, marvelling at this miracle, that he was alive, that they were all alive.

He'd spent the war in Russia, he said. He had gone willingly but things turned sour fast. Some time in a gulag, he wasn't specific. He still believed in communism but not in Stalin. He rejected him now. Somehow he got out. He made his way to Germany, from East to West, then across to Italy and finally here. Finally home.

'Home!' he said, and opened his arms wide, and held them both again. He took a big gulp of air. 'A country of our own,' he said.

Then he went away. Some sort of job, he said. Again, he wasn't specific. A lot of travelling was involved. The next time they saw him he drove to the kibbutz in a new car and his shirt was fresh and his shoes were polished. He took them to eat in a real restaurant, though Ruth protested. The waiter was quietly deferential. They had real coffee. He told them he was working in Tel Aviv.

So there they all were. Reunited at last. And yet separated by things unsaid. Shosh's war, and Yehoyakim's job, and whatever Ruth kept in her secret basement.

Shosh turned to Ruth, stroked her hair. Ruth smiled affectionately.

'We're here,' she said.

It was a quiet residential suburb, and *nice*. Houses built by German Templers and British traders and wealthy Jews. Houses meant to last, with cool stone walls and pleasant gardens, quiet in the starlight now. Ruth pulled the handbrake.

'I'll come back for you later,' she said.

'What will you do?' Shosh said.

'Run errands,' her sister said. 'I have things to do.'

Likely as not it was a man, Shosh decided. They said she had a British lover during the Mandate. Well, who could blame her. Shosh climbed out of the truck and helped the others down. When Arty Fenwick took her hand he said, 'You're warm!' in surprise, and Shosh said, 'I was sitting up front,' and Arty smiled, sheepishly, and said, 'Of course.'

Moritz came out of the house. He saw them and smiled.

'Welcome!' he said. His English wasn't as good as Shosh's but he could make deals in a dozen languages. They followed him inside. It was a handsome residential house. A couple in their late forties welcomed them. 'Eliezer and Paula,' Moritz said. 'They'll take care of anything you need.'

'They run this place?' Bill Goodrich said.

Moritz said, 'They work for me.'

Moritz touched Shosh lightly on the shoulder. 'You got the money?'

She stepped outside with him.

'Here,' she said.

Moritz took the bundle of dollars and counted. He peeled a note and passed it to Shosh.

'I want you to keep it for me,' she said. 'Be my bank.'

'You don't want the kibbutz to find out,' he said.

'I just need a backup, Moritz. Something for just in case.'

'You got it, doll.'

They went back inside. The men were sitting in the living room drinking. Eliezer and Paula served them. Music played on a gramophone. Nat King Cole, singing 'Mona Lisa'. The piano keys tinkled. Cigarette smoke rose in a blue cloud to the ceiling. There was an air of hushed anticipation, Shosh realised. They were all waiting for something.

The *something* materialised out of the kitchen door. First one girl, and then another. They looked like typists, just without clothes on. They were good looking, and John Hunt, the first AD, gave a whoop and said, 'Hot damn!'

'Language, Johnny,' Bill Goodrich said, then burst out laughing. The girls sauntered over. One draped herself over Hunt. The other slithered in between him and Arty Fenwick. Arty blushed.

Shosh had seen it all before. She found herself evaluating the girls' charms. They weren't Hollywood. But they were more than enough for a Friday night in Haifa.

'Which one do you want, Arty?' John Hunt said. 'I think this one likes me!'

Arty Fenwick raised his hands. 'I'll just stay here, I think,' he said. 'Thank you, no, oh! Please, though, no thank you.' He shot

Shosh an embarrassed glance. The girl next to him removed her hand from his lap and pouted.

'Then I'll take both!' Hunt said. He stood and lifted the girl from his lap and she squealed. He laughed and took the other girl's hand and pulled her from the sofa.

'Lead the way, ladies!' he said.

The girls, giggling in a way that said Moritz had tipped them generously, pulled Hunt along with them out of the door. Shosh could hear them trampling up the stairs to the bedrooms.

'And then there were two,' Bill Goodrich said. He swirled the ice in his glass. Ice, that was another thing Shosh hadn't seen in a long time. 'And then there were two...' His voice fell softly. He looked up. His lips parted. His eyes shone brighter. 'Well, hello there.'

A young man came quietly into the room. He stood framed in the door, one leg cocked slightly. He was young, maybe eighteen.

'Hello, Mr Goodrich,' he said shyly.

'Bill, come on,' Arty Fenwick said. He put his hand on Bill's arm, but Bill shook it off. He got up and went to the man in the doorway.

'And what is your name?' he said.

'Yosef,' the young man said.

'I'm Bill.'

The young man smiled.

'I know,' he said. 'You're famous.'

'Not here I'm not,' Bill said.

'No, sir. I mean, yes, sir,' the young man said, and Bill laughed.

'Where did you *find* him?' he said.

'Binyamin Garden,' Moritz whispered to Shosh. 'In a threesome with a French deckhand and an Italian bosun.'

Shosh laughed.

'Is it OK?' the young man said. Bill moved closer to him.

'OK?' he said. 'It's more than OK.' He touched the young man's shoulder lightly. 'Is there somewhere more private we can talk? Get to know each other a little better.'

'We have rooms upstairs,' Paula said. 'Very private, and with a well-stocked bar.'

'Then we shall go upstairs,' Bill said. 'Shall we?'

'Sure,' the young man said. Bill wove his arm through his and they walked out.

Art Fenwick, alone on the sofa, looked up at Shosh.

'This is some party, huh?' he said.

'Does he not like girls?' Shosh whispered to Moritz.

'Oh, I think he likes one girl,' Moritz said. 'Why don't you go sit on the sofa with Mr Fenwick? I have errands to run. I'll be back later. Ciao! Ciao!'

He whispered something to Paula and Eliezer and left. Paula came to the table, put down a bucket of ice, a bottle of whisky and a packet of new, unopened French cigarettes, and left the room. Her husband followed meekly.

'I guess it's just us, then,' Art Fenwick said.

Shosh sighed and went to sit beside him on the sofa.

'I guess so,' she said.

34

SHE MUST HAVE DOZED OFF AT SOME POINT. ALL ARTY FENWICK wanted to do was talk. He talked about his childhood, about the war, about movies, but mostly he told her about L.A. The sun and the oranges and the big cars, the tanned girls and muscled boys, the parties and the drinks that never stopped. Shosh couldn't get enough of it. She could imagine herself there already. From time to time she heard the creak of bedsprings upstairs, and loud grunts and a girl yelling in false ecstasy. But at some point, with the drink gone to her head and Fenwick warm next to her, she just fell asleep.

When she woke it was sudden and she was alert. Something had startled her. Something wasn't right.

It was very late at night or very early the next morning. Everything was quiet. Fenwick snored beside her on the sofa. Even in sleep his face looked kind. She wondered if he would make a good husband. The room was dark.

Something creaked upstairs.

Not like before. A sound like someone moving quietly. Like they didn't want to be heard.

Shosh stood. The room spun. She grabbed the arm of the sofa, steadied herself. How much had she had to drink? Her mouth tasted of ash. How much did she smoke?

That sound again. She crept to the door. Looked up, saw nothing. She took the stairs one at a time. She was the only one there awake, dressed and relatively sober.

There, did that shadow just move? She froze. Where were the brothel keepers? No sign of Paula and Eliezer. She climbed another step, stopped, did it again. She came to the landing.

Three doors, two closed. The third was very slightly ajar. Shosh crept forward. She pushed the door open—

Bill Goodrich lay naked on the bed, snoring. He was on his back. His penis flopped against his thigh. His arm was thrown over the equally naked body of the young man, Yosef.

A bright flash of light went off with a '*pop!*'

Shosh screamed.

As the light faded all she could make out was a man with a camera, standing over the bed.

He turned, saw her, and lunged.

Shosh put her hands out but the man knocked into her and she fell back against the wall. The man rushed out onto the landing and down the stairs.

Shosh recovered her bearings and ran after him.

'Stop!' she shouted.

Did that ever work? she wondered.

The man didn't stop.

He ran out onto the street. A car idled outside. The man jumped in the car and the car drove off.

Shosh stood on the doorstep panting.

'Son of a bitch!' she said.

She went back in. Arty was still asleep on the sofa. Shosh reached for the cigarettes. She lit one as Bill Goodrich, still entirely naked, came down the stairs and into the room.

He stood and stared at her curiously.

'What's going on?' he said.

'Put some fucking pants on, Bill,' Shosh said.

Bill scratched his chest.

'What?' he said. 'Alright.'

He turned around. She admired his buttocks as he left the room. She heard him go upstairs. He didn't come down again and when she went up to look she saw he was back in bed and fast asleep. Shosh had a headache coming on.

She went downstairs, located a phone and called Moritz's number. Somebody answered. She didn't know who.

She said, 'Tell him to get here fast. We have a problem.'

By the time Moritz got there Ruth had also showed up. Light began to smudge the horizon and the birds were making a ruckus in the trees.

'They have to be ready for the shoot at eight,' Shosh said.

She sat with Moritz and Ruth in the kitchen drinking coffee.

'Tell me again what happened?'

'I told you what happened. What kind of shit are you running, Moritz? I trusted you!'

'It has nothing to do with me, Shosh!' Moritz looked genuinely upset. 'No one should know about this place,' he said.

'Other than the people who do,' Ruth said.

'Well, obviously, yeah. I mean. But it's *exclusive*. It's not some flophouse down in the Check Post. It's a place with class!'

'This is a real fucking problem, Moritz,' Ruth said. Ruth didn't much like Moritz. Nobody much liked Moritz, other than Shosh. And she was beginning to wonder about that herself.

'This is, what, blackmail?' she said. 'He's a *movie star*, Moritz!'

'I know that!'

'Naked, with a guy? In pictures? It will ruin him!'

'I know, Shosh!' He did look upset. 'I will take care of it, I promise.'

Ruth took one of Moritz's cigarettes.

'The question is who,' she said quietly.

'Who has the motive?' Shosh said.

Ruth waved the cigarette. Smoke eddied.

'Means, motive, opportunity,' she said. 'It's classic Marxism. *Who profits?* That is always the question.'

'Is the motive money?' Shosh said.

'Isn't it always?'

'Maybe it's power,' Shosh said. 'Having a movie star owe you, that's something.'

'Hollywood's far. Who is he useful to?' Ruth said.

'Could be, you know...' Moritz lowered his voice. 'The security services.'

That made more sense than Shosh liked to admit. Influence in America would be useful to the new state.

'It feels a little clumsy to me,' Ruth said. 'The execution. Amateur.'

'Then who?'

Ruth said, 'Someone who knew he'd be here. And knew what he liked. What happened to the guy, by the way?'

'I let him go,' Moritz said. 'He won't talk. Believe me. That boy is shtum.'

'I believe you,' Ruth said. 'But somebody still has a picture of both of them with their cocks out.'

'I don't see the big deal, myself,' Moritz complained. 'It's just dicks.' He brooded.

'This isn't black market stuff,' he said.

'Not rivals?'

'Nah. I earned my territory. No one's coming on my patch like that. Not without bringing guns.'

'Then who?'

'Someone had to know,' Ruth said, with finality.

They stared at each other.

'You mean the crew,' Shosh said.

'It won't be one of us,' Ruth said. Meaning the kibbutz.

Shosh hated to admit it, but it made sense. Someone had to know. Someone had to tell. Which meant... what, exactly?

'Why would someone in the crew sell Bill out?' she said.

'Who knew about the party?' Moritz said. 'Start with that.'

'Everyone knew we were going,' Shosh said. 'It's a small set.'

'But not everyone knew *where*,' Moritz said. 'Or even *what*.'

Shosh tried to think.

'It was Bill's party, so it was his call. He invited the AD and, um, Arty... It was a boys-only thing. The director didn't want anything to do with it but he knew, Bill invited him. Oh, who else... The writer, I think?'

'What writer?' Ruth said.

'The guy who wrote the movie. Bill wanted him to give him new lines. Some real zingers, as he put it. So I think he invited him along to butter him up, but the guy wasn't interested.'

'I didn't even know there was a writer,' Ruth said.

'Well, there has to be,' Shosh said. 'Someone has to write the dialogue and stuff.'

'You gals start with him, then,' Moritz said. 'I'll check things this end. They'll have to develop the photos, have a darkroom. If they used colour they'd have to find a specialist lab, so I'll try that, too. We'll get there.'

Ruth stubbed out her cigarette. It was time to go. The film people trouped outside and stood miserably by the truck.

'You alright?' Arty Fenwick said to Shosh quietly.

'Yeah.'

'I'd like to see you again.'

He really was sweet.

'I'd like that, too,' she said, and he smiled.

They got back on the truck. Ruth drove. Shosh stared out at the road. The sun rose over pines and cypresses. Sheep chewed grass in the hills. The mountain slopes rose and fell.

A new day. It was pretty.

Sometimes she forgot the goddamned place was so pretty.

And someone had a picture of Bill Goodrich that was worth more than money. It was worth a life.

'We'll wait for the blackmailers to get in touch with what they want,' Ruth said.

'You think they will?'

'Why else take the picture?'

'He's not even rich, you know,' Shosh said. She wasn't supposed to tell anyone. 'I mean he's on salary from the studio but he spends everything as soon as he gets it. Even his house in L.A. is just a rental.'

'He can get money if he needs it,' Ruth said.

'I suppose,' Shosh said. 'Yes.'

'I want to talk to this writer,' Ruth said. Her hands gripped the steering wheel. Shosh knew her sister. She didn't like the film crew but it didn't matter. They were the kibbutz's guests. Which made them *her* responsibility. Ruth would burn down the Carmel if she had to on her way to getting the truth. She always wanted to *fix* things. To remake the future. While the past squatted behind her like the shadow of a vast beast from which neither she nor Shosh could escape.

The film set was active when they got there. Lights set up and cameras pointing and men dressed in police uniform idling around, and for one scared moment Shosh thought they had come about Bill's compromising photo, until she remembered today they were shooting the police scene. They had finally tracked down Goodrich's character to the kibbutz and were going to hold him under siege until he surrendered. This was a pivotal moment in the film. Would he come out firing? Or would he willingly surrender?

'*There* you are,' Eddie Dmytryk said. He sounded relieved. 'I was getting worried. John, you look like shit.'

'I can work, boss.'

'And Bill, you look even worse. Go to hair and makeup.'

'OK, Eddie…' Bill said.

'Jesus, Shosh. Look at the state of them.'

'I did my best, Eddie.'

'Well, at least they're all here in one piece and on time,' he said. 'In this business I'd count it as a win. Alright everyone! Positions please! Peter, how are we doing on the light?'

'All good, boss,' the lighting guy said.

'Hey, Eddie,' Shosh said.

He turned around and glared. He'd already forgotten her.

'What!' he said.

'Where's the writer?'

'Who?'

'The screenwriter.'

'Ben? He's doing rewrites in the coffee tent.'

The coffee tent was set down-slope from the set. Shosh headed over there. There was a samovar inside and tea and coffee, and she made herself a drink. The writer was in the back, hunched over pages of manuscript. He wasn't much to look at. He had thinning hair and a small moustache and he dressed like a schlub.

'What?' he said irritably when Shosh went over. 'Oh. Thanks.' He accepted the coffee she'd made him.

'What are you working on?' Shosh said. She sat down. A cigarette smouldered in a tin ashtray at the writer's elbow. 'I'm Shosh, by the way.'

'I know who you are.' He caught himself. 'Sorry. I'm Ben.'

'I know.'

She smiled. He smiled back, reluctantly.

'Can I take one of your cigarettes?'

'Help yourself.'

Shosh did. 'So what are you working on?' she said again.

'Some rewrites on the big speech,' Ben said.

'The big speech?'

'Every movie needs one,' Ben said. 'Hell, every star *wants* one. Justice and fairness and triumphing against the odds. That sort of stuff.'

'How come you didn't come to the party?' Shosh said. 'I heard Bill invited you.'

'I had to rewrite the speech for him. Besides, I'm not big into these sorts of parties. Girls and booze. In fact, I was thinking about your life here. Maybe I should try it. It seems so... peaceful.'

She looked at him in surprise.

'It's a hard life,' she said.

'Living is hard,' Ben said. 'At least you do it for a reason. To make a better future. A better world. That's worth struggling for, isn't it?'

'Is this part of your speech?' Shosh said, and he looked suddenly embarrassed.

'Well, yeah,' he said. 'But that doesn't make it any less true.'

She didn't know why but she liked him. Ruth would have liked his speech. Ruth would probably like the movie. Shosh didn't think it was going to amount to much. She preferred a comedy.

She said, 'I have to ask you. Did you tell anyone about the party? Who was going, where it was?'

He pushed his glasses up on his nose. 'Why would I?' he said. 'No. Why, did anything happen?'

Shosh stared at him hard, but he really did seem oblivious. Could they be wrong about the source? She stood up.

'I'll see you again,' she said.

He looked up at her.

'I'd like that,' he said.

35

THAT NIGHT THE SHOOT WENT ON LATE AND SHOSH WAS exhausted by the end of it. She'd caught a nap in between takes. When she woke up she was startled by a vulture. It stared at her through the bars of its cage.

'I thought we finished with the bird scene,' she said.

The bird man stood nearby, watching Goodrich and the Italian girl who wasn't Gina Lollobrigida. The girl was pleading with the man to stop. To come in from the cold. The man was running away. He had been running for a long time and he was going to keep on running forever. Even the love of a beautiful woman won't stop him trying to escape his horrors. This was more or less the dialogue.

'What do you think?' Shosh asked the bird man.

He shook his head.

'I've seen better,' he said.

When it was all over it was late and everyone was tired. Bill seemed subdued. He took Shosh aside.

'Do you have anything yet?' he said.

'We'll take care of it,' Shosh said.

'You better.'

He went to his quarters and left her there. Shosh went home. She just wanted to sleep. But Ruth was waiting for her by her room.

'Do you have anything?' Shosh said.

'I called a friend of mine,' Ruth said. 'Almog. He used to be in intelligence, still is for all I know.'

'Almog?' Shosh said. She had to smile. 'Like in those books?'

'What books?' Ruth said, looking annoyed.

'You know, *Der Hebreisher Detektiv.*'

'Oh, that,' Ruth said. 'I suppose so, yes. Anyway, he said he didn't know, but there were rumours about the film crew.'

'What sort of rumours, Ruth?'

'That some of them are known communists.'

Shosh burst out laughing.

'*We're* communists,' she said.

'*We're* socialists,' Ruth said. 'Well, Yehoyakim is a communist. Or was. And of course the inherent doctrine is sound. Stalin's a great man. But Israel leans west to America, not to the USSR. Almog said there is worry about Soviet agitators reaching out to communist groups here. America and Russia are great powers, Ruth. And we're caught in between them.'

'I don't understand,' Shosh said. But she was beginning to.

Russian spies. It would explain the lack of blackmail demands so far. Not money but *power*, not now but in some future point.

Poor Bill, she thought. But it seemed so farfetched.

She said, 'How will we find them?'

'Oh, we'll find them,' Ruth said. 'Our communists like to make themselves known. But forget about this for a moment. There's something I've been meaning to show you.'

Shosh just wanted to go to sleep. She'd sleep well for once. Instead she followed Ruth. The path was paved now. The dining room under construction loomed half-formed in concrete. They went past, and past the rows of not-yet-houses, down the hill to the place where they kept the horses. There were two now, not Arabian stallions but some local breed, short and stocky and practical. There used to be a donkey but he died.

'I'm not sure I want to see it,' Shosh said. 'Whatever it is.'

'You want to see it,' Ruth said. 'Listen.' They stood by the little shed where the hay was kept for the horses. 'I know you, Shosh. It's hard here and you were always softer than me. I see how you look at the men from America. How you lay out plans. Don't. Your future is here. Your home is here. And you're harder than you'd like to think of yourself.'

Shosh thought of Anna Klug lying in a pool of blood in the cellar in Landsberg. She thought about the camps. The world had fashioned her into a weapon, but she could choose not to be one, she thought. She wanted light, and music, and pretty dresses and, and *things!* She wanted *things.* She wanted a man who never said 'proletariat'. She wanted a child to belong to her, not a kibbutz.

But she couldn't tell any of those things to Ruth because Ruth wouldn't understand.

She watched as her sister lifted the hidden trapdoor. Watched as she went inside. Followed her, shaking. She didn't want to go down there. She didn't want to see whatever awful thing Ruth had done.

It smelled below. It was small and enclosed and she breathed panic. There was a door. She didn't want to see what lay behind the door.

'You can't make me,' she said.

'I did this for you. For us.'

'No. No.'

Ruth turned a key in the lock.

'Go on,' she said.

Shosh took a deep breath and regretted it.

'Fine,' she said. She pushed the door. She went inside.

A thing – a man – sat in a chair. His hair had fallen out and his eyes were sunken, his clothes rotting and filthy. He was shackled to the chair. Shosh gagged. The thing – man – raised his head and looked at her with hopeless eyes.

'Shosh?' he said.

'Oh, my God,' Shosh said.

She stared at Nathan Deutsch. She couldn't move. She felt Ruth behind her, a dark hovering presence.

Shosh was trapped here, caught by her sister. She went to Nathan Deutsch. She knelt beside him.

'What *happened* to you?' she said.

'She did.' His voice was hoarse with disuse. His eyes were madness bright.

'I thought about you all the time,' Shosh said. 'In the camp, and after. I blamed you, I was… I tried and tried, but I could never hate you.'

'I hated him for you,' Ruth said behind her. 'I hated enough for the two of us.'

'You can't do this,' Shosh said. 'This is monstrous.'

'What happened to you, what happened to Mama and Papa, that was monstrous,' Ruth said. 'This? This is just payback.'

Nathan Deutsch's eyes filled with tears. Shosh couldn't watch anymore. She stood. For just a moment she touched his hair, what was left of it.

He had been so beautiful once.

She went outside. Every step was heavier than the one before it. It felt like a hundred years before she reached the top. She threw up against the shed wall. When she straightened up Ruth was there.

'How could you?' Shosh said.

Ruth said, 'How could I not?'

'You had no right.'

'I had every right! Do you know how long I looked for him? How long I looked for *you?* We're family, Shosh. We can't bring back what we lost. But we can make a new life here. A better life.'

'Yes,' Shosh said. Her voice felt hollow.

'Think about it,' Ruth said. 'That's all I ask.'

'Yes,' Shosh said. She walked away. She couldn't bear to look at her sister. She got back to her room and closed the door. She lay in the bed. She started to shake.

'I have to get out of here,' she whispered. 'I have to get out of here, I have to get out!'

36

In the morning everything was normal. The sun shone. The birds sang. Shosh made herself forget what she saw. She was good at making herself forget. She'd tried to do that every night, for years. Focus on today. Focus on right now. Today will be a *good* day.

Breakfast in the dining room was good. There were leftovers from the film crew. And there were fresh eggs. She ate her hardboiled egg. She smeared margarine on her bread. It was *good* bread. The members chatted around her. She had made few friends here, in all this time. She wondered where Renata had got to. Her American must have taken her away, he must have. She would be living in a house with an electric oven and a white picket fence and have two kids. She was probably so fat now. It made Shosh smile.

'Nice to see you smiling,' Tsilla said, going by. Tsilla ran the kitchen and now doubled up feeding the film crew. 'You're pretty when you smile, Shosh. It's time we found you a new man.'

'I'm good, Tsilla,' Shosh said.

She took a detour on her way to the set. Past the children's house. The children were playing outside. Yael saw her. She came running for her mother.

'Shalom, Shosh!' she said.

'Shalom, Yael.'

The children were not allowed to call their parents 'mother' or 'father'. Shosh's throat constricted. She knelt down to hug Yael. The metapelet saw them.

'Hi, Shosh,' she said. 'Yaeli, it's time to go inside now.'

'Bye, Shosh!' Yael said. Shosh held on to her hand.

'I have to go now,' Yael said.

'I know you do, sweetheart,' Shosh said. 'I know you do.'

She watched her daughter go back. The metapelet gave her a thin-lipped smile and all the kids trooped in. Shosh walked on. She had to walk on. She went to watch the Hollywood folk make *The Vultures*.

'Living is hard,' Goodrich said passionately. He held the Italian girl's hands. 'At least you do it for a *reason*.'

Vultures circled overhead. The bird man watched the scene, entranced. Everyone was silent, watching. The actors dressed as British cops hovered just out of shot.

'To make a better future,' Goodrich said. 'A better *world*. That's worth struggling for, isn't it?'

He imbued the last with so much meaning. As though asking for himself, a man seeking a place in this new land. Shosh held her breath.

'We can do it, together,' the Italian girl said. She was very pretty. She held Goodrich's hands. She looked deeply into Goodrich's eyes.

'Stay,' she said.

The moment lengthened, one, two beats. The camera zoomed in on their faces as Goodrich leaned in for a kiss—

'And cut!' Eddie Dmytryk said. The couple relaxed, looked back to the camera.

'How was it, Eddie?' Bill shouted.

'Terrific, Bill! You guys were terrific!'

'Yeah? You really think so?'

'It's good!'

'If you say so, Eddie.'

There was the usual hubbub of activity now as everyone got

ready setting up for the next scene. Ben, the writer, came and stood beside Shosh. He was smiling.

'So?' he said. 'What do you think?'

'It's great, Ben,' Shosh said.

'Well, I mean,' he said. Somehow they were standing side by side. Somehow the backs of their hands were touching. 'It's alright, isn't it.'

Why were film people so *needy?* Why did they always need *praise?*

'You wanna go someplace?' Shosh said.

He turned and looked at her. Unspoken words. Shosh didn't want to talk. She just wanted to forget.

'Sure,' Ben said.

She lay on his bed and reached for his cigarettes. She lit up for them both. The sheets were humid. She said, 'This was nice.'

'It was.'

'I have to go,' Shosh said. She got up, cigarette in mouth, and began to dress.

'Stay,' Ben said.

For some reason that was very funny. She started to laugh. He did too.

'But I mean it,' he said.

She leaned in and kissed him hard on the lips.

'Thank you,' she said.

She was smiling when she went outside. She went to find Ruth. Ruth was by the truck. There was a man with her. He had a military bearing. Shosh didn't mention the previous night. It never happened.

'Shosh, this is Almog.'

He looked different than she imagined him when reading his made-up adventures in Yiddish. He was just some guy.

They shook hands.

'Well?' Shosh said.

'I may have something,' Almog said. 'We can take my car.'

Shosh sat in the back of his car. Ruth sat up front. She and Almog had an easy familiarity between them.

'So?' Shosh said.

'There's a small communist newspaper published in Haifa,' Almog said. '*The Voice of Freedom*. Here.' He tossed over a paper. Shosh opened it – black and white and cheaply printed, a single broadside sheet folded into four pages. The headline said, 'PM Ben-Gurion Pulls the Cart of American Imperialism'. Below, with a grainy photo: 'Saifuddin Kitchlew Awarded Stalin Peace Prize'.

'Page two,' Almog said.

Shosh turned to page two. At the bottom she found it: 'American Film Crew Makes Movie in Israel'. The article was small but overall supportive. 'With a writer and a director both known for their communist sympathies one can only hope *The Vultures* brings more viewers to the cause.'

Finally, a small photo of the barn set and a smiling indistinct man gesturing at it, and a caption underneath: 'Set designer shows off his work to our reporter.'

'That's Arty Fenwick,' Shosh said. 'Son of a bitch!'

'Yes,' Almog said. 'He made contact with the folks at *The Voice* as soon as he landed, we think. We monitor them periodically. I think it most likely someone there hatched the plot, perhaps even at Fenwick's suggestion.'

He drove fast. The sea on their right. The car took the incline up to the lower city *fast*. Almog stopped with a screech of tyres. He parked. Across the road was a cloth store and a grain store and a car garage and sandwiched somewhere in between them was a small faded sign that said *The Voice of Freedom*.

Moritz materialised out of the shadows of a municipal rubbish bin and came towards them.

'My boys are ready,' he said. 'There should be no problems.'

'We just want to talk to them, Moritz,' Almog said.

Moritz shrugged. 'Then there should be no problems,' he said.

Almog nodded. Shosh scanned the quiet street, noticed Moritz's 'boys' idling: there a moustached heavy in a too-tight shirt smoking a rollup, there a skinny kid with a bicycle leaning against the wall, cleaning his nails with a small sharp knife. She followed the others across the road. Almog pushed the door open and they all went inside.

A young man standing beside a running printing press looked up in surprise.

'Can I help you?' he said.

'You know me?' Almog said.

'Stern Gang,' the man said with distaste. 'What do you want?'

'I'm looking for a photograph.'

'Try a photo studio, then, asshole,' the man said. 'And who are these? This is private property.'

'I thought all property belongs to the collective,' Almog said.

'Don't be a smartass. Hey, Moshe! Come over here!'

Another, older man appeared in the back of the shop and ambled over, a cup of tea in his hands. He wore a shabby suit and a trilby hat.

'What's this about?' he said.

'This fascist here is making trouble,' the younger man said.

Moshe, the man in the trilby, studied them with sad eyes.

'Almog,' he said. He sounded resigned.

'Moshe.'

'What do you want?'

'I'm looking for a photograph.'

'Is that supposed to mean something to me?'

'I don't know,' Almog said. 'Does it?'

Moshe shrugged. 'It does not,' he said. 'Is it something from our archives? If so, you are welcome to have a look through them.'

'It's more of a custom job,' Almog said. 'I believe.'

'Cryptic,' Moshe said. 'David, you know what he's talking about?'

'Not a clue,' the other man said. He looked jumpy, Shosh thought. He was checking the door as if he were going to make a run for it.

'Maybe you need our photographer,' Moshe said. 'But he's not in.'

'Where is he?'

Moshe shrugged. 'Rousing the workers, I hope,' he said. 'That, or taking pictures someplace. David, you know where he is?'

'Even if I did I wouldn't tell this bastard,' the other man, David, said.

Moshe adjusted his trilby. He took a sip of tea.

'Will you...?' he began to say.

He didn't quite finish.

Somehow Moritz was right *there*, in David's face. Somehow David was raising his fist, and somehow Moritz ducked it, and grabbed David's arm behind his back, and *twisted*. David yelped in pain. Moritz's face was next to his, his chin resting on the man's shoulder.

'Where is the picture, David?' he said.

'Let go!'

'Where *is* it!'

David screamed. The man in the trilby hat stared at them aghast.

'What are you doing, man!' he said. 'Let him go at once!'

'Where is the picture, David? Where the fuck is it!'

'Alexander has it!' David said. He was crying in pain now. 'Alexander has it...'

'Alexander is the photographer?'

'Yes. Yes...'

'Where is he?'

'He has a place by the harbour. Let me go! Please!'

'How many copies are there?' Moritz said.

'I don't know! I was just driving the car, I didn't...'

'What is the meaning of this!' the man in the trilby hat said.

'Dirty pictures,' Almog said. 'Blackmail, Moshe. Blackmail.'
Moshe turned pale.

'I knew nothing of this,' he said.

'I believe you,' Almog said. 'We just want the picture recovered, nothing more. We can keep this whole thing quiet.'

'Then do. We are communists, not gangsters. Here.' He placed his mug on a nearby desk, reached for a pen and paper and scribbled a note. He passed it to Almog.

'Alexander's address,' he said.

Moritz released the captive man. David sagged to the floor.

'You broke my fucking arm!' he said.

'It's nothing,' Moritz said. He whistled. Two of his boys came in, the ones Shosh saw earlier.

'Take him to the Italian Hospital,' he said. 'Go the scenic route. Make sure he doesn't talk to anyone.'

'Yes, boss.'

They dragged David away. Moshe watched him, tight-lipped.

'Boys will be boys,' he said.

'You better hope we recover the picture, Moshe,' Almog said. 'Or we'll come back.'

'You think you scare me?' Moshe said.

'I hope I do,' Almog said.

'You ain't shit, Almog,' Moshe said. 'But I didn't authorise whatever rogue operation they were running. We're a legitimate political party. We don't work like this.'

'You keep believing that, Moshe,' Almog said. He turned to leave. They followed him out. Into the car, and down to the harbour. Ships in the water, workers on the docks unloading cargo.

The photographer's place turned out to be a dilapidated warehouse. They stood outside the doors.

'On three,' Almog said.

They broke down the door and went in fast. The place was dark. Someone said, 'What the...?' Shosh saw a shadow moving. The photographer, Alexander, trying to flee.

Bodies moving in the dark. Footsteps running, someone breathing hard, another set of footsteps and a grunt as two bodies collided and tumbled to the ground. Then Moritz turned on the lights.

Red lights overhead cast the place in gloom. Everything was ghostly, seen through a sheen of thinned blood. The photographer was prone on the ground, Almog sitting on top of him.

'Stay there,' he said.

Photos hanging from washing lines overhead. Tubs of chemicals on the working surfaces.

Shosh stared.

There was Bill Goodrich and there was his cock. He looked peaceful lying there next to the young man. An enlarged copy on the wall made her smile.

'Well, damn,' Moritz said. 'The guy is hung.'

'It's *kompromat*,' the photographer said.

'No shit,' Moritz said. 'What were you going to do with it, ask for money?'

'We were going to send it to Russia,' Alexander said. He seemed happy to talk. 'Leverage on a film star. You know?'

'You know anyone in Russia, do you?' Almog said.

'There's a guy—'

Alexander shut up.

'What guy?' Ruth said.

'Just some guy. I don't know his name. He told us to do it.'

'You better talk,' Almog said. 'Or it will go bad for you.'

'I don't know anything!' Alexander said. 'It's all compartmentalised to stop us revealing anything. All I know is I was to develop the photo and put it in a drop and it would get where it's supposed to.'

'And did you?' Ruth said.

'Not yet.'

'Get all the copies and the negative,' Almog said.

It was all right there. It was almost too easy, Shosh thought.

They tore the place down bit by bit looking for copies. Shosh found one stashed in a drawer. Just a small six by four. No one was looking. She hid it on herself.

'I could take you to the police,' Almog told the photographer.

'You can't do shit,' the photographer said. 'Unless your movie star wants to go to the police. Which we both know he doesn't. So just take it all and go.'

They were all bathed in red. Almog smiled. He looked like a ghoul.

'There is only one way to make sure,' he said.

The photographer cried without sound. Shosh took in deep gulps of fresh air. Gulls cried overhead and she could taste the tang of salt before the smoke began to rise from the warehouse.

They stood there and watched the place burn.

37

'It's a wrap!' Eddie Dmytryk said. There was scattered applause. Already the heavy camera equipment and lights were being dismantled, and the bird man stood forlorn with an unlit cigarette in his mouth, watching from afar.

Shosh went to join them.

'How do you keep the birds from flying off?' she said.

He shrugged.

'I feed them,' he said.

Arty Fenwick flew back to L.A. two days earlier. He didn't say goodbye. Shosh still hung around the film set. Bill still needed his tea. The last of the vultures came down to land and the bird man ushered them into their cages.

Shosh felt sad she wouldn't see them again.

But she still had some things to do.

She sat in the kibbutz dining room with Ruth. She put a spoon of honey in her tea – a special treat. Ruth said, 'It's over and now we can get back to our real lives.'

Shosh nodded.

'It's a relief,' she said.

She reached across the table and touched her sister's hand.

'I love you, Ruth,' she said.

By nightfall the crew were gone to Tel Aviv. A night in a comfortable hotel and then a flight home. Shosh decided to walk. It was a nice night. She followed the path from the gate to the main road. The wadi below. Jackals howled in the distance.

She lit a cigarette. The stars shone overhead. She watched the dark road. A single pair of headlights passed, then slowed. She went over.

'Well?' Moritz said.

'I'll show you.'

There was a back gate to the kibbutz near the place for the horses. Moritz picked the lock. They drove in without lights.

They went to the enclosure. Shosh lifted the hidden trapdoor.

'What's down there?' Moritz said.

'Hell.'

She went in. He followed. He unlocked the door for her. Shosh hesitated before she opened it.

The man who was once Nathan Deutsch sat in the chair. He didn't stir.

'Meyn gat,' Moritz said.

'Can you get him out?'

Moritz was sweating. He picked the locks.

Shosh said, 'Nathan? Nathan, can you hear me?'

The man in the chair opened two hopeless eyes.

'Shosh,' he said. He started to cry.

Shosh and Moritz held him. They lifted him up. Dragged him up to the surface.

'Get him in the car, quick,' Moritz said. He was still sweating. 'What do you want me to do with him, Shosh?'

'Take him to the harbour. Put him on a ship. Get him somewhere far, far away from here.'

She went to Nathan. She said, 'Can you hear me?'

'I can hear you, Shosh.'

'Get out of here, Nathan. Get out and never, ever come back.'

He tried to smile but his ruined mouth wouldn't form the shape.

'I will,' he said.

She shut the door on him. Moritz got behind the wheel. He gunned the engine and was gone.

*

'Dear Ruth,' Shosh wrote. She stared at the postcard.

'What is it?' Ben said. She looked at him in affection.

'Just trying to say goodbye,' she said.

He nodded and signalled for the stewardess to refill their drinks.

'Goodbyes are hard to write,' he said.

'I met a man and I love him dearly,' Shosh wrote. 'We are on our way to America. Please look after Yael. She will be happier with you.'

She promised herself she wouldn't cry. She looked out of the window. She had never been on a plane before.

'I love you,' she wrote. And she signed it as she always did. 'Your sister, Shoshana.'

The stewardess came with their drinks. Shosh sat back in the chair, resting her head. She closed her eyes. The engine thrummed comfortingly all around her.

The postcard in her hand. She turned it over and over and finally put it away.

She thought, she'll post it for sure once she got to America.

PART SEVEN

CALIFORNIA

Yael

Kibbutz Trashim, 1956

38

YAEL CRAWLED UNDER THE BROKEN TRACTOR IN THE playground. Beneath the chassis they had made a secret place. Mud walls and bark and leaves, and carefully placed discarded cloth. From the outside it looked like nothing much. The adults paid it no attention. The other children knew tacitly to leave it alone.

She dug in the secret place until she found the secret box. She brought it out. Faint sunlight broke through from the gaps in the walls. She opened the box, which once smelled pleasantly of tea, and which said *Wissotzky* on the lid. She took out the bundle of faded postcards.

Each one had been torn into pieces and thrown in the rubbish.

Each one carefully picked up and repaired as best as Yael could, in secret, with glue and Sellotape. She didn't understand the words. The writing was in Hungarian. At least, she thought it was Hungarian. It didn't matter.

It was forbidden – to look at, to ever mention.

Not to Ruth; not to anyone, but especially not to Ruth.

Yael placed the postcards on the ground and stared. She couldn't read the handwriting but she could see the pictures. Orange groves and sparkling seas, palm trees, golden beaches.

Greetings From Sunny California! the postcards said in English.

It must be heaven, Yael thought, where they came from. Or as close to it as to make no difference. She reached in her pocket for a slice of bread. Her front teeth were all grown up now, she was proud of that. She nibbled on the bread. She was always hungry. She touched the front of the postcard, the one with the giant motorway and the big cars roaring past. They seemed impossible. There were no roads or cars like that here.

The flap opened and a small figure slunk in. Ophek, a year younger, gave her a smile full of missing teeth.

'Not these again!' he said.

Yael put them quickly back together and back into the box.

'What do *you* want?' she said.

'I got something,' Ophek said, still grinning. 'For the treasure box.'

'What is it this time?'

'Look!'

He opened his palm like a magician. Yael stared.

It was a pocket watch, the metal smooth and polished. It ticked in Ophek's hand.

'You stole it?'

'There was a man from the unions here this morning,' Ophek said. 'From the Histadrut. He wore a beret and he had a big moustache. And this watch!'

'You can't keep *stealing* things!' Yael said.

'He didn't even notice,' Ophek said. 'It's not my fault.'

'If Ruth catches you again...' Yael said. Ophek lost the grin.

'She won't,' he said. 'I'm getting better.'

'That you are,' Yael said.

'I'm going to be a magician when I grow up,' Ophek said. 'This is just, you know. *Practise*. It's called *sleight-of-hand*.' He said it so self-importantly. He was always reading books about magic. Yael knew with a sinking heart he was going to mention Houdini.

'Houdini could take the watch from off your wrist and you would never even *know* it,' Ophek said. 'Houdini could escape from handcuffs and prison cells and, well...' His eyes shone. '*Everything!*' he said.

'Yeah?' Yael said. She took the watch and turned it over,

admiring the quality, then put it into the treasure box, alongside
the brass ashtray with *Palestine* etched on the bottom, a horseshoe,
a broken rock with crystals growing inside it and other precious
things. 'Could he escape from the kibbutz, though?' she said.

'Why do you want to escape from the kibbutz?' Ophek said.
'It's home.'

'I want to go *there*,' Yael said. She stabbed the packet of
postcards with her finger. 'To *California*.'

'Alright,' Ophek said. 'So let's go there.'

'Go there how!'

'We'll just go.' He looked up at her with those big bright eyes
that meant he never got into trouble for long. 'It can't be that far.
Look.' He pointed at the postcard. 'The sea, right? We could just
walk there.'

'We'd get in trouble,' Yael said.

'No one will know,' Ophek said. 'They won't even miss us.
Besides, we can come straight back.'

This made a sort of sense. Yael nibbled on the bread. She said,
'We'll need supplies.'

'We can pick fruit on the way and stuff,' Ophek said.

'On the way to where?' someone else said. The flap opened and
Yoram came in.

'Yoram!' Yael said. She jumped into his arms. He held her and
smiled. At eleven he was all grown up. Just one year shy of moving
to the regional school, and already in the underground for the
youth movement (though that was still a secret) and Israel already
let him drive a tractor. Yoram's hair fell down to his shoulders.
Yael felt so safe with him around.

'To the sea,' Ophek said. He shot Yael a look. 'We're going now,'
he said.

'You can't go,' Yoram said. 'It's really far.'

'Well, we're going,' Yael said, pulling back. 'It's an adventure,
like in those Avner Carmeli stories in *Our Country*.'

'Who?' Yoram said. Yael looked at him pleadingly.

'Oh, *please*, Yoram,' she said.

He sighed, and caved in.

'I'd better come with you, then,' Yoram said.

Ophek whooped and Yael clapped.

Yoram smiled.

'We'll need water,' he said.

They set off beyond the water tower and down to the wadi half an hour later. They had a military backpack from Israel's closet, with bread from the dining room and five hardboiled eggs, two military canteens filled with water, a compass and a Swiss army knife.

Both the compass and the Swiss army knife came from the treasure box. Yoram wore the canteens on Israel's military belt, which he'd had to put on its farthest notch. It was still too loose around his waist, and he kept adjusting it.

Down the hill and along the wadi, wild za'atar growing in the fallow fields. They followed the brook, chewing on small green khubbayza fruit.

'Used to be an Arab village with that name round here,' Yoram said. 'Khubbayza.' He nibbled a handful.

Yoram knew everything. He even claimed there was a secret slick under the horse enclosure, but it wasn't for guns, it was an empty prison cell, he saw it once when he was secretly following Ruth. And he remembered the woman who sent the postcards, a little. The woman called Shosh. But Yael didn't care about Shosh, not anymore, maybe not ever. She didn't even *need* a mother, she had Ruth and the kibbutz.

But she still wanted to see California.

'What happened to it?' Ophek said.

'The village?'

'Aha.'

Yoram shrugged.

'I don't know,' he said. 'I guess they just left.'

Yael lost interest. The sky grew overcast. Ophek went behind a tree to pee. Yael didn't need to pee. They didn't see anyone else around. Once a tractor in the distance, driven by one of the farmers from the moshav up ahead. Soon they came to the old caves. They were set into the side of the hill. A ring of stones for a fire had extinguished coal still within it. The caves were cool and dark. It started to rain and so the three of them went inside the largest cave and waited. Yael ate one of the eggs. Yoram, who knew everything and was also good with music, played his pocket harmonica. Ophek practised making a small stone appear and vanish in his hands. He really was very good, but it got boring fast, watching him.

After a while the rain stopped. They went outside and started walking again. Yael felt the first tinge of excitement. She'd never gone beyond the Hill of Caves before. The ground was damp and snails came out. She stepped over the snails. In kindergarten they raced snails sometimes, for fun. Put a lettuce leaf at the finish line and watched them slither. After the rain snails came out and danced with each other and their bodies stuck together sometimes. She looked at Yoram. He strode ahead. Ophek said, 'I'm tired.'

They stopped at the crest of a hill. Down below in a valley stood a gaggle of lonely homes. Yael shivered. This wasn't California. She didn't know what it was.

They sat down on rocks. Yoram passed around the water canteen. Yael put out the bread and eggs. Ophek contributed a pomegranate. It was small and wizened. This wasn't the season. They ate the food and broke the pomegranate against a rock and picked the tiny bright red seeds with dirty fingers. Their lips were caked in juice.

'We'll keep going,' Yoram said. 'It can't be far.'

He didn't sound certain. Down they went. Yael stumbled into stinging nettles. She cried out and Yoram steadied her.

'Don't cry,' he said.

'I'm not crying!'

He poured water on the rash. His fingers were gentle. He looked at her and smiled.

'I'm fine,' Yael said.

They kept going. The clouds grew in the sky. In moments it rained again. They ran down to the houses below. The houses seemed empty. A dog barked once, then fell silent. Yael could see no one around.

'What do we do?' she said.

'Knock on a door,' Ophek said.

They tried the first house but got no answer. Empty windows, closed blinds, no sound in that place. They tried the second one, the same.

'I want to go home now,' Ophek said. He took Yael's hand. Bitter disappointment rose in her throat, like bile the time that she was sick.

'But we're nowhere near the sea,' she said. 'I want to see California.'

'California isn't here,' Yoram said.

'Then where is it?' Yael demanded.

'In America.'

'I don't care,' Yael said. 'I want to see it.'

Yoram went up to the third house and knocked. He knocked again. He knocked three times. The door was snatched open. A woman stood in the doorway in a grey dress. She held a baby wrapped in a blanket. She stared at the three of them.

'What do you want?' she said.

Yael didn't know why Yoram blurted it. Why he didn't ask for help. Why he didn't tell her they were cold and it was raining, and would she let them in?

Yoram said, 'What's the time?'

The woman said, 'The time?'

'Yes, please,' Yoram said.

ADAMA

The woman went inside. She must have had a clock. She came back. She said, 'It's five o'clock.'

'Thank you,' Yoram said.

The woman nodded.

She shut the door.

Yael and Ophek looked at each other.

'What do we do now?' Yael said.

'We go on,' Yoram said.

They walked away. The houses vanished behind them, small grey specks in the midst of fields. Yoram checked the compass. Yael went to pee behind a bush. It got colder, but then the clouds parted and she saw the sun come out. The sun warmed their faces. Yael smiled. *Welcome to Sunny California!* the postcard said. She kept the top one in her pocket for the trip.

'Here,' she said. She passed Ophek the last egg.

'Thanks, Yael,' he said.

They walked on.

They made camp that night under cold bright stars. Yoram played his harmonica. They built a fire together, then sat around it. There was no more rain. The sky was clear.

'Tell me that story again,' Ophek said.

'What story?' Yael said.

'The one from *Our Country*. The Avner Carmeli one about the kids who have adventures.'

'*The Young Detectives*?' Yael said. She couldn't really remember how it went. It was a new series in *Our Country* magazine. The young detectives were Eli and Shosh and Pinhas. They went on all kinds of exciting quests. Settling in the wilderness and fighting Arabs and always getting into trouble and—

'Well,' she said. 'One day the Young Detectives decided to go exploring in the wilderness. They were chasing, um, a bank robber—'

'Why?' Ophek said.

'What?'

'Why were they chasing him?'

'He was a bank robber,' Yael said.

'Doesn't mean he was bad,' Ophek said. 'Maybe he just liked robbing banks. Or he was doing it for a good reason. Like to help people with the money he stole.'

Yael wasn't really sure what money *was*. It was something people had to use outside the kibbutz, and they kept it in banks, and people sometimes robbed the banks. This was in all the stories. She didn't really understand why people *needed* money, though. Some people were poor and didn't have food, but then, if they didn't have food couldn't they just go to the dining room?

'*Anyway*,' she said. 'The Young Detectives went after the robber, and they travelled many kilometres on foot. Soon it started to rain, and the Young Detectives were cold, and tired, but they never gave up. They never gave up!' Yael said.

Ophek yawned. He lay on the ground, his head in her lap. Yoram played softly on the harmonica.

'On they marched,' Yael said, 'until they saw, far in the distance, a collection of awful little houses in the middle of the wilderness, and they knew some terrible people lived there—'

'Not people like us,' Ophek said, with certainty.

'And they knew the robber was hiding there. And so, gathering all their courage, they approached the settlement—'

'Guns drawn,' Yoram said. He put down the harmonica.

'Guns drawn,' Yael said. 'The robber burst out firing! But the Young Detectives took cover, and they fired back, and—'

'He's asleep,' Yoram said.

Ophek snored. Yael stroked his hair, then pushed his head off her lap onto the ground. Ophek said, 'Oof!' then turned on his side and went back to sleep.

'I'm scared, Yoram,' Yael said.

Yoram looked up. The fire danced in his eyes.

'There's nothing to be scared of,' he said. Yael shifted until she sat next to him. She put her arms around him. He felt so warm and so strong.

'There are no robbers,' Yoram said. 'No dangers. Just us. Go to sleep, Yael.'

She nestled into him. She felt warm and sleepy.

'Can you sing me something?' she said.

'The wind blew through the cypress trees,' Yoram sang. His voice was high and reedy. 'In the distance the jackals howled. And you were beautiful, so beautiful, as you sat by the campfire beside me...'

Yael drifted off to sleep.

The next day the sun shone bright, and Yael stretched as high as she could go, and the air smelled of fresh pine needles. That was a nice smell. They didn't brush their teeth and their clothes smelled of the smoke from the campfire. Yael liked it. And still they saw no one. They marched on, and soon came to an orchard and stole the fruit from the trees and gorged themselves, and drank from the single irrigation pipe that ran into the trees. Out of the orchard they came to wheat fields and walked through them, and the sky stretched blue and faint with cloud whites to the horizon. Beyond a range of hills they saw riders.

Yoram froze. Ophek and Yael stopped with him. The riders were far away, on horseback, moving in a row. They were framed against the sky.

'Do you think anyone is looking for us?' Ophek said.

'They must be,' Yoram said. 'They would have noticed we were gone when we didn't come back to the children's house after dinner.'

Yael hoped they were. Someone must miss them. Ruth would notice. Ruth noticed everything. But the world felt so still.

The riders vanished behind a hill. The children went on.

By midday they came to a road. The road was covered in black asphalt. It went north-west, Yoram said after checking the compass. They walked along the road for a while. No cars came. Further down the road they found a bus shelter. They sat under it and waited. A car came by then, a small white car. It puffed slowly along the road. When it came to the bus shelter it slowed. A pale hand holding a lit cigarette dangled from the open window. A pale face with a shock of black hair looked them over behind dark sunglasses.

'You kids lost?' the driver said.

Yoram shook his head.

'You need a ride?'

Yoram shook his head.

'Don't talk much, do you?' the driver said.

Yoram shook his head.

The driver smiled.

'Cute,' he said. 'Give you a pound to come sit in my lap. Or that little girl with you, she'll do in a pinch.'

The driver seemed nice and he was smiling but somehow the pit of Yael's stomach was knotted in ropes and she held on to Ophek's hand tightly.

'What about me?' Ophek said. 'I could sit in your lap.' His eyes were fever bright again. 'A pound,' he whispered.

'Go away,' Yoram said to the driver.

'Or what?' the driver said.

Yoram picked up a rock.

'Go,' he said to Yael. He didn't look at her. She pulled Ophek away. They ran.

She didn't look back. She heard Yoram scream. Then the sound of glass smashing, and the man cursing, and then the sound of the little white car speeding away.

Yael stopped. She breathed hard.

'Yoram?' she said. 'Yoram!'

She ran back. Yoram was under the bus stop. He had a cut on

his arm, and she ran to him, but when she tried to take his hand to look he pushed her away.

'It's fine,' he said.

'What did he want?' Yael whispered. 'Why was he like this?'

'It doesn't matter,' Yoram said. 'But let's stay off the road.'

They walked on. Ophek complained about losing out on a pound. A whole pound! They could have put it in the treasure box. Yoram didn't say much. His arm stopped bleeding. He had a determined look in his eyes. They weren't going back. They were going to finish what they started. He stalked ahead of them and Ophek struggled to keep up. Yael kept pulling him on.

'Yoram, we have to stop!' she said. 'We're tired.'

'We're almost there, Yaeli,' he said.

'Ophek can't, Yoram.'

'He can! It's like in that story you told him last night. The Young Detectives. They wouldn't stop. They wouldn't let anyone stop them!'

'But it's just a story,' Yael said. 'It's not real.'

'And your California is real?'

Yael froze. Ophek sat down on the hard ground. Yael balled her hands into fists.

'Stop it!' she shouted.

They stared at each other. Yoram was crying, Yael realised. This made her more afraid than she had ever been.

'Yoram...' she said.

'We will find it,' he said. 'You wanted to go, so I'm taking you.'

'We can't...' Yael said.

She sat down on the ground next to Ophek. She felt so helpless. Yoram stared at them both. There were tears on his cheeks but he didn't make a sound.

'The Young Detectives went on,' Yael said. She used her story voice. Ophek perked up, paying attention. 'They passed many perils.' She wasn't sure what 'peril' meant but the author of the Young Detectives liked the word a lot. 'The bank robber held them at gunpoint from a car he stole, but Eli defeated him and the robber lay wounded on the ground. "You will go to prison now!" Eli said.'

'But the bank robber isn't a *bad* guy,' Ophek said. Yoram came over. He sat down on the ground with them and just listened.

'On and on the Young Detectives marched,' Yael said. 'Until, in the first light of dawn, they saw something amazing. They went over the final hill and saw the sun rise – rise over the sea. It was a beautiful sun, warm and yellow like the tastiest egg yolk—'

'I wish we had an egg,' Ophek said dreamily.

'The Young Detectives ran into the water!' Yael said. 'Eli and Shosh and Pinhas. They splashed in the warm, beautiful sea, and then built castles in the sand all day and lay in the shade of the orange trees. There were beautiful people everywhere they looked. They had beautiful clothes and beautiful cars and beautiful teeth. And the mayor came out and shook all their hands and said, "Thank you for saving my town from the bank robber. Welcome to sunny California!"'

Yael closed her eyes. She leaned against Yoram and he put his hands around her. She felt safe with him. And in this way they sat together by the side of the road.

She must have fallen asleep. It was near dark. Her tongue felt furry. Her mouth tasted like a mouse had died there. She heard a car engine, the tread of wheels in the dirt. Headlights blinded her.

'It's them! We found them!'

Running footsteps. Tall figures of some giant beings standing above her. Ophek started to cry. Yael was pulled up. She blinked and made out Israel's worried face.

'You gave us such a scare!' he said.

He hugged her, so tightly she thought she would burst.

'Enough, Israel.' Ruth's voice, cool and tight, from behind the glare of light. 'Children, go sit in the back of the truck. Don't spoil the produce. You're going home.'

Israel put Yael down. He patted her head awkwardly.

'You heard her,' he said.

Yael nodded. She went to the truck. She climbed on and sat between crates of cucumbers and tomatoes. Yoram joined her there. Ophek, she noticed, had worked his charm: he was allowed to sit up front between the adults.

Yael didn't say a thing all the way back to the kibbutz. No one did. They took them to their respective children's homes and dropped them off. The metapelet sent her to the shower and then to bed. Yael climbed into her bed in the room she shared with the others.

'Where did you go, Yaeli?' Gideon whispered from his bed by the window.

'Go to sleep, Gideon.'

'Everyone was looking for you.'

Yael thought of the postcard. Ruth took it from her when they got back. She didn't say a word. She just snatched it from her hand and then she walked off.

It didn't matter. Yael didn't need the postcard anymore.

She'd already been to California.

PART EIGHT

PURIM

Yael

Kibbutz Trashim, 1964

39

ON JUST TWO DAYS OF THE YEAR THE KIBBUTZ WAS
transformed and became a carnival of sorts. One was Independence Day: hayrides and swings and sweets for the kiddies,
flags everywhere and meat on the grill. Yael still remembered
the Independence Day celebrations soon after she and the others
walked to the sea. They'd sung the anthem and marched with the
flags for the eight-year-old nation. The country was Yael's age. Just
a little girl in pigtails like in the song.

But that was long ago. And Yael was all grown up now. She
was more like the girl in the Song of Songs. Black and comely, O
ye daughters of Jerusalem, as the tents of Kedar, as the curtains
of Solomon. She was tanned from the sun, and her bare legs were
long and her shorts were short, and she knew the way all the boys
looked at her.

She was sixteen, with long hair in a braid just like in Solomon's
song, and the more scholarly-minded of the boys would quote the
Bible at her, telling her how her breasts were like two young roes
that were twins which fed among the lilies.

Boys! She didn't want boys. She was sick with love, like the
nameless girl in the Song of Solomon.

Tonight, she thought. With the music, in the dark.

Tonight—

There were just two days in the year when the drabness of the
kibbutz was replaced with party dress.

One was Independence Day. It was nice for the kids.

LAVIE TIDHAR

But the other one was Purim and, on Purim, you got *drunk*.

Not that Yael was sure what being drunk was actually *like*, but she was going to make sure to find out. The thought of tonight made her excited, and a little scared. In the Bible, Esther's feast saved the Jews of the Persian Empire, and to commemorate it the Jews were commanded to drink-until-they-knew-not.

Esther was a nice name, Yael thought. She liked the ring of it. She looked in the mirror.

Paula and Malka, who were her sort-of older sisters, had recently taken on the role of Purim seamstresses for the entire kibbutz. They spent months hand-making costumes for the party. The Adloyada, the until-they-knew-not. Sometimes she was so tired of *knowing*! Being drunk must be marvellous, she thought. To not know, or care, to just be *free*. She tried on the dress.

A princess out of a fairytale looked back at her. She set the crown on her head.

She barely recognised the woman in the mirror.

Perfect, she thought.

Night fell, and torches were lit on the way to the dining room. Kids in costumes ran and shrieked everywhere. Yael took it all in:

Maccabees mixed with Greeks, cowboys with clowns and pirates with soldiers. Two kids dressed as Stalin and Karl Marx with competing moustaches had a heated argument by the rose bushes. The little kids were cats with ears and whiskers, sailors, trees, police officers.

She passed a Moshe Dayan complete with eye patch, boys in blackface and girls made up as China dolls with knitting needles in their hair. More girls, the older ones, her age: nurses and Red Riding Hoods, Snow Queens and Indian maids. Standing to one side: one Moses with a long white beard awkwardly holding the tablets of the Ten Commandments.

In two short years she'd go to the army, Yael thought. She would wear a uniform for real, a gun that wasn't made of wood. There was no *point* dressing up as another soldier. That was one costume everyone was eventually going to wear.

'Yael!'

She turned at the sound of her name and smiled. Ophek, dressed unsurprisingly in a magician's outfit, complete with tall hat and sequinned sleeves. Malka and Paula very rarely spoke but they doted on Ophek the way they did on no one else. There was just something about him. Everyone liked Ophek.

'Do you like it?' he said self-consciously, spreading his arms.

'Tell me you don't have a pigeon in your pocket,' Yael said.

Ophek looked momentarily embarrassed.

'You *promised!*' Yael said. 'After what happened last time...'

'It's different now!' Ophek said. 'She's comfortable. You'll see.'

'You're doing your act later?'

'Sure.'

'I heard you've been doing shows all over,' Yael said. 'Other kibbutzim, even Haifa.'

'Yeah.'

'You get paid?'

'Yeah.'

'But you give it all to the kibbutz, right?'

Ophek grinned.

'Sure I do,' he said. 'Besides, Israel has to drive me.'

Yael looked at him suspiciously but decided to say nothing.

'Have you seen Gideon?' she said.

'Your boyfriend?'

'He's not my boyfriend!'

She felt herself blushing.

'You do it yet, Yael?' Ophek said.

'Did you?' she said.

'I fingered Daphna in the pool last summer,' Ophek said.

'You're disgusting, Ophek!'

'What!' he said, giving her those innocent eyes until Yael couldn't help but laugh.

'Come on,' she said. 'Let's go in.'

Inside, the dining room was momentarily transformed. The decorations committee had done their job with zealot enthusiasm. The lights were dim and streamers hung from the ceilings and cut-out silhouettes of wise queen Esther, faithful Mordechai, foolish King Achashverosh and the evil vizier Haman loomed in the corners. The opulence of a Persian court was summoned in the form of glitter and gold foil, and plates of Haman's Ears – which Ruth kept slipping and calling Hamantashen, like in the diaspora, and having to correct herself every time – sat on the tables that were pushed to the side to allow for the stage and the dancing area.

Ruth stood talking to Yehezkel from the falcha under the board where all the baby quilts were on display. Every baby born on the kibbutz had a special little patch quilted for them. They hung overhead. Yehezkel from the falcha eyed Yael with a sort of hungry appreciation that made her uncomfortable.

'Not a baby anymore, are we?' he said. She stood away from his wandering hands.

Ruth smiled at her, but only with her lips.

'You look very pretty, Yael,' she said.

She was always kind but she was never loving. She changed when she turned to Ophek. The smile was in her eyes then, and Yael could see all the love Ruth had inside her, spilling out.

Growing up, Yael kept wishing some of that love would spill on her, too. She was parched for the few drops that splashed her way.

'You look too much like her,' Israel once told Yael. Yael didn't ask who. She still had the postcards, even though no new ones came. They had stopped a long time ago, and with them her dreams of going anywhere. Her home was here.

'I'm going to find my friends,' Yael said.

'Don't do anything I wouldn't do!' Yehezkel said and leered, then stopped when Ruth shot him a glance. Ophek vanished to the backstage and Yael went to stand by the cut-outs of Esther and Achashverosh.

She saw Gideon just then, standing with his friends near the kitchen entrance, and she almost ran to him but then stopped and hovered nonchalantly and waited for him to notice her.

Which he did, and quickly enough. He came over and said, 'Wow, you're like a real princess.'

She looked at his shabby jacket and shirt, and the budding moustache he couldn't quite grow yet.

'What are you supposed to be?' she said.

'I'm Bill Goodrich!' he said. 'You know, from *The Vultures*?'

She hated that movie.

'Well, you look very handsome,' Yael said.

'Really? You think so?'

Gideon was a sweet guy, so eager to please. Gentle, too. He never pushed her to go all the way. He was happy to wait. He would always wait for her. Now he beamed, as eager as a puppy.

'Want to dance?' he said.

'It isn't dancing yet,' Yael said.

'Well, when it is.'

Gideon nodded to the tables.

'You want some punch?' he said.

'We're not supposed to…' Yael said, and he grinned.

'No one'll notice,' he said.

She watched him go. He was right. No one was supervising. He poured them both drinks into dining room glasses and brought them over. She took the glass. She took a sip. It was sweet and fruity but there was something under it… She coughed.

'Take it easy!' Gideon said, laughing.

Yael took another, more careful sip. It went down easy.

'What do they *put* in it?' she said.

'Fruit juice syrup and vodka and cherry liquor,' Gideon said. 'I saw Israel mixing it earlier. He always makes the punch.'

'It's good,' Yael said. 'I think.' Her head swam funnily. She took another sip.

'Just drink it slow,' Gideon said. 'Hey, they're about to start the programme.'

He took her hand. It was nice to have a boy hold her hand in public. They were going steady, as they said. She followed him to the back of the dining room. The lights came on the stage. First the kibbutz secretary, saying, 'Comrades... comrades! Your attention please—'

He was pelted with eggs and fled the stage. Someone came on to mop. Then the children from third grade recreated the meeting between Esther and Achashverosh with some of the finest acting Yael had ever seen. She giggled. Her glass was empty.

'Gidi, can you get me another one,' she said.

'Shh,' he said. 'Later. It's too early.'

'But I like it.'

The kids got off. Ophek got on.

'Ladies and gentlemen, chaverot and chaverim!' he said. 'Prepare to be dazzled!' He raised his arms dramatically and a white dove flew out. Everyone clapped. Yael breathed a sigh of relief. Ophek had killed more birds than any fifteen-year-old ever should. The rest of the magic show went on. Ophek took a bow to enthusiastic applause and flashed his smile to the audience, then vanished in a puff of smoke. She had to give it to him, he was getting better. She wondered where he got the smoke bomb.

Then the costume competition. Moses and Moshe Dayan had a fight for second place and Moses lost his beard and Dayan the eye patch.

'And the winner is...!' the kibbutz secretary said, and Yael groaned.

She stared in hatred at the stage as Galya came on to collect her

prize. She was older and prettier, dressed as an El Al stewardess
in a blue and white outfit she first wore three years earlier and
was much too short for her now. No one seemed to mind. The
assembled men and boys whistled appreciatively. Galya smiled
and took a bow, those long brown legs, those perfect tits, that
smile that lit the darkened dining room like sunshine.

No wonder Yoram fell for her.

Yael just wished Yoram was there.

After the costume contest was finally over a group of singers
came on in white shirts and sang 'Rose of Ya'akov', which Yafa
Yarkoni had recorded only a couple of years earlier. The happy beat
got the mood going. Yael *definitely* wanted another glass of punch.
Gideon lit a cigarette and puffed on it inexpertly. The singers
finished to scattered applause and Funny Itzik went on stage and
started telling jokes everyone had already heard. By then nobody
cared. He got a roaring applause and the kibbutz secretary came
on and announced that this was the end of the artistic portion of
the evening.

The applause he got *this* time nearly brought the roof down.
The metaplot began to usher the smaller kids out of the dining
room and to bed. The lights dimmed further and this time Gideon
did make a dash for the punch and he came back with two refilled
glasses and it really *was* smooth going down. Then the record
player hooked up to the speakers Israel got in the flea market in
Jaffa came alive, and the Cockerels sang 'Everything's Gold' and
then 'When You Say No (What Do You Really Mean?)' and 'Just
Like That', and everyone started shrieking 'Yabayeh! Yabayeh!'
like lunatics. The tables were pushed further and people started
to dance, a Stalin with Golda, Haman with Esther, Esther with
Esther, policemen with nurses, cowboys with Indians. Yael felt the
music move her as of its own accord. Her limbs felt loose and light.
Old and young danced together and each one danced alone. When
Gideon came back with another drink she took it from him and
downed it in one. The warmth spread through her. She pushed

him against the wall and pressed her lips to his, her tongue sliding into his mouth, tasting cigarette smoke and punch. Her body pressed against his, she felt his hardness, pressed herself against it, moaned into his ear.

'Yael,' he said, so softly, 'oh, Yael—'

Couples were pairing up all around them. It was Purim, the one night of the year when there weren't any rules. She took his hand and led him to the walk-in cold room in the back. Their breath steamed in the cold air. She ran her hands through his hair, fumbled under his shorts and took hold of his penis. She had never done that before.

'Oh, Yael!'

She'd never seen him like this, not even when they were dry humping. His penis was so hard and yet warm and it felt weird and his eyes were lost in something she couldn't see. Then he seemed to stutter, and his penis *moved* in her hand and shot out white sticky stuff all over her hand.

She felt him deflate. He looked mortified.

'I'm so sorry,' he said, 'I wasn't ready...'

'It's all right,' Yael said. She wiped her hand on his ratty jacket. She smiled.

'It was nice,' she said. She kissed him, and he kissed her back, but he was different now, not filled anymore with that hot need she still felt.

'I'm going to dance,' she said. She left Gideon looking both embarrassed and pleased as he adjusted his trousers in the cold storage room. Outside felt hot, humid, bodies pressed together, the music changed to some American song and couples slow-danced close together. Yael snatched a fresh glass of punch and went outside, where the air cooled her feverish skin. Motti from the year above her was throwing up all over the grass. Smaller kids, having snuck back out after bedtime, stood around him in a half-circle and watched curiously.

'Motti did a puke!' they chanted. 'Motti did a puke!'

Motti groaned and lay on the grass. Yael thought he looked peaceful, lying there. The world spun pleasantly. She laughed.

'Yael?'

She turned and her heart lifted and she ran to him.

'Yoram!' she said. He laughed and lifted her up. He smelled musky, of sweat and gunmetal oil and powder. He was in uniform, his gun in a strap over his shoulder.

'I missed you!' Yael said. 'What are you doing here?'

'Like I wouldn't come to Purim?' he said. His cheek was rough with the start of a beard but she liked it. He smelled nothing like Gideon – like a man, not a boy. 'Besides, Galya said she had something to tell me.'

Galya.

Yael's heart dropped.

'What?' Yoram said. He let her go. 'Oh, come on, Yael.'

'I'm glad you're back,' she said. 'Is it true you're going to be a pilot?'

'I'm trying to be!' he said. He looked boyishly excited. He loved his toy planes as a boy. Israel made them in the carpentry shop. He made them for all the children to use, but everyone knew they were Yoram's. Israel was Yoram's dad, even if Yoram didn't look anything like him.

'I almost got my ten,' Yoram said.

'Ten what?' Yael said.

'Ten solo flights!' he said. 'It's a… Well, it's sort of a big deal.'

'*You're* a big deal,' Yael said. The world swam. Yoram smiled.

'I'll see you in a bit,' he said. 'I'm just going to go find Galya.'

She watched him go inside, lugging that army-issue gun on his back. He must have come straight from the gate, not even got changed. A soldier could not leave his gun unattended. She wanted something. She didn't know what she wanted. She went back inside. Ruth and Israel were dancing. She had never seen Ruth dance before. But this was Purim, and on Purim the rules were different. On Purim, there were no rules.

'What did you think of my show!' Ophek said, materialising beside her. He beamed. 'Good, right?'

'You put the dove back?' Yael said.

'Sure I did.'

'It was good, Ophek. You're getting good.'

'Hey, Yael, are you drunk?'

She laughed. The room swam.

'Why?' she said. 'Do I look drunk?'

'You're kind of swaying,' Ophek said. 'Hey, Yael, what is it like?'

'It's nice,' she said. 'You didn't try the punch?'

'I've got to stay sharp,' Ophek said. 'A magician is always prepared.'

'Show me a trick, then,' Yael said. Ophek pulled the blue silk handkerchief from his jacket pocket.

'As you can see,' he said, 'there is nothing up my sleeve—'

Yael groaned.

'Not again,' she said. 'You need some new material.'

'I want Israel to build me a saw-the-lady-in-half,' Ophek said. 'But he won't do it.'

'I want another glass of punch,' Yael said.

'I got something better,' Ophek said. He waved the handkerchief over his open palm; when he removed it there was a rolled-up cigarette in his hand.

'What's the point of that?' Yael said.

Ophek whispered, 'It's hash.'

'What?'

'Hashish! You want to try it?'

'Where did you get that, Ophek!' Yael said, shocked.

'I found it in someone's room.'

'You've *got* to stop stealing, Ophek!' she said.

'But I'm good at it, Yael.'

She shook her head and the world tilted.

'Come on!'

They ran, past Micha and Pnina making out against a pine,

past Dubi from the avocados throwing up against a rose bush, to the new bomb shelter on the southside lawn of the dining room. Behind it, invisible to anyone watching, they sat down with their backs to the wall.

'So? Do we do it?'

'Let's do it,' Ophek said.

Purim. Until-they-knew-not. Ophek lit the cigarette with a fancy lighter. The smell was strange, earthy. Ophek took a drag and almost immediately coughed. Yael burst out laughing. Ophek was belching smoke.

'What!' Ophek said. 'Leave me alone. You try it.'

'Alright.' She took it from him. She felt so grown up. She took a drag. She had smoked cigarettes before. But this came *deep*. She held her breath. Felt the smoke reach into her lungs and *open*. Her mind changed, somehow. Became clearer, calmer. She exhaled and felt the world itself being exhaled. The grass shimmered in the starlight. She took another drag and held it longer in her lungs this time.

'...What?'

'I said, are you just going to hold it? It's gone out.'

'Oh. Here.' She passed it to him. It seemed to be an effort. Ophek re-lit it. When he smoked this time he didn't cough.

'...Whoa,' he said.

'Where did you get the lighter?' Yael said.

'I found it.'

'You've got to stop finding things.'

'But I'm good at it.'

He passed her the cigarette. She smoked. The world wavered, then steadied. The hill sloped down to the brook.

'Yael?'

'Yeah?'

'What do you...?'

'What?'

'What?'

'You said what do you...?'

'I don't know.'

'What?'

'I forgot,' Ophek said.

'Forgot what?' Yael said.

'I don't remember.'

The cigarette was finished. She threw it on the grass. The dew lay on the grass. The night was dark. The stars were bright. Purim, 1964. She felt her whole life laid ahead of her. The future opened, full of twisting paths. She staggered to her feet. Ophek sat slumped against the wall. He snored softly. She blew him a kiss, adjusted the crown on her head and staggered back towards the dining room.

She grabbed a glass of punch off a table and drank it. It was warm and cloying. She drank some more. She looked at the bodies around her. Nurses and school teachers, laundresses and kitchen workers. She could be anything, she thought. She staggered into a cowboy who twirled her round then passed her to an Arab sheikh who sent her flying towards a group of teenage soldiers. She felt their hungry eyes on her and swivelled to avoid them and their groping hands. The music came to a screeching halt and someone shouted, 'Hey!' and then the needle whispered on the new record and the Beatles erupted through the speakers with 'I Want to Hold Your Hand'.

The dancers went into a frenzy, the forbidden music of this English band bounced off the dining room walls and took Yael with it and spun her round and round and round until-she-knew-not and was lost in the harmonies. Moshe Dayan grabbed her ass and a Stalin made a lunge for her boobs and they brought her out of her trance and she drifted like a mote of dust along the dance floor which she would have to clean tomorrow morning – she was on dining room duties all week.

She sought refuge at last in the cold storage room. The air felt freezing on her feverish skin. As her eyes grew accustomed to the darkness she became aware of another figure standing there against the far wall with the crates of tins, its back to her. She started and the figure turned.

'Yael?'

Yoram, still in his uniform, and she went to him, put her hands on his face as if to make sure it really *was* him and not some fevered dream she had—

'What are you doing here?' she said.

'I was thinking.'

'You don't want to do that,' Yael said, and then she was somehow pressed closer against him, needing his warmth, and her own breath came ragged and excited at his closeness.

'Yael, no—'

But she felt him respond and she reached down and held him and he was hers, for just that moment, and then they didn't speak again. He undressed her hurriedly, she pulled down his pants, felt his hands on her bare skin and as he lifted her up she felt so safe.

She cried when he entered her and he stroked her face and kissed her and she moaned into his kiss as he began to thrust against her, *with* her, mute, his face as known to her as her own, and she was lost in his eyes as a tide came over her and a wave lifted her up and threw her against some impossible, distant shore.

They didn't speak. Yoram pulled his trousers up and buckled his army belt. Yael put on her underwear. She touched her head and realised she had lost her crown somewhere; but it didn't matter. She smoothed down her dress. There was a cold wetness on her thighs.

'What did Galya want to tell you, anyway?' she said.

Yoram had his hand on the lever for the cold room door. He didn't look back at her.

He said, 'She's pregnant.'

PART NINE

SCHLAFSTUNDE

Yael

Kibbutz Trashim, 1965

40

THE BABIES WERE LINED UP ON THE LOW SHELF, LYING ON
their backs in identical, small transparent boxes. They were all
asleep. They had just been fed. The new mothers, dazed themselves
with the feeding and the heat, hovered. Yael pulled down her
shirt. Ruth always said babies deserved their mother's milk, not
powdered, none of that weak stuff city kids got. Only natural milk
was good enough for kibbutz babies.

'Look at the little darling,' Galya said. She stood over her baby.
A handwritten note attached to the box said *Lior*. 'Doesn't he look
just like his daddy?'

All the other mums murmured in agreement. Yael looked at
her own child. Esther lay in the box, as cute as anything. She loved
her so much. Everyone said how much she looked just like Gideon.

'Yael, are you coming to Ruth's room later?' Galya said.

'Sure,' Yael said.

'I'll see you there, then.'

She drifted outside to light a cigarette. Yael just wanted to
stay in the baby room with her baby. But the metapelet came
and scowled at the mothers who were tarrying behind, so she left
Esther and went out.

It was afternoon time, *schlafstunde*, that time between two and
four when everyone slept. The kibbutz was so still.

'Can I bum one?' she said to Galya.

'Sure.'

Galya passed Yael a cigarette and lit it up for her with a match.

Yael took a grateful drag. It was hard work being a mum. Not something she'd planned on, but then like they said, a child was a blessing. She had expected to be tired and she was, but it was a different, good sort of tired, like after a long day picking apples.

The birth was long – the ride from the kibbutz, Ruth driving like the wind to the hospital in Afula, the dark straight road from Armageddon to the hospital, the stars above, the businesslike nurses and the doctor with a breath of smoke, he had cold hands. Then the contractions, the pain, like a wave that tossed and threw her in a tide, and then the baby.

'Esther,' she whispered.

Galya turned her head and smiled.

'It's so hard to believe sometimes that they're here,' she said.

But Esther was a gift: that was the only way Yael could describe her. From the moment they cut her umbilical cord and placed her on Yael's chest, to hold, like a present wrapped for months and finally opened. That smell of babies, the smell of fresh life. The way her tiny skull pulsated when she touched the top of her head, that soft spot there. The first time the baby drew breath, the first time she fed, the first time she pooped, expelling the last of the food that she got in the womb.

Yael realised with some surprise that she was *happy*.

'What are you going to do next year?' Galya said. 'Are you going to join the army?'

'Of course,' Yael said, surprised.

'I deferred for a year, with the pregnancy and all,' Galya said. 'But I'm going to do teacher soldier training. It's a good path, you know. You get to work with kids and help them. You should think about trying it.'

'Maybe I will,' Yael said. She put out the cigarette. 'I've got to go to work,' she said.

'See you at Ruth's later, then.'

'See you, Galya. If not there then for feeding time.'

Yael floated down the kibbutz side roads. She felt as light as air and filled with radiance. Galya was right, she thought. She could do a soldier teacher course, and this might come in handy down the line when she finished her service. The kibbutz always needed teachers and people to look after the children. Gideon wanted to get married and then they'd get their own room, really a little house all of their own. She could have a kid with Gideon. Give Esther a little brother or a sister in a few years' time. It was so quiet walking down the little roads. The lawn was coming along nicely. The new sprinklers kept it green. It was nothing like it used to be before. There were nice houses and they kept building more. All the new couples and all the new babies. This new generation. Her generation.

She came to the library and unlocked the door. It was cool and dark inside. She flicked on the light. The head librarian, Tzippi, was away that week, so it was just Yael. She tidied the returned books and went over the borrowing slips. She noted to leave Ruth a reminder notice in her mailbox in the dining room – she was overdue on a book.

Ruth drove her to the hospital, she was always the driver. She was there when Esther was born. Her face had softened then, there was a genuine love in the way she held Yael's hand in that moment. Or maybe Yael imagined it. Ruth went away then and Yael was left alone with her daughter. That was all she had. That was all she needed.

She pulled up the blinds and opened the door, where three children were already queuing outside, books in hand. They came in and their quiet chatter filled the dusty air, and Yael lost herself in stamping the returned books and filling in the catalogue and checking the listings of new books available to order.

The kids were chattering excitedly about the latest volume of *The Young Detectives*, whose latest adventures involved the mystery of the diamond of the Queen of Sheba and the mystery of the atom bomb, respectively. The atom bomb was much in the news just then, and only recently she'd heard that Ruth's brother,

Yehoyakim, had been arrested by the internal security services; though no one knew why, there were dark mutterings about nuclear secrets and Soviet spies, and everyone knew Israel had been trying to build atom bombs on a secret base in the desert, which sounded as fantastical as any children's book.

Yael stamped the books for the kids. For a moment she admired the childish illustrations of the gang, by M. Aryeh, who illustrated so many of the juvenile books they had in the library. When the kids left a couple of guys from the factory came in and got a stack of *Ringo* westerns and *Tarzan* adventures. The factory was new, they'd just started to build it on the far side of the kibbutz, uphill from the stables. Gideon worked shifts in the factory. But he was going to the army soon. So would she, she decided. It was unthinkable not to serve. She would do it not for herself but for her newly born daughter. To protect her and keep her safe.

Yoram came in. He stood in the doorway, framed in light.

'Hey,' he said.

'Hey.'

'How's the baby?'

Yael smiled. 'She's good. I'll bring her to Ruth's later.'

'Galya told me.'

It was easy between them. Nothing needed to be said.

What difference did it make anyway?

The children were the kibbutz's children. They were daughters and sons of the kibbutz.

'I heard you got your wings,' Yael said.

He smiled again. Why did he smile so goddamned *easily*?

'I want to fly a Mirage,' he said. 'Right now they just have me on the Pipers.'

'Is it good?' Yael said.

'What?'

'This Mirage?'

'It's the best, Yael! It's ultrasonic.'

'Then I'm sure you'll get to fly it,' Yael said.

'Got anything good to read?' Yoram said. 'They have me cramming so many textbooks right now, I need something easy.'

'There's a new *Young Detectives*,' Yael said, and Yoram laughed.

'I'm a little old for that now,' he said.

'Then have a look.'

She watched him browse. He eventually picked up a murder mystery, one of the new pocket books that small publishers in Tel Aviv were putting out. Tzippi frowned on keeping cheap literature in the library, but do what she could to get people to read Shamir or Yizhar, inevitably people came to ask for the latest romance or a good detective story. Yael stamped the book and Yoram left without looking back and time passed and she closed the library.

The day stretched out before her, slow and filled with small happinesses. She went back to the baby room and picked up Esther and held her and marvelled again at how small and how soft she was. The baby touched Yael's face with her podgy fingers. She fed her and then took her to Ruth's, only for a little while, to say hello. Ophek was there, entertaining everyone with his latest tricks, and Israel cooked coffee on the stove. Then Yael went to her room, where Gideon waited. They put the baby in her cot and made love on the single bed, then lay there as the late afternoon sun faded towards evening.

They ate together in the dining room. The comforting chatter of the members swapping tales of their day, the easy camaraderie. Baby Esther looked at everything with bright, interested eyes. After supper Yael kissed Gideon, whose turn it was for night guard duty on the gate, and she and Galya went back to the baby room, where they put Esther and Lior to sleep together.

Outside, Galya lit a cigarette and Yael said, 'Can I bum one?'

'Sure.'

Their little ritual. The streetlights came on. The stars were faint in the sky. The air was still and the jasmine blossomed, filling the world with a sweet, peaceful scent.

Yael said good night and went back to her room and lay in bed. She missed her baby, but her baby was safe.

She wrapped her hands around a pillow instead and turned to face the wall and closed her eyes.

She thought, It had been a good day.

PART TEN

EILAT

Yael

Eilat, 1967

41

It was hot. It was always hot. She thought of that day a couple of years back when she was still just seventeen and Esther was just a baby. It seemed so long ago now. It was hard to think in Eilat. It was always so hot.

The heat lay like dust over the dry hot houses where sluggish fans pushed air around like cops with a guilty suspect. It lay over the dry and dusty streets of the small and dusty town that lay on the shore of the most beautiful sea Yael had ever seen. When the sun was high its light reflected off the distant red mountains and when it fell the colour of the mountains changed like a spell. When Yael swam in the sea small colourful fish swam beside her and corals fanned open like flowers just below. When she got out of the water her feet left marks in sand that often had no other marks in it. She wished she could show it to Esther, but Esther was back in Trashim. She would see her soon. She was going to drive back across the desert with Israel and Ophek.

Her heart lifted in excitement at the thought of seeing her daughter again. Esther, so confident on her feet now, talking, laughing. She was a fat, happy little thing, three years old and waddling confidently across the kibbutz pavements. God, how much Yael loved her.

It was so very very hot. She didn't think she'd ever get used to this desert heat. She took a salt pill and swallowed it with her glass of cool soda from the little kiosk that perched on this side of the beach. You had to take the salt pills or your teeth would become loose.

Flags drooped in the still air. Blue and white, blue and white. Men who were former convicts and now wore Sanitation Department jackets swept up the sand from last night's victory party: bottles of beer and vodka, condoms and cigarette butts, somebody's bra. Eilat was built by convicts. It was go south or go back to jail, so most of them, given the choice, went south.

It wasn't such a bad place, really. Just a gaggle of low-roof houses and a dusty airport and a handful of half-built hotels. That, and the harbour.

It was all going to change, anyway, now that they'd won the war.

She had been so afraid of the coming war. Everyone was. The Arab states were going to invade – Egypt, Syria, Lebanon. Instead, when the war came, it ended in six days and now Israel was double the size it was before, what with all the seized new land.

All of the west bank of the Jordan, East Jerusalem and Gaza, the Golan Heights and the entirety of the Sinai Peninsula up to the Suez Canal. She heard Yoram was one of the pilots who bombed the Egyptian planes on the ground. The entire Egyptian Air Force wiped out in an afternoon. She had been so afraid before the war, everyone was.

Now it was just one long victory party, night after night.

She drank her soda. Israel and Ophek came trudging along the beach. She watched them inch their way like ants across the sand. When they came to her they stopped. Israel mopped sweat from his brow.

'It's hot,' he said.

Ophek hopped from foot to foot. He was tanned and tall and beaming with pleasure. Yael couldn't get over how big he was. He'd just shot up like a young tree. All the girls loved Ophek. His hair was down to his shoulders. He was growing it like a hippie.

'I love it here!' he said.

Yael looked at him with affection. She couldn't wait to go back with them to Trashim. She missed Esther. But she loved what she was doing here, serving, a teacher soldier, working with the kids. Even in this heat, even with the way Eilat was, not quite a city, not even a real town but like some sort of lonely outpost. Soldiers, convicts, a handful of bars where if you stayed up late enough there was usually a fight. Then there were the hippies who started to come after the war and slept on the beach and bought hash from the Bedouins.

'I want to go to Sinai,' Ophek said.

The swift victory in the war had taken everyone by surprise. Before, Eilat was a sole spear point to the Red Sea, nestled uneasily between Jordan and Egypt on both sides. Now, the new Israel extended for miles and miles of desert and prime coast all but unexplored.

Yael could see the spark in Ophek's eyes. The dream of virgin beaches, hidden coves, of Bedouins on their camels riding in the secret pathways of the mountains of Sinai. God handed Moses the Ten Commandments there.

These were not enemy territories occupied – these were the old lands of Israel *regained*. Or that's what everyone said. You could drive down to the Dead Sea, could visit at last the ancient towns of Jericho and Bethlehem and Hebron. The Western Wall and Temple Mount, Joseph's Tomb and Jacob's Well. Ancient names she only knew from books, suddenly right there. She took another sip of her soda but it had already gone flat and sickly-warm. She tossed it on the sand. The cleaners swept it up with sullen indifference.

'It's hot,' Israel said, and mopped his brow.

'I wish I got to fight in the war,' Ophek said. 'It was over so quickly.'

Yael smiled. 'You're joining up when, in two or three months?'

'Yeah.'

'You'll get your chance.'

'To fight who?' Ophek demanded. 'We *won*, Yael. We got all...' His hand swept the sea, the mountains, the desert in the distance, 'This.'

'Can we find a coffee and some shade?' Israel said. 'Is there anywhere open?'

'There's a bar not too far from here,' Yael said.

They walked slowly across the dusty road. Away from the beach the town hovered, dead in the heat of the day. It was the sort of town you could cross in twenty minutes, population six thousand and change. A few ships hovered in the harbour, some navy, the others Zim ships laden with cargo containers. Fishermen's boats were moored to the pier or beached on the sand. You could rent a glass-bottom boat and take a pleasure cruise and look down at the fish. Yael had done that when she first got to Eilat.

Now she just had her routine, teaching during the day, a swim afterwards in the lagoon to wash off the day. She roomed with two other girls, and some nights she joined them going out to the Queen of Sheba hotel bar or to the nightclub at the Red Rock that was popular with weekenders from Tel Aviv, who came on the Thursday flight and went back Sunday. She missed Gideon, but everything was so far away from Eilat and when she got lonely or restless it was easy to find someone to spend the night with. Eilat wasn't the sort of place where you felt guilty about things. Everything was in the present, and all there really was to life was the heat of the sun on your bare skin, the whisper of cool water when you swam in the sea, the soft touch of a breeze in the early evening.

And there were stars, so many stars overhead, reflected in the sea at night; you could drown in their ancient light. There was no light like in the desert.

The bar was dark and a fan whizzed on the countertop when they stepped inside. The proprietor came out of the back room. He was an old German Jew. He spoke Hebrew with the broken cadences of a man who'd never found comfort in this new adopted land. He had a number tattooed on his arm that he hid with a long-sleeved shirt but that she saw, once, when he had rolled up his sleeves.

'Hello, Jacob,' she said.

'Yael,' he said, without much interest. He mopped his brow with a handkerchief.

'It's hot,' he said.

'It's hot,' Israel agreed. 'Do you have coffee?'

'I have coffee,' Jacob said. 'In Eilat you have to have coffee. You want coffee?'

'Please,' Israel said. 'And maybe something to eat?'

'I can do you an egg sandwich,' Jacob said.

'I'll have a soda,' Ophek said. He looked bored now. He'd been out every night since he and Israel got to Eilat. There were Scandinavian girls on the beach, sunbathing topless, with no care in the world. Yael envied them. Long white bodies turning brown in the sun, and Ophek couldn't get enough of them any more than they could get enough of him. To the Swedish and Danish girls he was something exotic, charming: this sabra with his lithe brown body and innocent eyes. Yael warned him not to thieve, not here. There were too many ex-cons in Eilat and she didn't want Ophek beat up over some worthless junk.

'I was here in '49,' Israel said unexpectedly. He wasn't a man who talked much, usually.

'Yeah?' Jacob said. He didn't sound interested. 'Anything here back then other than sand?'

'Nothing much,' Israel said. 'A small Arab village and an old British police station. We stuck a hand-drawn flag on the station building and told the locals to leave and that was that. That's how we won the Red Sea.'

'And what a victory that was,' Jacob said. 'Here's your egg sandwich.' He brought it over, along with three cups of coffee.

'I asked for a soda,' Ophek said.

'Coffee's better for you,' Jacob said.

Yael didn't complain. It didn't do any good in Eilat. She sipped the coffee. It was strong and bitter. She thought about seeing Esther again soon.

'When do we start tomorrow?' she said.

'Early,' Israel said. 'Before it's too hot. It's a long way back.'

'But I wanted to go out,' Ophek said.

'You can sleep in the back of the jeep,' Israel said.

They drank their coffee. Israel paid. He counted out the coins carefully and left them on the Formica top.

'No tip?' Jacob said.

They walked back to the room Israel had rented. It was in a row of houses on the edge of town. Ten pounds a night but it was clean. And ten pounds was still a lot of money for a kibbutznik.

There were few people out. A police jeep cruised past and left in a cloud of dust. The late afternoon plane flew overhead. A dog barked somewhere in the distance. Yael could see the flat-roofed houses of Aqaba beyond the invisible border line that was all that separated Israel from the Kingdom of Jordan. The mountains in the distance changed their colour, became dull copper. The first of the stars was out in the sky.

Three men appeared ahead of them. They moved slowly but with purpose.

'That's him,' one of them said. He pointed at Ophek.

The men stopped. They stood and waited. Israel, Yael and Ophek stopped too. They stood facing the men, a track of dusty street between them.

'You know these people?' Israel said.

'I don't recall,' Ophek said.

'He stole my watch,' the man who pointed said. He didn't sound angry. Yael bit her lip. She'd *told* Ophek not to thieve. But he never listened.

'Do you have this man's watch, Ophek?' Israel said. He didn't sound angry either. Everyone was being so reasonable. But the men were still blocking their way.

'What watch?' Ophek said.

'He stole my watch,' the man said again. His two friends didn't say anything. The dog barked again somewhere in the distance.

'He says he doesn't have it,' Israel said.

The man spat on the dusty ground. He looked at Israel. He didn't say anything.

Israel's hand dropped to his side. The man saw the pistol hanging there in its holster. He licked his lips.

'Do we have a problem here?' Israel said.

The men looked at each other. They seemed to confer silently.

'You should leave Eilat,' the man on the right said finally. He turned away and the other two followed him.

Israel didn't move. They watched the men walk away until the dust swallowed them.

'I *told* you not to, I *told* you!' Yael said.

Ophek looked sheepish.

Israel said, 'We'll leave before dawn.'

42

THEY LEFT BEFORE DAWN. THE NIGHT WAS TAR-BLACK AND GULLS cried far in the distance. The jeep shook and jerked on bad suspension. In moments they were past the houses and then the airport, and the sea was left behind them. Then there was only the desert.

Yael had slept poorly. She packed her kitbag and a present for Esther from Eilat, a seashell she found on the beach. If you put it to your ear you could hear the sea. She couldn't wait to give it to her to put in the old tea box. The night was hot and she tossed and turned. When she heard the jeep arrive at last she ran straight out. Ophek lay asleep in the back. Yael rode shotgun. The jeep shuddered and jerked.

They came to the Timna mines where the machines were silent under the sandstone cliffs. The desert road stretched out before them, heading north. There were no settlements other than, once, an isolated kibbutz far in the distance.

Israel drove fast, hands on the wheel, Ophek snoring in the back. The stars shone overhead and the air was mercifully cool. A great silence spread out in all directions and Yael took a deep breath and felt herself relax for the first time since she'd come to Eilat. A bridge ahead, over a dry wadi.

A goat stepped into the middle of the road.

It came out of nowhere. Yael stared, not quite comprehending. The goat's eyes were caught in the lights of the car. The jeep screeched as Israel hit the brakes, the goat stood frozen, the jeep sped on, the brakes unheeding of their urgent need—

The impact was like the sudden break of glass at a wedding. Yael felt herself *lifted* into the air, for a moment she imagined she was flying.

Then a tonne of jeep came down on her.

She couldn't breathe. The pain was everywhere, like a spider web of cracks through broken glass. She opened her eyes. She tried to move but couldn't. The stars above, the road invisible. She was down in the wadi. The broken jeep pressed her down. She screamed.

She couldn't. The air was crushed out of her. She moved her eyes. Saw Israel dangling through the broken windshield, his face a lifeless clown mask of chalk-white skin and blood. She screamed again. Nothing came out but pain. It took her and tossed her here and there and smashed her down on the ground again.

She wasn't going to make it.

The certainty suffused her with a sudden clarity. She saw the night and heard the silence. There would be no help, not now, not in time.

The pain cut through her and the stars came down and burned holes in her body. She whimpered. A tiny bit of air escaped and with it blood.

'Yael? Yael!'

She heard movement. She couldn't move. Only her eyes. She saw a shadow rise above her. He strained against the jeep, trying to move it off her. She could have laughed.

Ophek, the magician. Entirely unharmed.

He heaved and metal groaned and Yael could have screamed forever, into the dark void that rose before her eyes, and all the bones and all the nerves throughout her body shrieked with the agony. She tried to think of Esther then, but it was hard, it hurt too much, and she shied away. She looked at Israel, upside down.

Saw the gun still on his belt.

She tried to speak.

'What? Yael, I'll get you out, I promise, I…'

She realised Ophek was crying.

She didn't have *time* to comfort another crying boy. She blinked desperately. He came closer. She saw his face, dusty, innocent. She moved her eyes, hoping for him to follow.

'What?' He looked at last. Looked back uncomprehending. It was like he didn't even *see* Israel hanging there above them. Didn't, couldn't. She blinked helplessly. Stared *up*, at Israel, at the gun.

'Yael, no.' His voice filled with horror. She had no pity for him. She had nothing left but this, the overwhelming desire to be rid of the pain. No sound in the desert beyond. No cars, no ambulance, no help. There was nothing, there never was anything but this moment, the darkness and the cold indifferent stars above.

'I can't,' Ophek said. He spoke so softly she could barely hear him. She closed her eyes, defeated. It was too hard. The pain washed through her in endless waves. Please, Ophek, she thought.

She heard something. Heard a holster popping open, something heavy slipping out.

She opened her eyes.

Ophek stood above her. He was crying. He should learn not to cry so much, she thought. Boys shouldn't cry. He held Israel's gun in both hands, aimed it at her.

You need to take the safety catch off, she thought.

She looked into his eyes, willing him to do it. She couldn't take it anymore. This was worse than giving birth to Esther, worse than anything, and there was no one there to fix her, no one there to make the pain go away before the end.

No one but Ophek.

Do it, she thought. Do it. She closed her eyes.

She heard the safety catch click.

She waited, wondering if she would hear the final sound when the gun went o—

PART ELEVEN

YOM KIPPUR

Lior

Kibbutz Trashim, 1973

43

'WE REGRET TO INFORM YOU...'

The voice crackled on the telephone in the dining room foyer. Lior could hear it, standing beside Ruth. She pushed him away.

'What is it?' Esther said. Esther watched Ruth on the telephone. Lior watched Ruth on the telephone. He saw how white her fingers were where she clutched the hard plastic receiver.

'It's my dad,' he said. 'I think he's dead.'

Esther bit her bottom lip, hard. Lior hated when she did that. Esther drew blood. She licked it off.

'My mum's dead,' she said.

'I know.'

'But your dad's a pilot, Lior.'

'So?'

'So he's, like...' She waved her hand. 'A hero.'

Lior watched Ruth. Ruth put down the receiver. She stared at the wall. Lior was scared. He didn't want to approach her. When Ruth turned to the children her face had that hard expression on it he didn't like. She took three steps towards them and stopped.

'Yoram was shot down over the Hermon,' she said abruptly. 'Your father is dead.'

Lior wasn't sure who of them she was addressing at first, him or Esther.

'But he could parachute,' he said.

'He didn't have time to parachute.'

'How do you know he's dead?'

'They told me. He was hit by Syrian artillery over the Hermon. The plane went down in fl— There was a crash.'

'Maybe he survived,' Lior said. 'Maybe he's just a prisoner now. In Syria.'

They were at war with Syria and he knew the Syrians were taking prisoners. Maybe Yoram was in prison right now. Being taken care of. They'd have to, he thought. There was a Geneva Convention. They learned about it and everything.

All the men were gone from the kibbutz. Only the very old, the very young and the women stayed. It was a weird time.

'He's dead,' Ruth said. She knelt down and hugged him. He felt how strong she was. She held him so tight it hurt.

'I'm sorry,' Lior said. He didn't know what he was apologising for. He had to be a man. He had to be strong. Yoram lifting him up and throwing him in the air, laughing. Yoram turning steaks on the grill on Independence Day, letting him have a slice of meat thick with blood when no one was looking. Yoram taking him for a ride on the tractor through the fields, letting him hold the steering wheel.

Lior started to cry.

'No,' Ruth said. 'Don't you cry.'

'I'm sorry,' Lior said again.

'And never apologise,' Ruth said. 'Shit. I have to go tell Galya.' She let go of him.

'You will be all right?' she said. She took his chin in her hand, turned his face, wiped his tears off with her wrist. 'Go play with Esther until it's dinner time.'

She walked away, not looking back. He saw how straight her shoulders were, like she was holding herself up with an effort. He wanted to be more like his grandmother. Strong like her.

'How do you feel?' Esther said.

'I don't know,' Lior said. 'It doesn't...' He shrugged.

'Feel real?'

Her eyes were dry. She reached and touched the side of his eye, where it was still wet.

'Did you cry?' Lior said. 'When Yael died?'

'I guess so,' Esther said. 'I don't remember. I mean, they're just parents.'

She took his hand.

'Let's just go play,' she said.

They were all listening to the radio. It crackled and echoed through the dining room hall. Galya sat like a rag doll in the hard dining room chair. The nurse had given her something. Lior wanted her to hug him. He pushed himself into her unresponsive arms.

'We're trying to listen!' someone said.

Lior gave up and went to sit with Esther and the other children.

'This is the news from Jerusalem. The battle for the Hermon rages on as Syrian forces move across the Golan Heights, leading to intense fight—'

The announcement crackled, was replaced with the sound of sirens on the radio. A monotonous voice repeated code words: 'Stew Pot. Stew Pot. Stew Pot.' The announcer returned.

'Full mobilisation is in effect. Our forces are tackling the aggressors. All sirens are true sirens. Tank units are moving across the Sinai, encountering heavy Egyptian presence. A UN ceasefire is not in effect. Prime Minister Golda Meir speaks from Jerusalem—'

The radio crackled. The adults leaned forward in their chairs. Someone got up to go to the toilets and left a napkin dispenser on the seat to reserve it. Lior was bored.

It was scary and exciting at first, when the war was announced. All the men got together by the gate, ready to go. They got into cars and drove to war, and the rest waited for a bus to come get them.

Golda came on the radio. She talked slowly, with that accent that wasn't from here and the smoker's voice that was.

'This war was not of our choosing,' she said, 'but we will fight it, and we will be victorious.' She sounded like Ruth, he thought. The sort of grandmother who calmly sent men to die.

He had run to the gate, when he heard the men were leaving. But by the time he got there Yoram was already gone.

Esther took his hand. Her hand was sticky.

'Let's sneak out,' she whispered.

'Yeah,' Danny said, leaning in. He sat on the other side of Lior. 'I'm bored.'

'I want to listen,' Lior said.

'Did they find your daddy?' Danny said.

'Shut up, kids!' someone said. The old man who left the napkin dispenser came back from the toilets and sat down again. Golda spoke some more.

'No,' Lior said. 'Just what was left of the plane.'

'But there has to be a funeral,' Esther said. 'Yael had a funeral. I think it's the first thing I really remember.'

'I don't know,' Lior said.

Maybe Yoram wasn't really dead, he thought. If they hadn't buried him then he couldn't be, could he?

'…Fierce battles on both the Syrian and Egyptian fronts…'

He got up, crouching, and sneaked away. The adults didn't care. Esther and Danny caught up with him in the foyer. They went outside.

'What should we play?' Esther said.

'Let's play soldiers,' Danny said. 'I'll be Israel. You can be Syria.'

'But I don't want to be Syria,' Esther said. 'I'm always Syria.'

'You're a girl,' Danny said. It was compelling logic. Lior had to agree.

So did Esther. Her shoulders drooped.

'*Fine*,' she said. 'But you'll never catch me!'

She ran away, laughing. Lior and Danny went in hot pursuit.

'Pew pew!'

'Pow! Pow!'
'Pew pew pew!'

He lay on his back in his bed, eyes open. He stared at the ceiling. Danny snored in the next bed over. Crickets chirped outside.

He dreamed awake:

Planes flying over a snowy mountain. The sound of artillery, *boom! boom!*

Soldiers swarming onto a crusader fort at the peak. The sound of gunfire. Tracer bullets lighting up the skies. One soldier drops, red blood blooming against white snow. But the darkness swallows him. Another one dies, silently. Airplanes fire on artillery batteries. Mortars fire shells. Fireworks explode in the skies above. The planes roar past. They fly as high as birds.

As close to heaven as you can ever get, Yoram once told him. When you grow up you could be a pilot just like me.

Lior didn't want to be a pilot. He didn't know what he wanted to be. He wanted to lash out and hurt someone. He wanted to inflict pain for the pain he felt and couldn't speak. You had to be a man. Land demands sacrifices. Ruth's voice, Ruth's words. And dead men's pictures on her shelf.

He couldn't sleep.

Galya, sitting alone in her room, just sitting there all day. She didn't even go to work – the one sin on a kibbutz you couldn't get away with. They had the doctor in. He gave her medicine to take. When Lior went to their room she didn't even get up. It was like he wasn't there. Just some ghost.

Well, he didn't need her. He didn't need anyone.

'Lior, are you asleep?' Esther said.

'Yeah.'

'I can't sleep.'

'What's it like, not having a mum?' Lior said.

'I don't know. It doesn't matter, I guess.'

LAVIE TIDHAR

'Do you remember her?'
'A little. She smelled nice.'
He stared at the ceiling.
'Lior?'
'Yeah?'
'Are you asleep yet?'
'Yeah.'
'All right. Good night.'
'Good night.'
He heard her turn, the thin blanket scrunching over the sheet. He stared at the ceiling. The crickets outside. Esther's breathing became even. Danny farted in his sleep. Lior stared at the ceiling.

Esther must be happy there was a war, he thought. The man who sometimes came in the night also went to the war. Maybe he wouldn't come back, Lior thought. After all, people didn't.

He fell asleep cheered by the thought.

'If you watch carefully...' Mishka said. He held a stick in one hand and used it to turn over a rock in the field. 'You will note that – here it is! Quick!'

A small scorpion darted from under the rock but Mishka was quicker. He pinned it with his stick.

'*Leiurus hebraeus*,' Mishka said in satisfaction. 'The Hebrew Deathstalker, children, to give it its scientific name. Commonly known as the yellow scorpion. Observe the colour, children.'

Mishka walked with a limp from the War of Independence. Mishka wasn't going to war again any time soon.

'Danny, the Guide, please,' he said.

The scorpion writhed under Mishka's stick. Danny hurried to open the guide. He had been trusted with the dog-eared volume, Mishka's proud possession. His name was on every line of the borrowing slip taped to the front endpaper.

'Well?' Mishka demanded. The scorpion writhed.

Danny said, 'It's the most dangerous scorpion in Israel, and one of the most poisonous in the world.'

'Correct.'

'Present in all parts other than Mount Carmel and the shore planes,' Danny said.

'Well done,' Mishka said.

'Also common in Jordan, Syria and Lebanon?' Danny said.

'Correct!'

Mishka lifted the stick. The scorpion darted away very fast. The children jumped back.

Mishka waved the stick in the air.

'The Hebrew Deathstalker!' he said. 'Small and dangerous, he only attacks when he feels threatened. Be the scorpion. Have heart. We will win this war like we won all the others. I myself—'

He digressed into his tale about the war in '48. They'd all heard it a hundred times. And they'd all seen scorpions before. They knew not to turn rocks over without being careful.

'...And that's how I got shot in the leg!' Mishka said. 'Now. Let us continue. Perhaps we will see a deer, if we are quiet.'

He led them on, over the hill and to the ruined mill on the wadi. Later, they picked sabras from the cactuses that grew in profusion in the abandoned Arab village.

There was no radio. There was no more talk of the war. Lior didn't have to think about his father. They made a fire and sang some old song about cypress trees.

'Lior?'

'Yeah?'

'Are you asleep?'

'No.'

'Me neither,' Danny said.

'Danny?'

'Yeah?'

It was Esther.

'There's a movie in the dining room tonight,' she said.

'Yeah?'

'We could sneak in.'

'What if we get caught?' Lior said.

'We won't get caught. It will be dark,' Esther said.

'I'm in,' Danny said.

'I'm in too,' Lior said.

They got dressed with the lights off and snuck out. Not that there was anyone to check. The one remaining night watchman didn't come around much. They walked along empty roads and only saw one other person and kept clear. They reached the dining room and dashed through the foyer into the dark inside.

Cigarette smoke rose and eddied lazily through a beam of bright light. It threw moving pictures on a screen made out of a sheet hanging from the wall.

Esther was right. No one saw them. No one paid them the slightest attention. All eyes were on the movie.

They crept along the back wall and found three empty chairs and sat down behind the adults, masked by the dark.

Lior watched. There was a piano player in a smoky bar. He wore a black jacket and a white shirt and a black tie. The movie was in black and white. It had subtitles. It was a real movie, from America or France, one of those places. The man had a sad face. His fingers danced across the piano keys, white and black. A woman came into the bar. She looked at the piano player like she wanted to shoot him. Everyone was silent in the dining room. The cigarette smoke eddied in the beam of the projector's light.

Men with guns came in. They wanted to shoot the piano player. The piano player pulled out a gun. Lior couldn't really follow the story. It didn't matter. He forgot about Yoram, forgot about war: for just a moment he was transported to another world.

★

'Son. Your father served his land with honour.'

The officer's hand was calloused. He shook Lior's hand.

'You should be proud of him.'

'Yes, sir,' Lior said.

The officer saluted. He looked tired. He turned to Galya and Ruth, sitting side by side on the sofa.

'We were able to recover this from the site,' he said. He presented them with a small box. Inside it was Yoram's watch. It was a stainless steel Omega, a pilot's watch. It was dinged and blackened but intact. Galya started to cry. Ruth was mute.

'The remains are only now ready for burial—'

Galya cried out. Lior ran to her. She held him in her arms. He felt her sobbing.

The officer wiped sweat from his forehead.

'I understand he wished to be buried on the kibbutz,' he said. 'Military protocol—'

'It is all arranged,' Ruth said.

'Yes,' the officer said.

'Did we win?' Lior said.

'Win, son?'

'Did we win the war?'

The officer made an attempt at a smile.

'We're getting there,' he said.

'Lior!'

Big hands lifted him up and into the air.

'Uncle Ophek!'

Ophek beamed at Lior. He looked different. He had a thick black beard and his face was browned by the sun. And he was in uniform.

'Didn't have time to shave,' he said, at Lior's look. Lior pulled on Ophek's beard.

'Ow!'

'I thought it was fake!' Lior said.

'It's not a *prop*, kid!'

He put Lior down.

'Where are you stationed?' Lior said. 'Are you in the Golan Heights?'

'Nowhere in particular,' Ophek said. 'I move around.'

'What do you do?' Lior said. He felt suddenly excited. 'Is it something secret?'

Ophek smiled, amused.

'I'm just a driver,' he said.

'Oh.'

'Don't look so disappointed! Hey, I brought you something.'

Ophek did that magician thing he did. One moment his hand was empty. Then he had a small metal object in it.

'What's that?' Lior said. He took it from Ophek and turned it. It was a medal, with Arabic writing and crossed swords over a winged anchor, all between two olive branches. It had a dull rusted spot. Lior rubbed it but it wouldn't go away.

'Is it Syrian?' Lior said.

'It's a general's medal,' Lior said.

'How did you *get* it!' Lior said.

Ophek shrugged.

'Magic,' he said.

He knelt down, put his hands on Lior's shoulders, looked him in the eyes. He was no longer smiling.

'Are you alright, buddy?' he said. His eyes filled with tears.

'Are you?' Lior said.

Then he started crying too.

The coffin was lowered into the ground. The soldiers stood with guns at the ready. They fired the honour salute. The military rabbi read out the prayers. The kibbutzniks stood politely until he finished.

It was when the coffin was lowered that Ruth – Ruth of all people, Ruth who stood there and welcomed the mourners, Ruth who told Lior to stand straight, who acted, all this time, as though this was just another event in the smooth-running calendar of the kibbutz – who suddenly threw herself forward and fell onto the coffin. It was Ruth who beat her fists against the closed casket, and it was Ruth who howled in a wordless cry of pain and rage that made the bulbuls fly from the branches of the trees overhead, and Lior squeezed the dead Syrian general's medal until it dug so deep into his palm it drew blood, and he just wanted her to stop, he wanted her to stop screaming, he wanted—

It took three of the soldiers to pull her off. The coffin was lowered to the ground. The first clumps of dirt were thrown and old men with shovels filled the grave until a mound grew over the earth.

Here lies Yoram, May His Memory Be Blessed. Died in Service of His Country, Month of Tishrei, in the Year 5734.

And that was that.

'I water this land with the blood of my men,' Ruth said. She spoke to Uncle Moritz quietly by the samovar. Uncle Moritz wasn't really Lior's uncle. He was just some outsider Ruth didn't even like much. But he showed up.

People milling about in the newly built social club building, mixing instant coffee into cups, talking in low voices about the deceased. Lior had a sudden sense of déjà vu, but he had never been here before. The last funeral he went to was Yael's, and all he remembered of that was the strange, faraway look in Esther's eyes.

'I'm still here,' Ophek said. He gave his mother a hug and she returned it.

'And the children,' Ophek said, looking to where Lior and Esther stood.

'The boy,' Ruth said. Lior didn't know what she meant.

Something unspoken between her and Ophek. She let go of her son.

'You will be careful,' she said.

'I am always careful,' Ophek said.

He had a gun on his belt. He patted it and gave his mother that dazzling smile of his. 'See?'

He turned to the kids.

'Hey, Lior,' he said.

'Yeah?'

'Want to learn to shoot?'

'Really?'

'Sure,' Ophek said. 'Just don't tell your grandmother.'

He knelt down and stroked Esther's hair.

'You alright, sweetheart?'

Esther nodded.

'You want to learn to shoot?'

Esther's eyes lit up.

'Can I?' she said.

'You'll learn sooner or later anyway.'

Lior thought uneasily of what happened to Israel and Yael. He wasn't supposed to know. They died in a car accident in the desert, that's all there was to it. But he'd heard the stories.

'I'm sorry about your dad,' Ophek said.

Lior wasn't sure for a second which of them he was speaking to. Then Ophek took their hands in his and said, 'Come on, kids,' and led them away, and Lior was grateful. He didn't think he could stomach another second in that place with the echoey feeling of death and incessant murmurs of empty condolences like the singing of mermaids down in the deeps.

They walked to the field beyond the cemetery, overlooking the wadi. Nothing but stones and a view of the reach, and Ophek stopped, not smiling this time, and said, 'This is where we went once, me and your folks, we tried to make it to the sea on foot—'

He stopped and for a moment Lior thought he looked like a

child, lost. Then he took out his pistol from the holster on his belt and showed it to them, how to take it apart and how to put it back together, and he put in a round of bullets and pointed to the lone cypress tree, as old as time, that stood guard against the view of the hills.

Lior stood like Ophek showed him. He gripped the pistol with both hands and when he fired the explosion threw him back like a punch and he staggered, and Ophek laughed. The tree was unharmed. Lior tried again and on the second try he was calmer, and thoughts of his dad, and Ruth's ungainly display on the coffin, and the smell of coffee, all vanished and he found his mind clear. He fired, once, twice, three times, and the air filled with the smell of gunpowder and a bullet hit the trunk of the cypress tree with a soft *thunk*.

'Nice!' Ophek said. He took the gun from him and Lior stood back, breathing heavily, and he thought with some surprise that firing a gun was *easy*. It had seemed to him such a hard thing to do before.

He watched Esther. When she took the gun from Ophek she was different. Calm, almost like... She reminded him of the man who did the accounts for the kibbutz. He sat in a little office, all on his own, with a pen and a slide rule and sheets and sheets of paper and he added and subtracted numbers all day and made them line up. That's how Esther held the gun. She took aim, lined up the target and drew a breath she let out *slowly*—

The shot rang. The bullet hit the trunk of the tree and bark shot out, and Esther smiled.

And maybe that was it, Lior thought. The air felt clear and the light so exact that it picked every strand of her hair, reflected off the gun metal and onto her face, catching her smile and the spot of blood on her lip where she bit it, maybe that, he thought in wonder, the way he felt that moment, wishing it would never end—

Maybe that was love.

PART TWELVE

END OF ROAD

Ophek

The Sinai, 1976

44

'We can't find her, Ophek.'

It was Roni from his class. They shared a room all through kindergarten and up to third year. She had the left bed by the window. He had the right bed by the door. She talked in her sleep. Now she taught the kids geography and was on the decorations committee.

'Who?' he said.

'Your mother, Ophek.'

'Ruth? You can't find Ruth?'

'She was supposed to open the room for us,' Roni said, sounding irritated. But then she always sounded irritated, even back in kindergarten. 'She has the key.'

'That's not like her,' Ophek said.

'Can you, I don't know, go and find her or something?' Roni said. 'And what's with this outfit, anyway? It's not Purim yet, you know.'

'It's my stage costume,' Ophek said. Not like she didn't know. Not like she didn't make fun of him a hundred times when they were growing up, for doing magic. 'I've got a gig later tonight.'

'A *gig*,' Roni said, in the tone of voice that said this was the most ridiculous word she'd ever heard. 'What are you, Uri Geller?'

Ophek hated it whenever people brought up Uri Geller. Geller hit the newspapers in *Davar* in 1970, and in a year he went from being an underwear model to playing kibbutz dining rooms, from there to the clubs in Tel Aviv and from *there* to touring in

Europe. There was even a photo of him with Sophia Loren, but Ophek heard it was a fake. Not that it mattered. Now Geller was in America going on *The Johnny Carson Show*.

'I'll see if I can find Ruth,' he said. 'But if I were you I'd just move the meeting somewhere else, Roni.'

'It's the *principle*, Ophek,' Roni said. She was always big on principles. 'If you say you'll be somewhere then you should be there or you let everyone else down.'

'And we wouldn't want that, would we,' Ophek said. He walked away.

'No, we wouldn't!' Roni said. Her voice carried.

Yeah, yeah. God, he hated still being here. Still having to do a day with the sheep, or getting put into kitchen duty or gate guard duty or whatever else the work coordinator decided he should do, because as far as the kibbutz was concerned, the other stuff Ophek did, his *performing*, well that was just a hobby, even if he got paid for it and the money all went to the kibbutz. If you wanted to be an artist that was fine, but work came first: first and last. He was so sick of it.

If only he could leave.

He went past the factory and found the stables. He looked for the place. It'd been years since he saw her do it, and he never told, but he knew it was there. He found the trapdoor and pulled it up and went down, shutting it behind him.

Ruth sat in a chair in a small, dank cellar. A slick, he remembered they used to call them. Back when his mother and her generation hid weapons from the British. Somehow Ophek didn't think this slick was ever used as a weapons cache. Or that anyone on the kibbutz knew about it.

His mother had secrets. He liked that about her. It was hard to have secrets on a kibbutz.

'How did you know I was here?'

She had an unlit cigarette in her mouth. Her face was older. Her eyes, which could be so hard, were sad.

He said, 'I saw you once.'

'You were always a good watcher, Ophek.'

'It was a long time ago,' he said. 'But I remembered. You've been vanishing a lot, recently.'

'I need a place to think, sometimes,' Ruth said.

There were old dark stains on the floor. Ophek didn't need to ask what they were.

'You ever miss them?' he said.

'All the time.'

'Me, too.'

'I've given everything for this land,' Ruth said. 'And now that it's ours, sometimes I wonder why I did.'

'Not everything,' Ophek said. He tried to smile. 'You still have me.'

She held her hands out to him. He came and knelt beside her and she hugged him.

'You won't leave me like they did,' Ruth said.

He let her hold him, in that room that smelled of death.

All he could think of was wanting to escape.

'Tonight, chaverim, we have a special treat,' the culture coordinator said. 'He's not just a magician, he's a kibbutznik, too! Please give a warm welcome to the Amazing Ophek!'

Scattered applause. The members sat on hard chairs in the darkened dining room. Ophek was on a kibbutz in the lower Galilee. He stepped onto the makeshift stage.

The smell of liver and onions lingered in the air. The spotlight was bright and hot on his face. This was what he loved, and it didn't matter if it was here or some arena like Geller now got. It was the art he loved.

He started with some simple coin tricks, then silks, then the linking rings. He wanted to save up for a saw-the-lady-in-half, he had a guy in Haifa who could make it custom for him if only he could come up with the money. He got a volunteer from the audience and did some mind-reading. Someone in the back shouted, 'Bend a spoon!'

Ophek flashed them his good-natured smile. 'No destruction of kibbutz property, please,' he said, which drew a polite laugh. Since Geller hit big Ophek got the spoon bending line nearly every show. He smiled through it, ran through his patter, did the cups and balls and the card out of a lemon and finished with the Miser's Dream, which always went down well when performed on a kibbutz.

Later, in the kitchen, he collected the envelope with cash inside it and wrote out an invoice.

'We had Uri Geller here a couple of years back,' the culture coordinator said.

'He's something,' Ophek said.

'You should get an assistant,' the culture coordinator said. 'Someone pretty, in a short skirt, you know.'

'Right,' Ophek said. He pocketed the money. 'See you, Omri.'

'See you, Ophek.'

He stood in the parking lot and drew in air. The night silent, only the crickets chirping. He didn't smoke, never touched the things. But on a night like this sometimes he wanted to.

He got back in the car. The guard let him out of the gate. This was Ophek's favourite part: driving alone along an empty road at night, only the headlights shining the way home.

Ruth taught him to drive, sitting him on her knees, letting him turn the wheel when he was just, what, seven? Eight? Before the bad things. She never judged him. She was there to pick him up after Eilat. When he was hiding in the hospital, shivering inside the darkest janitor's closet he could find, she found him.

'You did what you had to do,' she said. 'You did the right thing.'

But how could it be the right thing? He could never scrub that morning from his mind, the jeep bouncing along the road, the sudden swerve, and suddenly he was flying through the air. Why did it have to be him who survived? And why couldn't Israel and Yael die on their own? They had no right to do that to him, to be *dying*, to make him do what he did.

Then a few months later in the army, the instructor in sniper training saying, 'The first one's the hardest,' and looking at Ophek then. 'But that's not an issue for you anymore, is it?' he said.

A dark road, a shape darted across and was caught in the headlights. A wild hare. Ophek slowed down, drove around it.

Turned out the instructor was right. The first job they sent him out on… It just wasn't that hard. So much easier, in fact, staring at someone so far away through a telescopic sight. feeling the air, finding the right time, then that perfect moment of connection as he *squeeeezed* the trigger.

And then, all he had to do was walk away.

After fifteen minutes he turned on the overhead light and checked the address on the note. Not that he needed to. He'd gone twice earlier. He turned off the light and then the headlights and drove in the dark, down a dirt track, until he came to the small moshav. A few lights were on in the houses. A dog barked. Ophek hid the car under a copse of pines behind the fence. The fence was not well maintained and he got through it easily. He wore black and the night swallowed him. He found the house, which stood alone against the wood behind the fence. There was a light on. He waited.

The light went out. Ophek waited some more. Everything was still. He went to the back door. It was locked but it didn't take long to open. He crept in. He was told there would be no one in other than the occupant.

He couldn't hear anyone moving. It was a nice house. They got pretty rich, some of those moshavniks. It wasn't like a kibbutz, they each had their own land, nice big houses, they were more like the old farmers Ruth and Israel had to work for when they first started Trashim, when they had to work in the Jewish farmers' orange groves for money. When they lived in tents and stuff. It all seemed so long ago.

Kitchen, empty. Living room, empty. He went up the stairs. Slowly, but not too slowly. Going too quiet made too much noise, as someone once told him. People registered slow creaks but not sounds they were used to. He came to the landing. The master bedroom door was closed.

He pushed it open softly. It swung on oiled hinges. A small figure lay in the big bed. A set of teeth sat in a glass of water on a dresser. A wig hung from an old-fashioned hat stand. The figure snored softly.

Ophek crept closer. An ancient woman lay asleep in the bed. She looked like a doll, almost, but there was something hard around her eyes that reminded him of Ruth. He didn't know the client's motives. He didn't ask. It was always something boring. Money, or some ancient hatred. That sort of thing. He picked up a pillow. The woman opened her eyes.

She stared at him, eyes hard and mean.

'You son of a bitch,' she said. 'Whatever he's paying you I'll pay you double.'

'It won't hurt,' Ophek said. Then considered.

'Much,' he said.

He pressed the pillow down. The woman thrust under him. Then she went still.

Ophek puffed up the pillow and put it back where it had been. He arranged the blanket over the woman. Sometimes the clients wanted to send a message. Sometimes they just wanted it to look natural.

He let himself out and relocked the door behind him. He went out of the fence, found his car, and drove away with the lights off until he got to the main road.

45

'You doing all right, kid?' Moritz said. He slipped the brown envelope across the Formica laminate on the table. Ophek took it. He didn't bother counting. He put the money away.

'I'm all right,' he said.

'You need a bank, kid,' Moritz said. 'Too much cash, it draws attention.'

'I don't need a bank, Moritz. Thanks.'

Moritz shrugged.

'Don't listen to me,' he said. 'What do I know?'

Ophek sipped the strong black coffee. They were in the lower Hadar in Haifa, sitting outside at a falafel place Moritz liked. Buses crawled past, belching fumes. Taxis honked their horns. Soldiers stood perched on counters with stuffed pitas in their hands and tahini on their chins, staring at the girls go by in their shorts and mini-skirts. Haifa, which never quite changed. He finished his coffee.

'Listen, kid,' Moritz said. 'So what's your plan?'

'Huh?'

'What's all this for? Are you going to leave that kibbutz of yours or what?'

'It's killing me, Moritz,' Ophek said. 'But I can't leave her. You know I can't.'

'She's a cold one,' Moritz said.

'You still keep in touch with my aunt?'

Moritz shrugged, reluctant.

'Lost touch,' he said. 'She must be getting on a bit, now. I prefer to remember her when we were both still young.'

'You ever tell her about… You know?' Ophek said.

'You can say it, kid. No one is judging you. Some of the things we do, they aren't nice, but there's no use pretending otherwise.'

'About Yael,' Ophek said.

'I did not.'

Moritz dabbed his lips with a paper napkin.

'So what *are* you going to do with the money?' he said.

'I don't know, Moritz!'

Ophek could feel his temper fraying. Moritz had that effect on him. Moritz looked like a piece of dried beef, like rubber. He'll live forever.

'I don't know,' he said. 'I have to make a decision.'

'No point stretching it out, kid,' Moritz said. 'Ruth will understand.'

'She won't,' Ophek said. 'She doesn't.'

He got up. Moritz stayed seated. He barked an order at the guy behind the counter to get him another half-portion of falafel. The guy hurried to obey.

'Well, don't be a stranger,' Moritz said.

He barely slept, then three hours with the sheep. He didn't like the milking parlour. The smell of hay and shit and antiseptic. Pulling on the teats like the ringing of bells. He hated sheep's milk.

It ruined his hands. His fingers were meant for dexterity and grace. For making coins vanish and cards fan like peacocks' tails. The blue overall he wore was drab, his boots were caked in mud. Then lunch in the dining room, of boiled potatoes and bony chicken pieces in bland sauce. There had to be something else, he thought. There had to be something better than this?

Paula and Malka serving behind the food trolley. He flashed

them the grin that always worked on them and Paula gave him an extra portion, just like when he was a kid.

He sat alone. People came and went around him. The volunteer girls from Sweden laughed and smoked in one corner, the guys from the falcha smoked and watched them from the other end. Tired mums pushed fat little babies, the founders gathered around two long tables and drank their tea.

He saw Ruth. She smiled his way and continued arguing with Mishka, about what he didn't know or care.

He finished, scraped his plate clean in the bin and put the tray, plate and cutlery into the new machine that washed it automatically on a long conveyor belt. He went back to his room and lay on the bed, just for a moment.

'…Uncle Ophek?'

He must have fallen asleep. The door to his room was ajar, and Lior stood by the kitchenette looking worried.

'Lior? What… what time is it?'

'It's four o'clock.'

'I didn't hear you come in, kid.'

'It's Ruth,' Lior said. 'She's not in her room and I can't find her.'

Ophek sat up. He rubbed his eyes.

'Not again,' he said. 'She keeps doing that.'

'Can you help me find her?'

'What for?' Ophek said. 'You have other things to do, don't you? Go see your mum.'

The boy looked down. What was wrong with him? Ophek thought, irritated.

'You didn't hear?' Lior said.

'Hear what?'

'You know she's been coughing and that,' Lior said. 'Like, a lot.'

'She got a cold?' Ophek said.

'Test came back last week,' Lior said. Talking quietly. Still staring at the fucking floor.

'It's cancer?' he said.

'Shit, kid,' Ophek said. 'I'm sorry.'

Lior shrugged. 'She'll be all right. She'll get through it. Right?'

'Right,' Ophek said.

He got up.

'Come on,' he said. 'Let's take a walk.'

He wasn't really looking for Ruth. He was just looking to get away, somewhere quiet. To make a decision everyone in the place was trying to stop him from making. They would always need him. But he didn't need them.

They went through the kibbutz, members emerging into the open, fresh from their afternoon nap. He asked if anyone had seen Ruth. Finally someone pointed them towards the end, where the graves grew in profusion under the trees.

They found her next to Israel and Dov's graves. She didn't look up when they came, their feet treading softly in the pine needles.

'Won't anyone ever give me peace?' Ruth said.

'You can't keep going off like this, Savta,' Lior said.

'You should go play with your friends,' Ruth said. She turned then, her eyes cold and furious. 'Go, Lior! Go play!'

Lior stared back, his fists bunched up. Then he turned and ran.

'His mother's dying,' Ruth said passionlessly. All the anger drained out of her. 'Everyone dies and leaves me.'

'Come on, Ruth,' Ophek said.

'What do you want?' she said, with that same emotionless voice.

'I need to talk to you.'

'About what?'

He took a deep breath.

'I was thinking,' he said. He spoke quickly now. 'I want to take a year out. Just a sabbatical. Go on the road. I can't keep doing it from the kibbutz. I need to do it full time. I'll rent a place somewhere. Get my own car. I'll come back for every Friday night dinner. Passover, Purim. But I just need to do this. And I can't keep doing it if I don't...'

He fell quiet. She said nothing. Her eyes were closed to him.

'Only a year...' Ophek said.

She turned her back on him. Stood between Dov and Israel's graves, her hands on their headstones.

'Everyone leaves me,' she said.

He took it to the next members' assembly. They voted. Ruth voted against. But he got the majority. The kibbutz agreed to let him go on sabbatical.

It was not uncommon. People got restless, after the army. They wanted to see what society outside the kibbutz was like.

Everyone knew the math. Not everyone came back. But you had a year to decide, and if you came back it was like you never left.

But for now he was on his own.

'I'll come back,' he told Ruth. They were in the dining room. A public sing-along of all the old classics, led by a woman in a white dress with an acoustic guitar.

'The wind blew through the tops of the cypress trees,' everyone sang. Their voices rose in the air of the large hall. 'In the distance the jackals howled. And you were beautiful, so beautiful my darling, as you sat by the campfire beside me.'

Ruth shrugged off his hand.

'The boy's mother,' she said.

'Galya?'

'You will come to the funeral, Ophek.'

He felt so sad then.

'Too many funerals,' he said.

'You can run away,' Ruth said. 'But I know who you are. What you are. I gave birth to you. When all this was just...' She waved her hand. 'Dirt.'

'It was never just dirt,' he said, angry. 'There were villages, there were people living here—'

'And now they don't. So *you* would have a home.'

'I didn't ask for that,' he said.

'No!' Ruth said. 'You didn't *have* to.'

'I'll be back for Friday night dinner,' Ophek said.

'No,' Ruth said. But she said it gently. 'You won't.'

He walked away as she joined in with the singing.

'The night grew long, and soon we'd go to battle, and you would stay behind to wait for me...'

He walked to the parking lot. The little beat-up car he'd bought from Moritz, his few possessions in the back. But it was his. He *owned* something.

It felt strange, but good. And he was a little ashamed to feel that way about owning things.

A small figure ran in the night and caught up with him before the gate opened. Ophek rolled down the window.

'Lior,' he said.

'Take me with you.'

'I can't, kid. You know that.'

'I'm going to leave one day, too,' Lior said. He stared at Ophek with defiance.

'I'm not leaving,' Ophek said, 'I'm just taking a year off—'

'What*ever*!' Lior said. He was crying now, but he turned his head away from Ophek, so Ophek wouldn't see. The guard opened the gate. Ophek hesitated. Then he pressed the gas and left, and the gate closed slowly behind him.

46

THE BLACK TELEPHONE RANG ON THE DRESSER. IT RANG TWICE before Ophek picked it up. The blind beggar outside on Allenby was singing. No one could ever shut him up.

'Yeah?' he said.

'How are you finding life in the city?'

It was Moritz.

Ophek stared out of the window. The whores were out early, and soldiers and machers and chasids and thieves all intermingled. A bus went past belching smoke, a taxi driver shouted curses at a streetwalker, a group of spectators gathered around a three-card-monte man sitting on a crate. Some boys from Jaffa, barefoot, went past with a catch of fish dangling from their shoulders. Cruising men gave each other soft glances and furtive signals and vanished into darkened alleyways together.

'It's different,' Ophek said.

Moritz barked laughter. It turned into a smoker's cough. Ophek waited until he recovered.

'So?' he said.

'How would you like to take a holiday?' Moritz said.

'A holiday where?'

'Eilat.'

'I was there in '67,' Ophek said. Not really wishing to remember it much. The Sinai, just before it, was much happier in his memory. He'd loved it there: the desert and the endless sky and the shimmering heat over the sea. Sage tea and hashish and Bedouin tents in the distance, and hidden coves with blue-green water, and European girls in bikinis going past. He'd planned to go back but then what happened happened and he never did.

'Besides,' he said. 'I have gigs.'

'I know a guy runs a nightclub there,' Moritz said. 'You could do a spot.'

'I don't know, Moritz.'

'How do you like the flat?' Moritz said, changing tack. 'It was your uncle's.'

'Yeah, I know,' Ophek said.

Yehoyakim went to prison in '64 for spying for the Soviets. That's what Ophek heard, at any rate. He barely remembered him. Yehoyakim came to the kibbutz sometimes to visit Ruth. He was always travelling. Some sort of travelling salesman, Ruth always said. Then one day he just stopped visiting, and no one ever mentioned him again; not when Ruth was around, anyway.

Looking in the cupboard when he first moved in, Ophek had found a secret compartment in a false wall, and inside it a faded photograph of two naked men in a bed, one of whom had movie star good looks. It took Ophek a moment to recognise him as the actor from that old movie, *The Vultures*.

What the old photo was doing there or what it meant Ophek had no idea.

'Let me buy you a coffee,' Moritz said. 'Think it over. It's an easy job. Make a holiday out of it.'

'I'll think about it.'

'Don't think too long,' Moritz said and hung up.

Fuck you, Ophek thought. He got changed. Put on his new black velvet suit and the top hat. Checked the secret pockets for props. Twirled in front of the mirror.

'Abracadabra,' he said.

★

He came on after the comedian but before the strippers. The girls backstage wandered around in bras and panties but that just felt like the showers on the kibbutz, only the underwear was nicer. The comedian drew a laugh. Ophek came on stage.

'Bend a spoon!' someone shouted from the back. The audience laughed.

He did his routine but he was distracted. The patter failed to land. The light rig was too low and the spotlight kept missing the mark. He finished with a disappearing act that did get good applause, but then the strippers went on and the audience went wild.

The manager handed him an envelope backstage. There was no receipt.

'You should get yourself an assistant,' the manager said. 'Someone pretty.'

Ophek pocketed the money and left.

'Moritz?'

He stood at the phone box. Somewhere on Allenby, with the smell of the sea in the distance and the blind beggar singing. He'd been singing since the war and he was never going to shut up.

'Yes, bucher?'

'I'll do it.'

'Then get your ass south,' Moritz said. 'Ask for Gidi at the Red Rock.' And he slammed the receiver down.

He could be like Uri Geller, Ophek thought. He could make the show bigger, he could go to America, he could reinvent himself just like Geller did. He just needed more money.

He got in the car. He liked the car. It was the best part of the job. He drove slowly out of Tel Aviv. The headlights caught cats in the bins, their eyes shining as they looked at him indifferently.

It had been a long time since he drove this way. The landscape changed past Jerusalem, the hills where Solomon chased girls with eyes like doves and breasts like fawns gave way to a dead sea and cave-riddled cliffs where ancient books had lain hidden for two millennia.

He drove past Ein Gedi which the Sicarii once robbed, riding down from their fortress of Masada to the oasis to plunder and ravage, stealing the oasis's store of balsam and murdering the weak, the women and the children, some seven hundred souls Josephus Flavius recorded. What were Ophek's crimes compared to these ancient violences, what was he if not history rewriting itself, just a line on a page that had been written over and over again?

It was hot. He cranked down the window. Hot air on his face. The sun began to rise. Lot's wife turned to salt and the cities of the plain burned with sulphur and fire as the dead sea receded in the rear-view mirror. Then it was just the desert and the road.

A truck passed him going in the other direction. An army jeep overtook him. Bedouin herdsmen drove goats in the distance. He stopped at a petrol station and filled up the tank and bought a coffee from the sleepy attendant and heard nothing but silence all around him in all that sand. He wondered what he was looking for then. What was he trying to do. He was a sentence that had been written until it was overused and dying. 'I water this land with the blood of my men.' Well, Ruth, he thought savagely, this is not your blood to spill.

He finished the coffee and got back in the car and drove on, through all that empty land. This was his land, he thought, but he had not asked for it. All he wanted to do was saw a lady in half on the stage in Carnegie Hall. All he wanted to do was go on Johnny Carson.

Fucking Geller, he thought. Go bend a spoon. He gripped the wheel, the sun was higher, sweat got in his eyes. He passed the recently abandoned site of King Solomon's mines and approached Eilat.

One last job, he thought. He'll take the money and run until she couldn't find him.

*

By the time he drove into the city the plane from Tel Aviv had come in to land and the sea sparkled blue in the bay. The mountains were red in the distance. He parked outside the Red Rock Hotel. It was built beside the spot where the old British police station still stood, where Israel and the others had erected the ink flag back in '49. Israel had dragged him to see it when they came to visit Yael that time.

Back then there was nothing much there. Now the hotel sat cool against the rising sun, a lurid red rock decorating the entrance, a reference to Petra on the Jordanian side. A garden grew before the hotel. Ophek walked inside, saw couples going in to the breakfast room and girls in bikinis already heading to the pool, the new Scandinavian tourists who had started to come to Eilat on charter flights. For a moment he looked at the girls with longing. Then he approached the reception desk.

'Can I help you?'

'I'm looking for Gidi.'

'I'm Gidi.'

The guy had a pencil moustache. For some reason that annoyed Ophek.

'Moritz sent me,' Ophek said.

'You're from Tel Aviv?'

'Aha.'

'Here.'

Gidi slid him an envelope. Ophek opened it. Inside was a picture. A very beautiful woman, not much older than him. Blonde, with sad eyes. He was a sucker for sad-eyed blondes.

'She staying here?' Ophek said.

'She was,' Gidi said. 'She checked out last night.'

'Know where she went?' Ophek said.

'Where do they all go?' Gadi said. 'The Sinai.'

'She tell you that?'

'She was a good tipper,' Gadi said. 'You?'

'Not so good,' Ophek said.

Gidi stared at him. Read something in Ophek's eyes and shrugged.

'She said she was heading to Ophira,' he said.

'Thanks,' Ophek said. He pocketed the photo. 'Did Moritz book me a room?'

Gidi smirked.

'Did he, fuck,' he said.

'What the hell, Moritz?' Ophek said. He was standing at a phone box. Eilat grew around him: new hotels done in Brutalist architecture, paved roads, signs advertising the new piano-bar at the Red Rock and the nightclub at the Neptune. He fed another token into the machine.

'You can do your gig when you come back,' Moritz said. He sounded distracted. Ophek could hear voices in the background at his place.

'Are you having a party?' he said.

'Something like that.'

Someone screamed in the background. It was cut short.

Ophek said, 'Who is she, anyway?'

'What's it to you, bucher?' Moritz said.

'Just asking.'

'Just do your fucking job.'

Moritz slammed the phone down. Again. He was getting tetchy, Ophek thought. He took the photo out again. The girl in the picture looked at him with her sad eyes.

Her name was written on the back of the photo.

'Ursula,' Ophek said.

He liked the sound of that.

47

DRIVING AWAY FROM EILAT HE PASSED RAFI NELSON'S VILLAGE
nestled against the sea in Taba, where people lay under the straw-
and-mud huts, smoking joints and talking, and someone played
the Beatles on guitar. Snatches of music and the smell of hash
wafted through the open window of the car, and Ophek had
a sudden longing to join them there, but he drove on along the
coastal road and past the old border stone that no longer mattered
to anyone.

The world as he knew it vanished behind him as he drove.

Here there was only the sea and the desert, and the narrow
band of coast in between, where Bedouin tents and straw huts
stood here and there, and fishermen dozed next to their boats in
the sun. The last time Ophek came this way the road had not been
laid yet.

The silence settled and the further he went the more it felt like
he was driving to the very end of the world.

He kept blinking sweat out of his eyes. The sun beat on the
tin can car mercilessly, baking him inside it as it rose. It rose fast.
The road swayed. A jeep came from the other direction, honked
loudly and swerved onto the sand, throwing dust in the air. It was
loaded with young people, shirtless, laughing as they picked up
speed again.

Ophek figured he needed to stop.

The mountains rose dramatically on his right. To his left was
the sea. Just ahead he could make out the new settlement of Neviot,

which sat side by side with the Bedouin village of Nueiba. He saw the sign for a petrol station and a kiosk and drove until he got to it and stopped. The engine steamed. He wiped the sweat from his eyes and staggered out into the shade.

'Give me a soda,' he said.

'Sure thing.' The girl behind the counter reminded him of Yael at seventeen. She put syrup into a glass and pressed it to the soda machine. There was no ice when she handed it to him but it was miraculously cold all the same. He drank it in one go and felt brain freeze and he pinched the bridge of his nose until it stopped.

'Travelled a long way?' the girl said, without too much interest.

'Yeah.'

He handed her coins.

'Anywhere I can sleep?' he said.

'Anywhere you like,' she said.

'Thanks.'

He left the car there and wandered down to the beach. A few huts, and hammocks that were strung between the trees. He found one that was empty and fell into it. Someone played the Beatles on guitar. He didn't even like the Beatles. He fell asleep to a bad rendition of 'Let It Be'.

He woke up to a bad rendition of 'All You Need Is Love' and into a late afternoon with the sun lower in the sky. He felt better but he needed water. He wandered up to the kiosk and drank from the hose until he was sated and then washed his face and splashed water on his hair.

'The sea's right there,' the girl at the kiosk said. She didn't look like she had moved all day. She had a hardback book face down on the counter. He couldn't make out what it was from where he crouched.

'Wasting water?' Ophek said. 'Sorry.'

'I finish in half an hour,' the girl said.

'You live here?'

'Yeah.'

'How old are you?'

'Old enough to have seen a few things.'

Ophek stood, shook water from his hair. He couldn't read this girl at all. He stole a glance at the book. *Parapsychology: The World Beyond Our Five Senses*, by C. H. Berendt.

'Hey,' he said, pointing at the book. 'I'm a magician.'

The girl said, 'I don't care what you do.'

She picked up the book again and began to read.

'Can I get a sandwich?' Ophek said.

'Got hardboiled egg left, or cheese and tomato.'

'I'll take hardboiled egg.'

The girl put the book down, vanished in the back, came back a few moments later with a sandwich. She handed it over to Ophek and went back to her book. Ophek perched on the counter and ate the sandwich. He stared out at the lonely homesteads of Neviot, stuck there in the middle of the sand. It didn't look like much of a place.

It wasn't. He finished the sandwich, handed over more coins. The girl took them and made them disappear, not looking away from her book.

'You seen a blonde girl pass here recently?' he said. 'German?'

'Lots of blonde German girls pass through here.'

'Well,' Ophek said. 'See you.'

'Aha,' the girl said.

Ophek got back in the car. It was hot in the car. He felt like things were slipping from him. Another hundred and fifty kilometres to Ophira. He put the car in gear and followed the road. It had to end somewhere. All roads did.

By the time he passed the army base in Dahab the sun was setting. The road was very dark. There were no lights and there were too many stars overhead, too distant and impossibly old, and under them he felt unravelled somehow from his old life. He had not travelled far and yet he felt he had journeyed some impossible distance. It occurred to him suddenly that on the drive to Eilat he did not stop at the place where the accident happened, when he'd first had to kill. But in truth he couldn't even tell which bridge it was or over which dried wadi. There wasn't anything left.

He followed the road blindly until it took him to Ophira and there it stopped. The end of the road, the end of the world, and all that quiet. It was nothing like the quiet on the kibbutz. On the kibbutz there was always someone listening in the silence.

Here the mountains and the sea swallowed human voices and cast them away into nothing, into an immensity of peace. Lights were on and the houses of the settlement were made out of prefab concrete blocks but they were spaced apart and the whole place had the air of a half-abandoned western town, like in those Italian movies that had American actors shoot each other in Spain. He parked the car and stepped out drunk on the warm air and the smell of hash and the sound of laughter and the surf.

Fires burned on the beach. No one played the Beatles.

He suddenly felt like he was home for the first time in his life. He couldn't explain it.

He wandered down to the beach, past the prefab blocks and young mothers pushing babies in prams, past a single shop selling basic supplies, a barber's that was shut, perhaps for good, the police station that had one uniformed cop sleeping in the shade, a nursery and the public phone.

Down on the beach someone had strung up light bulbs on a wire and plugged them into the power supply. A makeshift kiosk had crates of beer stacked on the sand. Down here the settlement ended. A couple of Bedouins smoked a sheesha next to their kneeling camels, perhaps waiting to offer rides to any tourists with a few shekels to spare. Past the electric lights the fires burned and hash smoke rose sweet in the air. Bodies moved about more or less in the nude. There was not much point to wearing clothes, not here, not in this heat. A tinny radio on the kiosk counter played a song that had nothing to do with the wind in the cypress trees. Ophek grabbed a beer and popped the cap. The beer was warm but he didn't care. Someone passed him a joint and he took it in and coughed, then passed it on. A great sweet rest settled on his limbs.

That was when he saw her. A woman stepped out of the dark sea and rose onto the sand, her blonde hair wet, her skin shining in the moonlight. She wore no clothes and her feet left wet imprints in the sand as she walked up to the kiosk and took a beer. She had sad eyes.

Ophek's breath held still and he watched her and the way her body contoured.

'You been here long?' she said, not looking at him.

'Not long,' he said.

'I'm Ursula.'

'I know.'

She looked at him then. Really looked. Something like understanding was in her eyes. Then she smiled.

'How do you know?' she said, like it was nothing.

'I just know.'

She came closer and he could feel her wet body almost touching his and he stood still.

'I guess you do,' she said. 'What is your name?'

'I'm Ophek.'

'Ophek,' she said. 'What does it mean?'

'It means horizon,' he said, and she nodded very seriously and said, 'But this is the place beyond the horizon.'

'Is this why you came here?'

'Yes,' she said. 'I think. Why did you come here, Ophek?'

'It's the end of the road,' he said. 'There is no more road after this.'

She burst out laughing and he realised she must be a little stoned and so was he. He went and spoke to a guy a little further down the beach and came back with a fresh joint. Ursula smoked it with small quick puffs, like a bird pecking at seeds. She passed it back to him and he inhaled more deeply now, letting the smoke fill him from the inside.

'Why did you come here, Ursula?' he said. He wondered how he would do it. He could drown her, he thought. She was so light. She would float.

'I was married,' she said. 'He died.'

'People die,' Ophek said. She looked at him in some surprise.

'Yes,' she said. 'People die.'

She took his hand and led him down the beach, away from the lights, into the darkness. Only the stars above, and the black waves beating against the shore. Couples made out under the stars.

'Where are we going?' Ophek said.

'Somewhere quiet.'

She led him along the beach until the lights vanished and the sand was undisturbed by people. Into a cove where the waters rushed in and nothing else stirred. He would do it here, he thought.

They finished their beers and put them down on the sand. The joint had burned down to nothing. The stars shone down.

Ophek whispered, 'Why did you bring me here?'

Ursula said, 'Why did you come?'

She waded into the water, not waiting for him, not looking back. He watched her naked back.

After a while, he followed her in.

48

Sun, sea and sand: in the shade of a palm tree Ophek did beten-gav, front and back, flipping over periodically like a chop roasted over slow coals. From time to time he took a sip from his beer, but you couldn't drink it fast enough before it turned into a warm slushy thing.

He'd called Moritz and told him the job was done. He left the car parked in Ophira and got a plane up north from the small airfield. He collected his money.

'What did she do, anyway?' he asked Moritz.

'Do?' Moritz said and spat. 'She didn't do nothing. Where can I find you after this?'

'I'm going to be in the Sinai for a while,' Ophek said. 'No more jobs, Moritz. I'm through.'

'Suit yourself, kid.'

And that was that.

There was nothing in the Tel Aviv apartment for him. He never made it back to Friday night dinner on the kibbutz. He collected a few things. He got a flight back to Ophira from Ben Gurion. He hired a room in one of the prefab buildings, but most of the time he just slept on the beach.

And that should have been it, with the days bleeding into the nights, the days merging into weeks like the tributaries of a river flowing into one vast and featureless sea that smelled faintly of camels and hashish. He didn't even need to perform magic anymore. The magic was already here.

So why was it that he began to feel unease? Why was it that unwelcome thoughts began intruding into the dreaming mind which wished only to live in the present?

He called Moritz.

'You think you can fuck me?' Moritz said.

'Excuse me?'

'You little pisher,' Moritz said. Sounding distracted. Muffled voices in the background. 'Don't say I didn't warn you. Now it's out of my hands.'

'What did you *do*, Moritz?' Ophek said, and the sense of dread, which he had been avoiding, coiled about him like a desert snake.

'Fuck off, Ophek,' Moritz said, and hung up the phone almost gently.

Ophek wandered back to the beach. Ursula walked up then, handed him a fresh beer and smiled.

'What is it, love?' she said.

'Something is coming,' Ophek said. 'But I don't know what it is.'

She sat next to him on the sand. Ophek watched the skies. Was it his imagination or was that a cloud far on the horizon? It never rained in the Sinai.

'Tell me if you see any strangers,' he said.

'There are always strangers,' Ursula said. 'We're all strangers here.'

'Who was your husband?' Ophek said.

She lost the smile.

'You know I don't want to talk about this,' she said.

'I need to know.'

'He was an executive,' she said unwillingly. 'A businessman, that's all.'

'Was he rich?' Ophek said.

'Well, yes,' Ursula said. 'His family is very wealthy. He was on the board of... Well.' She stopped.

'Tell me.'

'He worked for Hoechst,' Ursula said.

'What's that?'

'The Amis split up IG Farben after the war and—'

'The company that made the gas for Auschwitz? Zyklon B?' Ophek said.

'And other things,' Ursula said defensively. 'It was just a pharmaceutical company. Then he had a heart attack and I was left a widow.'

'But you inherit him? What? Stocks, shares?'

'Yes.'

'So you are rich.'

'I suppose so,' she said. She frowned. 'I don't like to think about it.'

'And if you die? What happens to it?'

'His family get it, I guess,' Ursula said. 'I don't like them much. They are what you would call—'

'Nazis?'

She laughed.

'They are rich,' she said. 'The rich joined the Party when it was beneficial to them, and they abandoned it when it was not. They're old money, is what I was trying to say.'

It made sense now to Ophek. He watched the horizon with a sense of unease. Something was coming. He could feel a cold wind. But no one else seemed to notice. And the sky was bright blue, like the sea. And the sun still shone. He reached for Ursula and pulled her to him.

He said, 'Just let me know if any strangers show up.'

Another day, another night. Two jeeps pulled in full of holidaymakers from Tel Aviv, the men in beards and shorts, the girls in bikinis. A couple of European beatniks ambled up, having walked all the way from Dahab. They set up a tent on the beach and promptly got stoned. A group of soldiers from the nearby base also came in. They bought a crate of beers from the store and went skinny-dipping. It was the weekend. Ophek perched against the wall of the police station.

'You're gonna be busy tonight,' he said.

'I'm busy every night,' Eyal said. He was the new policeman, up from Eilat. He sat on a chair, watching the small town as it came alive at night.

'Aha,' Ophek said. 'Listen, Eyal. Do me a favour?'

'Aha,' Eyal said.

'Keep an eye out for any strangers, will you?'

'You expecting something, Ophek?' Eyal looked at him curiously. 'Something I should know about?'

'Just got a feeling, that's all,' Ophek said.

'This is a quiet place,' Eyal said. 'But sure. I'll keep an eye out. You want a coffee? I was just about to make a coffee.'

'Sure,' Ophek said.

He drank his coffee and listened to the night. Something was wrong with it. The stars, he thought. He couldn't see the stars. The wind pushed at him, coming out of nowhere. It felt suddenly cold. He'd forgotten what cold felt like.

'Do you hear that?' Ophek said.

Eyal frowned. 'What is that?' he said.

From down the beach came shouting, and figures ran for shelter in the night as heavy drops began to fall.

'Rain?'

'Rain!'

The call rose up all over Ophira.

'Well, that's a new one,' Eyal said. 'I thought it never rained here.'

'What do we do?' Ophek said.

'Do?' Eyal looked at him strangely. 'We wait for it to stop,' he said.

★

But the rain didn't stop. Thunder boomed across the bay all night, and lightning flashed in the black skies overhead. Ophek and Ursula lay in the bed inside Ophek's rented room. The thick concrete held back the storm outside.

'But what about the others?' Ursula said. 'What if the rain doesn't stop?'

'It will stop,' Ophek said. He held her close.

'I love you,' he said.

'I love you, too.'

The power was out. A candle burned on the table. They made love as the world drowned.

Morning came with more heavy rain. Ophek braved a run outside to get supplies.

The town was unrecognisable. A flood in the night pushed everything not locked down into the sea. The tents blew away in the wind. Power was out everywhere and the sea rose high over the beach.

'There are people missing,' Eyal said. 'At least two. There's no help coming, either. The planes can't take off or land until the storm's over and the coast guard can't come close. I'm on my own here.'

'I'll help,' Ophek said.

He went back to the room to tell Ursula but she was already dressed.

'I'm coming with you,' she said.

'It's too dangerous,' Ophek said.

'I don't care.'

He didn't argue. They made their way to the beach with the others. A group of permanent residents and some of the beatniks and the tourists. They made an unlikely company.

'Stay close,' Eyal said. 'It isn't safe. If it gets worse go back inside and find shelter.'

They moved slowly along the beach. The water kept rising. A flood from the mountains rushed down to meet the sea.

'I got one!' someone shouted. One of the beatniks who arrived the night before lay half buried in the sand. Ophek rushed over. He felt for a pulse, found one.

'He's still alive!' he shouted.

'Take him back to the clinic,' Eyal said. 'We'll keep going.'

Ophek and two of the men lifted the tourist. They carried him back.

'You'll be all right,' Ophek said. 'You'll be all right.'

In the clinic the harried nurse, more used to surfers, kids and maternity matters, ordered them to put the man on a bed. Ophek went out again. The sky had turned dark again and the water rose dangerously fast between the houses. He couldn't see the search party. He wandered down the beach. The hole where they had dug out the tourist had vanished.

Ophek shouted, 'Ursula!' but his voice was lost in the storm.

A car came out of nowhere and nearly hit him. It drifted on the flood and into the sea. There was someone still inside it. The car, tossed on the waves, began to drown. The person inside it didn't move.

Ophek tried to swim to it, to rescue them. The sea pulled at him and he panicked, knowing then that it was futile. He managed to get back to shallow land and find purchase again. The car vanished from sight.

He went on, desperately.

'Ursula!'

He thought he heard a scream.

He ran. In between rocks he thought he saw two figures in the water. An electric pole came drifting on the flood trailing cables. Ophek jumped over a rock, made his way to the figures he glimpsed, but could only see one now. He dove into the water.

When he rose, gasping for breath, he saw Eyal, the policeman, with his hands around Ursula's throat.

She was under water. Ophek jumped on Eyal and the man, startled, whirled around. For a moment they stared at each other.

'You?' Ophek said.

'A job's a job,' Eyal said. His fist smashed into Ophek's face. Ophek fell back and then Eyal was on him, those two hands with wiry strength closing on his throat, the thumbs digging in with merciless intent.

Ophek choked, the air trapped in his lungs. He kicked blindly under water. Eyal smiled. His hands like a vice closed on Ophek's throat and Ophek knew then that he was dying.

He closed his eyes.

But death didn't come. When he looked again, a look of dumb surprise filled Eyal's face. His hands slackened on Ophek's throat and Ophek gulped in air and sea water and choked again. What was wrong with Eyal? A line of blood like a smile grew on his neck.

Ophek trod water. Eyal fell into the sea and didn't rise again. Ursula stood behind him, a piece of jagged corrugated iron in her hand.

'We have to get out of here,' she said.

She dropped the metal. They swam to each other, their feet no longer finding purchase on the sea floor. The water kept rising. Eyal bobbed on the waves and vanished into the sea. Ophek thought he wouldn't be the only one that day to vanish.

He held Ursula close. The waves tossed them like seaweed. He tried to find land.

Lightning flashed, too close. Thunder exploded. In the brief light he saw the coast. It wasn't far. They swam together, holding hands, kicking against the tide. But the closer they got the more the sea pushed them away, and it seemed to Ophek they would never reach the shore, were doomed to spend their last few moments in the world trapped in the water together.

A wave rose and threw him and he had to let go of Ursula and when he rose again, gulping air, he couldn't see her. He tried to cry out her name but his voice didn't work, the sky was black and the sea between the rocks became a pool that stretched away from him forever, and he knew again that he would die.

Then he heard a voice, somewhere in the distance, and something landed in the water beside him. He stared about him dumbly.

'Grab the rope!'

For a moment the words made no sense. Then the world rushed back in and he was still alive. He felt in the water, found the thick woven line and held on. His body jerked as the cable was pulled.

He let it drag him, holding on as the sea churned. The shore was so close. Suddenly he was back on land. He lay there on his back, spluttering water, and when he turned his head he saw Ursula lying by his side.

'You'll be all right,' a voice said. Ophek couldn't see him. 'You'll be all right.'

The figure moved on and vanished into the dark.

'We have to get out of here,' Ophek said. The water was already rising again. Ursula reached for his hand and held it. For a moment they lay there, staring up at the starless skies.

'He was trying to kill me,' Ursula said. Her voice was soft.

'Yes.'

'What will happen now?'

'Nothing will happen,' Ophek said. 'He will vanish in the storm.' He got to his feet. Everything hurt. He helped Ursula up and together they limped away from the sea.

It all came to Ophek then. They will vanish too. Tomorrow or the next day the storm would cease. He didn't know how many died or were still to die, but when it passed no one would account for the missing.

He led her back into the town. Their room was flooded. He waded in and found his magician's jacket in the trunk. He ran his fingers down the lining, felt the small hard diamonds he had hidden there. His bank.

He took Ursula's hand and together they went past the town

and the sign that said 'End of Road'. The car was no longer there. He didn't expect it to be. He found a jeep still standing and hotwired the engine. The road was flooded and the nearest airport was Eilat. He found a blanket in the back and wrapped it around Ursula's shoulders.

Germany, he thought. He could start his act again there.

He put the jeep into gear and it took off, and Ophek drove away into the storm.

PART THIRTEEN

SAVTA

Ruth

Kibbutz Trashim, 1989

49

RUTH SAT IN THE CHAIR. THE ROOM WAS IN DARKNESS. THE
television screen flickered static. She thought she heard Shosh
saying, 'I miss you.' She shooed her away. Back to the shadows.
The television light projected on the wall. Shapes moving in a vast
distance. Her mother standing in a kitchen that no longer stood,
the radio on, playing Vivaldi. Her mother made szilvás gombóc.
She could taste it now, the hot plums inside the potato batter, sugar
and cinnamon mixing on her tongue. Her stomach rumbled in
longing. Her mother smiled and teased Ruth's hair.

'Look after your sister,' she said.

'I will, Mama,' Ruth promised. The television flickered in the
dark. Bill Goodrich pulled out a gun. He started firing at the
approaching policemen.

Bang! Bang! the gun went.

'Bang, bang,' Ruth whispered.

She was startled awake, the bangs coming from the door. They
let themselves in, stood there in the dark.

'Ophek?' Ruth whispered.

'It's us, Ruth.'

She turned on the side light.

'Boys,' she said.

Yuval stood waiting, Gadi and Peleg behind him. Their faces
were grim.

'Well?' Ruth demanded.

'It's done,' Yuval said.

'Make some coffee,' Ruth said.

'Thanks, Ruth.'

Peleg went into her kitchen. He rummaged about for coffee and filled up a pot.

'Where?' she said.

'The khirbe.'

She felt a terrible sadness then.

'I tried to reason with him,' she said.

'We all did, Ruth.'

'Does Esther know?'

'The police are there now,' Yuval said.

'Who—?'

'Cohen.'

'Good,' Ruth said. 'Then there will be no problems.' She could smell the coffee cooking now. 'And Esther?'

'They will speak to her. It was best if we...' He shuffled his feet.

'Didn't, yes,' Ruth said. She turned off the television. The flickering lights vanished abruptly. Peleg poured black coffee into glasses. He handed them round. Ruth took a sip. The coffee was bitter.

'He was a nice kid, Danny,' she said, distracted. What had she been thinking of? There were fleeting shadows in her mind but when she tried to concentrate they vanished. It didn't matter. 'It is a tragedy when we lose one of our own.'

'We mourn as a community,' Yuval said.

She gave him a sharp look.

'We do,' she said. 'It is no easy thing, what we do.'

Her phone rang. She picked it up. It was Almog on the line.

'Yes,' Ruth said. She listened to him shouting.

'It's taken care of,' she said. She listened to him some more. 'No,' she said. 'It won't affect the shipments. Yes. No. All right. Goodbye.'

She hung up.

The boys were looking to her.

It was nearly dawn. The light pushed in through the blinds. She drank her coffee.

'Well, go,' she said. 'I'll see you at the funeral.'

Yuval nodded. They vanished as they had come, though they knew to rinse the cups in the sink before they left. They were good boys, she thought. She sat in the chair. She waited for the dawn to come.

She never missed meals in the dining room, not if she could help it. It was important for the social cohesion of the kibbutz. It was the beating heart and soul of the commune. The sound of cutlery clinking and people talking, but today their voices were hushed. Word of the death had spread already. She saw a police car parked by the dining room when she went over in her scooter. She didn't see Esther.

It was not easy, becoming a widow. Ruth knew. It was women's lot to go on when their men died in service. Danny died in service too, she thought. The individual gave up his life so that the commune could live on. She wished there had been another way, but you couldn't make an omelette without breaking some eggs. She had two hardboiled eggs from the serving counter and vegetables for a salad. She sat down in her usual place. She chopped the cucumber into tiny tiny pieces.

'Did you hear, Ruth?' Uzan said. Uzan wasn't kibbutz born. It shouldn't matter if one was or wasn't, but it did. He also couldn't keep his goddamned mouth shut.

'I heard,' Ruth said. She chopped the tomato next. Uzan looked like he wanted to keep talking.

'Do not dawdle, Uzan,' Ruth said. He had his mouth open to speak. He thought better of it and moved on to spread his gossip elsewhere.

She chopped the onion. It didn't make her cry. Very little did, these days. The other elders came and joined her. They knew death. They spoke of other things. She didn't see Esther. She didn't see the man from America, who sometimes ate in the dining room too. Ruth did not care for America. She did not wish for the Americans' money. They had built the factory themselves, with their own hands, and now to have to prostitute themselves for others' money sat bitterly with her, but she was a realist.

You could not tell it, not just then, but she knew the kibbutz was slowly dying. This generation now wanted to take their children out of the communal houses and into their own homes. They wanted to break the social structure. The last few kibbutz meetings had been stormy. The other kibbutzim were struggling financially, worse than Trashim. There was little support from the government or even from the main office of the movement. They were on their own. Other kibbutzim were talking about privatisation. She couldn't let that happen here.

She mixed the salad and added olive oil and salt. The doctor told her to cut out salt. What did doctors know. She peeled an egg. She put salt on the egg. The boys did what they could. It was not what she would have liked, this disco and whatever else they had going. But it was necessary. The ends justified the means. She bit into the egg. A sombre mood in the dining room. It was always sad to lose a member; one of their own.

At work her mind drifted, her fingers putting labels onto boxes, labels onto boxes. How did time pass so quickly? It was only a minute before that she drove the kibbutz truck down the dirt road past the Arab village, only a minute ago that she was in the Casino in Haifa, plotting revolt against the British... The last time she saw Almog he was an old man. Out of the service, but still connected. She had not seen him in years. He had called, and she had gone to see him. The Casino long gone, they sat in an air-conditioned café in the Check Post shopping mall.

Almog explained what was needed. She had heard rumours

of the hashish transports in past decades, grasped instinctively the value of the operation. Only the target now was not Egypt but the Palestinians, and the drugs were now hard drugs, that would otherwise flow in through the porous border with Lebanon and reach the wrong hands, the hands of young Jewish boys and girls.

She said yes. They went to another place, down the road, and drank whisky. Then to a small hotel with mildewed sheets where things took their course, even if that course took a while.

Later, lying there, Ruth lit a cigarette. She could hear the trucks pass outside, whooshing along the main road, and she thought of other rooms like this, in other times. The cigarette tasted good. She coughed. Almog, beside her, scratched his belly.

'You were always a good-looking man,' Ruth said.

He turned on his side and smiled at her.

'And you always lit up any room you walked into,' he said.

'Flattery,' Ruth said.

'It's true.'

She took a drag and listened to the trucks whoosh outside.

'I was good-looking once, too,' she conceded. He laughed.

'We would need to discuss the financial arrangement,' Ruth said.

'Of course. You would want to bury the paperwork,' he said.

'The factory, I think,' Ruth said. 'It would keep it clean.'

'Is it profitable?' Almog said.

'The factory?' she shrugged. 'It gets by.'

'We all get by,' Almog said. She turned over too, looked into his eyes.

'For how long?' she said.

He looked at her in silence, almost puzzled.

'We will endure,' he said at last. 'We have waited two thousand years for this moment.'

'My grandson, Lior,' Ruth said. 'He's in Lebanon.'

'My grandson, too,' Almog said. He took the cigarette from

her, took a drag and gave it back. 'He was wounded in the battle for Beirut. Lost a leg.'

'I'm sorry.'

'Yes, well.' He looked into her eyes, searching for something, she didn't know what. 'You lost more than I ever have. But you still believe.'

'I gave up everything for this land,' Ruth said. 'I sacrificed.'

'Just as Abraham sacrificed Isaac,' Almog said, a little pompously.

'Isaac lived,' Ruth said.

'Let's not have a theological debate,' Almog said. Ruth put the cigarette out in the ashtray. She listened to the trucks whooshing past on the road outside.

'I will make the arrangements,' Ruth said.

'Good.'

He reached for her. She pushed him away, but fondly.

'You don't have it in you,' she said.

'The fun's in the trying,' Almog said.

She smiled and got dressed. She walked out to the car. She couldn't walk as well but she could still drive. She made her way past the Check Point intersection and down the silent road below the Carmel and along the sea, and she thought of other nights, just like this one; and for a little while she was content.

50

SHE TRIED TO READ A BOOK BUT IT WASN'T GOING ANYWHERE good. The door opened without a knock and Lior came in. She stared at him, the black trousers and jacket, the unshaved cheeks. He'd grown since she last saw him. When he left he swore he'd never come back. She could see herself reflected in him. When she left her home in Hungary she vowed the same.

'Lior? Why did you come back?' she said.

She put the book down. She watched him. He reminded her so much of Israel, of Yoram. Blood of her blood, flesh of her flesh. She knew what he was going to say even before he said it.

'I came back for Danny.'

'You came back for Esther, you mean,' Ruth said. She had tried to keep those two apart all those years. Now he was back for all the wrong reasons. She shook her head.

'Are you staying here tonight?' she said.

'I was hoping to.'

'You can take the sofa.'

It was good to have him back, she realised. She asked him to make her a cup of tea and cadged a cigarette. She wasn't supposed to smoke but it felt good to.

When he made the tea he sat down on the sofa. He looked like a little child again. She saw him looking at the framed photo on the table. The Passover seder, so long ago, when her children were still alive.

'Are you still working for those gangsters in Tel Aviv?' Ruth said.

'Savta...'

She wasn't going to judge. The kid wanted to make his own way in the world. He'd never fitted in with the collective. He reminded her of Ophek in that way.

She made Lior show her his gun. It felt good in her hands. It had been a long time since she'd used one. She gave it back to him.

'When you carry a gun,' she said, 'you've got to intend to use it.' She listened to him protest but they both knew it was true.

'Dead men don't need guns,' she said. But he wouldn't listen. She had a terrible feeling then. She wanted him gone from there, for his own good. Well, she thought. She'd make sure he went back to Tel Aviv after the funeral.

'Get some sleep, Lior,' she said. She patted his hand.

'Savta loves you,' she said.

He was asleep on the sofa. She watched him sleep. He looked like a little child then. She dialled a number. Yuval answered.

'Lior is back,' Ruth said.

'So?'

'So Danny was his friend.'

Silence on the other end of the line.

'What do you want us to do?' Yuval said at last.

'You could talk to him.'

'You think talking will do it, Ruth?'

She sighed.

'I hope so,' she said.

She hung up. She watched her grandson sleep.

Sunlight broke through the blinds. She put the radio on.

'Get up,' Ruth said. 'It's time to go.'

'Go where?' Lior said. He didn't look happy.

'Stop dreaming and get up,' Ruth said. 'We're going to the dining room.'

Her grandson groaned. She hid a smile.

He came with her to the dining room. She saw the way people looked at him. In that undertaker outfit and those shiny shoes. Ruth chopped her salad small. Lior went to get a coffee. She saw the boys approach him. She pursed her lips. She skimmed the front page of *On Guard* half-heartedly. When Lior came back he didn't say anything.

'Well?' Ruth said. 'We have a funeral to go to.'

She took him with her to work first. Sticking labels on boxes wasn't much but it was honest work, and as long as you worked you were *valuable*. Lior chatted to the nurse, Ronena. Ruth watched them. The boy needed a girl. He needed to get over Esther.

When work was over it was time to go to the funeral. She rode her buggy. Lior walked beside her. They followed the black Chevra Kadisha car all the long way to the cemetery. It was a road Ruth knew too well, it occurred to her. The boys carried the coffin in. Ruth and Lior walked slowly. She held onto his arm. They passed the gravestones for Yoram and Galya and stopped.

'Do you ever miss them?' Ruth said.

Lior said, 'No.'

They spoke some more. She barely noticed. Lior put pebbles on the graves. Ruth saw Esther in the distance. The girl was crying. The coffin was lowered into the ground. Then it was over.

'A good funeral,' someone said.

She tried to get Lior to come with her to the social club but he had eyes only for the girl.

'Don't come crying to me when it all ends badly,' Ruth finally said.

'Yes, Savta...'

He wasn't even listening.

She got back on her buggy. She drove down to the social club but she didn't stay long. She drove out as Lior came in. She went down to the stables. The disco, now. She found Yuval inside. He was dressed in blue overalls.

'The stuff needs to go out *tonight*,' Ruth said.

'I'm on it,' Yuval said. He was counting money.

'And try to keep my grandson out of the factory.'

'He won't see anything in the factory,' Yuval said.

'Just...' She took a deep breath. 'I didn't want mess,' she said.

'Stuff will be out tonight,' Yuval said. 'Danny's gone. And Lior's going to go back to Tel Aviv sooner or later. He hates it here. You worry too much, Ruth.'

'You're a good boy, Yuval,' she said. She patted his hand. 'Is this money clean?'

'It will be.'

She left him to it. Drove to the dining room. She wasn't hungry but it didn't do to miss a meal. She had rice and a bit of boiled chicken. She wished she had a cigarette. Then back to work, sticking labels for an hour.

She didn't see Lior but he was up to something. She knew her grandson.

She went back to her room. Arab workers were busy painting the neighbours' block. Ruth shut the door behind her. She sat in her chair and turned on the television. *The Vultures* was just coming on, it's been on repeat on the kibbutz's local cable channel. She watched the titles, the ship coming in on the rough sea in the night, the British policemen waiting on the shore to arrest the refugees from Europe. Bill Goodrich appeared on the deck, his chiselled face belonging to a different era. He'd died a few years back, she'd read about it in the paper. Heart attack.

'Oh, Shosh,' she said. The music swelled and then the ship arrived and the policemen shouted, Goodrich punched one of the officers and made a run for it. He vanished into the night. Ruth fell asleep. She didn't dream. She thought she heard Lior come in, then go out again. When she woke up the movie had ended and birds called outside. For a moment she wasn't sure where she was.

'Dov?' she said. 'Israel?'

But there was no one there.

51

Lior came back in the afternoon. He didn't say much and she didn't ask. He slept for a while. When he woke up it was dark and Ruth was frying eggs.

'Eat up,' she said. She slid the eggs onto a plate. She buttered toast. She watched her grandson eat and helped herself to one of his cigarettes.

'You're going to get yourself killed,' she said.

'Doing what?' Lior said.

'Whatever it is you're doing.'

He mopped up egg with his toast. She watched him eat. He reminded her of Dov, of Yoram. Doomed men.

She brought out his gun. She had missed holding one, she realised. She said, 'I oiled it for you.'

He got up, kissed her on the top of her head. When he reached for the gun she stopped him.

'They don't allow guns there,' she said.

'Guns where?' Lior said.

'The disco.'

'Who said I'm going to the disco?'

Ruth shrugged. 'It's night on a kibbutz,' she said, 'and you're not even married. What else are you going to do?'

Lior nodded. 'Alright,' he said. 'I'm going to the disco. Like old times.'

'I'll keep the gun for you, then.'

She wanted to keep him safe. He went out and the door closed.

She hoped he would leave the next day. Go back to his gangsters in Tel Aviv. She washed the dishes.

Usually there was a guest lecturer or a show in the evening, but not today, what with the funeral. Esther would be sitting shiva, and in *On Guard*, in the death announcements section in the back, there would be a black-bordered notice of Danny's death and the arrangements. Or was that yesterday? She tried to read a book but her mind wandered. There were gaps in her memory now, she'd noticed. Sometimes she didn't know where she was, and people's faces changed without warning. It was like clouds passing overhead and casting shadows. She shook it away. She liked the feel of the gun in her hands. She put it away in her bedroom closet.

Maybe Lior will meet a nice girl in the disco and that would be that. The boys would know to keep him away from anything sensitive. She went back to her book but it was no use, she never had much interest in fiction. She watched the international news instead.

America had a new president. The Soviet army left Kabul after nine years of occupation. An ayatollah in Iran put out a death sentence on some writer. An oil spill in Alaska. Student protests in China. The Colombian president has been assassinated with Israeli-made machine guns and two kids in California murdered their parents.

What was the world coming to? she thought. In comparison to that, Kibbutz Trashim was a green island of serenity, standing proud and alone upon its hill. The winds of the world may buffet it, but like a cypress tree it stood against the storm.

In the morning Lior was fast asleep on the sofa and she didn't want to wake him. She watched him sleep. He tossed and turned and there were rings under his eyes. She went out for breakfast and ran into Yuval in the dining room foyer by the post boxes.

'Shipment's gone,' he said. 'The silo's clean.'

'Good,' Ruth said. So that was that, she thought.

She ate and went to work, then to lunch, then an hour at work again and back to the room. She watched the teletext channel. Her mother was in the kitchen cooking goulash. The gramophone played Vivaldi. Yehoyakim and Shosh were play fighting upstairs. She could hear their voices. Shosh screamed, 'Mum!'

'You must look after your sister, Ruth,' her mother said. She stroked her hair.

'I will,' Ruth promised. 'I will.'

'Savta?'

'Who?' Ruth said. 'Who? Ophek?' she stared at him in incomprehension.

'I'm Lior, Savta! Lior!'

'Lior?'

His face came into focus.

'I was asleep,' she said angrily. 'You woke me.'

'You weren't asleep, Savta,' he said. She could hear the worry in his voice.

The Vultures came on the television again. Lior sat and watched it with her for a while. It felt nice, sitting there with someone for a change. Why was she so alone? Sooner or later everyone left her.

All she'd done, all she'd sacrificed to give them a land of their own.

She couldn't concentrate on the screen. Her thoughts wandered. Ghosts walked in the rooms. Yoram made coffee in the kitchen. Dov and Israel argued good-naturedly by the window. Shosh smiled at Dov from the chair by the radio, cradling Yael in her arms. A shadow by the closet – Ophek, practising card tricks. An overwhelming wave of happiness washed over Ruth. Her family, the way she'd always dreamed it, all gathered around her, all together at last.

'See you later, Savta,' someone said. But when she looked there was no one there.

*

She only had a sense of how bad things got when she went to the kolbo on her buggy later. Everything was quiet and peaceful, the mothers pushing their prams and the children playing hopscotch on the road. She parked the buggy and was on her way to the shop when the ground shook and smoke and fire rose high into the sky, followed a split second later by the rolling sound of the explosion.

The windows of the kolbo shattered. Ruth stood frozen. Children screamed. The smoke billowed in the sky over the factory. Everyone seemed sluggish, confused.

God *damn* it, Lior, she thought. What have you *done*!

Some of the men ran towards the factory. Another explosion erupted. The silo, Ruth thought. It had to be that. Thank God it was empty.

She really didn't think her grandson would be this *stupid*!

She got back on the buggy, feeling for a moment like she did back in... When was it? Back when she had the truck and bounced along the barely paved road to Haifa, running guns... Screw this, she thought, and gunned the engine as much as the tiny buggy could handle. It didn't move fast. She drove past the shocked parents and the crying children and along the road to the factory, where the men trained in firefighting were running to the factory.

'You can't go here, Ruth!' Uzan said, stopping her. She stared at him.

'Fuck off, Uzan,' she said. He stared at her open-mouthed and she drove away, smoke in the air, wind in her hair, feeling alive for the first time in what felt like decades.

Lior blew up the silo, she thought. Therefore Lior will be after the rest of the boys. She knew where he'd go. She drove down the hill to what was still achingly clear in her mind as the stables and was now this idiotic disco that pumped out loud music even on weeknights. She didn't care for this new music much, and for townies coming in to the kibbutz, all kinds of unsavoury elements treating her home like it was some playground.

But it was necessary, the money it brought in. The boys did their best for the kibbutz. She parked the buggy.

The disco seemed quiet. What was Lior doing? She hoped he was still alive. She stepped cautiously to the door. She pushed it open without a sound.

'Yuval,' she said. He turned from the bar counter, a shot glass in his hand. He nodded tiredly.

'We got him,' he said.

'Don't hurt him,' Ruth said. The words came out before she had a chance to think.

Yuval downed the shot and put it on the counter. He stared at Ruth mutely, ash on his face, streaked with sweat.

'He's become a liability,' he said at last.

She heard it but she didn't respond.

'He killed Peleg,' Yuval said.

Still she said nothing.

'I have to go clear out the cache,' Yuval said. 'Ginge is with him. We're keeping him in the cellar for now.'

'Yuval...'

'It's for the good of the kibbutz,' Yuval said.

Ruth said nothing. Words didn't come. Shosh laughed in a corner of the room, Yael and Ophek walked hand in hand onto the dance floor. A sad song played as they began to dance: The night grew long, and soon we'd go to battle, and you would stay behind to wait for me.

'Do what you have to do,' Ruth said. And then she turned and left there.

She drove back. She heard fire truck sirens. The smoke billowed from the burning silo but it was easing now.

She went back to her room and she sat there and time lost its meaning and became an open chasm she fell into, where all her ghosts were still alive. She came to a hard dry land marbled with rocks, where wild za'atar grew. Israel came and walked beside her and she took his hand, and they walked through the hills and wadis as the sun set slowly and red poppies bloomed.

When the phone rang she was startled. It sounded like a jackal in the valley below the kibbutz, and it took her a long moment to answer. She wasn't sure if it was day or night.

'Ruth?'

'Who is this?'

She could hear him hesitate.

'It's Uzan,' he said.

'Uzan?'

'I'm on night guard duty. I was... It's about Lior,' he said.

'Lior?'

'There's been...'

She could hear sirens now, in the background.

'What happened?' she said.

'The boys,' Uzan said. 'They're all dead. Esther's gone. And Lior is... Lior is...'

'Spit it out, Uzan!' Ruth said.

'They're taking him to hospital now, Ruth. But... But they don't think he'll make it.'

'I need to see him,' Ruth said.

'Of course. I could drive you... They're taking him to Haifa. There's a lot of police here, Ruth. I don't know what to tell them. I don't understand anything. Ruth?' he said. He sounded like he was about to cry. 'Ruth?'

But she hung up the phone. She put her fingers in the blinds, between two slats, and pushed them open. It was dawn. Bill Goodrich sat at her kitchen table. He drank whisky from a dirty glass.

'Living is hard,' Goodrich said. 'At least you do it for a reason.

To make a better future. A better world. That's worth struggling for, isn't it?'

'You were always a shitty actor, Bill,' Ruth said, and Goodrich laughed.

Then he was gone, of course; and she was all alone.

PART FOURTEEN

PARABELLUM

Ruth

Tel Aviv, 1993

52

'SHE'S AN OLD DEAR, REALLY,' THE NURSE SAID. THEN, LOWERING her voice, 'She can be difficult, of course. As I'm sure you noticed.' This to the younger nurse. 'She has no visitors.'

'It's sad,' the younger nurse, who was new, said. The other one shrugged. Ruth watched them from her bed. They spoke about her as if she wasn't even there.

'Age creeps up on you,' the older nurse said. 'They say she was really something, once.'

With that concluded, the final line delivered like an epitaph on a gravestone, the two nurses dispersed. Ruth put the television on. She didn't resent the nurses, who were hard workers on the whole. Outsiders, though. The kibbutz, having constructed this assisted living block for people like her and put it on the outskirts, happily hired strangers to look after the old. She was more lucid than they thought, though. She just didn't have a need to show it.

Rabin and Arafat shook hands on the White House lawn on the screen, the American president beaming between them. Disgraceful, Ruth thought. After all the blood that spilled, to just... pretend it could be different. She knew better. And they would find out in time.

It was then that she saw it. It was the news of some dignitary visiting Israel, the camera moving jerkily across the arrivals hall in Ben Gurion. Ruth wasn't interested in the report. But then she saw it, the camera panning in passing across tired men and women arriving with their luggage through the security doors—

Her lips formed a bloodless white line and if the nurses saw her just then they might have been frightened of the expression she wore, but they never really saw her, they only ever saw the old woman who could not remember names.

Well, *Ruth* saw. An elderly couple exiting the doors, the man in a bowler hat, wearing a cheap, old-fashioned suit. His shoes were shined. His face was ravaged by time and some past suffering, his eyes sunken, his hair a distant memory. He shuffled forward, trying to drag a too-heavy suitcase in his wake.

None of that mattered to Ruth.

The decades peeled away and only a pure, raw emotion remained, as hot as it had ever been, and she realised with some surprise how she had missed it: hatred, so strong it was like the blackest coffee.

On that fuzzy television screen, glimpsed in passing, a minor detail in the background to someone else's story, there he was.

Nathan Deutsch, the man who sold her parents and her sister to the Nazis.

Then he was gone, and Danny Roup was there on the screen instead with the weather report.

Ruth stared at the screen, but she didn't see the handsome young weatherman anymore, or the programme that came after, a cookery show with Ruth Sirkis—

Her mind worked furiously. He came back.

He came *back*!

The years peeled away and she was busy planning, working out the angles. She found herself humming that Yehoram Ga'on song about the girls of yesteryear, in their Russian sleeveless dresses and their long hair tied in braids. The ones who rode horses and carried a Parabellum in their bras. She was once one of those girls. She still had a Luger Parabellum hidden away, in a cache of weapons buried years back. It might still work.

The years vanished as she made her plans. Information – logistics – execution. She'd have to find him, then do what had to be done. She thought of Almog. Almog would help her. She would have used the boys but the boys were buried in the cemetery. She had a phone on her bedside table. She dialled nine for an outside line and then Almog's number. A woman answered after several rings.

'Hello?'

'Is David there?'

'Who is this, please?' The woman sounded young, and a little harassed.

'My name is Ruth. I'm an old friend of his.'

'He is sleeping now,' the young woman said. 'He had a heart attack during the Gulf War and, well. He never fully recovered. And now with the cancer...'

'I didn't know.'

The war was back in '91. The Iraqis kept firing rockets on Israel but none of them came anywhere near the kibbutz, and some of the kids used to climb up on the rooftops when the alarm sounded, to watch the rockets in the sky. You had to go into a room and put a wet towel against the door in case it was a chemical attack. Ruth had found the entire affair bothersome.

'I do need to speak to him,' she said now.

'Perhaps you could call again later?'

'I would like to speak to him now.'

Ruth hadn't spoken to Almog since the debacle in '89 permanently shut down the operation they were running. They kept it out of the papers as much as possible. The military censor helped and the fire in the factory and the subsequent deaths were blamed on improperly stored chemicals.

Ruth grieved, but she was used to grieving.

The money dried up and the kibbutz voted to sell a majority share in the factory to an American company. Ruth didn't know where Esther was, and she didn't care. Those who left, left. Shosh, Ophek, Esther. Those who got away. She thought of them as the landless, if she thought of them at all.

LAVIE TIDHAR

A pure hatred suffused her again, as hot as it had always been. Nathan Deutsch came back. She didn't know where he was or how long he came for.

She would need to move fast.

'I really must insist,' she said.

'Hold on...' The young woman sounded tired. A nurse? A granddaughter? Ruth didn't know. She didn't much care. After a while Almog came on the line.

'Hello?' he said. 'Who is this?'

'It's Ruth,' Ruth said.

'Ruth? Ruth who?'

'It's me,' she said, listening to his cough – his voice sounded different, much older somehow.

'What do you want?'

'I need your help.'

He laughed. It turned into another cough.

'I can't help anyone,' he said. 'I'm dying, Ruthie. They won't tell me but I know. We had some fun, didn't we? You and me? We fought...' He coughed again. 'We fought for this country.'

'I need to find a man,' Ruth said. 'You helped me find him once before.'

'Check... Check the phonebook,' Almog said.

'He won't be in it,' she said patiently. 'He is visiting. From overseas.'

'Then check the hotels in the *Yellow Pages*,' he said, and hung up.

She stared at the phone.

Bastard hung up on her!

'Right,' she said. There was no one there. She climbed out of bed and got changed. It took her a while. She stepped out. The young nurse was in the common room.

'Where are you going, Ruth?' she said.

'The library,' Ruth snapped. She walked out. Her buggy was parked where it was always parked. She got in it. They didn't

374

like her driving it anymore but they didn't dare take it away. She cranked up the speed as high as the engine would go and nearly ran over the older nurse who was having a cigarette outside. Ruth cackled and sped away.

It was only a short way to the library. She walked in, grabbed the latest *Yellow Pages* book and walked out. She drove to the public phone in the dining room and dragged a chair across the floor until she could sit down, and then she started to dial. Deutsch could be staying with family or friends; but she didn't think he had family, or friends. From the quick glimpse she caught of him he didn't look rich, either.

So a hotel, but a cheap one.

She figured it was a long flight – his suitcase looked heavy and he'd looked tired. So he'd be staying somewhere in Tel Aviv tonight. Why *did* old Jews come to Israel? Jerusalem, the Western Wall?

Christians always went to Nazareth and the Jordan, to be baptised. Muslims didn't come if they had any sense, not unless they had to. And only the Baha'i ever went to Haifa. No one ever thought that place was holy other than for them.

She tried the beachfront hotels first just to be thorough. Deutsch might not even be using that name, she realised. She gave a description, as much as she could. An elderly man. Hungarian accent. Arriving that day or just arrived. Nothing at Dan Panorama, nothing at the Hilton or the Sheraton. Her small bag of tokens was getting lighter. There was a queue forming to use the phone. Someone tutted. Ruth turned and glared and the people waiting decided that maybe it wasn't that urgent and they could come back later. They had phones in their rooms now, anyway. She could have called from the assisted living facility herself if she wanted to. She didn't want to. She didn't want people butting into her business. She fed more tokens into the phone.

She was down to her last token when the phone rang four times before it was picked up. It was a cheap pension on Allenby Street.

'Yes?'

'I'm looking for someone who might be staying with you,' Ruth said. 'An old Hungarian man—'

'Ah, yes, Mr Deutsch,' the woman said. 'He is resting now. He's just arrived from New York with his wife. Are you a friend of theirs?'

Ruth stared mutely at the phone.

He was *there.*

'Hello?' the woman from the pension said.

'Yes,' Ruth said. 'An old friend.'

'That's nice,' the woman said.

'I would like to surprise him,' Ruth said.

'He will be here until the day after tomorrow,' the woman said. 'He wants to visit the Western Wall, after.'

'Thank you,' Ruth said. The tokens ran out just then. She stared at the phone.

'Ruth?'

A voice, speaking close in her ear. She startled from a void, stared about her helplessly. A woman, her face in shadow.

'Shosh?' Ruth whispered.

'It's me,' the nurse said. 'Ruth, do you know where you are? You've been sitting here for over an hour. People were worried.'

'I'm fine!' Ruth said. She glared at the nurse. It was the older one, the one who smoked menthols.

'Let's get you back home,' the nurse said gently.

'I *am* home,' Ruth said. She could see people staring. It was dinner time and they were all coming into the dining room. The nurse reached for Ruth's arm to help her get up. Ruth staggered.

'I built this place!' she shouted. People looked away. Ruth shook off the nurse's hand, raised her arms shakily. 'With these two hands. *Look* at me! You want to bury me away but I am here!'

'Let's get you back, Ruth,' the nurse said. She helped her out. Put her on the buggy and sat down herself.

'I'll drive you home,' the nurse said.

'You all want to bury me,' Ruth said.

The nurse drove slowly back. Manicured lawns and people shuffling to dinner and sprinklers whooshing gently as they watered the grass. Fat babies and lights switched on in the kindergartens, and teens walking in blue-shirted groups to their movement activities.

The kibbutz did not need her. Life went on and she was put away like an old tattered dress. She let the nurse take her back to her room. She let the nurse give her the medicine. She let her put out the light.

She waited.

Then she spat out the pills and put on her sturdy work boots and her coat. She took a torch she always kept by the bed, and the getaway bag she kept hidden under the false bottom in the cupboard.

She snuck out and wondered if that was how Lior felt on those nights as a kid in the children's house when he snuck out with his friends. She felt the excitement run through her. She took the buggy and sped away before they would notice she'd gone. She left the lights off and used the side roads until she got to the edge of the settlement and into the cool and quiet dark of the cemetery. She parked and went inside.

The headstones to her dead rose in the dark all around her. She shone her torch on the ground, over pine needles and fallen pinecones. Large mushrooms grew in the base of the trees. She found the grave she was looking for, then stuck her fingers in the dirt of the empty lot beside it. Her fingers were stiff these days, and kneeling there on the ground like a gardener she felt every ache of the decades that passed creep up on her, but she persevered.

At last she found it, buried deep. She pulled out the sealed bag and cleaned her hands on her trousers and opened it. Wrapped in oilcloth and kept there all these years. She took out the Luger. It felt good in her hands. She aimed it at the tree.

'Pow,' she said. 'Pow.'

53

She had to get out of the kibbutz and get to Tel Aviv. But it was night and there wasn't a bus until morning. So that was no good. Ruth drove herself to the car park along the ring road and parked in the shadows and watched the gate. It was Uzan on guard duty. Uzan always did guard duty. Truth was he wasn't good for much else.

Ruth walked to the dining room. Dinner was over and there was no one there. She went to the car noticeboard and checked the lists. There were five keys left hanging on the board, cars unclaimed by any members for the evening. She pocketed one. A Subaru. The kibbutz bought them in a single lot a couple of years back. Japanese cars. They were all white and all had the kibbutz's name plastered on the side.

She went back to the parking lot. It was no good having Uzan in the guard booth. She came over.

'Ruth!' Uzan said, surprised. He was trying to hide a used copy of Israeli *Penthouse* that had been sitting open in his lap.

'I heard noises,' Ruth said. 'In the admin block just now. I was walking past.'

'So?' Uzan said.

'It could be thieves!'

'Ruth, I watch the gate. No one's come in.'

'They could have come in through the fence,' Ruth said.

'Come on, Ruth,' Uzan said. 'Shouldn't you be back in the... I mean... Your room?'

'You think I don't have it anymore, Uzan?' Ruth said. She spoke softly, as softly as she could so as not to scream. 'You think I'm a crazy old woman?'

'No, Ruth, I didn't mean that—'

'Then what *did* you mean, Uzan?'

'Look, Ruth, I can't go, what if someone needs me to open the gate?'

'I'll stay here,' Ruth said.

'But you're not the night watchman, Ruth—'

He saw her face.

'I'll go check,' he said. He couldn't get out of the booth fast enough.

Ruth smiled. Ruth waited until he vanished towards the admin block. Then she hit the big button that opened and closed the gate.

The gate opened.

And *this* was why they gave Uzan the night watchman job week after week after week.

Because even he couldn't fuck *that* up.

She went to the car and put the key in the ignition and the engine started with a soft purr.

They took her licence a couple of years back when her little memory lapses got worse; but that didn't matter now.

She pressed the gas pedal *aaaall* the way down and shot out of the still-opening gates and down the dark road, away from the kibbutz.

There were two pairs of eyes caught in the glare of the headlights. Ruth slammed on the brakes. The Subaru, tyres protesting, came to a halt on the smooth asphalt road.

The eyes stared at her mutely in the headlights. She reached for the Luger. The Arab village was on her right.

She opened and closed the door, softly. She stepped out, gun extended.

'Who's there?' she called.

No answer, just two pairs of eyes, disembodied. She could not make them out in the dark. She crept closer. The night was quiet. But there they were.

'Come out,' she said. 'Slowly!'

Two shadows darted into the beams of the headlights. Ruth held back a Hungarian curse.

Two apparitions, like small and white-faced ghosts. Their faces were devoid of all expression.

Two baby jackals. They stared at Ruth, then fled across the road into the corn field.

Ruth drew a breath. The night was silent. The Arab village, now little more than piles of stones where Danny blew his own brains out back in '89 and Lior took his last stand, stood muted with its rings of cactuses. Ruth got back in the car. She drove away, more slowly.

Past the intersection and onto the main road to Tel Aviv, her window down and the smell of the fields on the breeze. A police car passed her going the other way, blue lights flashing.

At the petrol station near Zikhron she stopped, the gas being low now since some inconsiderate kibbutz member did not refill the tank after returning the car – it was the sort of thing that really highlighted the degeneracy of standards in the commune, she felt. She paid for the gas and bought herself a pack of cigarettes from the shop and a black coffee, and she stood there against the hood of the car, inhaling tobacco smoke, and thought she was free for the first time in years.

They wouldn't be looking for her straightaway. The nurses thought she was asleep in her room and the car wouldn't be missed until morning.

She breathed in the humid sea air and the smell of oil and warm asphalt. She remembered when there was nothing here, when Zikhron was just a gaggle of houses on a hill, when the road was still being built. She remembered trips to the beach in Tantura with the kids, and later with Lior, and she remembered stopping here for years, when she was still the driver, and filling up the tank and stopping for a coffee and a smoke...

'Giveret? Giveret, are you all right?'

She came to, not sure for a moment where she was. The apologetic face of the young gas station attendant loomed in her vision.

'What?' Ruth said.

'You burned yourself,' he said.

She stared at her hand. The cigarette had burned down to the filter, left an ugly mark between her fingers. She dropped the stub.

'I'm fine,' she said.

'You've been standing here for twenty minutes,' he said.

'I said I'm fine!'

'Whatever you say, giveret.' He looked at her dubiously. 'Drive safely,' he said.

'Mind your own business!'

She got back in the car and slammed the door. She sat there staring at the steering wheel.

She could do it, she thought. She just had to *concentrate*!

Where was she going? For a moment she couldn't recall the road. Then it came back to her. Deutsch, Tel Aviv, the pension on Allenby. She started the car.

She was fine.

The road to Tel Aviv stretched on before her. She drove in silence as sleeping settlements came and went, and the isolated streetlights whooshed by as she drove. Past Caesaria, past the fish ponds where they found that dead girl back in '75. The Hadera chimneys came into view on her right but she could smell them even before she saw them, that awful stench of the coalworks. Then villages and orange groves and train tracks and bus stops, until the suburbs began to appear, first Netanya, then Herzliya, and the houses began to congregate all together into the single white mass of the city.

Teens were out on the streets, ripped jeans and long hair and pierced noses. Ruth remembered another Tel Aviv, a more modest one, or at least she liked to think she did, but the city always had its ugly underbelly and the sound of gunfire and bombs was not uncommon there when she was young.

How did she get *old*! It made no sense to her. And the kibbutz she had built and the country she made – what had *happened* to them? She tried to find her way through the streets but the roads were confusing and she struggled to see the signs. The traffic was heavy now that she was in the city. She was not used to the traffic. People honked their horns at her. Someone rolled down their window and screamed at her. Cars were coming towards her from the other direction and cars were beeping behind her and she no longer knew where she was. She had crossed over the Yarkon River. She thought she was near the bus station. Music blared out of speakers set outside, playing Zohar Argov. She hated that kind of music.

Where *was* Allenby? How would she get to it? A bus rumbled past her, the driver honking, frightening her suddenly.

She had to get away.

She took a hard right. Cars swerved to avoid her and she found herself rushing headlong into oncoming traffic on a one-way street. Shwarma stands and flower stalls and people selling cassette tapes from blankets on the ground, soldiers and men in suits and streetwalkers and black-clad Orthodox men and long-haired teens with acoustic guitars slung over their shoulders.

She didn't know where she was.

She didn't *know* this country.

She looked for a street sign, for anything to tell her where she was. Where was the damned *sea*? To her left? To her right? Straight ahead? The buildings grew shabbier and busier and the cars beeped at her furiously and she saw a police car parked outside a jewellery shop, its lights flashing, and she turned at random, onto the next street, where laundry hung from the balconies overhead and the streetlights were broken.

She heard an awful, keening cry as her car slammed into a moving body.

The car stalled. Ruth let go of the wheel. The sound carried, this awful broken sound. She couldn't bear it. She stepped out of the car.

A dog lay on the road. It lay in a pool of blood. Bright feverish eyes regarded her with nothing but pain in them, all the pain Ruth felt inside her.

The dog cried. It was broken all over.

She couldn't bear it. She just couldn't *bear* it! She wasn't conscious of doing it, yet somehow the old Parabellum was in her hand. Somehow it was aimed straight at the dog's head, straight between those big wet eyes, so full of pain.

Somehow her finger tightened on the trigger.

The gun went off, an explosion of gunpowder and metal, and the bullet, that had sat all those years under the earth in the kibbutz cemetery, flew true. It burst through the dog's skull, right between those bright eyes, and it took away the pain.

Brain matter spurted and the dog went limp. A shard of bone sliced a line of hurt across Ruth's cheek.

She dropped the gun. She stared at the dog.

She didn't know where she was.

There was a car with stencilled letters on it that said Kibbutz Trashim. Hot tears fell down her cheeks and she didn't know why. She turned her back on that place and walked away, blindly, stumbling as she went.

Out on to a street filled with people and the smell of cooking shwarma, and music blaring out of speakers, and a police car parked outside a jewellery store, its blue lights flashing.

'Hey, giveret,' a policeman said. He stopped her. 'Are you alright?'

'Ophek?' Ruth said.

A second policeman came and joined his partner. She saw the way they looked at her.

'What's your name, dear?' the second policeman said.

'My name?'

Her lips moved but no sound came.

'Where do you live?' the second policeman said.

'Live?' Ruth said.

'Do you have an ID, giveret?' the first policeman said. Less kindly now.

'I have to... I have to find him,' Ruth said.

'Who is that, dear?'

'The... his name...'

Why was she *crying*?

'You'd best come with us, giveret,' the first policeman said. 'We'll get you a nice cup of tea at the station.' He took her arm gently; but not so gently that she could shake him off.

'I have to... Shosh,' she said. Overhead vultures circled, flying silently in the sky above the white houses of Tel Aviv. She blinked. They were gone. 'I have to find...'

'Come along, dear.'

The second policeman took her other arm. Together they walked her to the waiting car.

The tears just kept falling and she didn't even know why.

PART FIFTEEN

THE BEGINNING

Hanna

Florida, 2009

54

THE MOON SWAM IN THE SKY ABOVE THE HIGHWAY AND THE light caught the eyes of a raccoon who watched her silently from the roadside, then vanished in the rear-view mirror like it didn't exist. A police car went past Hanna, its blue lights flashing, going the other way. Hanna focused on the road, her hands gripping the steering wheel. She'd been driving for hours.

She should have been sitting shiva right now. She knew that much. Instead she was on the road, travelling towards something she didn't quite understand, trying to outrun ghosts.

She raced against the dawn as traffic grew along the highway, truckers like shadows in their cabins drifting on the currents of the road passing her by. She wasn't sure where she was anymore, Miami behind her and her destination half a continent away.

She needed food, a bathroom, sleep. Her window was rolled down and hot humid wind pushed in and her hand dangled out of the window with the butt of a cigarette, which she let go and let it float away like a dandelion.

Esther, who were you? she thought. We never know our parents until they're gone. Two people must have met and come together in some way for her mother to be born, and the same for Hanna, her father some mysterious stranger she would never now know.

The old photos sat in the tea box on the back seat. People from a past she didn't know, their light captured and etched onto paper, now fading, and who were they all? Did they, too, love and hurt, did they lead messy lives or good? What had they seen? What did they know?

Her eyes stung. The lights of an oncoming truck blinded her momentarily and they were followed by the loud scream of the horn, making her jump. She needed to find a place to lie down for a few hours. Dawn was breaking across the sky. It made her think of her mother cracking an egg in half, the yolk sliding across the pan and the cloudy white bubbling.

She was somewhere near a small town called Marianna. On the side of the road she saw the sign for a Motel 6 and she pulled in and parked and then sat for a long moment in the driver's seat, just sitting there, not really seeing anything.

Where was she going? She couldn't even say just then. She went into the office and paid for a day and the clerk gave her the keys to an empty room, which was all she'd wanted.

She went in and shut the door and collapsed on the bed.

Sleep. Shower. Mid-afternoon sunlight peeking through the closed blinds. She brushed her teeth. She stared at herself in the mirror. Grief hit her unexpectedly. Esther, sitting up in her bed, Esther with the bright eyes, the mother she knew all her life but now she thought she never knew at all. How could it be, that horrible absence? Was it like losing a tooth, with the tongue still trying, in futility, to probe for, forgetting it was no longer there? How could someone *be*, and then cease to exist?

What were they, then? she thought. When they were gone. A handful of memories and faded pictures in a box, and secrets? She wandered back into the room and sat, leaving a wet imprint on the bedsheet. She upended the box her mother kept. Sorted through the photos, placing them one next to the other, trying to fit together pieces of a puzzle that wouldn't fit.

A young couple with a grey sea and barbed wire behind them,

the woman in a white dress and the man in khakis, both looking nervous. The woman was visibly pregnant.

Dov and Shoshana, 1948.

A boy with a wide smile in a magician's outfit, pulling a rabbit out of a hat. Spiky handwriting on the back. *Ophek, 1961.*

Side by side: a handsome soldier and a pretty princess, who looked so much like her that Hanna's breath caught. *Yael and Yoram, Purim 1964.*

She wished she could make sense of it all. A young woman in khakis posing in front of a truck, smiling, a gun in her hand.

Ruth, 1934.

She looked so happy in the picture. There was a family resemblance there, too. A hill with rocks behind her, and smoke rising in the distance from a place Hanna couldn't see.

Hanna was hungry. She put away the old photos, back in the box. She went outside. Parked cars and the constant hum of traffic on the road. She lit a cigarette. The motel had a pool no one was using. It had a drinks machine. She saw there was a barbeque place over the road from the motel. Her stomach growled. When had she last had a meal?

She crossed the road on foot and sat down at a booth and had a burger. People came and went around her. Truckers eating alone, families on a road trip tucking into ribs and sodas. A few bikers. It was a popular place. She picked up her phone.

'Hanna?'

'Hi, Alex.'

Alexandra sounded different this time. What time was it in L.A.? Her voice echoed weirdly on the line.

'I just wanted to talk,' Hanna said.

'Listen, Hanna, I'm sorry about the last time,' Alex said. 'You caught me by surprise and I was… with people.' The way she said it made a spike of jealousy shoot through Hanna. It still hurt.

'It's really awful about your mother,' Alex said. 'How are you holding up?'

'I'm fine,' Hanna said. 'I think. I don't know... Alex, I want to see you.'

'But I'm in L.A.,' Alex said.

'I thought maybe I'd come see you. I don't... I don't really have anywhere to be.'

She fell silent. Alex was somewhere in the background, not saying anything. Why wasn't she saying anything?

'Oh, it was silly—'

'I'm worried about you—'

They both spoke at the same time.

'I'm fine, really,' Hanna said.

'I'm glad.'

'It's just... a lot, you know?' Hanna said.

'Are you really coming to L.A.?' Alex said.

Hanna thought of the miles and miles of road ahead. She thought of the place her mother called home just the once, when she died. You could fit seven Israels into Florida alone and still have change left.

'Maybe,' she said. 'I don't know.'

'We could get a coffee,' Alex said. 'We could get a coffee or something if you do come.'

'I'd like that,' Hanna said. 'I'd like that a lot.'

Her cheeks were wet and she didn't know why.

The sun was setting by the time she crossed back to the motel. She packed her bag, the television flickering in a corner of the room. Some black and white movie with Bill Goodrich in it; but Hanna had no time for old films. She put the bag into the car and got in and then she just sat there for a long moment, staring at nothing, and wondering what she would do and where she would go.

There were ghosts all around her now, but she didn't see them.

Dov leaned against a streetlight, smiling with his arms crossed while Israel tied a shoelace, crouching down. Shosh sat in the window of the barbeque place, doing the crossword puzzle, and Ruth sat across from her and waited patiently. A shadow sitting on the counter might have been that of Yehoyakim, the uncle no one really knew.

Yoram chased Yael to the motel's swimming pool, both of them shrieking and laughing. Esther sat in the passenger seat next to Hanna, studying the map. Behind her sat Lior, looking at his nails, and Ophek, the magician, was hiding in the trunk, of course.

And they were all so happy. They were a family.

She imagined them, for just a moment, who they were and what they did and what secrets they hid so deep inside them. Then she started the engine and the car purred to life and Hanna rejoined the highway and drove towards the setting sun, until she, too, vanished.